Praise for *The Sins on The*

"Samotin's breathtaking debut is a Gothic, deeply Jewish tale about love's power to both wound us and set us free. Passionate and gruesome, heart-pounding and poignant, this story will be carved into your very bones."

—ALLISON SAFT, *New York Times* bestselling
author of *A Far Wilder Magic*

"*The Sins on Their Bones* is a novel of grief flayed open with surgical care, a story like a broken bone healing stronger than before. From war-torn shuls to opulent palaces to hidden rooms with cold secrets, Samotin has created a queer Jewish fantasy world that feels real enough to step into. The journey is dark, but never lonely."

—LAUREN RING, World Fantasy Award winner and Nebula finalist

"Samotin's debut is both epic and intimate, both sharp and sumptuous, both painful and ultimately hopeful, with Jewish magic in its bones. Novo-Svitsevo will linger in my heart for a long time."

—REBECCA PODOS, Lambda Award-winning
author of *From Dust, a Flame*

"Intense and visceral, with a romance that showcases the restorative power of love on the wounded, this stunning debut will leave you spellbound from the first page."

—ADEN POLYDOROS, author of *The City Beautiful*
and finalist for the World Fantasy Award

"*The Sins on Their Bones* is a book that will break your heart and then fuse it back together, stronger for having been broken. It's a story of agency and abuse, about what we deserve and what we owe ourselves, about finding the strength to forgive ourselves and to accept the forgiveness of others. Samotin is a powerful new voice in the genre, with this queer dark fantasy that reminds us that there is always, always a light in the dark."

—KAMILAH COLE, bestselling author of *So Let Them Burn*

"An enthralling story that never flinches away from its darkest moments— Dimitri, Vasily, and even Alexey will carve themselves into your hearts and linger with you long after reading. With impeccable world-building, gut-wrenching prose, and a deeply compelling plot, *The Sins on Their Bones* is a must-read book of 2024. I can't wait to read whatever Samotin writes next."

—LILLIE LAINOFF, author of *One for All*

"Gothic and glorious, *The Sins on Their Bones* is the dark Jewish fantasy I've been craving. Novo-Svitsevo will stay with you long after you've finished the last page." —NATASHA SIEGEL, author of *Solomon's Crown*

"An implacable tangle of dark histories and intense passions, damaging desperation and many kinds of healing love."

—DAVINIA EVANS, author of *Notorious Sorcerer*

"Samotin has crafted a modern classic which explores love, family and loyalty whilst dabbling in dark magic, high octane sexual tension and a web of romance that I will never stop thinking about. *The Sins on Their Bones* is a book that you will devour with ease, but be careful, because it too will devour you—soul, heart and mind."

—BEN ALDERSON, author of *Heir to Thorn and Flame*

"Set in an imaginative, lived-in world steeped in Jewish mysticism, *The Sins on Their Bones* walks a tightrope between darkness and light, between heavy themes and levity, between escaping the monsters from your past and becoming one in the present. Get ready to fall in love with Samotin's characters—even the villain! *Especially* the villain."

—GENOVEVA DIMOVA, author of *Foul Days*

"A heart-wrenching tale of love, loss and the long, difficult road to healing, *The Sins on Their Bones* is an unmissable debut from a powerful new voice."

—K.M. ENRIGHT, author of *Mistress of Lies*

"Wrenching, brutal, and fiercely loving, *The Sins on Their Bones* is a remarkable and unflinching fantasy debut."

—EMILY SKRUTSKIE, author of *Bonds of Brass*

"Clever and inventive, Laura R. Samotin's debut novel filled me with giddy nostalgia for the heady days when a younger me first discovered fantasy adventures, deliriously unhinging my jaw to devour entire books whole in a single night. Which is exactly what I did with *The Sins on Their Bones*: it was simply too much fun to put down! It's left me desperately craving both blinis, and the second book in the series!"

—ROSE SUTHERLAND, author of *A Sweet Sting of Salt*

"Rich in wrenching intimacies, *The Sins on Their Bones* is a paean to healing and endurance against all odds."

—FOZ MEADOWS, author of *A Strange and Stubborn Endurance*

"*The Sins on Their Bones* is absolutely unique and potently atmospheric. The darkness nearly wafts off the page."

—ARIEL KAPLAN, author of *The Pomegranate Gate*

"Immersive and original, *The Sins on Their Bones* is the Jewish fantasy I've always dreamed of reading. Samotin has created a world that is rich and evocative and absolutely steeped in Jewish folklore, and a cast of wounded, messy, enchanting characters that grab you by the heart and never let go. Every page took my breath away, and the ending left me absolutely clamoring for more. This tender, violent, breathtaking debut will keep you on your toes until the very last word."

—SHELLY JAY SHORE, author of *Rules for Ghosting*

THE SINS ON THEIR BONES

LAURA R. SAMOTIN

RANDOM HOUSE CANADA

www.penguinrandomhouse.ca

Random House Canada and colophon are registered trademarks.

Library and Archives Canada Cataloguing in Publication

Title: The sins on their bones / Laura R. Samotin.
Names: Samotin, Laura R., author.
Identifiers: Canadiana (print) 20230519504 | Canadiana (ebook) 20230519512 | ISBN 9781039007567 (softcover) | ISBN 9781039007574 (EPUB)
Subjects: LCGFT: Novels.
Classification: LCC PS3619.A45 S56 2024 | DDC 813/.6—dc23

Text design: Talia Abramson
Cover design: Talia Abramson
Cover images: matrioshka / Shutterstock
Interior image credit: Ashe Arends

Printed in Canada

2 4 6 8 9 7 5 3 1

Penguin
Random House
RANDOM HOUSE CANADA

To all those who have lost a throne
and think that it's their fault.

My beloved is mine, and I am his.

דּוֹדִי לִי וַאֲנִי לוֹ

SONG OF SONGS 2:16

We are so lightly here.
It is in love that we are made;
In love we disappear.

LEONARD COHEN

The Sins on Their Bones is a story about love in all its forms—the transformative and the destructive. It centers themes of intimate partner violence, sexual abuse, and the PTSD, anxiety and depression that can follow life's traumas. While these topics are treated, I hope, with sensitivity, I have also chosen as an author not to flinch away from the reality of what so many of us have experienced. I trust that if you are not ready to face these topics, you will save this story for a time when it will heal instead of harm. My author website contains additional information and resources.

ONE

DIMITRI

Dimitri pulled the velvet dressing gown tighter around his bare chest to ward off the chill from the nighttime breeze.

As he moved, vodka sloshed out of the goblet he held, splashing onto the cobblestones of the street below. He drained the rest of the alcohol in one long swig, then let the crystal drop from his fingers in a tinkle of shattering glass. A disgruntled shout sounded from below, but he couldn't bring himself to care. Perched on the roof of the townhouse as he was, it wasn't like anyone could scale up the facade to reprimand him.

Although at this point, it would've been preferable to face an angry citizen of Wilnetzk—maybe even preferable to get into a light fist-fight—than to be alone with his thoughts for one second longer.

You always were a weak one, Alexey murmured in his ear, the memory of his voice low and smooth as silk. *You never had what it takes to rule.*

Dimitri wished he had thought to bring the entire bottle onto the roof with him. Copious amounts of vodka were the only thing that would silence Alexey's voice on nights like this, the only thing that would stop him from feeling like his beating heart was being ripped out of his rib cage and devoured.

The window creaked and Dimitri jumped, half expecting Alexey to be leaning over the sill, his shirtsleeves rolled up in that familiar, intoxicating way of his, pointing a pistol at his head.

But it was only Annika who slipped through, her silk dressing gown whispering over the shingles. "*Moy Tzar*," she said, dipping her chin, as if he still sat on a throne. As if they weren't two best friends, perched on the roof of a shabby townhome in a disgusting, backward city, all because his piss-poor choices had led them here.

"Are you here to tell me off for being on the roof?" He tried unsuccessfully to stop his teeth from grinding together.

"I'm here to find out why you're not in bed," she replied. "I could hear the creaking of the roof from the second story of the house. Not to mention the little explosion you just created." She winced and shame washed through him. His highest-ranking general, the woman who had led his armies, his brightest and best soldier, still hated sudden loud noises almost a year after the end of the war.

Her long, dark curls whipped across her copper skin in the icy wind, and he reached out to brush them behind her ear in apology. She leaned into the touch, then nudged him over so she could scoot off the window ledge and onto the roof proper.

"Couldn't sleep," Dimitri replied. "Nightmares. I needed fresh air."

"Most people who can't sleep and need fresh air take a walk, not sit on the roof like an overgrown crow." Her tone was light and teasing—she was always cheerful, even when he wanted her to rage at him—but she threaded her hand through his and gave it a squeeze. Annika had always looked out for him, even when he didn't want to be looked after. Even when giving him a little push off the roof would bring such an easy end to all their troubles. They could bury his corpse and perhaps then he would finally find a moment's peace.

She looked at him, furrowing her brow. "The nightmares. Was it him?"

"Always," Dimitri said. "It's always him." He pulled a match and a cigarette out of his dressing gown's pocket. *Disgusting habit,* he heard an echo of his father's voice say. *Not befitting a member of the royal family.*

Dimitri dragged the end of the cigarette against his lips, then lit it with shaking fingers and inhaled. It was a delicious way of saying *fuck you* to his father's memory. The old bastard shouldn't have gone and died if he hadn't wanted his third son to shit on his memory.

"Are you sure they're just dreams?" Annika plucked the cigarette out of his fingers. "Just nightmares and not portents?" She fingered the bone amulet she wore around her neck, the one she always claimed kept demons at bay, the one she clung to as she warred with her fear and guilt before every battle. Her family may have been followers of modern Ludayzim like Dimitri, but she still clung to some of the old ways, the ones with their roots in folktales and superstition. He'd never had the heart to point out that even with all her rituals and charms and protections, everything was still fucked to hell anyway.

She brought the cigarette to her own lips, the tip glowing like a star in the dark when she took a drag. It was the only star that Dimitri would see tonight, with the fog and soot that always hung over Wilnetzk. One couldn't see the stars here, not like home.

Home.

Ever since the end of the war, ever since he had exiled himself, the thought of home was like a bullet lodged next to his heart, one beat away from killing him.

Dimitri bit the knuckle of his left index finger. His hand felt so light now, without his wedding ring. So empty. Wrong. "It's not a warning," he said, letting out a long, slow breath. "I'd know the difference between a nightmare and a missive from the Lord, Anna. These are fueled by regrets, not the hand of God."

Annika handed him back the cigarette with a long-suffering sigh. "It's not your fault, you know. Scream, cry, rage at the Almighty. Let yourself fall apart. You are allowed to grieve. You are allowed to let the pain of this bring you to your knees and lay you bare. It's been a year, Dima, and I've never once seen you fall to pieces." The pity in her eyes made him flinch. "You're going to have to forgive yourself eventually. It's been long enough."

"Pray tell," he bit back, "how long is it supposed to take to forgive oneself for dooming one's country to the rule of a raving madman, killing hundreds of thousands in a war that one lost—badly—and then running off like a puppy with its tail tucked between its legs to save one's own sorry hide?" He stubbed the cigarette out on the back of his own hand and relished the searing burn. He felt so little worth feeling, these days, that sometimes pain was a relief.

"Not all of us can have good taste in who we bring to bed," Annika mumbled under her breath.

And suddenly, Dimitri wasn't on the roof of a townhouse in Wilnetzk. He was in the palace library, lying on the floor, his feet propped up on a stack of books, his knees falling open, his desire evident, heat coiling in his belly at Alexey's predatory gaze. Alexey's hand on his chest, pinning him down, the other opening his vest and then his shirt button by button, trailing a line of kisses down to his waistband that left him burning. Alexey's mouth on him, his fingers curled into Alexey's hair as he silently urged him for *more . . .*

Dimitri shook his head, clearing the ghost of old desire from his body. The last time he had seen Alexey, they were standing on opposite sides of a bloody battlefield. His pistol had been raised, aimed right at Alexey's heart, and he had failed to shoot. Because even if Alexey had become something worse than a man, all Dimitri could think about was how he had looked into Alexey's warm brown eyes, said words he had never said to anyone else, and thought, *This is the man I will let claim me for his own.*

Dimitri sighed. He really needed that bottle of vodka.

"Come inside," Annika urged. "You're no good to anyone if you fall off the roof in a drunken stupor and break your neck."

"I'm no good to anyone now, neck intact," Dimitri grumbled, but he followed her back through the window and into his bedroom, with its small, rickety bed and roaring fire and the striped wallpaper that was peeling in places from age and damp.

She shoved a plate of blinis in his face, which she must have brought up from the kitchen. "Eat," she said. "You're melancholic, and by the holy name of God, we all know why, but at least don't be sad on an empty stomach. That's simply pathetic."

He took a blini off the silver platter and popped it in his mouth, the hot cheese filling searing his tongue. It tasted like ash—like everything did these days—but he forced it down anyway. He made an obscene moaning noise just to see her smile and held her eyes as he licked his fingers one by one. He could at least try to seem normal, just for Annika, considering how often she sought him out and tried to cheer him up, even knowing that such a thing was impossible.

"Don't be unseemly," she warned. "I have more knives within reach right now than you have balls to cut off, Dima."

"Tzar," he corrected with a halfhearted wink. If he couldn't have anything else in life, he could still have this, taunting Annika gently until she rolled her eyes and huffed a laugh. Pretending, for half a heartbeat, that everything was still okay.

"Am I missing a party?" Vasily's baritone sounded from down the hallway, and he stepped through the doorway and into the light. He was fully dressed, his perfectly fitted navy wool suit muddy around the ankles, his warm bronze skin and dark curls painted gold in the firelight.

"Just a dressing-down," Annika said. "*Moy Tzar* was on the roof again, trying his best to die in an accident."

"Ah," Vasily said, stepping past Dimitri and trailing fingers across the back of his neck, causing him to shiver. Vasily sank into one of the two sagging armchairs by the fire, taking off his bowler hat and laying it on a side table on top of a collection of half-empty glass tumblers. "Well, if *Moy Tzar* wants to die, I'm sure he doesn't want to hear the news out of Novo-Svitsevo."

Dimitri tried to look disinterested, but he knew Vasily could tell otherwise. Vasily was an exceptional talent, after all, even among the best of spies, and was better at knowing what people wanted than the people themselves. It was why Vasily had been his most trusted confidant, his spymaster, when he'd ruled Novo-Svitsevo. And why he still was, even now that they'd fled to the hell that was the Free States.

So Dimitri acceded, sitting down heavily on his bed. His toes curled involuntarily into the worn antique rug on the floor. He should have put on socks, but it had been a long, long time since he had let his body be comfortable.

Not since that night in bed with Alexey. That last night.

"Do I need to wake Mischka and Lada?" Annika asked around a mouthful of blini.

"Let them sleep, Anna," Vasily said, unbuttoning his jacket and waistcoat before stretching his arms behind his head. "Bad news is always easier to bear on a full night's rest."

Dimitri's stomach dropped despite the blanket of vodka clouding his senses. "Bad news, you say?"

Vasily's eyes flashed. "Is there any other kind for us now?" His mouth was drawn, lines furrowed into his brow, the way he'd looked since he'd told Dimitri his spies had stopped reporting back.

"Vasya, the only good news I'm likely to get is that the Lord our God came down from on high to tell me there's no afterlife, so that when I die, I no longer have to exist," Dimitri said.

"You didn't lie," Vasily said to Annika. "Our darling Dima is in quite the foul mood tonight. Maybe we should snap his neck and put him out of his misery." He got up and came over to take Dimitri's chin in hand, angling his face back and forth as if studying it, then kissed him on the cheek. "Though I'd hate to waste such a breathtakingly pretty face, when those lips could start wars and those cheekbones alone could kill a man."

"Stop being an insufferable flirt." Dimitri frowned and his chest tightened. The more Vasily flirted, the more dire the situation usually was. "Tell me the news."

Vasily's smile wavered and he turned on his heel, then sat down in the chair once more. He pulled out the pack of playing cards he'd carried with him since the war, starting to shuffle the deck in one of his nervous tells. Dimitri's heart pounded just a little harder at the sight. "I've heard a whisper that Alexey Balakin is calling for people to come to Rav-Mikhailburg to volunteer for the army." He propped his ankle atop his knee. "Which sounds an awful lot like he's going to be building up his forces again. The tavern was full of panicked men trying to figure out how to buy their relatives remaining in Novo-Svitsevo passage to Lietuva."

Annika snorted. "As if that would work. The Pretender is calling up armies, but he's going to let a bunch of peasants cross the border into the Free States? No competent general would let that happen, not when he may need to conscript."

Dimitri had to admire her. She hadn't called Alexey by his name since the betrayal. She would have shot him dead on that battlefield if she'd been within shooting range, because unlike him, she'd been raised to kill, and he was a boy still half in love with the man who had ruined his life and his country.

Vasily shrugged. "People will always hope in the face of death. It's the human condition." He threw Dimitri a look. "Except our Dima. He's a master of being alive and utterly devoid of hope. Are you sure you won't let Mischka try their new tonics on you? Some medication might just hoist you out of your depression." He tugged on one of his black curls, winding it around his finger as his hazel eyes sparkled in the firelight.

Dimitri ignored the suggestion. "The question is," he said, throwing a rude gesture Vasily's way, "what is Alexey planning to do with an army?" He pulled concern from his alcohol-sodden brain like taffy.

"Nothing good," Annika said. "If Vasya's other information on Novo-Svitsevo's trade situation is correct, I would bet every last tolar to my name that the Pretender is going to advance on the Free States. It's what I would do. He has no route to the sea, not since he blew a hole in his alliance with the one region of Novo-Svitsevo that borders the ocean. It's not as if he's going to be able to cut a transport deal to the east with the Urushkins without getting his balls handed back to him on a silver platter with a side of caviar."

Dimitri blinked to clear the visions from his mind of what he and Alexey had done with caviar.

Annika pushed off the wall and came to stand next to him, resting a hand on his shoulder and using the other to pull his head into her chest. He knew it was supposed to be comforting when she did this, but her touch felt like a weight almost too heavy to bear.

"I would say there's another war coming," she said. He felt her heart beat just a little harder at that.

Dimitri shuddered against Annika's rib cage. He couldn't stop himself. Not at the thought of more bloodshed, more corpses, or having to walk through more fields littered with broken, mutilated people screaming for mercy. Not at the thought of acres of dead bodies riddled with bullets, so many they couldn't even bury them all. Not at the memory of the constant, aching fear that he would turn and find his friends in the dirt, bleeding out, torn to shreds by artillery fire or shrapnel. Not at the reminder of the horrific trembling in his hands that wouldn't go away, no matter how much he drank and pretended and tried to forget that they were all one bullet away from death or worse. He pulled away from Annika, shaking his head.

Vasily leveled a look at Dimitri, one that pinned him in place, anchoring him. "Do you want me to keep investigating? Or would you rather we all sit on our asses and slowly waste away from a diet of vodka and despair, waiting for the war to start?"

Dimitri closed his eyes. Tried to remember what it felt like to hope. Settled for remembering what it felt like to issue commands, to order people to do things that might save the country or might get them killed.

"Do it," Dimitri said. "But be careful. Alexey hasn't found us yet, and by God, I'm sure he's trying. Don't draw more attention than you need to." His gut twisted with familiar anxiety at the thought.

Vasily saluted, winked rakishly, and sprang up out of the chair. "Then I'm off to bed, *Moy Tzar*, so I can be a well-rested spymaster come morning. May I suggest you do the same? Circles under one's eyes are devilishly unattractive, even on you."

Dimitri rolled his eyes. Sleep only held dreams of Alexey. Nightmares of his failure. But he could pretend, at least, for what remained of his court. For his friends.

"I'll go," he said. "And when I wake up, I'll try to figure out what the devil is planning on doing to Novo-Svitsevo."

"That's *Moy Tzar*," Annika said. "See, I told you blinis would help."

Dimitri couldn't help but crack a grin. But he didn't move from where he sat rigidly on the bed. "I'll stay awake," he said, nodding to the fire, "to warm up. Just for a bit longer."

Annika gave him a wary look but didn't say anything, just spat three times into the fire in one of her endearingly old-fashioned gestures meant to keep him safe from curses and demons and the devil himself. She and Vasily left him alone with the worries haunting his mind.

He ran a finger around one of the glasses sitting on the table next to his bed, then gave in and poured himself another measure of vodka, throwing it back. It burned away some of the guilt that sat on his chest like a demon trying to suck the life out of him. Eventually, the alcohol sunk into his blood enough that his eyelids grew heavy, and he lay back against the pillow.

He reached into the drawer of the nightstand next to the bed, the motion so well practiced that he didn't need to look to close his fingers around the unadorned metal band hidden there. He thumbed it, the battered gold glinting in the firelight, and slipped it on. He hated that it made him feel whole again, that every time he did this it felt *right*.

Annika and Vasily, Ladushka and Mischa—they all thought he'd thrown his wedding ring into the Nevka River, that he'd gotten rid of everything that Alexey had given him in a fit of rage after Alexey's betrayal. But he'd lied to them.

He hated how keeping the symbol of his devotion to his husband should have shamed him, but didn't.

Dimitri closed his eyes and trailed his left hand down his stomach, ghosting around his navel, inching lower, trying to remember what it felt like when it was Alexey touching him, when it was Alexey holding him and soothing away his fears.

But Alexey would never touch him again. Because Alexey was dead. *His* Alexey was dead.

And it was all his fault.

TWO

ALEXEY

A lexey was cold, down to his very bones. The core of him had
been frigid since he had been made anew. And it didn't bother
him, except at times like this, when it made the work of running the
empire difficult.

He put down his fountain pen and flexed his fingers, working away
the stiffness. The candle at the edge of the desk was waning, but still
shed enough light for him to see the half-finished edict. The rest of
his formal council chamber was wreathed in shadow, the dark wood
of the walls absorbing the light, the thick crimson drapes and intri-
cately patterned carpet muffling any sounds from the nobles of his
court fidgeting in front of him as he worked.

"*Moy Tzar*," the lord standing nearest him said. "Would you like
assistance with the decree?"

Alexey leveled him with a stare, and the man flinched away. If eyes
were windows to the soul, his had turned into windows to Gehenna
itself. They were the most inhuman thing about him, two pits of
blackness within the blank whites. He'd used this stare to great effect
many a time since taking the throne.

The only way to rule this court was with terror in the hearts of its occupants, and respect for the sovereign they all served. Respect came from fear, and Alexey knew fear. It was, after all, what he was made of now.

Perhaps it was what he had always been made of.

Alexey picked up the pen again and finished writing, his penmanship perfect as ever, not a spot of ink out of place. He signed the parchment with a flourish, then passed it off to a waiting servant to dry the words.

"Lord Novikov," he said, turning back to the man in front of him and pushing back the dark hair that had fallen into his eyes as he wrote. "You'll take the decree to the garrison at Domachëvo. The captain there is to conscript for the front lines starting with known dissidents. They'll be the first to die in the next wave of assaults, and we can deal with two problems at once."

"Yes, *Moy Tzar.*" Lord Novikov bowed deeply as he approached Alexey's desk. "Your command is my duty."

Alexey stood as the parchment, now dried and bound, was handed back to him. He dribbled hot wax onto it, and then pressed his signet ring into the seal. When he handed the scroll off, he did not miss the slight shudder of revulsion that went through Novikov as their skin brushed.

He stood and snapped his fingers, and a servant sprang forth from the shadows to settle a richly embroidered cape over his shoulders. It was as unforgivingly dark as the bottom of a well and trimmed in the fur of a jet-black wolf.

Alexey dressed to fulfill his court's expectations of him, shrouding his iron-hard body in the darkest fabrics the royal tailor could acquire. He knew well what some of the nobles whispered about him since his return. That he was the prince of darkness, that he was a demon sent by the Holy One to punish them for their sins.

He was neither. He was simply a man who had dared to do what none had done before and had been rewarded for it beyond all measure.

He'd had to procure an entire new wardrobe anyway. Everything he owned from before smelled of Dimitri, no matter how many times it was laundered. It was a reminder Alexey could not stand. His biggest failing, his greatest regret. The one thing that had almost stopped him from becoming everything he knew he could be.

He rounded his desk and brushed past the crowd of lords and ladies who had been watching him work. He heard the rustle of fabric behind him as the court followed him and held up a hand. "Chancellor Morozov, with me. Everyone else, leave us."

They dispersed like birds startled out of a tree, murmuring to each other.

"Come," Alexey said. His chancellor followed mutely, for once not needing to fill the silence with idle chatter.

Once they had navigated to the opposite wing of the palace and reached Alexey's chambers—a grand, elegant space filled with the finest furniture and adorned with dark velvets and darker paintings of Novo-Svitsevo in nighttime—and a servant had closed them in, he turned to Morozov and raised an eyebrow. "So?"

"*Moy Tzar*," Morozov began. "We have tried the most advanced methods. None of them will alter their position."

"None?" Alexey crossed his arms over his chest and leaned back against the wall. "Not a single of the western nobles we managed to capture has been broken by a year in the dungeons and your . . . advanced methods?"

Morozov bowed his head. "I even found the journals of Mischa Danilleyev in their former workspace. We have tried all their . . . techniques. Some were . . . quite gruesome. None of them have produced results."

Alexey pinched the bridge of his nose. "What about the children?"

"The children, *Moy Tzar*?" Morozov's voice wavered.

"Where are the children?" Alexey fought to keep his voice even. What an irony it was, that now that his time in the lower realm was infinite, his patience had finally worn thin. "Where are they living now? Are they in the western provinces? Elsewhere? Can we abduct them?"

"Excuse my ignorance, *Moy Tzar*," Morozov said with a bowed head. "But what will we do with the children?"

"Torture their parents in front of them, you idiot," Alexey snapped. "Tell them that since their mothers and fathers declined to pledge their allegiance to me, they can do so and rule their houses, or join their parents in a cell while we move on to their next-born sibling. If you cannot break the body of the parent, break the mind of the child and bend them to our will."

Morozov straightened, his eyes gleaming with sudden under-standing, a smile twisting his lips. "Yes, *Moy Tzar*."

Alexey knew the pain of a broken mind well. Dimitri had done that to him, had ripped him apart with his unwillingness to listen to reason, to pay the proper regard to the Holy Science.

And everyone and everything in Novo-Svitsevo had paid the price.

*

Hours more spent reading reports from his spies around the empire did nothing to dull Alexey's focus. He should have been working in his study in the eastern wing of the palace, but after the interminable council meeting, he had needed the comfort of his bedroom fire-place. It threw off enough heat that sitting next to it at the small desk there, he almost felt warm.

By the time night fell, he could nearly taste the exhaustion of the man beside him, who was standing perfectly erect despite his fatigue, holding a pile of scrolls that he doled out one by one. When Alexey had unrolled the last report, had committed it to memory and tossed it in the fire, he watched as the young man's eyelids fluttered with exhaustion or boredom or both, just enough for him to see.

Ivan, with his high cheekbones and fine features and clear blue eyes, looked so much like his older half-brother Dimitri that, when the boy had worked among the palace staff, Alexey had sometimes mistaken Ivan for a younger version of his husband. It seemed that the former Tzar, Dimitri's father, had preferred to stash his bastard sons and daughters—there were plenty of them, and it was not as if his affairs were a secret—where he could watch over them all. Drawing Ivan in after Dimitri left had been useful, in several senses.

Ivan was younger than Dimitri by almost five years, and though his face was less angular, his skin devoid of Dimitri's light dusting of freckles, his frame slightly larger, there were enough common-alities that they might have been twins. Except when Alexey stood from his chair and rounded the table on quiet feet, letting his eyes trace Ivan's body, he caught the moment Ivan's gaze flicked from his chest to his belt. Alexey chuckled at the sight, causing a brilliant flush to spread over Ivan's cheeks, his head ducking in embarrassment. Ivan's interest, even if hidden away under bashfulness, was nothing like the way Dimitri would flinch away at the end, nothing like the way he'd shied away from Alexey's touch. Here, there was none of the repulsion that had rolled off Dimitri in waves, none of the fear.

Just because Alexey was cold, it did not mean he could not feel. And Dimitri drawing away from him day by day, becoming a shell of himself, avoiding Alexey's quarters, circling him like a specter—it had all been too much for Alexey to bear. It had almost been a relief when the war started and he could feel something for Dimitri that was not this deep, aching chasm of loss.

Alexey reached Ivan and lifted a hand to cup his cheek. The warmth of Ivan's skin was like the barest flush of dawn sunlight, but the way Ivan's eyes met his shot desire to the core of him.

This man craved his presence. Dimitri had been too weak to stand it.

"*Moy Tzar*," Ivan said, his voice nothing more than a breathy whisper. "You will dine with the court at the toll of the next bell. I could not cause you to be late for your duties."

Alexey drew a thumb over his lips. "Ivan," he said slowly, "I am the Tzar. No one tells me when to carry out my duty. The only duty I have now is to ask whether you desire me." He trailed his thumb lower, down Ivan's chin, and hooked into the collar of his shirt, feeling his pulse flutter, pulling him closer until their chests were touching. He was so fragile, so breakable, so *human*.

It was nice to hold someone who was intoxicated by his power and not repulsed by its cost. His time with Ivan had soothed something in him that had broken the last time Dimitri had pushed him away.

"Yes," Ivan breathed. "Yes, *Moy Tzar*."

Alexey spared a moment to take in the sight of Ivan, flushed and willing, then tore the jacket from him with one twist of his hand, leaving him in nothing but a waistcoat and shirtsleeves. He backed them up to the bed, then picked Ivan up, relishing the way he overwhelmed Ivan's smaller frame, the way the young man was as light as a feather in his arms, the way Ivan's desire was clearly evident.

When their lips met, Alexey almost did not think of Dimitri and how his mouth had tasted of vodka and sweetness and desire and the cigarettes he smoked when he thought no one could see.

Almost.

*

Alexey was indeed late to dinner. But walking into the dining chamber and seeing his court, fidgeting with their barely concealed agitation, made him smirk. He shrugged off his black cloak and threw it to a waiting servant, revealing a black damask jacket, a replacement having proven necessary after he and Ivan had thoroughly sullied the last one.

There was nothing wrong with reminding his court from time to time who controlled whom.

He trailed a finger against the backs of their chairs as he wound his way to the seat of honor at the northernmost point of the hexagram in which the tables had been arranged. He stood behind the ornately carved wooden chair, and only after meeting the gaze of each of the nobles around the tables did he motion for them to sit.

A servant approached with the ceremonial bread and a silver cup of wine, which Alexey took and raised high. "Pray," he ordered, and the court did, intoning their thanks to God for the fruit of the vine and the bread brought forth from the earth.

When the room had quieted, he raised a hand. "And now, to the Lord our God for the blessings of the Holy Science, with which He has protected Novo-Svitsevo. For this, we give thanks," he commanded.

They did. But Alexey did not miss that while many of his court prayed, they made gestures against demons or touched the bejeweled amulets they wore around their necks bearing the covertly hidden Seal of Zalman.

He knew what they were warding off, and it was not a demon. It was him.

The court at Rav-Mikhailburg was riven in two, and Alexey had not yet managed to forge it completely back together. So many of his lords and ladies had followed modern Ludayzim before his transformation, but during and after the war, many of them appeared to have harkened back to the supposedly protective customs of their foolish ancestors, full of empty liturgy and devoid of power and soul. So many in the court were terrified of what he had become, could not grasp that he had sacrificed his life to serve the empire and in the process had been blessed beyond measure. In secret, where they thought he could not hear, they called him a sinner, an abhorrence against the Lord his God.

But Alexey knew, even through his anger and frustration, that those who had fought against him and then retreated to their estates in defeat would eventually turn towards his rule. He would change their minds and educate them in their ignorance. He was, after all, the father of the empire, and he was merciful to his children. But if they refused to submit to him fully, he would be forced to send them to join their western brethren in the dungeons. And then, if they continued to disobey, he would dispose of them.

It would be all the mercy that traitors deserved.

"Lord Morozov," Alexey said once the first course had been placed on the tables, a delicate roasted quail that he would not eat. Food and drink no longer needed to pass his lips to keep him alive. He liked to remind his nobles that he was something they were not, a being who did not need to eat a single morsel in order to persist, and nothing said that better than plate after plate of untouched food. "You will deliver your report on the situation in the west."

"Yes, *Moy Tzar*," Morozov said, the sharp planes of his handsome face flushing with pleasure. He licked his full lips, running a hand through his golden-red hair. "We have grown the army in the southwest to fifty thousand soldiers. We have set up supply lines from Rav-Mikhailburg so that they can be fed and clothed adequately while they train."

Alexey tensed as Morozov began to detail the logistics of the supply convoy. The quail, left untouched on his plate, began to desiccate, slowly shriveling, the tiny bones cracking audibly.

Everyone in the room looked towards him. He breathed in, out, and reeled back the void that was beginning to open within him, itching to spill its magic into the lower realm. It had become more difficult to rein in, gradually becoming more insistent on seeking exit from Alexey's control, but he reminded it that he was its master, its creator, and he alone determined its use.

"Why," he said gently, ignoring the stares of his nobles, "can the army not supply itself in the field, Chancellor Morozov?"

His chancellor paused to wipe his mouth with a napkin. Alexey knew it was a ploy, so he could have a moment to compose himself. "There were . . . unexpected circumstances, *Moy Tzar*," he began. His green eyes shone with the tiniest tinge of fear, his narrow shoulders curling in on themselves. "A . . . situation has arisen in the countryside, which you need not concern yourself with."

Alexey raised an eyebrow. "A situation?"

"As I said, *Moy Tzar*," Morozov said with a dip of his head, "it is beneath your station."

There was a whisper to Alexey's left, and he whipped his head around, feeling his rage rise. "Lady Zakharova," Alexey said, watching the woman swallow hard. "Do you also feel as though details of *my* empire are beneath me?"

"No, *Moy Tzar*," Zakharova said quickly. Her eyes flicked back and forth between him and Morozov, as if she was judging whom it was safest to offend. She had always been significantly less astute at court politics than her daughter, Ladushka. Alexey had often wondered how the mother begat the child.

But for once, she chose correctly. "It is the peasants, *Moy Tzar*. They refuse to supply the soldiers. The peasants say that the soldiers deal in the Holy Science, and thus aiding them will offend the ghosts of the fallen, who speak to them."

Alexey fought to keep a straight face, burying his rage and vexation beneath a veneer of calm. So many of the empire's peasants clung to the old folk ways of Zalman's ancient line of Ludayzist teaching, fearing unburied corpses, believing that ghosts could possess living humans, all the nonsense that Alexey's own grandmother had peddled beside the fire. Foolish folktales for those who had neither modernized nor been awakened to the beauty of the Holy Science. So much non-sense and prejudice that stood in the way of progress. "I must enlighten them personally, it seems. Ready my carriage for tomorrow morning, Morozov. I will go to them and address their concerns."

He would drag this empire into the future, would enlighten its people about the miracles that men like him could wield with the right knowledge, the right ingredients, the right experiments, the right conditions. He would not let them continue to live in ignorance of all the Holy Science could do. He would not let them stop him from taking the power that was his right by the grace of God.

He stood from his chair, and the court of Balakin stood with him. It was the only time they did anything as one.

Alexey would change that. "We won a war," he said quietly, "against the boy who would have held Novo-Svitsevo in the past, crippled under the chains of ignorance. Against the boy who was not brave enough to seize the power that could have been his. Each of you has witnessed his failure. And each of you know that your holy duty is to assist me in rooting out that same failure among our people, no matter the cost. Science will replace superstition. Power will replace weakness. It is my pledge. So it shall be yours." He cast his gaze around the room.

His lords and ladies bowed before him. "Your command is my duty," they said one after another. But Alexey could tell from their flickering eyes and frowning mouths that many had faltering loyal-ties, and that he would need to strengthen the court before these cracks could show.

When Alexey wrapped his cloak around him and left the room, it was to utter silence.

THREE

VASILY

Vasily shivered in the late fall chill, pulling the collar of his thick woolen coat tight around his neck. The rain pattering down from the gray-clouded sky made him feel filthy, as if it was contaminated with soot and ash and all of the disgusting detritus that hung around the air in Wilnetzk. The Free States might have been part of no ruler's empire, but they certainly weren't free from the curse of being squalid.

If it weren't for Dimitri and the usurpation of the Novo-Svitsevan throne, he never would have been here, not even with all the spectacular brothels one had access to in this city.

Vasily arched his back slightly as he picked his way carefully down the uneven cobblestones of the street, keeping to the awnings of the various shops and taverns that he passed, his bowler hat and coat not doing nearly enough work to keep him dry. But it wasn't as if he had the luxury of going home to avoid the weather—there was far too much to do. He sighed, reminding himself that apparently, these days, he could not accomplish everything. There were too many enemies to ward off, and too much information to gather in order to keep his friends and his country safe.

But he would happily put work first. He'd pull out his own spine and wear it as a necklace if that was what his Tzar commanded.

He fingered the note in his pocket, the one from his latest spy, which he'd tucked in between a few of the playing cards he'd been thumbing through as he walked the streets. The boy had been sent to uncover the second-latest spy, who'd never reported back. There had, it turned out, been an obvious reason for this—the second-latest spy had been hanged outside the garrison at Rav-Mikhailburg, her tongue cut out in the mark of a traitor.

A familiar, itching anxiety made its way down Vasily's skin. He needed information. He had no information. None of his spies lasted long enough in Novo-Svitsevo to cultivate relationships, to extract truths to send back to him. And now he was left recruiting children to go find the bodies of his spies, because children were less suspicious. Until they became suspicious and he ended up getting children killed too. Just the thought of that eventuality made Vasily want to punch the nearest wall, then ruin the shine on his shoes by vomiting all over them.

He needed someone good. He needed someone who knew how to survive. Someone who wouldn't panic and give themselves away.

He pushed down the guilt he felt that the way he saw it, every person he passed on the street was a potential asset, someone who could be sent into the line of fire. Any one of them could be the spy he needed, the one capable of finally penetrating Alexey's court and figuring out what the devil was up to—or dying in the attempt. The pickings were slim—mostly men and a few women, bundled up against the rain, their heads bowed, scurrying around like rats trying to escape from the sewer. So he kept inching along down the street, unwilling to return home to his master without at least *something* to give him, some small scrap of hope.

Because what he had heard out of Novo-Svitsevo was very concerning indeed.

Vasily ducked into the next tavern on his mental list, wrinkling his nose at the smell of stale beer and the way the sawdust scattered on the floor to catch refuse crunched under the heel of his shoe. He wasn't pretentious—far from it, and certainly not compared to Annika or Ladushka, or, God knew it, Mischa—but now, after years spent lurking in the background in the palace, eavesdropping on nobles and uncovering plots, he could afford to have actual standards, ones that eliminated back-alley haunts from his list of preferred drinking establishments.

Still, despite the high pickpocket-to-patron ratio, these were the places where people whispered their fears to each other, and it was those whispers he needed to hear now.

Because while fears were often the result of minds spinning tales, they were also often based on kernels of truth. And Vasily's special talent was collecting truths, molding them together into stories, and using those stories to whisper to others. It was how he, a truly minor lord with few connections to speak of, had turned his brief stay at court into a job as the Tzar's anonymous, yet vital, spymaster.

So Vasily had pledged his life to Dimitri and never looked back. And that was how Vasily had come to learn that Dimitri was the best man he had ever met in the cesspit of the court—and still was, despite being a shell of his former self at the moment. Vasily knew every secret that the denizens of the court at Rav-Mikhailburg thought they'd kept hidden, and yet he'd never found so much as a hint of anything awful about Dimitri. He'd somehow managed to remain honest, and true, and surprisingly moral given the fact that he'd grown up as one of the jewels in the empire's crown and then spent almost a third of his life with Alexey Balakin.

Service to his country had saved Vasily, body and soul, in a way he could never repay. He'd made it his life's mission to protect Dimitri— the very heart of Novo-Svitsevo, the backbone of them all—from anything that might hurt him, be it assassination or civil unrest, or bruised ribs and a broken heart.

Vasily just wished he'd never seen Alexey in person. It was hard to reconcile knowing Alexey was evil with thinking that he was insufferably handsome. He wondered how Dimitri managed the dissonance.

Come to think of it, that could have something to do with Dimitri's depression. But Vasily shook his head to clear the thought. He had a job to do. And right now, he and four other people were all that stood between the country Vasily loved so much and utter disaster.

Vasily blinked in the low light of the flickering gas lamps, eyeing the few patrons lined up at the worn bar, the bartender pouring vodka from chipped bottles that looked older than Novo-Svitsevo itself. There was a woman in one of the corners of the room staring down at an untouched bowl of soup, her eyes puffy and red. Vasily's gut twisted in the way it did when he spotted a mark, someone whose pain and vulnerability he could exploit to his own ends. It made him feel terrible, but he couldn't bring himself to regret it, not when it kept his friends safe.

Not when the knowledge he gained could save Dimitri and his country both.

The chair across from her scraped over the floorboards as he pulled it back, dropping into it with a casually affected lack of grace. He pulled a handkerchief out of his pocket—cotton, not the one made of silk in his other pocket he would have offered to someone in a higher-class establishment—and held it out, twisting his expression into something sympathetic, perfected through hours in front of the mirror staring at his own completely forgettable face. "Are you all right?"

The woman took the handkerchief, and Vasily noted the cracking of the skin on her fingers, a sign of long hours spent outdoors in the winter. She used it to wipe at her eyes, then swallowed hard.

"I'm sorry." She spoke in accented Lietuvan, the way Mischa did—with the tones of someone who hadn't spent a lifetime with tutors, being taught other languages from birth. "I've had . . . a bad day." She laughed, but it came out like a gurgle, thick with tears. "Actually, more like a bad year. A fucking shit year."

That hit Vasily like a punch to the gut, and he had to fight not to let his smile slip. Hadn't they all.

"Is there anything I can do to help?" He let the strains of a rural Novo-Svitsevan accent slide back into his voice, letting her know that she was in the company of a fellow traveler, a fellow refugee— wherever her mind would take her, whatever her thoughts would paint onto the blank canvas that Vasily offered her.

"No, I just . . ." The woman fingered something on her lap and looked down, swallowing hard.

Vasily could tell simply from a well-honed gut instinct that this woman had some scrap of information for him, but that it would take time to unwind it from her. Pushing too hard would make her suspicious, when she clearly only wanted a sympathetic ear.

He preoccupied himself by raking his eyes down the woman's body—subtly, out of deference to her obvious state of distress. She was exactly the kind of woman he would have happily taken to bed, all plush curves and generous proportions, beautiful despite the cracking of her lips and the windburn on her cheeks. But he ignored the way his body responded to her, because he was working, and focused instead on the rucksack next to her. It was army issue—*their* army's issue—and so were her boots, peeking out of the muddy hem of her dress.

And that was check, and mate. Manufacturing shared trauma—a chance to bond if ever there was one—was one of Vasily's specialties.

"You served," he said. He toyed with the cuff of his coat between his fingers, worrying at the hole he'd intentionally picked into the too-fine-to-be-cheap wool with a knife. He'd really have to visit a second-hand shop if he was going to keep patronizing these kinds of taverns.

Her eyes widened, her mouth pursing. "What?"

"I did too." Vasily had, in a manner of speaking, served in Dimitri's army.

"Ah." The corner of her mouth lifted up. She held the object on her lap aloft. It was a shard of something on a string. "Today is the anniversary of the day my entire family died in the war. I would have placed a headstone on their graves today, but they don't have them. I wasn't there to bury them. I was too busy being shot in the ribs."

Vasily peered closer at what she was holding. It was a piece of bone. He shivered. "May their memories be a blessing." He passed a hand over his face. He almost hated to pry, but he needed to. "Do you have news, from home?"

The woman bit her lip, looking off to the side, anger flashing across her eyes. "I write to my village's rebbe from time to time."

He poked at her wound. "Where is home?"

"Voloski, to the south of the capital." She shook her head, picking up her spoon and fiddling with it. "Last I heard, the Tzar was calling up soldiers, sending them to the garrison at Domachëvo. And worse, villages are being ordered to turn over food stores to the army. But there isn't anything left to eat. There's no one to harvest the grain rotting in the fields. Too many died in the war." She recited it all in the way that people did now, deadpan, as if by showing no emotion the reality of war and pain and loss could never touch her.

Vasily looked down at his hands. Too many *had* died in the war. He had lost track of the names of those he knew personally who had met their end at the barrel of a gun. "Are you planning to go back? Is there anything left for you to go back to?"

"No." The woman shook her head, staring down into her soup. "No, my family home and my father's butcher shop were destroyed when the army went through. I'm entitled to compensation for the damage, but the capital can keep their blood money. A few tolar won't bring back what I lost. It won't bring back any of the people who made my house a home."

They sat for a moment in silence, the clinking of glasses and the low murmur of voices the only thing penetrating the horror of what she was saying. But as always, Vasily's mind began to piece together the puzzle. She'd mentioned a dead family and government benefits that had never been claimed. Maybe, if he was very lucky, she had a dead relative whose identity one of his spies could borrow for a trip to Rav-Mikhailburg, to do a bit of poking around.

Or . . . he licked his lips as his heart started beating faster. Or, if she had a dead male relative roughly his age, *he* could go instead. If she did, it would be the most promising lead by far that he'd uncovered in months, something to get him back to Rav-Mikhailburg, even if it got him no closer to Alexey's court. But it was something—he'd be able to spend some time in the capital finding a ruse to penetrate the palace . . .

But before he could prod her for more information, she asked, "Do you have news from home?" She handed back his handkerchief, wet with her tears. He took it, his fingers brushing hers, feeling the scrape of skin ruined, he surmised now, by too many days spent gripping a gun.

"No," he said bluntly. "Not a word. Everyone I knew who stayed in Novo-Svitsevo died." Horribly. He would never be able to scrub the image from his mind of his spies hanging from the bridge leading into Rav-Mikhailburg, their entrails pulled out and used to make the nooses roped around their necks. Vasily may have hated Alexey, but he had to give him credit—the man had boundless creativity when it came to pain.

"May their memories feed a revolution," the woman said, her voice thick with hate. She turned to her cabbage soup, starting to eat in a way that told Vasily she was done with this conversation, and done with him.

Vasily couldn't help the lump that lodged in his throat at her words.

"I'm trying," he whispered to himself as he stood, too quiet for her to hear. Because if his love and his grief for his country could lead an army, he'd already be at Alexey's gates.

He pitched his voice louder. "I come here every so often. If you need someone to talk to, I'll see you soon, I'm sure." It would be worth trying to see if he could manufacture a second meeting and make it look like pure coincidence, so he could ask her the questions he hadn't had the chance to.

She looked him in the eye, her mouth twisted with anger even as tears rimmed her lower lashes. "Thank you. Really. Maybe sometime."

He bid her goodbye and left the tavern, heading to the next one. And then the next. And the next. But everyone had the same story, the same news.

By the end of the night he knew, without a doubt, that the devil was coming for them and Novo-Svitsevo both.

*

By the time Vasily made it back to the townhouse, he was thanking God for the warmth and the dryness. He hung his sodden coat on the hook in the entryway, toed off his shoes, tossed his hat and suit jacket onto the upholstered bench by the door, and avoided the kitchen, where Mischa would undoubtedly be trying to bake something to tempt Dimitri with.

He loved his friends, but he needed Dimitri to hear his suspicions first. He wondered if he should broach with Dimitri the growing sense in his gut that no one would be as good at penetrating Alexey's court as himself and that he couldn't risk more and more people who he just knew wouldn't survive, but then shoved the thought aside.

Dimitri wouldn't take that well, not at all. One bit of bad news for his Tzar at a time.

He took the stairs two at a time, anxiety gnawing at him, his mind piecing together the information he'd gathered, constructing a story out of parts that he could tell to his Tzar. He passed the landing with his and Annika's bedrooms, then the next level where Ladushka and

Mischa stayed. He hesitated at the door to Dimitri's attic room, his hand on the cool brass of the knob, then let himself in.

Dimitri was hunched in the chair by his fire, the wood long since burned to nothing more than ashes. His cheeks were hollow in the light from a few last flickering candles, and his fingers toyed with an empty glass tumbler. He looked like he needed someone to hold him together, to keep him from shattering.

"It's freezing in here." Vasily's cheeks stung with the chill in the air of the bedroom. It was almost winter, far too late in the year to suffer anything except a raging fire at all times. Vasily crossed the room in a few steps, kneeling down to put more wood on the fire, stoking it back to life. When the wood finally caught, he stood up and gently moved Dimitri over in the chair with both hands, his heart clenching at how thin Dimitri was becoming, the way the ridges of his spine and arches of his ribs pressed through the fabric of the dressing gown he always wore, the one that smelled like another man's cologne even now. Vasily always tried to block from his mind the fact that he could tell exactly whose dressing gown it was that Dimitri clung to like a baby's blanket.

"I wasn't cold," Dimitri protested, but a shiver went through him all the same. He melted into Vasily's side as he sat down, Dimitri's head falling onto Vasily's shoulder, the shorn sides of his hair like velvet against the skin of Vasily's neck.

Vasily bit back the quiet urge to find something, anything, to soothe his Tzar's sadness away. Instead, he ghosted a thumb back and forth across Dimitri's knuckles and tilted his head until his nose was buried in Dimitri's hair, which he kept longer on top, inhaling the familiar scent to calm himself. He slung an arm around Dimitri's shoulders.

"The situation is bad." Dimitri whispered it, more a statement than a question. And Vasily's heart ached because yes, it was.

"Alexey isn't just calling up an army." Vasily stared straight ahead, looking at the ash on the lintel from the fire, the mantel decorated with discarded bottles of vodka. It was easier to give someone their death sentence when you didn't have to look them in the eye. "He's also laying down supply lines, the kind you'd need to move a very large army. I've heard twenty tales tonight from twenty refugees, all saying that their relatives back home are being ordered to supply the army with what food they have left. The supply lines lead all through Novo-Svitsevo. What he's planning is big."

Dimitri stilled, then reached up and wrapped his fingers around Vasily's forearms. Vasily's heart clenched. Even through the thick cotton of Vasily's shirt, Dimitri's skin was like ice.

The wind rattled the panes of Dimitri's window, like someone shaking the bars of a cage, and Vasily felt the other man jump at the sound.

"We'll see what Lada thinks in the morning," Dimitri eventually rasped. "She would know, and Anna too." He tilted his head up, staring into Vasily's eyes in a way that left him feeling helpless.

Vasily shook his head, an apology. "This can't wait until morning," he said gently. Which perhaps was true, but came more from the fact that he would not be able to sleep tonight without knowing that they could do something, *anything*, other than just sit there—lambs before the slaughter—to stop yet another war, yet another wash of soldiers sweeping over Novo-Svitsevo, decimating everything in their path.

Dimitri's entire body tensed, the light gone from his eyes in half a heartbeat. Vasily's chest hollowed out.

"Because, Dima . . ."

He cleared his throat, swallowing the scream that was trying to break through the veneer of calm he wanted—needed—to maintain for Dimitri. "Dima, most of the supply lines lead south. I think Alexey and his army are coming here, to Wilnetzk. I think they're coming for us."

DIMITRI

It was hard to remember how to be useful.

Dimitri dropped his head into his hands, digging the heels into his eyes until he saw stars. He had spent three years as Tzar, doing useful things every day, running a country and being what he hoped was a ruler for the ages, and now he was unable to get through even a simple strategy session with Ladushka. Even with Mischa continually poking his side to keep him awake, Dimitri's thoughts kept going back to Alexey. Where he was, what he was planning. And sometimes, traitorously, whether he was okay, whether he was safe, whether he was taking care of himself without Dimitri there to prod him to do so.

"Dima," Ladushka said icily, "do you need to stop? Because we have only been discussing Vasya's information for an hour, you and I, which is not very much time at all."

He looked up at her, her pale-blue eyes shining with disapproval, her back perpetually straight, and slumped backwards into his chair. He couldn't stand the disappointment in her expression, as if he'd been irreparably ruined and was now incapable of scheming with her. Ladushka had always had the power to make him feel like an idiot, even from the time they were both children growing up together in the royal nursery, similar enough in age that they had been paired for lessons, which had turned them into friends. Her lack of deference to him was part of why he loved her so, and why he had trusted her as his chancellor and political adviser, tasked with the running of his empire.

"I don't need to stop," he said. "I need a drink."

"Absolutely not." Mischa clamped a hand on his shoulder as he tried to stand. Dimitri struggled, but either he had gotten weaker or they had gotten stronger sometime in the last few months. "Unless you're looking to be crowned Tzar of Gaunt Cheekbones before you die of cirrhosis, you'll stop drinking and start eating."

"Who gave you the right to tell me what to do?" Dimitri asked sulkily, trying to bat Mischa's arm away.

"The Lord our God, and also you, you ass," Mischa said, flicking him hard on the cheek with their thumb and forefinger, then brushing imaginary crumbs from their vest and suit jacket as if Dimitri had gotten something dirty on it. "Taking care of your health *is* my actual job. It's the one you gave me after I saved your damned leg after that idiotic riding accident when none of the royal physicians could. And as your physician, I order you not to drink in the middle of the day, Dima, for God's sake."

"Mischka," Dimitri groaned. He slumped further down into the armchair, then curled on his side to rest his head on Mischa's shoulder, hoping the headache that was growing between his temples would somehow vanish. "You're going to be the death of me."

Mischa fell uncharacteristically quiet and didn't follow Dimitri's moaning with a sharp-tongued quip. Probably because they knew Dimitri wasn't truly angry about the effort to preserve his life.

No, it was more about the terror that ran through him at the thought of having to face his own sober thoughts. Of having to think on what he had done and who he had become. The failed leader who had been up to his ankles in blood when he retreated off the

THE SINS ON THEIR BONES

battlefield, the coward who had tucked his tail and run off to the Free States, exiling himself, abandoning his country to the rule of a monster. Or worse, having to think on what Alexey had become, all the blood from that night, the terror and the hope of waiting for him to come back. The heartbreak of realizing that when he did, it wasn't *him*, but someone—some*thing* else. Something worse.

"People," Ladushka said, her voice placid as always, the only hint of tension in the way she gripped her pen hard enough to show bone through the skin of her knuckles. "Pay attention, please, to what I am telling you." She gestured at the map of Novo-Svitsevo and the surrounding countries, which she had been marking up, trying to divine what Alexey's plans might be.

"Lady Ladushka Zakharova, master of politics, you have my full attention." Dimitri feigned a bow from his seat. He eyed the decanter of vodka on the sideboard but contented himself with reaching for his cigarette case, striking a match and lighting one with shaking fingers. He raised an eyebrow when Mischa snatched it from him to take a long draw, exhaling through their nose. "And Doctor Mischa Danilleyev, who knew you were such a hypocrite, you of the long diatribes about health and not poisoning our bodies."

Mischa arched an eyebrow and handed the cigarette back. "Fuck you."

Dimitri rolled his eyes. Criticism always made Mischa caustic.

"There are four possible outcomes, in my opinion," Ladushka said, ignoring them both. "And the problem is that they are all equally plausible. I am not as convinced as Vasya that the answer is obvious."

Dimitri's anxiety deflated at that. Ladushka's belief was that Alexey's supply routes leading straight to Wilnetzk might be nothing more than a clever feint. And while Vasily was the one who gathered and leveraged the information no one else could, Ladushka was the one who saw the path of empires, fitting people into bigger roles, understanding how the forces of countries moved and clashed.

She must have heard the sigh of relief that escaped him at her reassurance, because she frowned, just slightly, her rosebud lips turning down at the edges. She took a moment to straighten her perfectly pressed ruffled blouse and finger the buttons on her skirt, even though they were perfectly even too. Dimitri's nerves grew at the tiny tells. It never boded well when even Ladushka was nervous enough to show it.

"Do not become complacent, Dima. It is difficult to know Alexey's plans because we have no access to his court and he has not made any public declarations of policy or intent." She looked at Dimitri levelly, her eyes serious in the light trickling in from the window.

"It's almost like he knows that when you say your plans out loud, your enemies can hear," Dimitri said with a snort. "Alexey always did keep everything close to his chest. His plots were always for him and God alone, as if God would listen to a heretic." He ignored the stinging in his eyes at the thought of all Alexey had kept from him and took another drag on his cigarette.

Ladushka furrowed her brow. "It is completely evident what his immediate problem is. He has strangled his own trade routes. The western provinces are still loyal to you, Dima, to the best of our knowledge. Vasya keeps in contact with most of the nobility there—or rather, whoever is running the estates now that Alexey has arrested many of the lords and ladies—and they seem to be holding firm against Alexey. So he has no route to the water, and grain is lying to rot in the fields because it cannot be transported elsewhere for sale."

"Grain isn't the only thing rotting in those fields," Annika said quietly. She appeared in the doorway with barely there footsteps announcing her presence, her long hair swinging from her head in a horse's tail and her knives tucked into a belt slung around her hips, dangling like ornaments over her breeches. She settled into an empty chair, undoing the clasps of the leather vest she wore and straightening the sleeves of her blue cotton shirt. Vasily followed behind her, his shirt soaked with sweat and rolled up to the elbows, flipping one of Annika's knives between his fingers. Dimitri reflexively checked him for injuries, then stopped himself—he and Annika must have just been sparring. They, at least, hadn't given up trying to stay fit.

"I haven't forgotten," Dimitri said grimly. Annika reached out and clasped her hand over his, giving it a squeeze. She was the one who felt the pain of the war worst of all. She had never wanted to be the leader of Dimitri's armies, had only done it because of pressure from her father, a renowned general in Dimitri's father's court. She'd been recalled from her father's country estate after Alexey had pressed Dimitri to replace the man, insisting that Dimitri needed his highest-ranking general to be loyal to him alone and not to the memory of the former Tzar. She'd demonstrated a keen mind for strategy, but Dimitri had been puzzled that she'd been the one chosen to follow in her father's footsteps, and not her brothers—she'd been unfailingly kind and warm from the moment they'd met, two weeks into Dimitri's reign. A nurturer, not a warrior, despite her facility with knives and tactics. But he'd put his worries aside, because Annika had never once complained about her role, and he'd enjoyed her company too much to send her away. And in the end, Alexey had been right about both Annika's father's loyalty and her own; he'd turned on Dimitri when Alexey announced his intention to claim the throne, and she'd stuck by him all this time.

All the death they'd seen and caused in the war, though, had dimmed the light in her eyes in a way that made Dimitri's heart ache.

Ladushka moved her fountain pen over the map as Vasily came to stand behind her, leaving a precise line, impeccably straight. "So there lies one potential reason to raise an army—attacking the western provinces. The problem with that is the mountain range the western provinces crouch behind. It would take a massive army to breach. It remains the only reason they escaped the worst of the war."

"Yes," Annika said. "We all remember. They just shut the mountain passes and pissed off. So lovely of them to say they stayed loyal to Dima though."

Ladushka gazed off into the corner of the room and wound a strand of her flaxen hair around a stark white finger. Sometimes Dimitri wondered if she had any blood in her at all or if she was made up entirely of political knowledge. "It is what anyone would have done. If Dima had won, they would have been forgiven. We need them for trade too badly to hold a petty grudge. If Dima lost, then they would have held all the cards against Alexey. He either makes a deal with them to rejoin the empire, or they remain independent and get rich off their status as the only deepwater port between the Free States and the isles of the far north." She brushed her finger over the left edge of the map, where the ocean lay.

"Unless he crushes them with an army," Annika said. She examined her chipped fingernails idly. "It's not a chance I would take."

Ladushka shook her head and moved her pen along the stylized mountains that separated the western provinces from the rest of Novo-Svitsevo on the map. "It would be very difficult, given the terrain, and since the western provinces were not involved in the war, they still have large stores of ammunition—and healthy soldiers. I cannot conceive that it is a likely option. It is why he is trying to force their loyalty in other ways, why so many of the western nobles have been reported abducted from their homes, why Alexey is trying to replace them with their children who have sworn loyalty to him. Alexey is many things, but not stupid."

Of course he wasn't. He had tricked Dimitri into heresy of the highest order. He had clawed his way to immortality, to being whatever he was now, and then he had won a war that he should have lost.

Dimitri got up and stretched his arms behind his head, then began to pace around the room. Talking of war made it hard for him to sit still.

"Tell me about the other possibilities," he said, taking another drag on the cigarette, then passing it to Annika.

"Another possibility is that he is preparing for an attack through the eastern provinces, and is going to try to subjugate Urushka and establish trade into the far east." Ladushka drew another line on the map, from the center to the rightmost edge. "That would be a logical reason for a feint to the southwest. Urushka would potentially lose valuable time preparing for war."

Annika laughed. "Unlikely. And besides, that would be the best-case scenario for us all. He and his army can march into Urushka and the Urushkin cavalry can cut them down like grass under a scythe. I don't think the Pretender would stand a chance."

Dimitri closed his eyes. All this talk of Alexey was like being poked with pins, a discomfort just on the edge of pain. "Alexey can't be killed with a scythe, Anna. Nothing can kill him."

"You know what I mean," she shot back. "I don't think it's likely. I stand by what I said before. I agree with Vasya. I think he's coming here. Advancing on the Free States. It's easier terrain to cover, it's a path to the sea, and a rich little prize to conquer."

"It explains the supply lines," Vasily broke in. "I'm not as convinced as Lada is that those are a ploy." His grip on the back of Ladushka's chair tightened, and his evident tension tightened Dimitri's ribs unpleasantly too. He was flipping a tightly folded piece of paper through his fingers now, like he usually would with a playing card, frowning down at it like it held bad news. Maybe it did.

"It cannot be discounted as a possibility," Ladushka admitted, drawing a fourth line down from Novo-Svitsevo to the Free States that crouched below its bulk, hugging the ocean to their left. "It certainly is one. And maybe it is even the most likely."

Mischa's long fingers stilled from where they had been nervously tapping along the edge of the table. They rubbed a hand over their shaved head, their green eyes narrowing, the dusting of freckles across their normally tan skin showing bluntly now that they'd gone pale. "Look, Lada might be right. Vasya might not have complete information, or the move to construct southern supply lines could be a hoax." They cleared their throat and shifted uncomfortably. Dimitri turned to look at Mischa, a chill running through him.

"But he has another reason to come here," Mischa continued, inclining their head towards Dimitri. "Let's not forget that the true Tzar sits here. The one who by all rights should be ruling the country. As long as Dima is alive, he will be a threat to Alexey's reign. No one knows exactly where we are, but Alexey must suspect where we ran to. You could only have sought refuge in so many places, Dima—it won't take him years to search them all."

Dimitri sat back down heavily, grabbing another cigarette from the dwindling supply in his case and lighting it. His hand clenched the arm of his chair involuntarily as he inhaled the bitter smoke. The thought of Alexey, here, was too much. Another drag on the cigarette did little to calm his nerves. "He doesn't know where I am. He can't." He'd never mentioned the address of his grandmother's house to Alexey, not that he could recall.

The floorboards creaked as Vasily shifted his weight, his hand coming up to press over his mouth. For a moment, no one spoke. His court had never hesitated to tell him the truth, but none of them liked being the bearer of bad news.

"From your lips to God's ears," Annika said. "But we have to prepare for the eventuality that he'll find out. We can't stay hidden forever. And any one of us would be a prize." She looked around the room, grimacing. "We'd be paraded around the city before he killed us, just as a symbol of how he was crushing the old regime." Her eyes clouded over. "And Dima, I don't want to even think about what that monster would do to you."

Dimitri felt that like an arrow to the heart.

"There is one final option," Ladushka said, her gaze unfixed, her mind clearly wandering elsewhere, envisioning all the ways in which Alexey could thwart them. "Alexey could be planning something that none of us can foresee."

They all stared down at the map.

"How likely is that, Lada?" Annika asked.

"Who could say?" Ladushka replied. "We know he is raising an army. None of the ways in which he can use an army are immediately obvious as the clear choice. Perhaps we have not foreseen his plans." A tiny, repeated tapping of her forefinger on the pen was the only evidence of her discomfort at the thought.

Vasily bit his lip. "That's possible. He surprised us enough during the war. Like what he did at Vysoka."

Dimitri closed his eyes, and for a moment all he could see was miles of broken bodies and Alexey staring at him from across the field, swathed in black and with those bottomless eyes that did not belong to the man he loved. All he could feel was the weight of the pistol in his hand, his arm shaking as he struggled to pull the trigger. All he could hear were the screams, all he could smell was the blood and the guts and the gunpowder . . .

"Dima." Mischa's hands were on both of his shoulders, shaking him. Dimitri opened his eyes to look into their warm green eyes. Human eyes. "It's not real. You're safe. You're here. Breathe."

Dimitri tried, but his breathing was shallow, his body shaking, the terror of that day creeping up on him as if it was happening all over again. "I want that drink now," he said, hating the way it sounded like he was pleading.

Mischa gave a curt nod, and Vasily stood up to get everyone glasses, his face drawn and his eyes contrite. He poured each of them a measure of vodka, paused, and then filled Dimitri's cup to the brim. He put the stopper back in the bottle and raised his glass. "If I die first," he said, beginning the toast they had said over and over since the beginning of the war.

"I'll tell you the secrets of heaven," they all echoed. A talisman against the permanence of death, against being parted forever. A reminder that, even in the afterlife, they'd claw their way back to one another.

Dimitri drank, and the vodka slowly burned away some of the fear that had coiled in his chest. But now his court was watching him, and the way they studied his movements—like he was about to break down—made him sad in a way that he could barely comprehend.

"I'm tired," he choked out. "I'm going to lie down." He stood up too quickly for it to be casual and wobbled his way out of the parlor and up the stairs, betrayed by his shaky legs. He hoped none of them would follow him and was gratified when his footsteps were the only ones he heard on the stairs.

He made it up three flights to the townhouse's top floor, pushed open the door to his bedroom, and collapsed on the bed. He breathed, in and out, trying to master himself. But still, the panic came as it always did, mingled with shame and failure and fear.

If Alexey were here, he would have ordered him to breathe and take hold of his own mind. And it would have worked, because the part of Dimitri that was weak bowed to the whole of Alexey that was strong. And then Alexey would have gathered him up in his arms and taken him to the library on their estate, would have let Dimitri doze in his lap in front of the fire, the dogs at their feet, their cat perched on the back of the sofa. And while Alexey would have read a book for hours, unmoving so that he would not wake Dimitri, his face would have nestled into Dimitri's hair. And when Dimitri came to, the panic would have washed away and he would have known he was safe, and loved.

Alexey had been his shelter, and now he was gone. Dimitri was laid bare to the ravages of memory.

There was a knock at the door that Dimitri barely heard, and Vasily entered without waiting for Dimitri to speak.

"I need to talk to you." There was a pinched crease between Vasily's eyebrows, and Dimitri couldn't decide if he wanted to smooth it out with his fingers or yell at Vasily for barging in, witnessing his private pain.

Vasily folded his long legs and knelt on the floor, studiously ignoring the agony written on Dimitri's face. Dimitri sat up, looking down at Vasily, who reached out, paused, then hesitantly slid his palms up Dimitri's thighs, his presence warm and reassuring. Vasily searched his face for subtle confirmation, as always, that the touch was welcome.

Seeing Vasily kneeling there in front of him made something within Dimitri burn, but he pushed it away, even as Vasily's hands slid higher.

Dimitri could feel Vasily's heart beating against his knees. Vasily didn't move—he knew better than to join Dimitri on the bed. Dimitri had been clear he couldn't stand to share a bed with anyone now, not even his friends, not even during the day, not even if they were both awake and talking, unless he was being completely and utterly distracted by a good fuck. Otherwise, the heat of another person next to him in a bed was unbearable.

It was too much like that last night he had woken up next to Alexey.

"Dima." Vasily had been talking to him. Dimitri refocused.

"What, Vasya?" It came out tired and sad and cold. Vasily didn't meet his eyes, and suddenly Dimitri wasn't sure he wanted to know the answer to his own question.

Vasily drew in a deep breath, but it hitched in his chest.

The edges of panic crept back into Dimitri's mind. "Vasya, what?"

He bit his lip. "We need a spy in Alexey's court."

The panic fled, just a bit. "Fine. Find someone new. Maybe they'll even come back this time." Dimitri knew the jab was cruel as soon as he said it, but he couldn't help himself. He shook his head, trying to clear his thoughts of all the people who had died because of him— *for* him—in the last two years. It was far too many.

He brought his hands to Vasily's wrists, about to move the man's hands off of him, about to do something else, something to make himself small and vulnerable, because what he'd just said must have made Vasily upset and he couldn't stand the thought of that. With Vasily's pulse beating against his fingers, he wanted to drop to his knees and reach for Vasily's waist and offer something more. But Vasily simply flipped his hands and grabbed Dimitri's wrists instead, stopping him, his thumbs smoothing over Dimitri's veins.

"Dima." Vasily's voice was quiet, soft, cracking at the edges. "Dima, it's got to be me. I want it to be me."

"What?" Dimitri pulled away from Vasily, stunned. "You want what to be you?"

"The spy." Vasily pushed off Dimitri's thighs and rocked back on his heels, and Dimitri felt the loss of his warmth like plunging into an icy pond. "I want to penetrate Alexey's court myself. It's too dangerous and too uncertain, sending someone else. We know he never uncovered that I was the one you hired as your spymaster, and he won't recognize me as nobility, not as a lord from such a minor house. You said it yourself—no one else I've tried to cultivate has come back. We need to know what he's doing, Dima. We need to keep you safe."

"No." Dimitri didn't even have to think about the answer. It came from him as reflexively as his next heartbeat. "No. You're not going. I forbid it. If he finds you, he'll kill you. He'll do worse."

"I know the danger." Vasily stood and crossed his arms, staring down at Dimitri the way Alexey would have when he was chiding Dimitri for something poorly done. "We can't keep sitting here and doing nothing, Dima. If that's what we're going to do, we might as well all lie down at night and let the devil take our souls, because there's no point to living if it's like this."

Dimitri fought the urge to plead, to scream, to pick up the crystal decanter next to his bed and throw it at the wall, to scare some sense into Vasily the way Alexey would have. "No. I forbid it."

"You may still be my Tzar, Dima, but in truth you can't order me to do anything." Vasily's eyes fluttered shut, and he swallowed hard enough for Dimitri to hear his throat click. "I wouldn't just be doing this for you. I would be doing this for *us*. For all of us and for Novo-Svitsevo both."

"Fuck you," Dimitri spat, sudden fury making his cheeks heat.

"Don't be selfish," Vasily shot back. "Don't stop me from protecting the country. If I have to die, I want it to be while I was doing *something* about Alexey. I played my part in it, just like you did, and now I have to atone. We all do."

For a moment, the room was silent, still, as if Vasily realized he'd overstepped. Dimitri's anger shattered into something that felt like it was tearing pieces of his heart away. "I've been atoning for what I did every single day, every single moment since that night." There was a tremor in his voice and he didn't even care, couldn't bring himself to be ashamed. "How *dare* you imply I'm not doing enough."

Vasily sighed and turned to look out the window. "I'm going. You can't stop me."

He didn't move to comfort Dimitri, the way he usually would. Instead, he pulled out his pack of cards from the war, a gift from a soldier in Dimitri's guard—the first to have died—that he'd carried like an amulet ever since. He started shuffling, looking down at the worn cards marked with ink where he'd drawn on them, a frown on his face.

Dimitri wondered if Vasily thought him such a pathetic man now, angry at his role in the country's downfall.

At that thought, the pain became overwhelming and Dimitri's anger dissolved into aching, agonizing sadness. He gathered his knees to his chest, wrapping his arms around his legs as if that could stop him from breaking.

"Please don't leave me, Vasya." It came out as a whisper. "I can't do this alone. I don't know if I can *live* without you all." And that was the truth of it. He didn't know if he could survive losing yet another person he treasured. He had so few of those left, bereft as he was of both his entire family and his husband. All the people he cared for in the world could sleep in a single small townhouse. And now, Vasily was trying to leave because of him, because of something he'd done, and Dimitri would never forgive himself if—

"You have to." Vasily's voice was harsh as he pocketed the cards again and scrubbed a hand over his face. "You have the rest of the court. I'm the only one who can do this. I'm the only one with the skills to survive and come back with the information we need."

"Find another way." He wished he knew how to make Vasily obey his commands, because he could tell the other man disregarded him, his eyes glassy, shaking his head back and forth.

Vasily stepped forward and rubbed a tender thumb down Dimitri's cheek. "No. This is our best chance, and you know it. Please don't make this harder, Dima. It will already be hard enough, leaving you." He left with a pitying glance and not another word.

Dimitri forced himself to move once he was alone again, pulling his boots off, then divesting himself of his shirt and pants, all the while in a daze at Vasily's insistence on martyring himself. Then he wrapped himself in the dressing gown he had worn every night since their arrival in Wilnetzk.

But for once, he didn't take his wedding ring back out of the drawer and slip it on, thumbing at the gold.

FIVE

ALEXEY

As the night stretched on, Alexey spent his time studying the Holy Science, now that his court was asleep and he had no such base needs.

He flipped the edges of the book he had been trying to read between his fingers, using the repetitive motion to free his mind. It would be a long carriage ride to the nearest village tomorrow, and during the journey he would have to deduce how to deal with the peasants' concerns in a way that would both result in his desired outcome and allow news of his visit to spread so that he would not have to personally visit the entire countryside to goad peasants into complying with his edicts.

Morozov would come along, as he always did, and Alexey decided he would bring Ivan as well. Ivan could occupy Morozov with asinine questions if Alexey wanted to be alone with his thoughts.

Alexey sighed, already dreading the prospect of tomorrow, but leaned back in his chair, redirecting his attention to the book on his lap. His study was usually one of the few places in the palace that allowed him to forget the troubles of his fractured court and his desires to crush everyone in it and start anew. Here, there were no courtiers, no demands, no one in his bed or trying to capture his ear. It was just him and his library, and the connection he felt to God when he learned of yet another miracle he could carry out.

When Dimitri had become Tzar five years ago, Alexey had been gifted the suites that had belonged to Dimitri's mother, an amalgam of parlors and sitting rooms, and a large bedroom across from the one Dimitri took. It had taken weeks, but Alexey had remade them in his own image, swapping the abundance of floral wallpaper and hideous gold leafing for damask and velvets and the rich jewel tones that he favored, far more appropriate for the dwelling of the Tzar Consort. And an unused parlor was converted to a study, filled with shelves so that he could grow his collection of books on the mysticism of Ludayzist scholars that he knew was the key to Dimitri's future control over the country.

Alexey turned and walked around the room, trailing a finger along the leather spines of dusty books and his own copious journals lined up neatly on their walnut shelves.

He checked the cage in the corner that held a small demon with the wings of a bat and a coal-black body shaped like a cat's. It was curled up, its serpentine tail wrapped around its body, but it cracked an eye open and chirped when he reached in to scratch its velvet-soft head and check that its bowl of cream was full. It had fallen through a rift he had created during an experiment, injured, and he had nursed it back to health and kept it for company—and as a reminder of his newfound power. He lingered for a moment, stroking it back to sleep, but then an image of Dimitri playing with a litter of spring kittens bubbled up from the darkness. It sent a pang through his chest so strong that for a moment, he could hardly breathe.

He resumed his pacing and let himself fall into the deep well of his memories. And his regrets.

✳

Alexey often thought about how this all began, his ascent to power, and his dominion over man and the empire.

He knew how to run a court because he had done it all his life. His father had died young, and at nineteen Alexey oversaw a provincial estate governing Chernitzy, the most profitable region in the empire, enriched by its mines that yielded diamonds and gems, gold and silver and coal. And for years, he worked to ensure that taxes were collected, that the peasants were fed, that the region was peaceful and prosperous and secure.

He had done it. For nine years, he had lived up to his birthright and honored the legacy of his family, which had ruled Chernitzy for longer than written records existed. And then, when he was twenty-eight, he met his undoing.

Dimitri had come with his family on a tour of the region, barely twenty years old and bold and beautiful. The third and youngest son of the Tzar and Tzarina, Tzarevitch Dimitri was nothing, meant for little more than marrying well and bringing honor and wealth to the Crown.

Alexey had looked into those crystal-blue eyes, seen the corners of that rich mouth twitch upwards, the perfection of that cream-pale skin, and knew this was a man full of possibilities. That night, after dining with the family and realizing that Dimitri was intelligent—far more than any of them, including the Tsesarevich Fedyenka, the eldest son who by birth would rule the empire after his father's passing—Alexey decided that there was one more thing he needed to make his rule over Chernitzy complete.

A dutiful, brilliant, handsome husband, someone he could have on his arm at political functions with the members of his provincial court, someone who would be by his side as he ruled, a steadfast supporter. One more paving stone on the path of his inevitable rise to becoming the greatest ruler Chernitzy had ever known.

For that role, he chose Tzarevitch Dimitri.

The Tzar readily agreed to the proposal of marriage, on one condition—that Dimitri not be married before Fedyenka chose a wife. Marrying his sons out of order would be unseemly, when the future of the Abramovich line had yet to be secured through heirs. Alexey agreed. He did not need Dimitri to be legally bound to him immediately. He would achieve that in every other way.

And so, when Dimitri was left with him after his family departed, bewildered and naïve but willing, Alexey set about molding him.

*

Alexey blinked himself out of his stupor, quelling the desire that rose within him at the memory of those early days with Dimitri, his husband's fumbling eagerness, and the way that Alexey had fought not to laugh at Dimitri's attempts to seduce him. Alexey had never intended to care for Dimitri—he had engaged in a transaction for power, and feelings did not enter into such a thing—except, after a while, it had become inevitable.

Like so much about Dimitri, Alexey knew now that it had always been inevitable.

Dimitri's entire family had been assassinated by anarchists just three years after their meeting. Dimitri was only spared because he had been safely ensconced on Alexey's estate, being tutored in Chernitzy's regional politics and strategy so he could hold a conversation with Alexey's party guests, allowing Alexey to drape him in furs and jewels, being shaped into the exceptional man Alexey knew he could be.

But then all of that had been ripped away.

That evening, when the chancellor of the court had arrived with the news, the pain that flitted through Dimitri's eyes awoke something within Alexey. Something unfamiliar. Something despicable, a slight, faltering moment of weakness that made him just want to hold

Dimitri close and tell him that everything would be fine, even though he knew it would not be.

They had married before they left for the capital two days later. Alexey had looked at Dimitri, his eyes still bloodshot with grief, and made a vow before God and a rebbe to be his husband and care for him for the rest of their lives, which felt truer than any other promise he had made in his life. The night they'd been married, just the two of them alone in the garden of their estate, Alexey had finally realized that not a day of his life could go by now without Dimitri by his side. If Dimitri left, Alexey would crumble. It would be like removing a keystone from an arch and watching the entire structure tumble down.

That night, he had kissed away his new husband's tears as he cried because his siblings hadn't lived to see him wed, and then shed tears himself when Dimitri told that he would leave the Abramovich family name behind and start afresh as Dimitri Alexeyev, even though by custom and right Alexey should have been the one to take Dimitri's name, a mark of being subservient to a partner of higher status. His heart had been so full when Dimitri said, *I want to belong to you, in every way, I want you to be my family and for the world to know*, that he had thought he would never be unhappy again.

But he was wrong.

Because Dimitri was crowned Tzar of Novo-Svitsevo soon after, and that meant Alexey was no longer the one in control.

It meant that now, Alexey was Dimitri's, and not the other way around. Not the way it should be.

Alexey was never meant to be someone's consort, to be content with being the power behind the throne. But that was exactly what he had set about to do, toiling day and night to teach Dimitri everything he knew about ruling a nation, about inspiring fear.

And Dimitri had thrived—even now, Alexey could not deny it. He had been as strong on the throne as he was submissive when the two of them were alone in the dark. And while it was a special kind of power, to know that the most powerful man in the empire knelt only to him, was laid bare only to him, was taken and claimed only by him, Alexey had known Dimitri could be stronger yet.

And that was when it had all fallen apart.

*

His mind couldn't touch the years of pleasure and warmth they had shared. It hurt even more than remembering the pain of when it had all been taken away. Alexey rested his head against the shelf for a moment, forcing himself back into the present, feeling the slight warmth of the fire on the back of his frigid neck, the cushion of the plush Urushkin carpet under his boots, the smoothness of the wood under his fingertips, and breathing in the musty smell of his books.

Sometimes, it felt as though he was being pulled back into the past by the weight of what he had done. As if he had shed his ability to move forward when he abandoned his mortal body.

He ordered himself to forget Dimitri. And so, he set back to work.

The rays of dawn's first light were already pushing their way through the gap in the thick crimson velvet curtains, illuminating the motes of dust that swirled through the air. Alexey picked up a pen and consulted the last notes he had made, which were little more than a series of frustrated scribblings.

The text laid out in front of him was both clear in intent and vague in the details, a record of a Ludayzist mystic who had bound the souls of others to him. He had created what he called *zemonyii*, creatures under his control who could interact with the middle world—the realm between this lower realm of mortals and the upper realm of God—and command the demons within. They were the perfect generals, the perfect conduits. And they would have made the mystic the most powerful man in the world if they had not literally eaten him first, leaving blood spatters across the last filled page of the journal.

This was where Alexey's immortal, unbreakable body would be a definite advantage.

But Alexey had not been able to uncover the mystic's formula for the experiment, despite poring through all his journals. He was left to experiment himself, and none of the subjects he had attempted to alter survived.

He would have to perfect the formula on prisoners—maybe some of those recalcitrant western nobles—before he moved on to altering men whose fate he cared about. He was a scientist, not a butcher. He tapped his pen against the book, ordering himself to think harder, to solve the problem faster, to see the answer within the pages that must be there.

But the weight of time pressed on his shoulders. He knew that in order to solidify his power, in order to make an empire to outlast the ages, he had to move fast, had to carry out his ultimate plan before he was undone by mortal politics.

Uniting the middle world of demons and the lower world of men using the Holy Science would be no small feat. But if anyone could do it, it was him, Alexey Balakin. Because he was blessed by God and so commanded to perform miracles, so miracles he would wreak.

VASILY

Vasily had known that Dimitri wouldn't take kindly to the proposal to use himself as the spy. He'd been prepared for the rage that had flashed across Dimitri's face, and even the possessive refusal to let him do anything at all. It had been the same story for the last twelve months, every time they'd tried to coax Dimitri into taking action.

But Vasily hadn't been prepared for Dimitri's hurt and his pain, and the way he'd curled into himself like a wounded animal. Sometimes it was so hard to live with the idea that saving Dimitri meant hurting him, that the best thing for the country would be the worst thing for them. It was sometimes so hard to realize, Vasily thought, what one would give up to win.

He didn't want to die, but he would give up his life if it meant saving Novo-Svitsevo. He didn't want to die, but they needed information almost as badly as they needed air, and he was the only one who could get it for them. He knew it as well as he knew his own name.

Vasily's jaw cracked as he yawned, but the swirling mix of resentment and sorrow in his chest would make it impossible for him to sleep. Instead, he made his way down to the ground floor, the kitchen light like a beacon in the dark.

He pushed through the propped-open door to find Mischa at the stove, muttering curses. Ladushka sat at the table reading a book so thick it would break a foot if it were dropped from any height. He sidled over to the bubbling pot on the stove, evading Mischa's arm and dipping a finger into the pot. Then he stuck it in his mouth, pushed away the pain in his heart, and moaned with pleasure. "Mischka, what *is* this? It's going to kill me from one taste alone."

Mischa cracked a grin, but still used their hip to bump Vasily away from the stove. "It's the filling for honey cake. I'm glad someone appreciates it. Dima will just dump it into the waste bin when he thinks I'm not looking."

"The *filling*, you say." Vasily immediately made for the icebox, where he had a feeling the rest of the cake would be sitting unguarded, the perfect thing to salve his wounds.

"I will remove your kneecaps without anesthesia if you so much as breathe on my cake," Mischa added cheerfully, eliciting a rare chuckle from Ladushka. "It's for *Dima*. He's lost at least another couple of pounds over the last two weeks. You can have the leftovers." Vasily stopped in his tracks, chastened.

"Fine." He rolled his eyes theatrically, but was secretly relieved they all still had Mischa. It wouldn't do to have him be the only one worrying about Dimitri's health, not if he'd be leaving soon. "Get him to take that tonic you made, yeah? The one for his mood. We need him to."

"I'm fucking trying," Mischa said, taking the pot off the stove and setting the spoon aside. They scratched their head, leaving a trail of powdered sugar over their shorn hair, which cascaded down their cheek. "If it wasn't unethical, I'd strap him down and pour it into his mouth myself. But you know that Dima does what he wants and nothing more. Especially now."

Vasily clapped them on the shoulder, shaking his head. "I know what you mean." One of the most endearing parts of Dimitri's early reign had been watching him steadfastly refuse the requests raised by any member of the council save Ladushka and Annika. He'd also acted, on occasion, against his own best interests—like when he'd gutted the allowances paid to the highest-ranking nobility and used the money to start a food distribution program for the poor, insisting it was the right thing to do. Vasily knew the only reason that hadn't led to a coup had been that Alexey had quietly started to pay the affected nobility out of Chernitzy's provincial accounts. It hadn't been smart politics. But it didn't change the way Vasily's heart had grown seeing that and all of the other naïve, fumbling policies that weren't smart but were *right*—all of the other programs for the poor and the helpless and those that Rav-Mikhailburg had always forgotten, had always let fend for themselves.

Alexey reined Dimitri in, in the end. That period of Dimitri's head-strong, naïve, justice-minded decisions had lasted for a year. Then the policies got harder, less sentimental. They matched the bruises around the Tzar's throat and his ribs and scattered across the rest of him. Watching that part of Dimitri gradually be buried was one of the hardest things Vasily had had to endure.

He grew faintly nauseous at the thought, and turned away from Mischa and the stove, the smell of sugar turning acrid.

"So he refused your plan, then?" Ladushka chimed in, breaking him out of the memory of grief. "What a terrible shame."

"Were you eavesdropping, Lada?" Vasily's brows arched up in shock, but he wouldn't put it past her. Ladushka liked to know every-thing that happened in the townhouse, much the same way he did. Their shared, insatiable thirst for information was one of the things that had helped them first bond.

"Of course not. But anyone with basic knowledge of the situation and your personality could deduce that you would eventually offer to be the spy. And the way you came into the kitchen just now, looking like you were terribly upset, with that furrow in your brow and your shoulders hunched inwards, would lead one to believe that you had told Dima of your plan and he had refused." She flipped a page in her book, as if she hadn't just taken him to pieces the way he normally did a mark.

Needing a moment to think through a suitable reply, he dropped into a chair across from Ladushka, pulling out the cards in his pocket for something to do with his hands, shuffling them compulsively. He never played games with them, just flipped them through his fingers—he didn't want anyone, not even his friends, to see what he'd done to them. Fifty-three cards, with years' worth of aimless sketches, some of them funny, some memorializing the dead, others illustrations of dreams and nightmares and hopes. Four cards where he'd altered the faces to fit his friends: Ladushka, the queen of diamonds, for her sense of nobility; Mischa, the jack of clubs, for rising from nothing; Annika, the ace of spades, the death card, for always being in the winning hand.

Dimitri, the king of hearts.

He'd done a self-portrait on the joker. The extra card, the odd one out. The one that could be used to replace a damaged card, should the need come about. The trickster, the seducer. It had felt, after coming back from yet another spying mission, like it had fit.

"You fucking what?" Mischa dropped down heavily into the chair next to him, slapping their palms down onto the table. "For fuck's sake, no wonder he said no, it's *you*."

"What?" Vasily turned to Mischa. "What do you mean, it's me? I'm the damn spymaster of his court, of course it's me. Why would it not be me, if I'm the one who can get us the information we need?"

"So fucking oblivious, the two of you," Mischa huffed. "It's like you're two human-sized cocks with no brains attached."

"I don't—" Vasily trailed off and looked at Ladushka for a clue, but she merely shrugged.

"I'm going to bed." Mischa stood back up. "That filling needs to cool. I'll know if you touched it at all, Vasya. Don't even think about it." They pointed a finger threateningly at Vasily's kneecaps, and he cringed.

Vasily let the door to the kitchen swing shut before turning to Ladushka, crossing his arms. "Tell me how you knew." He needed to find any cracks in his facade.

"It had been brewing in you for weeks, Vasya." Ladushka's pale-blue stare cut through him, making him flinch. "With every failed spy you have become more desperate. And I do not mean it as a slight— far from it." She paused, pursing her lips, then slid the worn strip of leather she always carried with her off the table and placed it between the pages of her book.

"Are you going to tell me I'm wrong too? Try to guilt me into staying?" He couldn't help the way his voice rose. "Because I'm fucking sick and tired of just sitting here, sending people out to die in my place, doing nothing to help the situation, leaving Novo-Svitsevo and a hundred million citizens to starve to death if they're not killed in Alexey's wars." He gripped the edge of the table so hard it hurt.

He remembered what it was like to have no one to protect him, what it felt like to have the enemy come through the door yet again and know he was powerless to stop them. He didn't want anyone in Novo-Svitsevo to feel like that ever again, not if he could stop it.

"No," Ladushka said quietly. "I agree with you."

He deflated at the quiet way she looked at him, steady and unmoving. Here, finally, was someone who knew that his life was far less important than their people. The relief that bubbled up in him was immense, and he let out the breath he'd been holding. "Oh. Thank you."

An arch of one eyebrow was the only betrayal of her emotion. "Do we not have a duty to keep him safe, even if he could not care less if he lived or died? Did we not pledge our lives to him? To our country?"

"We did." Vasily let out another breath. How strange to be relieved by the thought of his friend telling him to commit treason, going against a direct order from his Tzar. "And I've tried so hard, for so long . . ." He trailed off, suddenly finding it hard to speak past the lump that had formed in his throat.

"I know." Ladushka reached across the worn wood of the table and clasped her hands overtop his own. "We know. And we love you for it."

He bent his head down to kiss her left hand, then her right. "You're a treasure, Lada." Another yawn escaped him, his body ready for sleep even if his mind still was not. "I should go to bed."

"Let me try to convince Dima tomorrow," she replied quietly. "You go and continue to finesse your plan. Figure out how to infiltrate the court. That way, if he agrees, you can move quickly with his blessing. And if he does not—" She paused. "If he does not, you will need the information anyway."

"Thank you," he repeated, his voice thick, gratitude making his heart clench. He had only come to know Ladushka after Dimitri had introduced him to her as his spymaster, an essential crack in the secrecy of his identity given their need to work together. Over the years, as he saw the way she'd acted on the information he gathered, he'd quickly come to respect both her intelligence and her quiet confidence, as well as the way that she clearly held an enormous amount of Dimitri's trust. "He'll listen to you. You've known him longer than any of us. He takes what you say seriously, he knows you think through all the options. If he hears you say that I should go, he'll know we have no other choice."

She merely ducked her head in response and went back to her book. Vasily stood, then swiped one more fingerful of sweetness from the pot before he left the kitchen. If he was about to walk into the lion's den, he was owed some good dessert first.

SEVEN

DIMITRI

Dimitri lay sullenly on the parlor floor, the early morning light filtering in through the window. He'd been woken by the door to the house slamming shut at an ungodly hour and had tried to go back to sleep, but to no avail.

Eventually, Annika had come and stripped him of his blankets, taking him by the arms and hauling him out of bed.

"We need to talk," she'd said in that kind yet firm way of hers, the one that brokered few arguments because its target would feel bad if they defied her.

"Except I don't want to talk," he'd insisted through the sinking feeling in his stomach. "I want to lie here in bed and chain-smoke and never have to talk again, truthfully."

She'd just smiled and yanked his nightshirt off his body without his permission, pulling clothes out of his armoire and dressing him like a disgruntled doll. And then she'd marched him down the stairs, which was how he'd found himself lying on the floor, because Mischa was taking up the entirety of the couch and wouldn't move. He was wedged between Annika and Ladushka on the carpet, both resting their heads on one of his shoulders. Ladushka was dozing, her eyes red-rimmed after presumably having been up all night, pacing, trying to figure out what Alexey was doing.

He knew he should have stayed up to help her. He'd actually enjoyed batting theories back and forth with her in the old days, Alexey's suggestion to replace his father's chancellor with Ladushka one of his better ones. They would haunt his candlelit parlor in the palace late into the night, grappling with the news out of a troublesome province, or some foreign threat, or the hunt for the anarchists who had murdered his family.

Not that he cared one whit about his dead parents, because they had never cared one whit about him; he had done it for his brothers and sisters, nieces and nephews, all of whom he'd loved. His father had barely ever looked at him, and he would have been surprised if his mother remembered the name she'd given him when he'd been born. He was the child to be discarded, the one they had left at a provincial estate at the age of twenty with a man who, they had kindly informed him right before leaving, was his new master.

He had fallen in love with Alexey by the end of their first dinner together, but Dimitri wasn't stupid. He knew that his father had sold him for political influence and access to the Balakin fortune, and that if Alexey had been a hideous old man that Dimitri didn't want to touch, he would have been ordered to marry him all the same.

He was the spare son, the chess piece who had become Tzar by accident. And sometimes, he wished that his parents and siblings hadn't died just so that he could have gone on living on Alexey's estate, ordering around the house staff and planning elaborate parties and otherwise being generally charming and sensual. His life would have been full of passion and pleasure and love, dinners with his husband under the stars, stealing kisses and dances when no one was looking, losing himself in Alexey's arms each night. He could have had endless long rides through Alexey's grounds on any one of his beautiful horses, hours of pretending like he had no idea how to shoot a gun, so that every time they hunted Alexey would laugh and roll his eyes but press his body firmly against Dimitri's to help him pull the trigger.

He would have been there to entertain Alexey, and Alexey would have been a ruler in his own right. They would never have moved to the palace, and maybe then, Alexey would never have met Morozov or been bored enough to study the Holy Science with him.

And maybe if he hadn't done that, Alexey would still be here, alive and whole.

Maybe the man Dimitri had fallen in love with, body and soul, would still be here to love him back.

Annika had thrown her arm over Dimitri's chest and was stroking Ladushka's hair, humming an old far-eastern lullaby. She had dragged him out of bed demanding to talk, and then let him settle on the floor, like she was lulling him into complacency before saying something awful. But he couldn't bring himself to care, not when the vibrations of her chest against his as she hummed and the weight of her arm across his ribs were solid, and real, and helped draw him back into the present. Which helped when his mind was fighting so desperately to go back to the past.

Because lying next to anyone reminded him of Alexey, and when he thought of their tender, quiet moments alone, his heart broke all over again. Alexey gazing at him across the pillows in the early morning light, the edges of his eyes crinkled in a smile. The way he would stroke Dimitri's hair, playing his fingers over the close-shorn sides and then running them through the hair Dimitri kept longer on top, making Dimitri close his eyes in pleasure. The way Alexey would worship him, kissing his knuckles and then his mouth and then the hollow of his throat. The way he would bundle Dimitri to his chest and hold him close against everything in the world that wanted to break him.

Until, of course, he was the one doing the breaking. Then Dimitri was nothing more than a glass under the heel of Alexey's boot.

"Stop thinking about the Pretender," Annika whispered. He turned his head to look at her and found her gazing up at him. "Your thoughts are so loud I can hear them from here, Dima."

He didn't answer. He was quite certain he didn't want to have the conversation he was sure she was about to broach, at least not while sober. His friends had a habit of ganging up on him when he least wanted them to.

"Let him go," Annika said, loud enough that Ladushka's eyes cracked open. Dimitri heard the constant rustling of paper from the couch stop, a sure sign that Mischa was listening in. "Please, Dima."

A lump formed in his throat. "I let him go a long time ago," he said, even though he knew deep down it wasn't true.

"No," she replied, her eyebrows drawing together, her lips pursing. "Vasya."

"Oh." The breath left him in a huff. Of course she wanted to talk about letting Vasily sacrifice himself senselessly. "Please stop, Anna. I've had this conversation with him. I made my decision. And he made it clear he's going anyway."

"Try not to be upset with him," Ladushka said, sitting up. "It is our best chance against Alexey, and we must stop him. Vasya knows the risks and he is happy to take them. Not just for you but for all of us. For the entire country. He wants you to see that. He wants you to trust him to take care of himself."

"She's right and you know it," Annika piled on, sitting up too. "He's good enough that he won't get caught."

"You don't know that," Dimitri bit back, shivering now that the warmth from the two of them was gone. The roaring fire wasn't enough to heat him up. The chill went down into his very bones, and he jumped as a log cracked in the fireplace, falling and sending up a shower of sparks.

"Do you actually *want* to stop Alexey, or not?" Dimitri turned at Mischa's words, his lips parted in surprise.

"Yes," he croaked. "He's deluded. He believes he decoded the old scriptures and discovered the secrets of God and His angels. Of course I want to stop him. He's the man who ruined everything." But even to his own ears, it didn't sound convincing.

"Dima," Mischa said, and though their voice was calm, it was laced with steel. "Is Alexey Balakin still truly a man? Is he the man you married? Is he the man you loved? Can you really look me in the eye and tell me that?"

Dimitri didn't know what to say. Because no one had ever put it to him quite like that, in a way that forced him to answer the question, not avoid it.

It took him several heartbeats to make up his mind.

"No," Dimitri replied, and ripped his pain open wide, exposing the wound that had festered within him for so long. "Alexey Balakin is no longer a man. He is a dead body reanimated through a perversion of the Ludayzist mysticism that he calls the Holy Science. His body is unbreakable and he cannot be harmed or killed. He believes he communes directly with God and with demons. He is stone cold, and his eyes are like the pits of Gehenna, like hell itself. There is no soul left in him."

"And why did you start the war?" Mischa leaned forward, their hands clasped together, their forearms resting on their thighs. "Why did you muster the army to try to retake the throne? What did you tell me the night we got you out of the palace?"

"I fought the war to stop a monster," Dimitri whispered, closing his eyes.

"Why?" they prodded. "Why not just let him take power? He'd already set a coup in motion and turned your own court against you. He'd already brought in his provincial soldiers from Chernitzy, knowing he might have to fight. You could have stopped the war before it started. Why not just walk away?"

"Because," Dimitri said, tasting bile on the back of his tongue, "he is evil. Because I knew if I walked away, he would do everything he's

doing now, ruling without mercy, without kindness, doing everything he can to grow his power and decimating anyone who attempts
to defy him. Because I wanted to prevent him from abusing Novo-
Svitsevo." He took a deep breath to avoid choking on the lump in his
throat. "And because I was the one who helped him become what he
is today. And I had not wanted to fail my country twice, not if I could
stop him. Not if there was even a chance."

"You know it's not your fault." Annika's hand caressed his hair.
"You hold on to so much guilt, but Dima, it is not your fault."

"You don't know what I did," Dimitri snapped, pulling away from
her, bumping into Ladushka and then skittering away until he was on
the other side of the rug, on his hands and knees like an animal they
were trying to cage. "You don't know how I—what I—did to his *body*.
You don't know."

Because of course he had never told them everything. He had told
them about the resurrection dome, how he had done what Alexey had
asked, had followed Alexey's instructions for an experiment to resurrect people from the dead. They were with him through those nine
long months of fear and uncertainty and grief, waiting for Alexey to
come back, fearing he never would. But he had never, ever told them
about what he had done between Alexey's death and his encasement
in the dome. He would never forget what he had done to help Alexey
achieve immortal life in an unbreakable body, all because of his desperation to see his husband again.

He simply could not deal with them knowing the extent of his
heresy, because if they did, they would never speak to him again.
Dimitri closed his eyes and tried to block out the horror creeping up
in his mind, the memory of when Alexey had emerged.

Because Dimitri had spent nine long months crying every night
and praying for Alexey to come back so he could make things right.
He'd spent nine long months terrified that the experiment would fail,
that Alexey had been wrong.

In truth, he should have been far more terrified that the experiment would succeed. Because when he had broken open the dome at the end of the fortieth week, revealing Alexey's rejuvenated body, the relief that washed through him had turned into horror the moment Alexey opened his eyes. Those eyes had looked straight past him and into his soul, and he knew in that moment that he had lost Alexey forever, and that what was before him was inhuman and wrong.

He acted like a man. He spoke like Alexey, and danced like Alexey, and presided over his court like Alexey, and fucked like Alexey. But inside he was different. Dead.

And furious. Because Alexey had wanted Dimitri to undergo the experiment too, so that they could rule together, immortal and indestructible. And when Dimitri refused, that was when Alexey had lost all control.

Dimitri started panting at the memories that washed through him, his ribs constricting, not enough air going into his lungs. Spots danced in front of his vision.

And then hands were grabbing his face, nails digging into his cheeks. The pain brought him back to himself, and he found himself staring into Ladushka's eyes.

"You have it wrong," she snapped, her jaw trembling with barely contained fury, angrier than he had ever seen her before. "Dima, you defied Alexey's base impulses for as long as you could. We all saw him making a grab for the throne, but you held him off longer than any of us could have. He wanted to rule. He wanted you to defy God. But you, Dima, you defied *him* instead. You defied his appeals for you to use his blasphemous Holy Science to strengthen the empire because it would spit in the face of God. And it was your defiance that caused the war. I truly do not care what you did before that point. All that matters is what you did after." She paused, breathing raggedly, her cheeks flushed. "You fought a war to put down a threat to the country, Dima. You conducted yourself with honor. You tried to save your people. What Alexey did was Not. Your. Fault. Not a soul in this room blames you for what happened."

The pinpricks of pain along his face where her nails were digging into him kept him anchored, long enough that her words could start to sink in. A shiver worked its way up Dimitri's spine, his lower lip quivering with the effort of suppressing years' worth of guilt and tears.

"Do you blame us for what happened?" Annika was sitting with her arms around her knees, staring at him.

"No," he choked out. "Why would I?"

"So why do you blame yourself?" she said, and it was so quiet and so sad and so desperate that something inside Dimitri finally cracked.

And for the first time since it all fell apart, he broke down. The barrier that had held back his grief, keeping him numb, keeping him alive and moving forward, shattered. He felt everything, all at once, as if every bone and muscle in his body were alight with suffering. He cried for the first time since Alexey's death, his agony washing out of him in a wave. Annika rushed forward to wrap him in a hug, and he sobbed into her hair. Ladushka took his other side, and then Mischa was rubbing his back, the three of them forming a ring around him as if they could protect him from the world.

"Let it out," Mischa whispered in his ear. "Your grief is poisoning you. Let it out."

He cried for what felt like hours, until he was an empty vessel, choking on hiccups, sniffling and wiping at his eyes with a sleeve.

"I'm scared," he finally admitted, his voice gravelly and hoarse. "I'm so scared. I don't want to lose another person I should be keeping safe. I don't want to lose any of you."

"That's the curse of ruling, my darling." Annika ran her thumbs across his cheeks, wiping away his tears the way his own mother never had. "That's the weight of the crown you wear. Loving the tools that you use to protect your empire. And some of those tools might break. Some of us might die. But your burden is that you must love the work of ruling most of all. You must love the empire more than any one of us. You are the father of one hundred million children, Dima, and their lives are more important than any of ours."

She bent down to kiss his forehead. "Please save them from the Pretend—no." She sighed and pulled back. "Please, Dima, save them from Alexey."

It was the first time she'd said his name since the coup. And it cut through his heart. He looked at her, looked at the worry written on her face, and he took a deep, shuddering breath.

He wanted to protect her. He wanted to protect all of them. He clenched his fists, biting his lip, letting cold, hard anger wash over the festering wound of his grief, protecting him from sorrow. Hardening over the part of him that wanted to kneel, and repent, and obey.

A bright-blue bottle clinked into his lap. Dimitri picked it up, listening to the contents rattling inside the glass. Mischa peered down at him. "These are short-acting remedies for anxiety." Another bottle landed in his lap. "Take one of these every day for the sadness. They should reach full strength in a few weeks' time."

Dimitri swallowed, staring down at the bottles, his throat dry.

"It's not shameful to seek help for a wound," Mischa continued. "Whether a wound to your body, or one to your mind."

He drew in a breath, the first clear one in what felt like months. And he popped the cork out of both bottles, shook out the pills, and put one of each in his mouth, the taste of raspberries bursting across his tongue. He sat and breathed as deeply as he could, until calmness descended on him like a blanket, stopping the trembling in his hands and the nausea that haunted him and the frantic beating of his heart.

"All right," he said when he felt steadier, shrugging out of Annika's and Ladushka's arms, brushing away Mischa's hand as they checked his pulse. "All right. We have work to do." He took in another breath and said it out loud. "Vasya is right. He has the best chance of finding out the information we need. He can handle thinking through how to get into the palace. What we need to figure out is how, after he gets there, we can stop Alexey for good."

EIGHT

ALEXEY

It was fully morning when servants knocked on the study door after far too short a time of contemplation, drawing Alexey away from his books. He rose from his chair to face them.

"*Moy Tzar*," his dresser said. "Your carriage for the countryside will depart in one hour. We are here to prepare you."

Alexey grunted and winced at the way his knees cracked as he walked. It never did well to show weakness, even these small moments in front of his servants. He allowed himself to be led to his bathing chamber, a richly tiled room in shades of rose with an enormous window in the ceiling looking out at the sky, where he was stripped of the last day's clothes and ushered into a steaming copper tub.

He relaxed against the towels that had been laid on the rim of the tub, letting the smells of the fragrant aloe and honey that were mixed into the water clear his senses. The warmth of the water seeped into his bones, one of the only moments in his day when he felt warm enough to be truly alive. He despised the way he craved it.

When his servants had scrubbed his body clean, he stood up and let the water sluice off him, down the hard planes of his chest and over his legs, his skin tinged blue from the way his blood ran cold, a side effect of his transformation. He was dried and attired in black breeches, a linen shirt under a stiffly embroidered black jacket with silver clasps, and his jet-black fox fur cloak.

When he stepped back into his bedchamber, he wasn't surprised to find Ivan waiting by his desk, nor did he miss the way that Ivan's cheeks flushed when Alexey raked his eyes down the boy's body. Ivan was neatly attired in a dove-gray suit, and the effect of the slender cut highlighted his form. But this was a time for work, and when Ivan, who had taken it upon himself to serve as Alexey's personal steward, handed him a scroll detailing the day's agenda, Alexey forced himself to refocus.

"*Moy Tzar*," he said smoothly. "Your carriage is ready."

Alexey ignored all the nobles who stooped and bowed as he made his way through the palace, stopping only at his study to retrieve the book he had been puzzling over. Morozov was waiting for them in the courtyard, looking testy as he stood in front of the team of horses, surrounded by soldiers at attention. Alexey surreptitiously pulled his cloak tighter around his shoulders at the chill breeze, tucking his chin into the fur instinctively, even though his body no longer threw off any heat to warm him with.

"*Moy Tzar*," Morozov began, bowing. "Are you sure you wish to do this?"

"Morozov," Alexey said, his hands curling into fists, "I get the sense that you no longer think I am fit to be Tzar, with all you keep from me and all of your questions."

Morozov's emerald-green eyes widened amusingly, his fear delicious. "I am here to watch out for the safety of *Moy Tzar*, and the peasants have been restless these days."

Alexey gave him a withering look as he stepped into the carriage. "I am capable of defending myself. The Lord my God is the only one who can cut me down, I assure you. Now get in." Morozov complied without another word, pulling himself onto the padded bench, Ivan following after.

Alexey had requested a visit to the nearest of the peasant villages whose people were refusing to supply his soldiers. In the nearly half a day it took them to journey there, he reread the section of the mystic's diary that detailed the method for choosing the people who would become *zemonyii*. The mystic went into excruciating detail about the horror that would befall those who did not use the right method for choosing subjects, but neglected to mention what, precisely, the method was. Only that those who were chosen must be righteous, and that they must hold a connection to both God and the mysteries of the middle world.

So Alexey was left stumbling in the dark. By the time they reached the village, his head was pounding. He praised himself for bringing Ivan along, as the boy had taken note of Alexey's mood and prodded Morozov in the side every time the chancellor had tried to open his mouth, no doubt to attempt to convince Alexey once more why this was a trip unfit for a Tzar.

A soldier opened the carriage door and announced that they had arrived at the small village of Oskina. Alexey blinked in the weak sunlight and swept out of the carriage in a rustle of fabric. The village was small, with new boards scattered over the facades of old houses, presumably destroyed in the war. He wondered if the villagers had claimed their dues from the fund he had established for rebuilding, or if they, like most peasants, had been too lazy to travel to the capital. A hard dirt road was all that led through the small main street, a shabby shul presiding over the town square where his carriage had stopped.

The peasants before him looked haunted and frail, bundled up in rags, but they knelt before him in the dirt and touched their fingertips to their closed eyelids, as if seeing something holy.

It was a relief to see that even if his court had not accepted the power he had claimed, his subjects knew who ruled them.

Now, it was time to discover why, despite that, they were defying him.

*

At first, the peasants were too timid to speak, so he sent Morozov among them to fetch the rebbe, who was pulled to the front of the group, shaking and bowing.

"*Moy Tzar*," he said, sweat beading on his brow despite the fact that it was even colder here than in Rav-Mikhailburg. "We are honored you would come to visit Oskina. We are but a poor community. We have only started to rebuild in the last several months since the war. But still, we seek to serve you."

"Why then," Alexey said with icy calmness, fighting to keep himself from frowning, "do you defy my orders to provide supplies for the army?" He pointed to the outskirts of the town, which were surrounded by fields full of dead stalks of wheat, which should have been harvested. "You have the means to pay your tithe—do you not have the labor to harvest the fields?" Alexey squared his shoulders and leveled the rebbe with a stare.

"No, *Moy Tzar*," the rebbe said, dropping into a bow again. "We do not. Most of our young people died in the war. And now the fields are haunted by their spirits. They walk among us, especially at night and on the sabbath. They beg for proper burials, which we cannot give because their bodies were never returned."

Alexey scowled at that. He had ordered the fields of battle burned after his victory, so that the corpses would not contaminate the land with disease. No one had had the time to offer burial rites to each and every dead soldier. And the ground had eventually become too frozen to easily dig graves.

Claiming there were vengeful spirits was nothing more than peasant superstition, something that these stubborn followers of the old ways of Zalman clung to. It was not as if the souls of the dead could haunt the living—to claim so was a fundamental misunderstanding. Small, parasitic demons that possessed human bodies were a separate type of creature made by the Lord Himself. The Holy Science provided the answer, allowing man, with God's blessing, to control these spirits that resided in the middle realm, using their power for divine work. They could only interact with the living if they were permitted to run amok.

"What does this *superstition*," he said, stressing the word to make his disdain clear, "have to do with your defiance of my order?" Alexey felt the void open within him suddenly and without his permission, felt his power reaching for the rebbe and the life throbbing within him, wanting to crush it. He reeled it back in, soothing it, telling it to wait.

"The spirits threaten that if we aid the soldiers who participated in their killings, they will possess us to prevent it." A single bead of sweat dripped from the rebbe's forehead onto the cracked cobblestones. "We have already had one *dubbyk* made, *Moy Tzar*, by an angry spirit."

"What happened to it?" Alexey narrowed his eyes at the mention of a *dubbyk*. Peasant lore explained it as a spirit that possessed a living human with the intent of doing harm. He knew better. The Holy Science proved *dubbykim* to be a form of parasitic demon that delighted in invading mortal bodies and feasting on their brains until the host went insane and died. Alexey could do much with a *dubbyk* that he could transport back to his laboratory.

"We attempted to banish it, but the *dubbyk* was too strong. The possessed man died, and we purified his body before burial to expel the spirit." The rebbe raised his hands to the heavens. "*Zikhrono livrakha*. May his memory be a blessing."

"Take me to the grave, Rebbe," Alexey said. He wondered if he would be able to sense the demon still, if it had remained in the area after the host was killed. Perhaps he could lure it back to court somehow.

"Come," the rebbe said. He led Alexey around the shul to the stone wall of the graveyard, pulling open the rusty gate and ushering him inside. The rebbe pointed to a freshly dug grave. "Here, *Moy Tzar*," he said, stepping aside.

There was a man standing at the foot of the grave in a prayer shawl, rocking backwards and forwards as he read from a prayer book. "What is he doing?"

"He is from the bloodline of Leyvin, *Moy Tzar*." The rebbe nodded to the man. "He is praying over the grave and fasting to prevent the *dubbyk* from continuing to haunt the spirit of the deceased."

Alexey cocked his head, fascinated. While he knew of the priestly lines, this was a piece of peasant superstition that he had never heard of. The Leyvin had mostly been mentioned in his study as those holy ones who could enact certain rites before God, all but forgotten in the modern age, and Alexey had not met any claiming to be of the line. It must, he reasoned, be something that rural Novo-Svitsevans had clung to, unlike the nobility. The scholar in him could not resist trying to understand. "Do they pray over all of the graves for this reason?"

"No, *Moy Tzar*," the rebbe said. "They are forbidden from sullying themselves with the digging of graves or the handling of corpses. This is a special case, to help the village and beg for protection from the Lord."

"I have read of this bloodline." The man's praying had not ceased, not even to turn to bow to his Tzar. Alexey could appreciate the utter devotion with which the man appealed to God to protect the village from vengeful spirits. "But I've never heard it associated with the repellence of demons."

"They are descendants of the priests of old," the rebbe replied. "Righteous men who held the spirits at bay with their prayers."

Alexey stilled, his heart pounding as the words echoed through his mind like a gunshot. Righteous men. A connection to the spirit realm—known to the Holy Science as the middle world.

"How many are there here?" Alexey asked. "Is he the only one?"

"Come," the rebbe said, after a brief hesitation. "I have a book."

✶

The inside of the shul was musty and damp, the frescoes painted on the walls depicting the Lord's deliverance of man chipped and faded. The holy ark was little more than a curtain covering a niche in the wall, but Alexey still took the time to touch the edge of his cloak to the holy scroll within and kiss it.

He followed the rebbe into the small office behind the sanctuary and held the ladder for the old man as he retrieved a book from a high shelf. It was old and faded, and bore no title.

"The lineage of the Leyvin, *Moy Tzar*," the rebbe said. "Births, dates of their *b'nai mitzvot* ceremonies when they came of age, marriages and deaths. The rebbes have worked hard to keep a record of the lineage. There may be more complete copies elsewhere in the empire. This merely records the Leyvin in our region."

Alexey picked the book up and turned it over in his hand. Holding it felt right, like the Lord his God had led him to this moment, to this place, to find this book.

He said a silent prayer of thanks, pocketed the book, and swept out of the shul and past the waiting peasants.

"Come," he ordered Morozov and Ivan, who were conversing with some of the villagers. "This is no longer our primary concern. Delegate it to a general or a noble or someone who can rein in the situation."

Morozov's brow furrowed in confusion. "But *Moy Tzar*, the supply line, you'd said—"

"Silence." Alexey cast a dark, spiteful look at Morozov, who bit his lip between his teeth. "We have far more important work to do now."

If his suspicion was correct, he had just found the key to create the generals he needed to command the holy army he intended to build.

NINE

VASILY

L ate fall in Wilnetzk was at turns bitterly cold and depressingly foggy. Today was one of the days when Vasily needed a fur-lined coat to ward against the chill as he crept out of the townhouse before anyone else had risen—and before Ladushka would have had the chance to make good on her promise to speak to Dimitri about him being the spy. The biting morning air was refreshing in a way, wiping some of the fatigue out of his eyes, the result of a terrible night's sleep spent tossing and turning.

He really hated when Dimitri was upset with him. Because instead of becoming incandescently mad, instead of turning their disagreement into an altercation where at least they could go down to the dining room and spar with each other to fight out the anger, Dimitri would suddenly shut down and backtrack, trying to apologize when he'd done nothing wrong. Trying to take it all on himself, trying to do things it was clear that he only halfheartedly wanted to do, all in a desperate attempt to make things right. And Vasily knew that impulse was something that could only have come from the years Dimitri had spent under Alexey's thumb, learning how to avoid Alexey's ire. It reminded Vasily of all those times before they'd fled Rav-Mikhailburg, when the sight of bruises on Dimitri's skin had made bile rise up in his throat. The thought of all the ways in which he'd failed Dimitri haunted him, pressing down on his chest, stopping him from drawing breath. He'd seen the signs, and he'd let him suffer.

But no. He shoved those memories back down, where they belonged, in the furthest recesses of his mind. Once again, there was work to do. He wouldn't even have to deal with Dimitri's twisted attempts at an apology for their argument if he didn't end up leaving, if he couldn't find a way into Alexey's court.

Not for the first time, Vasily offered up a silent prayer to God. *Give me a way in. Take my body, take my safety, take my life, just give me a way in.*

He followed his steps back to the tavern where he had met the woman the night before. Its door was locked, the lights off. But because he had no other leads, nothing else to go on, he amused himself by tracing her likely steps. He didn't want to wait until evening for their next encounter, to coax that next bit of information from her. He'd much rather arrange that chance meeting now, if he could find her.

He recalled that she'd had a rucksack with her, which told him that she had either just arrived or, more likely, didn't feel comfortable leaving her valuables in her lodging. She had also been alone, so it was unlikely she'd wandered far that night in order to eat—this part of town was not the safest after nightfall.

There was one inn nearby that he knew of, neat and clean and yet prone to small robberies. The kind of place that would give a single woman a room without asking too many questions about why she was unaccompanied by her spouse or guardian.

He made his way there, avoiding the early morning foot traffic beginning to gather on the narrow side streets, his hands in his pockets to keep his valuables firmly attached to his person, his eyes on the cobblestones.

He found the nearby square where the inn was located, found a street vendor selling steaming black tea out of a samovar in huge ceramic mugs, and bought a cup so that he had some excuse to be loitering, watching the door. Trying to look casual, like he belonged here, because nothing aroused suspicion faster than hints that some-one was intentionally waiting for something to happen.

Vasily leaned on a ledge opposite the door to the inn. If memory served him correctly, the inn had no kitchen—and so, if the woman wanted breakfast, she would have to leave to get it.

He let his eyes dart among the people crossing the square and making their way to work, the wealthy being shepherded by servants or valets. Two women dressed in silk crossed the square hand in hand, their matching wedding bands catching the light. Their bearing, and the way their valet scurried after them, head down, reminded him of every time he'd seen Dimitri and Alexey enter a ball with their backs perfectly straight and clothes perfectly tailored, servants trailing behind, the smile on Dimitri's face shining past the scowl on Alexey's. How everyone would stop, their heads turning, tracking the couple's movements through the crowd the way he was watching the two strangers crossing the square now.

For a brief, shining moment, the court at Rav-Mikhailburg had been a haven for Vasily, a harbor from the horrors of his life back in the no-name province he hailed from. He'd finally had a purpose that was his own, a role that was his own, safety, and a bed to sleep in at night without needing to keep one eye propped open, even if he still triple-locked his door in case the ghosts of the past came for him. But then Alexey had turned out to be a fuckwit, and it had all gone to shit.

He shook his head to clear the memory, just in time to realize that his hunch had been right. The woman emerged from the inn, cross-ing the square, heading his way. He quickly drained most of the tea, scorching his mouth, then stepped neatly into her path as she made her way by him. When her shoulder hit his, he dumped the remainder of his tea onto her skirt. She quickly jumped back with a snarl.

"I'm so sorry," he said, whipping out a handkerchief and offering it to her to blot at the small stain. "I'm clumsy this morning. The cold is murder on my fingers."

The woman patted at the damp patch of skirt, her brow furrowed in annoyance, then looked at him. "Oh, it's you." Her eyebrows melted apart and a hint of a smile lifted the corners of her mouth.

He put a hand to his chest. "You're from the tavern last night. I thought I recognized you. I'm sorry again."

"It's all right." She handed the handkerchief back to him but didn't immediately move away.

He sensed an opening. "Clearly, I owe you breakfast. As an apology."

"It's fine," she said, waving her hand in the air. "It's just tea, it will dry. It won't even stain."

"Still," he insisted, holding out his arm. "Allow me."

She shrugged and took the arm he offered. He returned the mug to the tea vendor, who nodded appreciatively at the woman he was now escorting. She grimaced. Vasily filed away that she was clearly not looking for romance or to be seduced.

At least not this early in the morning.

"What's your name?" He hadn't asked her yesterday. He steered her in the direction of a café he knew, with decent food that wasn't expensive enough to raise eyebrows but good enough to whet his nonexistent appetite.

"Zora Haleyvin." She offered her surname without any prompting, and satisfaction curled in Vasily's chest. This would be easy.

"Yuri Igoravich," he replied, pulling an identity out of his brain at random. Yuri had been a soldier in Dimitri's personal guard who'd ended up sprayed against the side of a trench when an artillery shell landed where it shouldn't have. "And again, I must apologize for my clumsiness."

"It's all right." She shrugged, her arm moving up, then down, in his. "And I guess I get a free breakfast out of it. I was just going to go to shul, but the only one I've found that would let me in alone was, well—it was strange."

"Which one?" Vasily's interest peaked at that. He kept tabs on most of the shuls in Wilnetzk, but he was one man and couldn't visit them all every sabbath.

"You don't want to go there," she said, shaking her head. "I'm sure you have other choices in the city. But it was the one on Strabinski Street, at the edge of the square."

He filed that away as they entered the steaming warmth of the small café, pushing through the crowd around the counter to a small table in the back. Vasily flagged down a waiter and ordered an indecent amount of food.

Zora cast her eyes around, the redness from the wind fading from her cheeks. She peeled off her coat—too thin for the weather, Vasily noticed—and rubbed at her face. "We had a café like this in Voloski. Mikhail and I would go every Saturday after shul."

This was too easy. She was practically offering up what he needed. But he wasn't too ashamed to take it. The waiter put a plate of eggs in front of Vasily. He picked up a fork. "Your father?"

"No." She shook her head. "Mikhail is—was—my younger brother." She gave the same small shake of her head, the one Vasily inferred she did when she was trying not to cry.

"The war?" He pushed a plate of toast towards her. He kept his voice clinical, the way she had last night.

She reached down to move her rucksack out of the way of a passing patron, then pushed a strand of dark hair behind her ear from where it had escaped her braid. When she straightened up, her eyes were watery again. But she blinked several times and her eyes cleared. "No. Mikhail wasn't conscripted."

"Too young?" Vasily ventured. He hoped that wasn't the case—he couldn't pass for a minor anymore.

"No, he was twenty-five." Zora picked up a piece of toast, toying with the rye bread, shaking off crumbs. "But he had this illness that would come and go. All of his joints would turn red and swell, and he could hardly move. He couldn't even help our father in the butcher shop. He was like that when the officers came to town. I was conscripted. He was given a medical exemption. My sister was too young to serve."

"Oh." Vasily tucked all the information away in his head, forming a picture of what this woman's life had been like, how the war had touched her. "So it was the Pretender's army, then, that killed your family." Dimitri had ensured his soldiers didn't prey on civilians. Alexey had no such honor.

"Yeah," she said, her voice hoarse. "They got half the people in our town at once. Mikhail and my sister. My parents. They were among them. Mass grave. I don't even have death certificates for them. It's like they never existed at all."

Vasily reached out and grasped her hand as her lower lip wobbled. He murmured sympathies even as his brain lit up with possibilities. He tried not to think about how her story was so unlike his own experience of loss, his parents and then siblings dying of consumption across the span of years, until only he was left, the pain blunted by the fact that it kept hitting him, over and over, until he was numb.

They ate and talked, and at the end of the meal, Vasily used the crowded nature of the café to covertly slip a rolled-up five-hundred-gir note into Zora's pocket, where she'd find it long after he'd gone. It was the least he could do for the way he had used her and would pay for several months of lodging somewhere far nicer than where she was staying.

After he had sent her on her way, Vasily stopped and ducked into an alley. He pulled his pen and a small, creased journal out of his breast pocket. He flipped through pages and pages of information about the dead, those who would no longer need the details of their lives. When he came to a clean page, he started writing.

First name Mikhail. Surname Haleyvin. Middle name unknown. Voloski. Twenty-five at outset of war. Likely dark hair, dark eyes if like sister. Butcher's son. Suffered from unknown illness which inflamed joints. Two sisters, eldest first name Zora, unmarried, served as soldier. Second sister unknown. No partner, no children at time of death. No site of burial. No death record.

He snapped the journal shut, weighing whether the story of this dead man fit him, whether he could pretend, one day soon, to be a butcher's son. Whether he could shed the mantle of an orphaned minor lord, brought up by an uncle who taught him about people and their tells through cruelty instead of kindness. Whether he could rearrange the broken bits of himself into a new shape. Whether that shape would be convincing enough to fool a mark one day.

At least he'd accomplished something this morning, added one more identity to his book, added one more bullet to his arsenal. He could use this to get back to the capital as he'd hoped, which might lead to something more. He tucked the journal away, leaning back against the wall, wondering what waited for him at home. It would be so much easier to face his potential death if he didn't leave Dimitri here, angry at him.

He sighed. He couldn't avoid it forever. Hoping that Ladushka had done as she'd promised, and at least tried to soften Dimitri up, he turned and made his way back home, his steps as hesitant as his heart.

DIMITRI

Dimitri was sitting on the open windowsill when the door to his bedroom cracked open, Vasily's familiar footfalls light on the carpet. He'd been waiting for this moment since discovering Vasily had left the townhouse early that morning, and after hearing him return some minutes ago. There was a pause when Vasily toed off his shoes, and then the soft thud of a jacket hitting the ground, followed by a vest.

Something low within him tightened with anticipation because he knew what this meant, but he kept his gaze fixedly on the street. This was how he could redeem himself. This was how he could fix the pain he'd caused Vasily.

Vasily closed the distance between them and pressed himself against Dimitri's back, sliding his hands over Dimitri's shoulders and down the planes of his chest. Dimitri shuddered, leaning into the firmness of Vasily's muscular stomach.

"I was told you took your pills and changed your mind about allowing me to go to Rav-Mikhailburg," Vasily drawled into his ear, breath ghosting Dimitri's neck and making him shiver. "Which in *my* mind calls for a reward."

"You sound happy about being allowed to go to your death." Dimitri flicked his cigarette onto the pavement below, affecting nonchalance, and turned his head. Vasily's pupils were blown wide.

Then Vasily raised an eyebrow. "Is it not clear that I'm offering to fuck you to reinforce positive behavior?" He bumped his hips against Dimitri's back, so that Dimitri could feel just how interested he was in this particular form of therapy. Dimitri bit back a groan at the feeling of Vasily nudging into his spine. "Besides, I need to think through some things. Spy things. And you know I think best when I'm moving."

He bent down to kiss Dimitri's brow, and Dimitri lifted his head, claiming Vasily's lips in a kiss, Vasily's stubble brushing across his cheek. Dimitri shivered, sparks jumping down his spine.

"That's fine," Dimitri said, pulling himself back through the window frame and grabbing the back of Vasily's neck. "I won't be thinking about you either."

He focused on unknotting Vasily's tie and held it up plaintively, biting his lip in the way that he knew Vasily found tantalizing.

They had done this many times before, first on the battlefield to work off tension, then in Wilnetzk to forget their sorrows. And when Dimitri had finally admitted that Vasily was the same size and build as Alexey, and could mimic the way Alexey mastered him, Vasily had just shrugged and suggested a blindfold to make the illusion more complete.

It filled him with guilt, pretending that Vasily was Alexey instead, but it was what he needed. And Vasily had never told him no, had never complained, and so he took and took and took, even as he wished it wasn't Vasily he was taking from.

Vasily drew in a breath and Dimitri could tell when he surrendered himself to the moment, the physicality and the pleasure of it. He pushed Dimitri up against the wall, Dimitri's smaller frame molding perfectly into Vasily's larger bulk. Dimitri pressed kisses along

Vasily's collarbone, Vasily nipping at the shell of Dimitri's ear, letting his hands wander down to Dimitri's waist, holding him in place against the wall with his thumbs digging into the hollows of Dimitri's hips, stopping his attempts to buck forward.

Eventually Dimitri couldn't contain the desire building under his skin any longer, the heat of it almost unbearable. He stopped kissing Vasily long enough to divest him of his shirt and then gasped as Vasily picked him up, Vasily's hands under his thighs. Dimitri's legs moved to wrap around Vasily's waist of their own accord, his arms tangling around Vasily's neck.

Vasily turned and walked until he hit the edge of the bed, dropping Dimitri down on the furs before shedding the rest of his clothing. He pulled the bottom of Dimitri's shirt over his head, stopping when the fabric was over his eyes, and tucked it in so Dimitri couldn't see.

Dimitri moaned, his hands coming up over his head, his wrists pressed together. Vasily chuckled and straddled him, taking the tie that Dimitri still held and binding his wrists together, knotting them to the headboard. Dimitri gave an experimental tug and found no give, which only made him stiffen even more.

Lost in the enforced darkness, it was easier for Dimitri to pretend. Vasily held him down with one hand on his chest, and by the sounds of it was fishing around in the nightstand for the small bottle of oil that Dimitri kept there.

"What do you want?" Vasily asked, his voice gravelly. "What would you like?"

Dimitri just whimpered and bucked up into the weight of Vasily's thighs, the other man chuckling.

"You're not going to use your words?"

"No," Dimitri gasped out, knowing he was being petulant but not wanting to give directions. Alexey had never asked him to make decisions in the bedroom, and this was about Vasily, anyway, about what he deserved. "Whatever you—"

Vasily sighed but didn't push it the way he usually did. "I suppose if you're due a reward, I'll make it proper."

Vasily popped the cork on the bottle of oil, sank down, and took Dimitri in his mouth in one smooth motion. He pinned Dimitri's hips to the bed with one hand while working him open with the other.

Vasily pushed him mercilessly, taking charge the way that Alexey would have, pulling pleasure out of him in a rush of heat and satisfaction. It was perfect, the way Vasily always made it, the way it had always been with Alexey from that very first night. Dimitri pressed back onto Vasily's hand, desperate for contact, desperate for *more*. He had always taken everything that Alexey would give—it had always made him feel useful, and complete, and whole. Watching Alexey come undone above him, his eyes closing and his mouth dropping open, was more power than Dimitri had felt even sitting on the throne of Novo-Svitsevo.

Vasily hummed at the same time he crooked his fingers, jerking Dimitri out of his fantasy. That wasn't something Alexey would ever do, searching for Dimitri's pleasure like that, intentionally trying to find the core of him. It was too much, and just enough, and Dimitri lost control of himself as he came in a wash of heat.

Dimitri let his head loll heavy on the pillow as Vasily untied his hands from the headboard, flipping Dimitri over and bringing himself to completion between Dimitri's clamped-together thighs, hands strong as they dug into the hollows of Dimitri's hips, but not strong enough to bruise.

Vasily collapsed on top of Dimitri's back, panting, the sheen of sweat that had built up on both of them making their skin slide together. Dimitri felt the tie around his wrists unknot, leaving his hands free. Immediately, Dimitri leveled himself up and ripped the shirt off his head, nudging Vasily out of the bed with an elbow. Vasily, his skin flushed from the exertion, swung his legs over the side and dropped down onto the rug, sprawling out and holding up his arms for Dimitri.

Dimitri assented, making his way off the bed and lying down, his head on Vasily's chest, one leg hooked over his stomach. Vasily ran his hand through Dimitri's hair, and Dimitri allowed it, despite the fact that he was itching to stand up and get a rag to clean them off, the way Alexey would have expected of him.

Vasily liked to cuddle, and it was the least Dimitri could do for him, after all the favors Vasily granted him. And some small, traitorous part of him enjoyed it and wished he could experience it with Alexey, one last time.

"Thank you," Vasily said softly, "for letting me go. I would have done it anyway, but I'll rest easier knowing you're not fighting me."

Dimitri swallowed, letting the bonelessness of his body in the wake of the sex weigh down his sorrow at the reminder that Vasily was going to have to let him go too. At the reminder that he was going to be left here again, alone, without anyone to hold him close like this.

"I mean it," Vasily continued, more open and honest when he was like this than at any other time. "I do. Thank you, Dima."

Dimitri couldn't respond. His throat was too tight.

Vasily rolled over, shifting Dimitri off of him. He bent down and pressed a kiss to Dimitri's forehead. "I'll leave you to dress. I have more work to do."

Dimitri merely closed his eyes as Vasily collected his clothes, the door clicking shut after several long moments. He thumbed the empty space on the fourth finger of his left hand, resisting the urge to reach for the ring hidden in his bedside table, and prayed to God that wherever Vasily's mission took him, he'd eventually find his way back home.

ELEVEN

ALEXEY

This was what he needed. He could sense it.

"Morozov," he said as he ran a finger down the book's list of names. "We must collect the rest of these records. Send couriers to every shul in the empire and have them bring back anything like this they can find."

The candles in his study were burning low, and the night was growing late, the shadows wrapping around him like a mantle. He felt more comfortable, now, in the dark.

"Yes, *Moy Tzar.*" Morozov ran a hand over the auburn stubble that was dusting the curve of his jaw, evidence of how long they had worked. "We will have to experiment on a peasant before we undergo a large-scale collection of the Leyvin."

"Of course," Alexey said, putting a strip of leather into the book over the section on the family Ivanova and snapping it shut. "Obtain one from that village we went to. Oskina. That man praying over the grave would do nicely."

"I sent a soldier to retrieve him this morning, *Moy Tzar,*" Morozov said. "I thought you might not want to delay your experimentation. He is in the basement laboratory."

Morozov's competence pleased Alexey, reminding him why he usually liked the man, and he cracked his knuckles. "I would like to try the method tonight. I believe this is the reason that the previous experiments have failed. The Lord my God would not want His Holy Science worked on the body of an animal or an impure person. The vessel must be righteous. The subject must be a Leyvin." He said this with surety, because something in him resonated at the thought, ringing like a pure note coaxed from a crystal glass. God was telling him that this was the path he had to follow.

"You are wise, *Moy Tzar*. Your knowledge of the Holy Science has well surpassed my own feeble understanding since we started learning these ways together. It is beyond the grasp of any other being save God Himself."

"And that is why I'm Tzar," Alexey retorted, standing up from his desk and wrapping himself in the black prayer shawl draped over his chair. He walked around the desk and sat in front of the fire, closing his eyes as the warmth of the flames played over his face and hands.

"The Lord my God," Alexey prayed, fingering the fringes on the shawl's edge. "Guide me. Guide my hand."

My son, the familiar, ethereal voice whispered in his ear. *You have done well, uncovering my secrets.*

"Yes, my Lord," Alexey whispered back. He wound the fringes of his prayer shawl around his right index finger and raised it up to his lips to kiss it. "You have helped me to open my eyes. Now I beseech you, help me in this endeavor of the Holy Science."

Anoint yourself, my son, God said to him. *Purify yourself so you may channel my power.*

"Yes," Alexey breathed. He rose and turned to Ivan, waiting in the corner. "The Lord my God commands me to purify myself. I must immerse before the experiment begins."

Ivan nodded and opened the door to the study. They took the hidden stairs that wound down into the bowels of the palace, until they came to a small and enclosed chamber, steam rising from the deep pool in the center of the room, fed by an underwater hot spring and surrounded by fat, flickering candles dripping wax. Alexey shed his prayer shawl, then divested himself of his clothing, and stepped across the white stone and into the pool until he was in the center.

Alexey cleared his mind, took a deep breath, and immersed himself in the water. In the quiet, it felt like he was back with God during his period of death.

He rose and took a deep breath, then prayed the holiest prayer. *The eternal is my God. The eternal is one.* Then he sank below the water once more, his limbs floating out from his body, the water washing him clean.

You are righteous, God told him. *You are holy, my son.*

Alexey rose from the water, cleansed and blessed. He was ready to wield the Holy Science. He was ready to become a creator in his own right.

*

The man from the graveside was chained to a chair in Alexey's laboratory, a gag in his mouth and a blindfold over his eyes, his head and his feet bare. But still, when they walked in, he began to struggle.

Alexey ripped the blindfold from his eyes and the gag from his mouth. "I am your Tzar," he said. "And I am here to offer you eternal life through the grace of the Holy Science and God. Do you accept?"

The man struggled against his bonds. "Let me go," he begged. "I have children, a spouse. Please."

Alexey ran a finger down the man's cheek, his nail threatening the skin, a twinge of annoyance furrowing his brow. "You would resist my offer to join with me in power?"

"Please," the man begged. "I don't know what you're talking about. I just want to return home."

Alexey stepped back, cocking his head. Would it matter, that the man was unwilling? But then, was it truly possible for anyone to be willing, when they could not possibly understand what Alexey was offering them?

He was a scientist, and the only way to answer these questions was through experimentation. He rolled up his sleeves. "We will begin."

The man started screaming and struggling even harder. The straps that bound him to the chair groaned in protest. "Morozov," Alexey commanded. "Quiet him so I can concentrate."

Morozov grinned, then punched the man in the temple, the man's head snapping to the right. Several more blows caused the man to slump forward, unconscious. Alexey crouched down to examine the Leyvin before him, sniffing him to see if he could sense anything different about his blood, caressing his chest to see if his pulse felt different from that of an ordinary man.

He found no difference, but he trusted the word of God. This would work. Finally.

Alexey straightened up and ripped open the man's shirt. "Instruments, please," he instructed. Morozov stepped forward with a tray, and Alexey selected a scalpel. He pierced the tip of his left index finger until blood welled up, black and sluggish. He drew the Seal of Zalman on the Leyvin's chest, covering his skin like a canvas, as a way to channel the power of the Divine.

Others called his power heretical, whispered that it was a sin, but Alexey knew the truth. The mystics were the only ones who had known true communion with God. Centuries ago, holy men had practiced mysticism in the consecrated temples of God—but then Novo-Svitsevo's leaders had quashed their power, fearing rebellion if the people accessed the secrets of heaven. Ludayzist mystics were branded heretics, traitors, evil. They were hunted. Their findings were almost lost to time.

Until Alexey had brought the knowledge back with Morozov's assistance, compiling documents and records from these long-ago wise men and uncovering its true name—the Holy Science. He would use this power for his country, for his people, and because it was the will of God.

As he inscribed, he felt the hollowness inside him rear its head, pushing to be set free. Suddenly, he knew with perfect clarity what he had to do. He was guided by the hand of God.

Alexey gave in to the void and reached within it, clasping hands with the shadowy figure who slinked through its edges. The room rippled around him and he swayed on his feet, but instead of collapsing, Alexey simply tunneled deeper into the magic that God and his own death had given him.

He was a living conduit to the middle world and all its power. So when he summoned forth the darkness, the darkness answered.

Alexey opened his mouth to pray and shadow spilled forth, winding its way in a sinuous ribbon to the chest of the Leyvin bound in front of him. It pierced the man at his heart and his back arched, his mouth open in a silent scream even as his eyes stayed shut. He convulsed, the power sinking into him.

Alexey collapsed to the ground at the same time the shadow stopped pouring forth from his mouth. His legs would not support him, and his head swam with lightness. He had not felt this weak since he was mortal, like he had been drained of his vitality. He panted, catching his breath, leaning forward to brace his hands on the cold flagstone floor.

"*Moy Tzar*," Morozov said, his voice full of wonder. "Look."

Alexey looked. And what he beheld made his heart swell. The man was awake again, blinking at him with darkened eyes. His mouth twisted into a snarl, and his hands twitched like he was about to strangle Alexey. But his feet—his feet were the true miracle. They were no longer human, but scaled and clawed, like the feet of a monstrous bird.

"It worked," Morozov whispered reverently.

Alexey straightened up, leaning against the long wooden table next to him. "I am blessed by God," he said. "Of course it worked. I am faithful, and so when I work the Holy Science, it answers my call."

The *zemonyii* he had made snarled and thrashed, and Alexey drew his pistol from where he had tucked it into the waistband of his pants and fired a single shot into its head, the sound ricocheting around the room's stone walls. The *zemonyii* slowed but continued struggling against its bonds, which were already fraying. So Alexey reached inside himself, feeling for that well of power that was at the core of him, and sent a tendril forth to pull the life he had gifted into the creature back into his own self. The form went rigid, then crumpled, the body dissolving into black ash.

"Good," he said. "I can create them, and I can also destroy them." He turned to Morozov. "Find every Leyvin in Novo-Svitsevo. Invite them to the palace. There is much to be done." He turned on his heel. "I have an army to make."

*

Lying in bed that night, flush from the success of his experiment with the Leyvin and how he had created a *zemonyii* at last, Alexey could hardly believe his victory, how much closer he had come to his ultimate goal.

"This is what I've sought," he said, drawing Ivan close and burying his nose in the boy's hair. "A way to use the power God has given me." He ignored the way that the boy's weight did not feel quite right against his body.

"Tell me, *Moy Tzar*," Ivan said, flipping over and raising himself up on his forearms, planted on Alexey's chest. He dropped his lips down for a kiss. "Tell me how you will use your power." He shuddered, and the fervor in his eyes sent a shiver through Alexey too.

Alexey drew a finger down Ivan's cheek, looking into those stunning eyes, as pale blue as winter ice. "I will break the wall between the worlds," he said. "I am a conduit for the power of God. His creatures are at my disposal. I will harness them for my army, and with God and the Holy Science, I will make Novo-Svitsevo into the most powerful empire the world has ever seen. We will be indomitable. We will be the righteous hand of God on earth."

"You will purge the world," Ivan breathed. "*Moy Tzar*, you will purify it."

"Yes," Alexey said. "All those who oppose the Holy Science, progress and faith—they will all fall to us. We will make the world anew."

"Will you allow me to be a part of this new world?" Ivan's eyes searched his, and the devotion there made Alexey crush him to his chest.

Alexey shoved away thoughts of another man he had begged to join him. Another pair of blue eyes, which had held only pain and contempt when he explained his plans, his theories.

"Yes," he said, "yes. If you believe, then you are a part of me and I will protect you."

"I believe, *Moy Tzar*," Ivan said, bending down for another kiss, then nuzzling his neck. "I believe in two things. In you, and in the Lord our God."

Alexey didn't correct Ivan that believing in him and believing in God were one and the same.

TWELVE

VASILY

V asily knew he should be at home, doing something to figure
out how he was going to make his way into the palace at Novo-
Svitsevo, but his second-best talent was procrastination, especially
when it came to avoiding difficult things. Hiding was practically an
art form of his.

He'd spent days in the townhome, avoiding Dimitri and brainstorm-
ing with Ladushka, but hadn't managed to concoct a plan that felt
right—or that wasn't immediately likely to get him killed. They were
running out of options, and time, and so in one last desperate search
for information or leads, Vasily decided to find the shul that Zora had
mentioned. He always thought best when he was moving, anyway.

Wilnetzk was a city more committed to the new modernity than
faith, but if one knew where to look, there were still shuls tucked
away—including congregations of refugees from Novo-Svitsevo,
keeping religion and connections among countrymen alive in shabby
basements and formerly abandoned shuls, too plain or broken down
for the rich of Wilnetzk who wanted to pray as a public show of faith
instead of inborn devotion. Vasily had visited them all, lurking in
the background, observing and occasionally introducing himself, but

mostly keeping to the shadows. Keeping an eye on things, in case the congregants had news from home that he could overhear. Whispers that he could store away.

Vasily shouldered through the crowds, cursing the congestion as he made his way to the street Zora had indicated, blinking away the season's first flakes of snow that were spinning lazily from the gray-hued sky. Everything was cramped here, and always covered in a dense fog from the factories along the river. It was nothing like the clean air and wide fields of home, but if he thought too much about Novo-Svitsevo, the pain struck him with the force of a bullet. So, like everything else that made him sad, he tucked the thought away. It never did to dwell on the things that had cut him into pieces.

The shul was partially hidden in the corner of the square. He poked his head inside the worn and unadorned wooden door. There were empty benches in the sanctuary, but there was indeed a prayer service going on.

He realized that this shul, like a few others in Wilnetzk, was dedicated to the Holy Science. It was no wonder Zora would have found it off-putting and strange.

These congregations, despite sending chills across his skin every time he sat through a service, occasionally told him about what was going on back in Novo-Svitsevo. So he snuck in and took a seat as the rebbe prayed the *kabbalat shabbat*, an early version of the Friday night service for those who had to work in the evening. Most of the Novo-Svitsevan refugees had joined the underclass of service workers in Wilnetzk—covering night shifts in factories, warming the beds of the rich in the gilded rooms of the city's many pleasure houses, sweeping the streets once everyone else had gone home, lighting the gas lamps along the avenues. Not everyone had the luxury of praying at the correct time of day, not if they also wanted to make a living.

The people around him kept their heads down, hunched together in the pews. He was alone in the back, but for a moment he closed his eyes. He could almost convince himself that the swell of voices around him were from his estate's small shul, his family and their villagers praying together to welcome the day of rest.

The thought made tears prick at the corners of his eyes, sharp and stinging, but he blinked them away.

The prayers went on and on, through the *amidah* and past the prayers for healing and strength. Then the rebbe started the sermon and began talking about Alexey.

"Tzar Alexey Balakin, *zekher tzadik livrakha*, has shown us the way forward, with the knowledge of the Holy Science that is gifted to him directly from God."

Vasily almost snorted. *May the memory of the righteous be a blessing.* As if Alexey was some kind of dead, revered holy man, instead of a dead, absolute cock of a person.

"We honor the Holy Science with our blood and our bones, and we will do our duty to the Tzar should he call on us." The rebbe raised his hands up to the sky, looking like he was going to cry, or faint with ecstasy, or maybe both. This was by far the most devout rebbe that Vasily had come across in his perusal of Wilnetzk's shuls. Vasily wondered if Alexey was paying him—and other rebbes across the world—to praise him.

It would be a smart move. He made a note to himself to suggest it to Dimitri.

He looked around surreptitiously and saw many of the congregants touching their hands to their eyes in the gesture of peasants when they saw something sacred. Then his gaze landed on an icon of Alexey Balakin propped up in the corner of the sanctuary.

That was new. And disturbing.

It had been easy to miss, in the shadows by the holy ark. It showed a man all in black, his hair curling around his forehead and brushing eyes that were as perfectly dark as a moonless night. He had both hands extended in benediction, and shadows were rippling from behind him.

The rebbe knelt down in front of the icon and kissed the painted feet of the new Tzar, and the congregants lined up to do the same.

Vasily stiffened. This went beyond praising the Pretender. This verged on idol worship, making Alexey the subject of the service, not God Himself. Vasily was far from the most religious person he knew, but he was devout enough to try and keep the sabbath most weeks and not to violate the commandment to worship no God but the Lord. But he wasn't about to be the only one in the shul who wasn't participating—no, that would be far too remarkable, and his job was to remain as unremarkable as possible—and so he lined up and knelt down in front of the icon too. He hoped no one noticed that rather than kissing the icon, he whispered a filthy curse to it instead.

At the conclusion of the service, he sidled up to the front of the shul, where the rebbe was talking to congregants. Vasily pasted a beatific smile on his face. As he walked, he replaced the cufflinks he wore with ruby-studded ones from his pocket that glittered in the candlelight. He rolled up the sleeves of his coat to reveal the silk lining and hide the holes he'd deliberately poked there, then pulled a gold wristwatch out of his pocket and slipped it on.

Then he pulled on a fake identity and became someone worth talking to.

"Sir." The rebbe gave Vasily a small bow and a sick smile. "Thank you for gracing a humble shul such as ours with your illustrious presence." He didn't miss the way the man's eyes flicked down to his cufflinks.

Vasily nodded back. "A beautiful service. I'm new to the city, and I'm gratified to find others who support the glorification of the Holy Science."

"Ah, a believer." The rebbe smiled broader. "We still do not have enough enlightened ones among the Ludayzist community of Lietuva."

Vasily dug a gold gir out of his pocket and flipped it to the rebbe, who caught it like a magpie, his eyes going wide. "For the upkeep of the shul," he said with a wink.

The rebbe drew closer. Vasily smelled wine on his breath, noted the greasiness of his long beard, and tried not to cringe at the way the man clasped his hands over Vasily's shoulders like they were old friends. Vasily flinched at the contact, fighting not to pull away. "What was your name again?"

"Mikhail Haleyvin," Vasily said. It was always good to practice using the identities of the people he might need to pretend to be, trying their names on his tongue, playing with the details of their lives. "From Voloski."

The rebbe's fingers tightened around his arms, and the man's gaze darted to the back of the room. "Come with me." Before Vasily could protest, the rebbe dragged him through a small door next to the holy ark and into an office, the walls lined with shelves stuffed with old and dusty books. Vasily fought the urge to sneeze and tried not to knock anything over.

"Haleyvin, you say?" The man's bushy brows furrowed together as he turned back to Vasily.

"Yes, rebbe." He fingered the switchblade he kept in his pocket, running a finger over the polished wooden handle. "Mikhail Haleyvin." He hoped that the man didn't somehow know Zora's brother. He was in no mood to kill an old man and then dispose of a body. But no— that would be too much of a coincidence. Vasily drew in a steadying breath and forced his heartbeat back to normal.

"Yes, yes. That means you're descended from the line of Leyvin, does it not? I think I recall seeing your family name in our registry." The rebbe muttered something under his breath as he turned to the desk, covered in papers. He fished around for a moment before drawing a newspaper out of a drawer, covered in food stains. He brandished it in Vasily's face. It was from Novo-Svitsevo, given the language. Vasily squinted at it, trying to read the words in the dim light.

"You said you're new to town, so you must not have a congregation yet. We would be pleased to welcome you into ours, my fine sir. A man of your stature, of course. And if you take the Tzar up on his offer, will you say you came from the congregation of Rebbe Rozinberg, and tell him this is where to send the payment? We need a new roof, you see, and the money would go a long way." The man grinned, showing several cracked teeth.

Vasily pried the paper from the man's hands. It had been folded to an advertisement, written in bold block letters.

The Tzar Alexey Balakin of Novo-Svitsevo
invites those of the holy and righteous line of Leyvin
to the palace at Rav-Mikhailburg to pray with the Tzar himself.
Donations to be made to the shuls of those who come to pray
for the upkeep and maintenance of their premises.
Rooms in the palace and board provided to those who come to pray.

Vasily felt as if the floor was dropping out from beneath him as a plan clicked into place, so simple and elegant it was as if God Himself had come up with it. And maybe God had. He sent up a prayer of gratitude to the God who still showed his Tzar favor, who had clearly guided his path and laid before him the steps he would need to take to protect Dimitri and Novo-Svitsevo, without Vasily even realizing what was happening.

He folded the newspaper and fought back a grin. "May I keep this? I'll be sure to mention this congregation if I do make my way to Rav-Mikhailburg."

"Yes, yes." The rebbe bowed his head, clasping his hands in front of him like a beggar. "Please, sir, please do."

"Thank you," Vasily said, and meant it.

THIRTEEN

DIMITRI

Dimitri picked at the roasted chicken on his plate, hoping it would disappear before he had to put it in his mouth, as his friends chattered around him at the old, chipped dining table crammed into the small kitchen.

"Did you come up with a solution?" Ladushka asked Vasily, when Mischa had poured them all glasses of wine from a bottle on the table and passed them around.

Dimitri flinched, upset they were going to have this conversation over lunch, but Vasily had walked in the door an hour ago, a grin on his face and a newspaper under his arm. Dimitri knew it meant Vasily had found something good. He turned to Vasily. "Did you?"

"He's going to invite me," Vasily said, intertwining his fingers with Dimitri's, squeezing his hand. Dimitri fought the way his brow creased and his breath hitched, focusing instead on how Vasily's hand was warm in his. "I'm going to walk right in through the fucking palace doors."

Dimitri's heart sank as Vasily outlined the plan—a stolen identity, an invitation to pray with Alexey—because he knew, he *knew* this was a trap that Alexey was setting for someone, somewhere, even if he didn't know to what end. Dimitri knew this plan was dangerous.

And he knew he was going to have to allow Vasily to do it anyway.

Annika was tearing the challah into suspiciously uneven chunks, handing the largest one to Dimitri, scattering breadcrumbs across the white tablecloth. "I think this will work," she said good-naturedly. "The part about getting Vasya into the palace. We'll figure out the rest, about how we'll stop the Pretender. I have faith."

"It *better* work, or Vasya here is in trouble." Mischa accepted their piece of the bread and fell on it like a starving animal. "Dima, *eat*, or I'm going to shovel that food into your mouth myself."

"I'm going to." Dimitri surgically separated a sliver of the chicken from the bone. He put it in his mouth and immediately regretted it. Everything still tasted of ashes, even with Mischa's medications unwinding the tension from his body.

"Stop making that face." Mischa frowned. "I'm not that bad of a cook. And you need to eat to get your appetite back."

"Says who?" Dimitri chewed and cursed at how much willpower it took to swallow.

"Says me," Mischa snapped, looking either truly irritated or deeply concerned. "The physician sitting at the table. You look ill. And if we're going to take back the country, you need to do it looking like the handsome, vigorous Tzar you were, and not something that just crawled out of a grave."

"Stop," Annika said quietly. She pushed an enormous dish of mashed potatoes over to him, which he accepted a spoonful of gratefully. She gave him a small smile, like she knew it'd be easier for him to eat. He thanked God when she subtly stole the rest of the chicken from his plate and started picking at it.

Ladushka raised an eyebrow at Dimitri in a way that scared him enough to take a large bite of the potatoes. "They are right." She pointed to him. "You cannot rule if you do not look the part. You know as well as I that half of ruling is the image of power."

Dimitri knew. He hated being weak, and yet he couldn't help himself.

"Here's my question." Vasily was chewing on the inside of his cheek, the way he did when he was deep in thought. "I need a way to communicate with the rest of you. If you figure out how to deal with Alexey, I need to know straight away, so that I can start putting pieces of a plan in motion."

Dimitri swallowed another mouthful of potato, wincing. "The way you'll communicate is by coming back."

"Sure." Vasily's voice cracked on the word. "But . . . before then, we'll need to share information. And I have a suspicion that Alexey will be very good at catching errant letters, which would lead him right back to me." He frowned. "It's likely why most of my spies were caught."

Dimitri didn't miss the way that Vasily averted his eyes from those at the table. He could see the guilt there.

"It's not your fault, Vasya," Annika said softly. "It's no one's fault but the Pretender's."

"And mine," Ladushka broke in, staring down unblinkingly at her plate. "I was Dima's chancellor. It was my job to protect us, and those who worked for us, from Dima's political enemies, even if they were the ones who shared his bed. And I failed."

"Lada," Dimitri said as gently as he could, because he knew the pain in that tone of her voice, from the way it cracked. "None of us knew what he would do. None of us. Not even me."

Mischa reached out a hand to grasp her forearm. "We all failed, Lada. I was the court physician and I failed to see how Alexey had lost his grip on reality. If someone is guilty, it's also me."

Annika opened her mouth, likely to admit her own guilt, and Dimitri couldn't bear it, because there was a part of him that recognized—truly—that this was none of their faults.

"All of you, stop." It was natural, now, to order them about the way he used to, his mind and his body having remembered how to command. The remaining members of his court quickly straightened up and turned to him. "We are here. Don't dwell on the past. And if anyone is to blame, it's me. So immediately cease speaking of this and focus on the current problem. I have an idea."

Dimitri fiddled with his spoon, tapping it against his plate in lieu of taking another bite. An idea had come to him, but one he decidedly didn't like. It felt too much like the kind of heresy he had fought a war against.

"There's . . ." He tested the words out on his tongue, then decided to spit it out. "There's a library, of sorts. Here, in Wilnetzk. Alexey spoke of it a few times and sent for books from the collection. It has—" He swallowed thickly. "It has information on Ludayzist mysticism. And it might contain a way for us to communicate unseen."

"We cannot engage in blasphemy." Annika's face had gone ashen.

Mischa cocked their head. "Is it truly blasphemy if we use it to depose Alexey and rid Novo-Svitsevo of the Holy Science?"

They all looked to Dimitri. He was, after all, the one who would have to decide how low they would stoop to recover the throne.

He ignored the twisting in his gut at the thought of doing anything even close to the horrors that Alexey had wrought with the Holy Science. It could corrupt him, the same way it had corrupted Alexey. He had been robbed of so much—his safety, his love, his country— that he couldn't imagine his humanity being taken too. But this was the cost of losing the war.

This was the cost of keeping Vasily safe.

He turned to the other man. "Vasya, find the library. We'll go as soon as we can. And if it contains a solution, we can debate morality then."

Vasily gave a tight nod. Ladushka sagged with relief. Annika just bit her lip.

"In the meantime, there's a problem we *can* solve." Mischa glared at Dimitri meanly, in the way they did when they were expecting to be obeyed. "I spent two hours making a high-calorie, nutrient-dense chocolate mousse, and you're going to eat it *all*."

★

Vasily returned as Dimitri lay on the sofa with a cup of still-steaming peppermint tea balanced on his chest, trying not to think about how awfully overfull he was.

"I see Mischka got you to eat their dessert." Vasily lifted Dimitri's legs up and sat down, then lowered Dimitri's legs onto his lap.

"Did you find it?" Dimitri took a sip of tea and instantly regretted it, his mouth searing from the burn.

"Of course." Vasily undid his tie and unbuttoned his vest. "It's in the river district. Although we might all catch lice going there. Mischka better prepare."

Dimitri didn't want to move, didn't want to set them all on this path, but he knew that if he didn't force them all to go now, he might lose his courage come morning. "Don't get too comfortable. We should leave now."

"Are you sure?" Vasily cocked his head at him. "If you need time . . ."

Dimitri set the teacup on the side table and sat up, groaning as he cracked his neck. "Of course I need time. But we don't have it. Go get the others."

Vasily looked at him askance, but merely nodded and stood up, disappearing up the stairs. Dimitri gathered his determination and went to fetch his coat, pulling it on as the others came down the stairs.

"Are you sure you're ready?" Annika laid a comforting hand on his shoulder, but Dimitri found himself resenting the implication. That he couldn't do this. That he was no longer capable of doing the hard things, making the difficult choices. As if he were not the one who sent soldiers to their deaths under his name, all through the war.

"I'm fine." Dimitri swallowed thickly, burrowing into his coat. "Let's go."

Before leaving, Dimitri took care to pull his hat down low and wind his scarf around the lower part of his face, obscuring it from view. His official portrait had never been disseminated around the empire, let alone abroad—he'd had no time, and he and Alexey considered that it might look as though Dimitri was happy he was Tzar, despite his entire family being dead—but one could never be too careful.

They bundled into the carriage that Mischa flagged down outside. The driver was none too happy when Vasily gave him directions, so Dimitri flipped the irate-looking man a bronze gir for his troubles before shoving himself in between Annika and Ladushka on the seat.

"I should warn you all," Vasily said, his lips pursed. "When I found the library, I had the chance to peek inside. The librarian is named Aleksandr. And he can be . . . tetchy, from my brief experience with him."

"Is he going to curse us?" Annika rested a hand on the knife she had tucked into her belt. "Am I going to have to cut parts of him off?"

"No, he's just . . . mercurial. Eccentric, shall we say."

Dimitri raised an eyebrow. "Care to explain?"

"Don't offend the head, and all shall be well." Vasily held his hands up. "Just don't offend the talking head."

Dimitri was relieved to see that he wasn't the only one in the carriage who looked alarmed.

"What the fuck have we gotten ourselves into?" Mischa said, staring out the window of the carriage. "What the absolute fuck."

Vasily waved dismissively. "It will be fine. But there's something else you should know—using the library isn't free."

Annika rolled her eyes. "I hope you remembered to bring some money."

"Ah." Vasily chewed his lip. "You can't pay in money. You have to pay in pieces of yourself."

"Stop the carriage right fucking now." Mischa made for the carriage door, but Vasily blocked them with an arm. "There's no way I'm letting any of us cut off pieces of ourselves to *read a book*."

"Fuck off, it's not like that," Vasily grumbled, shoving Mischa back down onto the carriage bench. "We have to pay each time with an object that means something to us. Like this."

He pulled out a handkerchief, worn down and yellowed at the edges, the lace curling in on itself. There were faint specks that might have been blood on it.

"What is that?" Ladushka raised an eyebrow.

"My mother's handkerchief," Vasily replied, winding it around his fingers before putting it back into his pocket. "One of the few things I have from my parents that made it with me to Wilnetzk. It was in my pocket the night we fled. I've kept it with me ever since."

Dimitri flushed at that, since he had never noticed. Guilt prodded him, that Vasily paid such close attention to him, and yet he was too busy grieving and getting drunk to return the favor.

"The Holy Science demands a cost," Dimitri said to distract himself from that particularly unpleasant train of thought. "Something must be given for God to grant power in return." Alexey had often said it—the greater the sacrifice, the greater God's reward.

"This is bullshit." Annika was chewing on her amulet, the chain in her mouth. "I can't believe we're doing this."

"You know what else demands a cost?" Dimitri stared her down. "Saving our country. And for that, I'm willing to pay any price."

✶

After half an hour of bumping across the increasingly uneven streets, the driver stopped and thumped on the carriage roof. "Here we are," Vasily said. "And please, friends, remember not to insult the head."

"May the Lord our God protect us from evil," Annika said as she stepped out of the carriage. She made the sign against demons, and then fingered her amulet.

"Did you bring an extra one of those?" Ladushka whispered, eyeing Annika's Seal of Zalman. "Because I think I might need it."

Annika mutely removed four more amulets from her pocket and started passing them out. Dimitri felt no better once he fastened it around his neck, because he was still standing out front of a dilapidated house by the river, sitting alone in what looked to be an abandoned industrial area, its roof slouching inwards and its walls sagging.

What was truly concerning, though, were the human skulls scattered around the wild-looking shrubbery.

"I thought this was supposed to be a library," Dimitri muttered. He wasn't sure what he had been expecting, but it was certainly something much different than this, a dwelling that basically amounted to a shack with an alarming garden.

"This is it!" Vasily exclaimed cheerily, waving off the amulet Annika was trying to fasten around his neck and prancing up to the door to rap on it jauntily with a fist. Dimitri sighed, convinced that Vasily was just excited that he'd finally been allowed to march to his own death and would be enthralled with any part of the process.

Nothing happened for a few minutes, and Dimitri was ready to call the expedition off and return home to nurse a nice cold glass of vodka when the door swung open to reveal a man with a gray beard and a mean look on his face, wearing an extravagantly patterned velvet smoking jacket and apparently nothing else. "You again?" He squinted into the sunlight. "It seems early. Library's closed."

The man tried to shut the door, but Vasily stuck his foot into the corner of the frame before it could slam. "It's late afternoon. Aren't libraries public buildings?"

"Not this one," the man muttered.

"What better time to research magic than the present, Aleksandr?" Vasily grinned. "I've brought my friends, you see. And I have a gift."

Vasily held out the handkerchief. The man plucked it from his fingers, sniffed at it twice, and then shoved it into the pocket of his smoking jacket.

"That will do. It's painful enough. I can smell it." The man peered around Vasily's bulk to sneer at them, but then stepped aside. "Come in, then."

Dimitri followed Vasily into the house, because he knew if he wasn't the next to go in, no one would follow, and Vasily would be left on his own.

The inside of the house was no better. It looked like no library Dimitri had ever been to. It was full of bunches of hanging herbs, which were giving the house an unbearably sickly-sweet smell. Books were crammed on either side of the narrow hallway in tottering stacks, and small piles of bones were scattered randomly around the moth-eaten carpet. Aleksandr led them to a small sitting room and swept some papers off a sofa. "Sit," he commanded. "You're going to make me nervous if you stand looming over me like that. You're all far too tall."

Dimitri had never been called tall in his life—fine-boned and of middling height were perhaps more apt descriptors—and he stood eye level with the librarian. He opened his mouth to argue, but then Vasily shoved him down onto the distressingly lumpy sofa with a large hand. "Of course we'll sit," Vasily said good-naturedly.

Annika crammed next to him on the sofa, and Mischa sat on her lap. Ladushka perched daintily on a small stack of books off to the side, and Vasily sprawled out on the floor, completely unconcerned by their surroundings—although a flash of longing crossed his face when Aleksandr took the handkerchief back out of his pocket and flung it unceremoniously behind him. Vasily's fingers twitched like he meant to grab it, but he quickly tamped the movement down.

Aleksandr sat down in the armchair by the fire. For a second, they all looked at each other mutely. Dimitri wondered if he'd have to bribe the man for access to the collection, beyond the price they'd paid to enter the library.

"I told you they'd be early, you *putz*," said a loud and grating voice from under a black velvet cloth in the corner. "You shouldn't have had so much to drink last night."

Annika jumped, nearly ejecting Mischa from her lap.

"Shut it!" Aleksandr grabbed for a cane leaning against the mantel and hit at the velvet.

"Hey, has anyone ever told you the joke about the trees?" The velvet cloth was rustling now, and Dimitri's unease was about to strangle him. Vasily was staring at them and shaking his head minutely, mouthing, *The head, don't offend it.*

This time, Aleksandr used the cane to flip the cloth off. Dimitri couldn't help but stare. There was the head of an old man, balding, with blue eyes and liver spots, set at the neck into a small table made of mahogany.

"What the *fuck*," Mischa said under their breath.

"Young one, don't think that because I'm old I'm also deaf!" The head glared at Mischa, who immediately shut up.

"My library of the mystics contains far more than just books," the librarian exclaimed proudly, waving his cane aloft. "I have the finest collection of mystic artifacts anywhere in the known world. This head tells the future." He shifted and his smoking jacket almost fell open, giving Dimitri an eyeful of shriveled skin.

For a moment, Dimitri was simply glad that Alexey had never come here. Because, if he had, the librarian's demeanor meant Alexey would have cheerfully murdered him and then shipped the entire collection back to Novo-Svitsevo, and they wouldn't be able to access it now.

"There are rules." Aleksandr wagged a finger at them. "Don't tear pages out of any of my books. Don't spill blood on any of my books. Don't let human tears touch the pages. Rat tears, those are all right— most of the time. Don't allow the books on the third shelf under the window to get anywhere close to fire, and you'll want to wear protective goggles when reading from the section on alchemy. The last researcher went blind when the books spat lead at her. Don't annotate any of my books. The last person to write in the margins of the mystic Shaul's books had their fingers—"

"The boy's the Tzar of Novo-Svitsevo," the head said suddenly, interrupting the increasingly disturbing diatribe, and Dimitri couldn't decide what part of the statement was the most alarming—the fact that it was accurate, or the fact that it was issued from the mouth of a severed head.

Annika straightened up beside him and tensed in a way that made him think she was a heartbeat away from throwing a knife into Aleksandr's chest. He put a hand on her thigh in warning.

"Yes, yes, you said something about that," Aleksandr grumbled. "But that doesn't change the fact that he *can't bleed on any of the books.*"

"We acknowledge your rules. We'll do our best to follow them, stop worrying." Dimitri threaded a note of old command into his voice. "I'd appreciate it if you let us in. Now." He stared the librarian down and was gratified when he shrunk back in his chair and averted his gaze.

Pride flared in Dimitri's chest. Perhaps he did still know how to command others to do his will.

"Through the door." Aleksandr snapped his fingers, then pointed to the left. When Dimitri turned his head, there was a door there that he swore hadn't been there before. He briefly wondered if he was somehow drunk, but the rest of his court had similarly stupefied expressions on their faces.

He thought of Alexey, muttering about how mysticism was not simply a collection of parlor tricks, and then stood and walked through the door.

*

The library itself was large enough that there was no practical way to explain how it fit into the small house Dimitri had observed from the street. He tried very hard not to think about how the house was, quite obviously, much larger on the inside.

It was full of so much dust that his eyes immediately began to water, his footfalls causing puffs of something unidentifiable to rise up from the musty carpet. The entire dimly lit room was lined from floor to ceiling with bookcases, ladders occasionally interspersed to help reach the tops of the shelves. There was a strange buzzing sound that filled Dimitri's ears as soon as he got close enough to the books to touch them, and he backed up, his thighs hitting the low wooden table in the center of the room, barely illuminated by sunlight struggling to enter the filthy window.

The rest of his court looked as horrified as he felt, even Ladushka, who normally would do anything to get her hands on a book she hadn't read before.

No one was making a move to start, so he took charge, clearing his throat.

"Split up," he said. They all fanned out.

Thus began a several-hour search. Some sections of the library were labeled, although in a nonsensical manner. Some were sorted by what Vasily eventually deduced was the age the author had been when they died, while other shelves appeared to be arranged in ascending order of the faded prices written on their spines. Dimitri and Ladushka worked together, combing through the sections and eventually finding enough books on various means of communication that they could create a healthy-looking pile. They divided the books among the five of them and claimed rickety seats around the long wooden table.

There were several false starts, where they thought they would find something promising but then developed sudden, splitting headaches when they opened the book's cover. One book wouldn't come unstuck, no matter how much they all tried to pry it apart. When they determined which books wouldn't cause them bodily harm, and deputized Mischa to put the dangerous ones back on the shelves, they got to reading in silence.

Dimitri thumbed through pages until his vision blurred. He passed through instructions for making one's voice louder in a crowded room, how to ostensibly talk to dogs and horses, how to turn smoke different colors for signals. Too many times he found his eyes snagging on something that reminded him of Alexey, his heart twisting in his chest.

The lamps in the room were burning low by the time he found something, in the back of a small book, almost an afterthought. He must have made a noise, because Vasily leaned over. He grabbed the book out of Dimitri's hands, then squinted down at the page. "A simple communication spell, requiring only the exchange of a piece of your soul with each other, bound together with the help of an angel. Fear not, we only need a minor one."

Dimitri clenched his thighs with his hands to stop his fingers from shaking. This was so close to what Alexey had been doing—too close. Dangerously close.

"It gives the name of an angel and says to call on him with an offering of a . . . stimulant?" Vasily's eyes widened, and Mischa grabbed the book from him.

"Cocaine? You're kidding." They dragged a hand over their eyes. "What kind of fucking library is this?"

"A sinful one," Annika muttered, closing her eyes.

Ladushka had removed the book from Mischa's hands and was studying it. "I think this is precisely what we need. You and Vasya would be able to talk to each other in your dreams every night. A perfect, and secure, way to communicate." She closed the book and handed it back to Dimitri. "I think we have retrieved what we came for."

Dimitri took the book and stood up. He needed to leave. He needed to purge his mind of everything he had learned about the Holy Science that afternoon. "Let's go." He dusted off his pants, which had accumulated a mysterious furry coating while he sat in the library.

He tucked the slim volume into his coat pocket and motioned for the rest of them to put the piles of books they'd accumulated back. It wouldn't do for the librarian to be able to deduce what they'd been researching. They obeyed, and then filed back out of the door and into the room with the head and the fire. The librarian was still sitting in his armchair.

"Did you find what you came for?" Aleksandr scratched at his beard. "You didn't tear any of the books now, did you?"

"No," Dimitri said tersely. "If you breathe a word of this to anyone, Annika will be paying you a visit, and she's not a nice houseguest when she's mad."

Aleksandr turned his eyes to Annika, whose smile spread wider into her cheeks, nearly wolfish. She winked, and he looked appropriately frightened.

"You'll be back," the head said. "Again and again, you'll always come back. He'll bring you back."

Dimitri shuddered at the way the head's eyes went black as it spoke.

"*Pssht,*" Aleksandr said. "Shut up. It's too early in the day for a prophecy."

Dimitri fled the room with his court trailing behind him and didn't look back.

✳

"I want to talk to Lada," Dimitri said when they arrived back at home. "Alone. Shoo, the rest of you."

Vasily shrugged, Mischa looked wary, and Annika just gave him a small squeeze on his shoulder before ushering the other two away into the night-darkened townhouse.

"Come," he said to Ladushka, ascending the stairs to the top of the house.

He pushed open the door to his room and kicked off his shoes, flopping down on the bed. Ladushka stood, looking at him, and then slowly closed the door. She crossed to the bed and stood next to it, knocking Dimitri's sagging chin up with her thumb. "What is haunting your mind?"

"Am I wrong," he asked quietly, "to do this, Lada? To use the horror of the Holy Science on another person, like Alexey would? To do it to *Vasya*?"

Ladushka let his chin go, and slowly slid down to a sitting position.

"I no longer know what is right and what is wrong." Ladushka leaned her back against the side of Dimitri's bed, and the wisps of her hair that had escaped from her braid tickled his bare arm. "I lost all sense of that when Alexey staged his coup. Dima, I do not think we can live like we used to anymore, judging right and wrong, weighing both sides. I think being righteous was what led us here in the first place."

"I was raised to be righteous." Dimitri reached his hand down, and Ladushka grasped it. "And it's pathetic to admit it, but I'm terrified of dying and learning that I've condemned myself to an eternity in Gehenna. I don't want to spend the rest of my eternal life in hell."

Ladushka squeezed his hand. "I am as well, Dima. But then I think that I would give my immortal soul for the chance to save the country, and then I wonder if being righteous sometimes means you must sin along the way."

"What if I hurt him?" Dimitri swallowed hard. "What if drawing him into this condemns him to be a sinner or turns him to the path of evil?"

"Vasya would do anything to save his country," Ladushka said, her voice harsh. "We are commanded to choose life, Dima. And now we must choose the life of our nation over the lives of one person. Even if it is our dearest friend. It is the only way we can make this right."

"I don't—" Dimitri's voice cracked, and he paused for a breath. "Lada, I don't know if I can do it. I don't know if I can still rule. I fear every day that I'm too broken."

She would tell him the truth. She had told him the truth every time he had ever asked her, and sometimes even when he had not. They had grown up together, two nearly forgotten children being looked after by the same nursemaid, the castoffs of the powerful of Rav-Mikhailburg. There was no artifice left between them. Annika would try to soothe him, and Mischa would try to fix him, and Vasily would just make it all into a joke to avoid the discomfort of the truth. Ladushka would tell him what he needed to hear, even if it wasn't what he wanted.

Ladushka pivoted so that she was facing him. "We are all broken. Dima, look at me." She grabbed his chin again and forced him to face her. Dimitri met her eyes, stern but kind. "You can do this. I know you can. If you take care of yourself, you will regain your strength, and then you will survive what comes, and you might even triumph."

He swallowed thickly. But somehow, what she was saying felt right.

The parts of their plan were moving into place, and it was past time for Dimitri to start piecing himself back together. When the time came to act, he'd be ready.

FOURTEEN

Alexey

"Give them rooms. Feed them delicacies. Clothe them if they come to us in rags." Alexey paced the length of his council chamber, then turned on his heel to walk down the line of his assembled household staff. "Treat them as honored guests."

The gray-faced palace steward nodded tersely, looking down at the carpet all the while, his face bathed in the flickering firelight from the grate.

"I want them watched at all times." Alexey passed the head of the palace guard and gave him a pointed stare. "Do not let them wander the palace without my permission."

The guard, chin up and eyes forward, saluted.

"I do not know how many will arrive, but all of them will be accommodated here, in the palace. Do not send them out into Rav-Mikhailburg to find lodging. Come to me if there are problems, and no one else, do you understand? The first could arrive within mere hours."

He could taste the fear coming off the chief chambermaid, a timid girl who shook where she stood. "Yes, *Moy Tzar*," she whispered when he stopped in front of her and grabbed her chin, forcing her to meet his eyes.

He dropped her face and she scuttled backwards, her back hitting the gilt edge of a painting of some ancient Tzar, making it tilt.

"The Leyvin are coming," he said, picking up his cloak from where he had discarded it on his desk and slinging it around his shoulders. "Make sure they feel at home."

★

"There must be thousands of them in the country, *Moy Tzar*." Morozov stood and gave a short bow when Alexey walked into the study. He was poring over the enormous stack of books that couriers had been bringing in from every shul they could reach in Novo-Svitsevo. He sat back down, hunching over the stack, a gleam in his eyes.

Alexey deeply appreciated having another scholar to rely on.

"Has anyone responded to the proclamation yet?" Alexey settled into a chair by the fire and wrapped his cloak around his legs. It did nothing for the chill in his bones, but the feeling of the silk around his body was comforting all the same.

"We sent it days ago to every newspaper in Rav-Mikhailburg, and some beyond," Ivan said from his position at attention in the corner of the room. "They should start arriving any day now, *Moy Tzar*, the locals far sooner than that."

In the shadows, he really looked like Dimitri. Alexey shivered. Part of him wanted to grab for the boy and take him right there, and part of him wanted to slap Ivan for daring to look so much like the man who had betrayed him. The clash of emotions overwhelmed him, forcing him to rip his eyes away.

"Soon the news will be all over the country," Morozov muttered. "They'll be banging on the palace gates. What peasant could resist the offer to come live and pray with the Tzar himself? And with the reward to their shul, the pressure to come from their congregations and their rebbes will be immense."

Alexey stared into the fire. "I do not need many. I need the ones who feel love for me, who will be my conduits. To command my armies, that requires devotion. But even before that, we must first learn how to make the perfect *zemonyii*."

Ivan shifted on his feet and cleared his throat. "*Moy Tzar*," he began, then trailed off.

"Yes?" Alexey cocked his head and raised an eyebrow.

Morozov filled Ivan's silence. "We have discovered something interesting about the bloodline of Tzar Abram Fyodorev, may his memory be a blessing. Dimitri's father."

Ivan's father, too.

"I know who he was," Alexey snapped. His father-in-law had been a cold man, an illusion of a perfect ruler. But then that ruse was revealed, and he died because he could not control his own country. It was that same failing that had taken Dimitri away from him, in the end.

"He appears to be of the line of Leyvin, *Moy Tzar*," Morozov said, pulling out a finely bound book with gilt edges. "This is from the royal shul of Rav-Mikhailburg."

Alexey tapped a finger against his lips. "Perhaps it gave his line their original claim to the throne of Novo-Svitsevo." It made sense.

"Which means anyone descended from the former Tzar would carry the bloodline of Leyvin as well." Morozov looked meaningfully across the room, to where Ivan stood.

There was hope and love shining in Ivan's eyes, and it made Alexey's stomach twist in a way that he hated, and that he did not care to interrogate. It reminded him how he had felt for Dimitri in those last, desperate months before his rebirth. Feelings that had driven him to push the Holy Science to its limits to protect the country.

To protect Dimitri.

He had been willing to help Dimitri transform into something holy, something beautiful, something righteous, not one of the twisted creatures he had been creating, more beast than man. Dimitri had been too good for that, and he could not do it to Ivan without seeing Dimitri in his place.

And Dimitri never would have offered. Dimitri never would have stood there, his face flushed with hope, his fingers twitching in anticipation. Dimitri never would have given himself up as Ivan was clearly doing now.

"Ivan," he said, standing up and grabbing him by the arm. "You will come with me." He turned to his chancellor. "Morozov, keep compiling the lists. And alert me when any Leyvin arrive. You will begin the interviews once they are made comfortable, and then we will commence the experiments."

Alexey towed Ivan out of the study and pulled him into the nearest empty room, closing and locking the door behind them. He shoved the smaller man against the wall, sliding a knee in between his thighs, pinning him to the plaster. "You would give your life and your soul to me?"

"Yes, *Moy Tzar*," Ivan said, his eyes closing and his head falling back, exposing his throat like he wanted Alexey to claim him.

"Just like that?" Alexey took what was offered, and bit down on Ivan's neck, hard, leaving a mark that would bruise and eliciting a moan. "With no fight, you would give me everything that you are?"

"Yes," Ivan breathed, and he was getting hard against Alexey's thigh, though he tried to hide it by shifting his legs. It should have aroused him, but instead Alexey found himself pausing.

This was too easy.

If there was one thing about Dimitri he had despised, it was how stubborn and steadfast he was. Dimitri had pushed back and fought him, clawed at him, despite all of Alexey's efforts to mold him. Dimitri had submitted to him at night, yet called him Lyosha lovingly in the dark despite Alexey's hatred of his childhood nickname. And then he'd gotten up in the morning and ruled the kingdom, ignoring most of Alexey's advice.

"I would give you everything," Ivan repeated, his eyes piercing underneath the fall of his silken hair. "Anything you ask, I will do. You are *Moy Tzar*. You rule me, in every way."

Alexey should have been praising the Lord his God for sending him such an exquisite lover, with the face of the man he had lost and a willingness to submit, which had always failed to truly take root within Dimitri when it mattered. He should have wanted to turn Ivan, to make him the general at the head of his armies.

And yet.

A deep sense of wrongness pervaded Alexey, twisting his gut. There was no challenge here. Nothing to dominate, because everything was freely given. There was none of the push and pull of his courtship with Dimitri, nothing to draw him in. It was just Ivan, offering himself up as though Alexey was everything he had ever craved.

It was too easy. It was too much.

Something about Ivan was missing, and the closer Alexey got to him, the more he feared that the missing piece was simply that Ivan was not Dimitri. Was not the boy he had shaped and the man who had defied him and the husband he had lost.

He pushed away from Ivan, walked out of the room, and did not look back.

✶

Alexey knew he would need to focus himself, so when the hours stretched late into the night, he sent a servant to fetch Ivan and made his way into the courtyard near his study. The energy that was coursing through his limbs needed an outlet, and sometimes the best outlet was pain. The wind nipped at his cheeks as he emerged into the blissful, silent dark of the courtyard, fetching the bow and quiver from the rack kept just outside the door. His body may have been made anew, but it still remembered the paces he had put it through in his mortal life.

Alexey relished the ease with which he could pull back his bow-string, as easy as if he was reaching his hand through air. The fletching of the arrow brushed his cheek, and he let out a breath as he released it.

It hit the bull's-eye of the target that was kept across the court-yard, and then punched through the straw to bury itself in the stone of the courtyard wall.

Alexey lowered the bow and said a prayer to God, as he always did when an arrow hit its target, whether an object or a living thing. *Thank you, the Lord who is my God, for granting me strength and power, so I may defend my country.*

Eventually, Alexey ran out of arrows, firing the last one into the dark. It was the dead of night now, and the wind rustled the autumn-hued trees in the training yard, skittering over the gravel lining the ground. Since being reborn, Alexey had used this hour, when mortals slept, to test the limits of his new form. And even now, when he knew exactly what he could do—climb the palace walls by finding the barest fingerholds, jump from the palace roof and land unscathed, crush a prisoner's windpipe with a single hand and barely a thought—he still relished exploring the power the Holy Science imbued him with. God's presence within him allowed him to far surpass the limits of a normal mortal shell.

The heels of his leather boots crunched on the loose stones as he made his way to the target, the wind whipping his black silk cloak around his legs. It was easy for him to see in the dark—a lack of light was no barrier now. Not since he had spent so very long alone in the dark, finding his way back to this form.

He wrapped a hand around one of the arrows buried in the wall and pulled it free with a crack and a crumbling of stone. Once he had regathered his quiver, he strode to the center of the courtyard and snapped his fingers twice.

Ivan stepped into the moonlight, holding his own bow and quiver of arrows. He licked his lips as he lit a torch, placing it in a metal holder against the wall. He was wearing nothing more than a light wool coat against the chill, and the flush that rose to his cheeks at the bite of the wind sent a pang through Alexey's core. Dimitri had always hated the cold. It seemed so wrong that Ivan did not mind it.

"Come here," he said, beckoning to Ivan. "Now you are going to practice."

Ivan, like the rest of the royal bastards, had never been taught how to shoot, neither guns nor arrows. Hunting was, after all, a pastime for the nobility, and he had never entered military service. In the last months, he'd become a better shot, but Alexey wasn't dedicating the time to lessons that Ivan would need to become a competent marksman. He made a mental note to hire the boy an instructor.

"Yes, *Moy Tzar*." Ivan nodded obediently and came to take up his place next to Alexey, across from the target. He inhaled and fired his first arrow, the point thudding into the outer ring.

"Relax," Alexey urged, stepping up behind Ivan and tilting his shoulders ever so slightly to the right. He ghosted his fingers down Ivan's ribs, tucking his hands into the front of his coat to reposition his hips. He left his hands there, pressing Ivan back against himself. "Breathe with me. Release the arrow when I say."

Ivan murmured his assent, drawing back the arrow. His aim, Alexey noted with pleasure, was better this time. He drew in a long breath, feeling Ivan's ribs move in concert, and when they exhaled together he bent his lips to brush across the shell of Ivan's ear and whisper, "*Now*."

The boy gasped as the arrow was released. Alexey didn't need to look up to know it had hit home.

He turned Ivan around so that they were pressed together, bringing their lips to meet, claiming him in a kiss. "Wonderfully done. Shall we move on to your second target of the night?"

He backed away a step, releasing Ivan's warmth. Ivan bit his lip.

His eyes met Ivan's, and Alexey held his stare across the courtyard as he reached up and undid the clasp of his cloak, letting it fall from his shoulders to the ground. His jacket followed, his fingers sure on the buttons, and then finally his shirt, until he was bare from the waist up.

"I think," Alexey said, "that tonight, we will begin with the liver."

It always helped to practice on a living target.

Ivan nodded, nocked an arrow, took aim, and fired from ten paces away right below his Tzar's ribs.

Alexey didn't stumble back at the force of the blow, but he couldn't help the hiss that escaped his lips. He was something more than human, but he still felt a human's pain. Although now, he could rise above it.

He reached down and grasped the shaft of the arrow, which had gone clean through his torso, and snapped it with a grunt. He dropped the shattered shaft to the ground and pulled the other half of the arrow out from his back.

He panted as he watched the hole in his stomach seal up.

"The heart," Alexey ordered when he caught his breath.

This time, when the arrow thudded into his chest, he swallowed a scream and bit his lip so hard that he tasted his own blood. There was fire running through him, emanating from the agonizing point where the arrow had struck. His vision blurred, and he looked at Ivan, whose eyes shining in the torchlight looked so much like Dimitri's that for a moment, he was standing in front of the man he had loved with all his heart.

Except it wasn't real. Dimitri was gone, and all that was left was Ivan and the blood dripping down his chest.

He breathed in and out through his nose, then reached down, snapped the shaft, and pulled out the arrow.

This healing was harder, and longer. He blinked away stars and said a prayer to God when he felt the beating of his heart return to its normal, sluggish pace.

"Again," he ordered, gesturing to his shoulder. Ivan's next arrow pierced it through, then at his nod another arrow joined it, and then another. He crushed the shafts with his hand and pulled the splintered wood through, reaching behind his back to yank the other halves out, looking down to see the holes in his shoulder vanish seconds later, only the mess of blood remaining as proof that he had been wounded.

"*Moy Tzar*," Ivan said, setting the bow and quiver down and approaching, his cheeks flushed. "You are a marvel of the Holy Science."

"I am a marvel of what men can become when they have no fear," he said, brushing his finger over the center of his heart in the firelight, his pride swelling at how no imperfections betrayed that, seconds ago, the flesh had been torn and ruined.

Ivan's quiet breaths and the crunching of gravel under his boots were the only sound in the courtyard for a long moment. Unlike so many, he had taken to the Holy Science immediately, rejecting the soulless, mainstream version of Ludayzim with which he had been raised. Alexey spared a heartbeat to appreciate the newfound devoutness with which Ivan approached the Holy Science and the Lord their God, until he could no longer deny the desire that was building at the base of his spine.

"And now," he said, beckoning Ivan with a crooked finger, "for your reward, for being such an excellent shot at such a late hour. You truly have improved at close range. Have you been practicing?"

"Yes, *Moy Tzar*. Thank you." Ivan looked around the courtyard, blushing and biting his lip. "But—out . . . here? Are you sure—"

Alexey stopped his complaint with a violent kiss, seizing him by the collar of his coat and pulling him close, relishing the way the blood still dripping off him smeared on Ivan and marked him as his own. The intimacy of earlier was gone, burned away by pain and the triumph of surviving what would have killed an ordinary man.

Ivan melted against him, his body warm and supple, and Alexey closed his eyes and tried to shake the vision of Dimitri out of his head, the way Dimitri would have gotten a wicked glimmer in his eyes had Alexey suggested something as daring as this. He blinked against memories of stables and gardens and empty hallways while the court was occupied with a ball.

But you lost me, Dimitri's ghost whispered in his ear. *I'll never be yours to conquer again. I'll never be yours to ruin with one glance, with one command.*

The memory of Dimitri's voice made him stiffen in a way he didn't care to investigate. So he set to conquering Ivan, reducing the boy to nothing more than a helpless, moaning mess. He hoisted Ivan up and felt his legs shiver around his waist, walking them backwards until Ivan's back was pressed against the stone wall of the courtyard.

With one touch of Alexey's power, the torches in the courtyard went out. In the dark, it was easier to pretend.

"*Moy Tzar,*" Ivan gasped as his pants were unbuttoned and Alexey took him in hand, but his voice was so different from Dimitri's rasp that Alexey couldn't stand it in the moment, and he silenced Ivan with another rough kiss.

Just for now. It wasn't weakness for him to pretend. It was strength, he told himself as he crushed Ivan to the wall, to remember everything he had sacrificed.

✳

Alexey drew them back to his bedroom, where Ivan had been staying more often than not of late, instead of in his own room across the hall. As soon as the door shut behind them, he ordered Ivan to strip and wait for him on the bed. He took off his bloodstained clothes and made his way into the adjoining bathing chamber to rinse a cloth under the tap, scrubbing away the gore that had dried tacky on his skin.

Alexey gripped the edges of the basin for a moment, shoulders hunched, staring at his own face in the mirror. He took pleasure in Ivan, in losing himself in Ivan's body, and yet every time he did so, he could not help but feel a nudging, insistent sense of loss. It was not like how it was with Dimitri, perfect and beautiful, Dimitri shaped exactly as Alexey had wanted, coming to him completely innocent, unlike Ivan.

The shuffling noises of Ivan rearranging the pillows and furs on the bed shook Alexey out of his thoughts. Ivan would have to do, for now. Not just to sate Alexey's bodily desires, which had not quelled since his rebirth, but as part of Alexey's larger goals. He could not draw Ivan in without this physical aspect, not when the boy was so obviously in love with him. This was no business arrangement to Ivan, and Alexey had to act the same, lest Ivan become unwilling to participate in the plan when he later learned his true role.

If Ivan did, he'd be so much harder to control, and Alexey had no time for such things. Bedding Ivan was worth the reminder that he had lost Dimitri.

Alexey flexed his stiff fingers, curling them into a fist. He had hardened his body. Now he had to harden his heart. There was no more room for Dimitri there, not when there was so much work to do to protect Novo-Svitsevo.

He reeled his feelings back inside and offered them to the void within him. Something reached for his love and his pain, and took them, swallowing them whole.

Alexey breathed a sigh of relief. It was never permanent, this numbing of his wounds, but it was better than having to suffer continuously and he was grateful for the reprieve. It was better not to feel. Because if he could not feel, he would not hurt.

Dimitri was gone, and perhaps Dimitri was even dead. It mattered not at all to Alexey, Tzar of Novo-Svitsevo. He controlled the world. Which mattered far more than his hold over any one man, no matter how precious.

Alexey left the bathing chamber and found Ivan splayed on the bed, one of his knees hiked up, a pillow already positioned underneath his hips. The firelight played over the perfect porcelain of his skin, marred only by the occasional constellation of birthmarks speckling his arms and legs. Ivan turned to him and blinked languidly, his arms above his head, hands fisting into the pillows.

He looked so much like Dimitri, positioned that way, that Alexey could hardly stand it. But he crossed over to the bed anyway and crawled onto it. He straddled Ivan and pinned his wrists to the mattress, shoving a thigh in between Ivan's legs. The boy moaned wantonly, and Alexey relaxed as his cock stiffened at the sound.

He bent down and claimed Ivan's mouth again, biting Ivan's lower lip until he tasted blood. Ivan bucked up underneath him, seeking friction and contact, and Alexey pinned him down with a hip, irritated at the way that Ivan was chasing his own pleasure first.

"Don't move," he ordered. Ivan stilled, the only motion his tongue darting out to lick the blood that was beading on his lower lip. When Alexey was satisfied that Ivan was not going to move, he reached for the drawer next to the bed, pulling out a jar of thick salve. He dipped his fingers into it and then pushed them into Ivan, who groaned and bucked off the bed.

"Stay *still*." It was harder to work when Ivan kept moving about. Dimitri had learned how to stay stock-still, completely unmoving, while Alexey prepared to take his pleasure. He wished that Ivan could do the same, but had no patience to train the boy. It had taken him years to instruct Dimitri into perfect submission in the bedroom, and that was far more effort than Ivan was worth. This would have to do, for now.

After a few moments, Alexey judged Ivan ready and withdrew his fingers. "Relax," he commanded, and Ivan did, drawing in deep, steadying breaths as Alexey pushed inside him. He ran his hand down the back of Ivan's thigh, bending it backwards until it was flush with Ivan's ribs, ignoring the way the muscles of Ivan's leg jumped and twitched. With Ivan opened wide, it was easier for Alexey to pound into him, and he did, taking his pleasure. It built up at the base of his spine, until he crested and tipped over the edge, his body shuddering as he convulsed inside Ivan's heat.

Alexey rolled off Ivan and closed his eyes, grunting in assent when Ivan asked if he could finish himself off. Alexey lay back against the pillow that Dimitri's head had once rested on, Ivan's stifled moans cutting through his heart. When Ivan was finished, and had gotten up to procure a wet cloth to clean them both up, Alexey sat up in bed and grabbed the cigarette case off the bedside table, along with the box of matches.

He'd never smoked before he met Dimitri, nor after—not until Dimitri was gone. He dragged the cigarette across his bottom lip the way Dimitri always did, then put it in his mouth and lit it, taking a perfunctory drag before passing it to Ivan.

"The whole thing," he ordered, closing his eyes again and letting the familiar scent of Dimitri's favorite brand of cigarettes soothe him, doing his best to ignore Ivan's coughs after each inhale. The boy truly had weak lungs.

Alexey breathed in deep, reminded of the taste of Dimitri's kisses, and drifted, wishing for once that he could sleep, and dream, so that he could be with Dimitri one last time.

FIFTEEN

VASILY

Dimitri was still half-asleep, blinking bleary eyes as Vasily slipped into his bedroom the next morning.

"You wanted to summon an angel?" He bent down and kissed Dimitri's head, Dimitri curling closer to where he was standing next to the bed, the way Dimitri was warm and trusting and sleepy sparking fondness in his chest.

Dimitri groaned and shifted in bed, stretching. "I need strength first." He pulled the blanket off. "And help to solve a personal problem."

"*Oh.*" Vasily smirked. It was early, and he was tired from having spent half the night plotting, but he couldn't ever resist this. He toed off his shoes and took off his jacket and vest, laying them on Dimitri's bedside table, which for once was clear of half-empty tumblers.

He hid his thrill that Dimitri had finally *asked* for something in the bedroom, vague as it was. Alexey had been Dimitri's first lover, and evidently had never once asked his husband what he enjoyed or encouraged him to give any indication of what he wanted. The thought made Vasily far angrier than was appropriate so early in the morning, so he pushed it down and covered it with a joke instead. "You know, the sages call the phallus the peacemaker of the home."

Dimitri rolled onto his back and reached out, pulling Vasily on top of him. Vasily let himself be pulled, careful not to put too much of his weight on Dimitri, lest he crush the other man. "Yes, Vasya, we all know that this home would descend into utter chaos if not for the salvation provided by your dick."

"It's a nice one," Vasily said, bending down to claim Dimitri in a kiss. "Admit it."

Dimitri groaned and bucked his hips up against Vasily's. "I admit it."

"Well then, *Moy Tzar*," Vasily said, peppering each word with a kiss down Dimitri's neck, leading to the spot behind his ear that always made him shiver, "before we try our hand at spells, let's make a different kind of magic first, shall we?"

Dimitri, apparently having exhausted his reserve of words concerning his sexual desires, merely tugged on Vasily's tie plaintively. It was Dimitri's signal to take that tie and cover his eyes.

His heart sank a little. But Vasily complied, knotting the blindfold behind Dimitri's head. He always did.

He just wished, so fervently that it made his ribs ache, that Dimitri would stop comparing him to another man, would open his eyes and look at him and stop pretending.

But no. This was, and had always been, a simple, mutually beneficial arrangement between two friends whose bodies needed release and who happened to be uniquely compatible. It had nothing to do with anything. That was what Vasily told himself every time.

Vasily took every tender feeling that he had for Dimitri, anything that could be mistaken for something inappropriate and so far beyond his station that it was almost funny, and shoved them all away, deep, deep down, as Dimitri blindly started undoing the buttons on Vasily's shirt. Every time Dimitri's fingers brushed his chest, he shivered, heat building in his core. He reminded himself that this was just the joining of bodies, just a very human need, and not something more. It would never be anything more, because Vasily was a nobody, a minor lord from a tiny, unremarkable province, and Dimitri was the Tzar of his country. Vasily was just here to warm the bed.

He consoled himself by thinking that sometimes he truly loved his job and the responsibilities that came with it.

Vasily watched Dimitri work, chewing on his lip. When Vasily's shirt was hanging open, he straddled Dimitri and rose up onto his knees, letting the shirt slide down his shoulders, unbuttoning his pants and shoving them down. Dimitri was dressed only in a nightshirt, which had already ridden up far enough to be indecent, the slim lines of Dimitri's surprisingly strong thighs on display. Vasily pulled it up further, ignoring the pang in his chest at the way he could see each one of Dimitri's ribs through his skin, the points of his hips standing out like arches, and concentrated on making both of them feel good.

They could have this, if only for a moment. A tiny bit of comfort in a world that wanted to rip them apart. And only God knew how many more times Vasily would get to do this if he was successful in sneaking into Novo-Svitsevo and bringing Alexey down, returning Dimitri safely to the throne.

He pushed away thoughts of an inevitable second royal marriage—likely to a snobby Urushkin princess to quell generations of tension between their two countries—as he worked Dimitri open, losing himself in the moment and in the way Dimitri spread his legs and threw his head back, his mouth falling open. When Dimitri was just barely ready to take him without being injured, Vasily flipped him over and dug his hands into the creases of Dimitri's hips, pulling him backwards. Vasily would have preferred to take more time, be more tender, open Dimitri up for him slowly, make him ready enough that he'd be able to truly relax and feel good. But that wasn't what Alexey would have done, and so it wasn't what Dimitri wanted, no matter how much Vasily tried to convince him that his husband had been, at best, an artless lover—and at worst, a completely selfish one.

But this was his role, and he played it, because even though it made him faintly sick to emulate Alexey's worst practices, Vasily couldn't resist the chance to be this close to Dimitri. So he moved, sinking into Dimitri far too quickly, in a way that must have surely hurt him. Dimitri whimpered, clenching around him, and that was Vasily's cue to order Dimitri to stay quiet and still, putting a hand on the small of his back to keep him from moving. Taking him roughly, the way Dimitri wanted, all the while wishing that he could teach Dimitri how to be loved so much better.

But eventually, with the tightness and the heat, he lost himself in the moment, and Dimitri did too, by the way his hands fisted in the sheets. Vasily's movements grew more erratic. And then, just as he was about to tip over the edge, there was a very loud thump from the door.

He whipped his head around, and saw Ladushka standing in the doorway, frowning. Vasily rolled his eyes, moving in and out slowly, trying not to let the interruption distract him. "Go away."

"It is past nine." Ladushka crossed her arms over her chest. "We are all waiting for you so we can begin the ritual, and here you both are, wasting time with frivolous physical activity."

"I'm working quite hard here, thank you," Vasily muttered under his breath. There was sweat beading on his brow, and he withdrew from Dimitri and plunged in again, chasing the sensation of perfect bliss.

Dimitri raised his head out of where he had buried it in a pillow, ripped off the blindfold, and groaned. "Are you serious, Lada? Ten more minutes. The angel can wait ten more minutes."

Vasily pulled back and flipped Dimitri over, propping Dimitri's knees over his shoulders. Dimitri made an impatient face that Vasily knew meant *keep going*, even if Dimitri would never ask for that.

"Ten?" Vasily thrust into Dimitri again. "Please, I take offense at that. I can keep going for another twenty." He turned to Ladushka.

"Can't you see you've interrupted an excellent fuck? Please come back later. I know things are urgent, but not *this* urgent."

"I really must insist," she said, rolling her eyes and giving what, for Ladushka, counted as a disgusted grimace, in reality nothing more than a subtle twitching of her lips downward, "that you finish up quickly. As I said, we are all waiting."

"Are you going to leave?" Dimitri scowled.

"It is simply bodies coming together. You both know I have no interest in such activities. I actually find intercourse and romance off-putting, you know I always have." She put her hands on her hips. "It is why I thank the Lord our God every day that the war interrupted the betrothal my parents arranged. Anyway, if I leave, you will keep going for longer than you truly need."

"Fuck you," Dimitri muttered under his breath as he pushed back against Vasily. But he arched his back just a little bit more. Vasily always got the sense that Dimitri, somewhere deep inside, enjoyed performing. And it wasn't as if Vasily had ever minded his friends knowing they fucked.

Vasily went back to work with a stifled moan, and then he came in a wash of pleasure. He kissed each of Dimitri's knees, then took Dimitri in hand until he felt the other man clench around him. He pulled out, then collapsed onto the mattress. "Was that efficient enough for you, Lada?" ·

"Yes, thank you," she said primly.

Ladushka bent down and retrieved Vasily's clothing, flinging it on top of him. "Get dressed," she ordered him, turning to Dimitri's wardrobe and pulling out a suit. "You too, Dima."

"Fine." Vasily rolled off of Dimitri and used the sheet to clean them both before slipping back into his clothes. He turned to Dimitri once he was dressed and rearranged Dimitri's tie. The other man always did it up crooked.

The moment they were both dressed, Ladushka flung the door

open wider, revealing Annika and Mischa standing on the landing too, wearing identical expressions of consternation.

"You told us to be ready to perform the ritual in an hour, Vasya." Annika was pointing exasperatedly at the clock on Dimitri's mantel.

Mischa stepped into the room and whacked Vasily in the chest with the back of their hand. "Did you really have to fuck for an hour, you absolute rake?"

"*Moy Tzar* ordered me to." Vasily grinned hugely. "And I am loyal to the death and could not possibly defy such an important command."

"Disgusting." Ladushka grimaced as she held up a hand. "Kindly cease speaking about your animalistic urges. I already had to be the one to fetch you both, and that is more than enough for me for today. Shall we summon the angel?"

"I—" Dimitri shrank into Vasily's side at Ladushka's blunt probing, his eyes going wide. Vasily could feel the anxiety coming off of him in waves.

"Give us just a minute." Vasily made a shooing motion with his hands at the rest of them. Dimitri didn't need everyone staring at him as he made himself even more vulnerable than usual.

Mischa discreetly tossed Vasily a small, bejeweled snuffbox—he fought the urge to ask where they had gotten it so quickly—and muttered, "Be careful," before forcibly dragging Annika out of the room, Ladushka trailing behind.

Some things were better done in private.

✳

Vasily never thought that the first time he'd get truly shitfaced with Dimitri would be before they summoned an angel, as opposed to finally trying to properly drown their sorrows. It was a pity, really.

"Have some faith, Dima," he tried to joke, but Dimitri's eyes were still steely. "What's a little blasphemy in the scheme of things?"

"What are the chances that Alexey will fall for it?" Dimitri's face paled, like the question had slipped out before he could stop it. "Fall for your ruse?"

Vasily threw Dimitri a filthy wink, trying to soothe his nerves. "I'm good at pretending." He pulled Dimitri down to the floor, where they nestled on the carpet, their backs resting against the bed. "Besides, we all know that seduction is one of my core skills. I'll get the information out of him, one way or the other."

It was the wrong thing to say, and Vasily cursed himself as Dimitri's eyes widened and his entire body flinched. "Vasya, no, you can't—" Dimitri swallowed audibly and dug his fingernails into his own thighs. "You can't, please don't—"

Vasily didn't know what hurt more: the wounded look on Dimitri's face that *he* had put there, or the fact that Dimitri was going to guilt him into feeling bad about doing whatever it took to survive. "You can't possibly be that possessive of him after all this." He waved his hand in the air. "After everything he's done to you and to us, you can't possibly want to, what, protect his virtue? You can't possibly be *jealous* at the thought that I might have to let him fuck me to get what we need?"

It was, once again, the wrong thing to say. Vasily fought back a groan. He really shouldn't speak out of irritation, not around Dimitri. The other man was still hurting, hardly healing, and here Vasily had ripped open the wound again. He could tell because Dimitri flipped over onto his hands and knees, his head hanging down, barely meeting Vasily's gaze.

He always got on his knees when this happened, and Vasily viscerally hated the sight of it, because he knew where the impulse had come from.

"No, I didn't mean it like that." Dimitri's voice wavered, like he was on the edge of tears. "I meant I didn't want him to hurt you. If you go to his bed, he might—you don't know what he'll do to you."

"Oh, Dima," Vasily replied, his heart softening as he put a hand to the side of Dimitri's face, cupping his chin, feeling his pulse beating underneath his fingertips. "I know what he would do. I know exactly what he would do, because I spent years watching him do it to you. I could draw the atlas of the way he hurt you."

It was a punch to the gut, the way that Dimitri leaned into his touch, the way that he replied, "I don't want him to hurt *you*. And I'm afraid he will."

Like his own hurts didn't matter. Like he was so worthless that he didn't deserve to be safe.

Vasily hummed, then slung his arm around Dimitri and tucked Dimitri's head into his chest, pulling him into his lap. "I'm going to be fine," Vasily said, stroking Dimitri's hair in an attempt to calm him. Dimitri was shivering now, the tremors shaking his frame. "I'll be fine."

"I'd ask God to protect you, but I don't think He's listening to me anymore." Dimitri looked down at his hands in his lap, his voice thick. "When I was on the throne, I knew that God was watching over us and guiding my hand. I prayed and He answered. Since Alexey betrayed me, it's just been this horrible silence. It's been so long since I felt rightness in my bones when I've prayed for guidance."

He took a moment to breathe deeply. Vasily pretended not to notice the tears tracking down his cheeks, focusing instead on rubbing soothing circles into the back of Dimitri's neck. "God used to shepherd me, in my prayers and in my dreams," Dimitri whispered. "He would send me signs. Now the only signs I get are ones that tell me how royally I've cocked it all up."

"I don't think God has abandoned you, or us." Vasily tightened his embrace. "What are the chances that Alexey would invite strangers into the palace right when we need to gain entry? What are the chances that I would have stumbled upon an identity that would allow us to take advantage of that very fact?"

Dimitri shook his head, nudging his face deeper into Vasily's chest. He didn't believe him, and Vasily had no idea how to fix it.

Instead, he focused on what he *could* do. He stroked a hand through Dimitri's hair. "God smiles on us even now, my darling." Vasily pressed the lightest of kisses to the top of Dimitri's head, chasing it with a sigh. "We are still among the blessed."

He pulled the paper with the name of the angel out of his pants pocket, shifting Dimitri on his lap. "Do you want me to prove it to you? Do you want me to show you that God is still present for us? We can do it right now. His archangels would never respond to someone that He has abandoned."

"I hate to admit that I have found myself questioning the Lord every day since my husband died," Dimitri said, his voice cracking. Vasily flinched at the way *husband* sounded in Dimitri's mouth, cold yet with undertones of longing. "Despite knowing that I shouldn't. Despite knowing that I should trust. This *has* to fucking work, Vasya, because if it doesn't, we'll get nowhere in figuring out what Alexey is doing. And if we don't know what Alexey is doing, I will fail the people I am supposed to protect."

"It will work, darling." He slid Dimitri off of him, nestling the smaller man against his side, an arm slung around his shoulders.

"What if it doesn't?" The question was soft, almost so soft that Vasily couldn't hear. "What if God knows that since we found this information, I've been asking myself, which shall it be? Honor a God who has asked so much of us, or protect a nation that I may still save?"

"Don't let this be a regret." Vasily reached out a hand and put it on Dimitri's knee, encouraged when Dimitri didn't shy away. "You're doing what you have to do."

Dimitri snorted. "I have enough regrets as is." He picked at a loose thread on the carpet next to him. "I didn't get to spend enough time with my family, for one. I hardly saw them in the years before they died. I should have been with them." He blinked, hard. "We all returned to Rav-Mikhailburg for the Founding Day celebration, every year. But that year, Alexey fell ill, and I stayed to care for him."

He paused and tilted his head back so he was staring at the ceiling, blinking rapidly.

"The bombing wasn't your fault," Vasily said to fill the silence. He would know—he'd caught most of the people responsible and sent them to very gruesome deaths. It was all the anarchists had deserved. They'd killed the Tzar and Tzarina, all of the royal children, and most of their spouses. And the one detail Vasily would never forget—the three royal grandchildren, all under the age of five, had also been killed.

An entire family, decimated in an instant, in one single flash. Just like during the war.

"I never met most of my nieces and nephews." Dimitri's voice cracked.

"I know," Vasily said, gripping Dimitri's knee harder. "I know. But there's nothing we can do for the dead. All we can do is try to save the living."

Dimitri shook his head. "I agree," he whispered, except he didn't sound like he did.

"We can wait," Vasily said, wondering if Dimitri was even ready for this, trying to decide whether he could afford Dimitri any more time.

"No, I—" Dimitri stopped and swallowed, his throat working. "If I'm going to damn myself with anyone, I would like it to be you." He laughed wetly, averting his eyes.

Vasily would bet anything he was trying not to cry harder. He studiously ignored it.

Tipping his head back against the bed, Dimitri sighed. "I just want to know what this will cost us, beyond a piece of our souls. And whether it will be worth it."

"Think on the bright side, my darling." Vasily chewed his lip. "If it works, I can still annoy you when we're both unconscious."

Dimitri glared at him, somehow managing to do it through the fringe of his eyelashes. Vasily's heart skipped a beat at Dimitri's stare, and he wondered for the first time what it would be like to share a part of himself with Dimitri in this completely new way. Every time he'd done it previously, been open and honest and raw, he'd ended up both lost and more sure of himself than he'd ever been. Every time, it flayed him open and laid him bare.

This would probably be a thousand times worse, and Vasily prayed to God that he wouldn't give too much away. That he wouldn't reveal too much of himself.

"There's no one I'd rather do this with." Dimitri closed his eyes and threaded his fingers through Vasily's, resting on his thigh. A muscle jumped there, and Vasily wanted to kiss it into stillness. "Truly. Thank you."

"You're welcome," Vasily said through the sudden constriction in his throat, because there was nothing else he could say out loud, was there?

They sat, silent, for long enough that Vasily wondered if Dimitri had fallen asleep. But right when he was about to shake him, those brilliant blue eyes blinked open again, and Vasily was adrift.

Dimitri took a breath, clenching his hands into fists and squaring his shoulders. "Let's start." He stood up and took a candle and a prayer shawl out of one of the dresser drawers.

Coming back to himself, Vasily stood up too, drew the shades and came to sit back down on the floor, cross-legged. For a moment, he hesitated, wondering if he should get the others, but then he scooted closer to where Dimitri had sat back down, the candle in front of him and the prayer shawl by his side. Vasily's skin burned where his shoulder touched Dimitri's.

Dimitri placed the paper down in front of them and lit the candle. He unfolded the prayer shawl, made of the finest silk Vasily had ever seen. "My father's," he said quietly as he kissed the fringes, then draped it around both of their shoulders. It smelled of sandalwood and tobacco, and Vasily breathed deep. "I found it here, with my mother's things. I'm glad to have something of his." Dimitri paused. "Whatever you could say about the man, he loved his country."

Vasily merely nodded his assent. There was anxiety twisting its way into his throat. He could face down any number of enemies, but there was no telling what this would actually entail, and it set his hands shaking.

Dimitri cracked the lid of the snuffbox wordlessly. Vasily took the pinch he offered on the heel of his hand, inhaled, and let it burn its way down his nose and throat. Almost immediately, his limbs and his eyelids grew heavy. It had been too long since he'd last imbibed and he'd forgotten how little tolerance he had for the stuff. He was dimly aware of Dimitri following suit, scooping up a pinch that Vasily was about to say was far too big, but Dimitri just inhaled with practiced ease, and Vasily thought he was going to be sick watching him do it.

Vasily closed his eyes. He drifted.

"Stay awake," Dimitri said from somewhere far away, and then a warm hand slipped into his to anchor him to earth through the fog.

He was floating in space, and he heard Dimitri praying, and his mind was everywhere and nowhere and nothing.

And then Dimitri said the name.

"Qafsiel." It echoed strangely, as though Dimitri had uttered it into a much bigger room. Vasily's head was spinning, and then there was something so bright in front of him that he cringed back instinctively and closed his eyes.

It wasn't speaking, but he knew what it wanted. *Do not look*, it was telling him.

What do you require? it asked Dimitri.

"I am the Tzar of Novo-Svitsevo, and I want to save my people." Dimitri's hand tightened in Vasily's. "And to that end, I ask that you bind us together so we may speak through dreams."

You are righteous men. Vasily felt tears dripping down his cheeks, and he wondered if Dimitri was crying too, but the presence in front of him was shutting down his mind, too much to comprehend.

The brightness grew, so that even through his closed eyelids he could see it, and then it was punching through his chest and he was screaming from the pain until something in him tugged and he was drawn to the right, like he was being sewn together with the man next to him.

And then the brightness was gone, the fog of the drugs lifting far too soon and much too completely for it to be natural, and he was bigger than himself, like there was more awareness inside of him than there had ever been, something else nudging against his heart.

He turned to Dimitri, who was pale and sweating and shaking under the prayer shawl, just as the door broke open. "Are you all right?" Vasily asked him, trying to check Dimitri for injuries as the room started to spin.

Then Mischa's hands were on him, and Annika was holding Dimitri up and cursing, but all Vasily could focus on was the fact that the piece of paper with the angel's name on it was gone, as if it had never existed. And then he finally gave in to the darkness crowding his vision.

∗

"That was obscenely stupid of you." Annika was trying to be stern, but her voice was too laced with concern. "Why'd you kick us out of the room? I thought you were just going to *talk* or *fuck again* or something *safe*. I never would have left you alone if I knew you were going to chance the ritual all by yourselves. What if you were hurt? You could have died! What if we had needed to help you?"

Vasily winced, but he knew the only way to get Annika to stop being upset was to let her work it out through a fit of chiding, like she was taking a schoolboy to task.

And it was all from love, anyway. Always from love, with Annika.

"Anna," Vasily said, except he wasn't the one speaking. It was Dimitri. Vasily had a moment of wild disorientation and then looked down at his hands.

Except they weren't his hands. He knew those hands, pale and fine-boned.

He was looking down at *Dimitri's* hands.

"It worked," Dimitri said. "It worked. Vasya, can you hear me?"

"Vasya is dreaming," Mischa said, who had moved to sit next to him—next to *Dimitri*—on the parlor couch. "Look at his eyes, the way they move under the lids."

"What—" Vasily tried to shake himself or move his hands. He couldn't. He looked over to the armchair by the fire, where his sleeping form was propped up under a blanket, Ladushka crouching next to him, passing her hand tenderly through his hair where the curls were falling onto his forehead.

It was the strangest sensation, looking at himself through someone else's eyes. It was so disorienting that he couldn't even make a quip about how handsome he was. Panic started rising up in his throat. This didn't feel like dreaming, not in the least.

"Calm down," Dimitri ordered. "Vasya, I can *feel* you."

Vasily almost made a crude joke back about just how much he wanted Dimitri to feel him, but it was dawning on him that yes, it had worked, and he was somehow inside Dimitri's mind. Pride flared in his chest, chased by panic.

Vasily quickly retreated his consciousness back into itself, because there were things about him that Dimitri could never know.

I'm here, he thought when he'd gathered himself up, resting somewhere in the base of Dimitri's skull, in a corner of Dimitri's mind, inside his consciousness. He could feel himself there, a thorn embedded in Dimitri's soul. He reached down and wrapped a tendril of himself around Dimitri's heart. *It worked. If you were also asleep, I assume we could communicate even more effectively.*

Yes, Dimitri replied. *I think this will do nicely.*

Dimitri turned to Mischa where they knelt next to the couch. "Wake him up."

✳

"Holy fuck," Vasily said when he opened his eyes. He wiggled his fingers and toes, just to make sure that he had control of his body. "Holy fuck."

Dimitri was looking at his hands, as if he, too, was checking to make sure they were intact. "I suppose taking the risk was worth it." His voice was calm, but his brow was furrowed. "I also suppose there will be no way to control it."

"When you sleep, you dream," Mischa said. They lifted their fingers off Vasily's neck, and then pulled his right eyelid down and peered into his other eye. He swatted their hand away and sat up. "But there are drugs one can make that will cause Vasya to sleep soundly enough that he won't dream. He can take it unless he has information to transfer to you."

"How long will that take?" Dimitri stood up and wobbled. Vasily lurched forward to try to catch him, but Annika put out a hand and caught Dimitri as he stumbled.

"It's already done," Mischa replied, a smirk twisting their lips. "I compounded it last night and dosed it to Vasya's weight after our visit to the library. Because no one is as bold as you, Dima, and I knew you'd be unable to resist getting yourself into trouble like this."

Dimitri looked at Mischa askance, then turned to Vasily and cracked his knuckles. "How long do you need to prepare?"

Vasily swallowed. How much he wanted to stay here, safe, with the people he loved. But there was work to do.

"No time at all." He smiled as if he was not ripping out his own heart by leaving. "I'll go at dawn."

SIXTEEN

DIMITRI

The sensation of Vasily's soul intertwined with his own was so strange that Dimitri could hardly bear it. The worst of it, though, was that they had done something blasphemous and now it felt *right*. It felt like he had slotted in the final missing piece of himself, like he was whole for the first time since that awful night.

He never wanted this to end. He wanted Vasily here, inside him, always curled around his heart. And that thought, that greed, made him sick. Nausea twisted its way up his chest, churning uncomfortably with the guilt.

After Vasily had woken up, Dimitri quickly found he couldn't sit here with the rest of them, plotting their next move, not while feeling like this, not while having to look Vasily in the eye.

Dimitri left the sitting room after mumbling that he was tired, making his way up the stairs to his bedroom. His entire body was exhausted, the muscles in his thighs trembling faintly with strain, like he'd spent all day on horseback, hunting, or doing a far different kind of riding. He ignored the detritus of the ritual—the candle they'd lit burning to a stub, ashes around it, his father's prayer shawl discarded on the floor—and crawled into bed, closing his eyes.

It felt like Vasily was in bed with him, right there, as Dimitri drifted off to sleep. And for the first time in a very long time, he found he didn't mind the company.

*

After waking up hours later, when it was already dark, Dimitri came down to the kitchen for dinner and found the rest of his court all gathered around the table, an open bottle of something horrifyingly green next to the gin and vermouth that someone must have dug out of the moldering boxes in the cellar. Mischa was mixing the contents of five glasses, squeezing lemon into whatever concoction they had made. Annika was peeling an orange with a knife, dropping the curls into the glasses behind Mischa's lemon squeeze. Ladushka was humming, smiling uncharacteristically, and Vasily had his arms folded on the table, his chin resting on them, staring at Dimitri with huge, unblinking eyes.

"I read the recipe in the paper," Mischa said with a giggle, looking up at Dimitri, their pupils blown wide. Dimitri's eyes drifted to the snuffbox, which was now sitting on the sideboard, the lid cracked open, conspicuously much emptier than it had been that afternoon. "It's called a *corpse reviver*, can you believe it? It's—" They hiccuped. "It's so appropriate for tonight. We were just about to wake you. We've decided to give Vasya a proper send-off."

Dimitri's chest tightened, hating the reminder that Vasily was leaving in the morning. So to dull the pain, and despite his earlier resolution to pull himself together, he picked up the snuffbox and took a hit. This had always been Alexey's vice far more than his, but he couldn't deny that the excited buzzing that rushed down his limbs felt good, washing away the panic. The last time they had done this, it had been their first night in his grandmother's house, surrounded by dust and sheets covering all the furniture, half-starved and terrified, and with Annika feverish and sick from a bullet wound to the gut that Mischa had done their best to patch up.

He'd been feral with fear over the idea of losing her, that night. It was the only thing that had convinced him to abandon the campaign against Alexey after Vysoka, leaving the rest of his soldiers to either surrender or be killed.

He choked on the memory as Annika dropped in one last orange peel and nudged the glass over to Dimitri, her eyes wide in the low light, like she knew what he was thinking about. He took out a cigarette and dragged the butt over his lip to moisten it, lit it, and took a drag to anchor himself. He picked up the glass in his other hand and took a tentative sip, grimacing when the alcohol hit his tongue. "God, Mischka, what did you *put* in here? This could kill a horse."

"You mean revive a corpse," Vasily corrected with a grin, downing half his own glass in a single swallow and then pulling out the chair next to him, patting the seat. Dimitri dropped into it obediently, sipping gingerly at his drink, trying to bat away the memories that were coming for him, the way that the past was wrapping itself around his neck like a noose.

Ladushka took the cigarette out of his fingers and put it to her lips, her stare glassy and far away. "You are thinking quite hard, Dima." She inhaled, the tip of the cigarette glowing. "What about?" Her voice was soft and slurred.

"That first night." He took another long drink, letting the drugs carry away some of the pain. "The first night we were here. The last night of the war."

"Ah." Annika grimaced as she reached across the table and plucked the cigarette from Ladushka's grip, clamping it between her own lips. "I much prefer this version. I'd like to never experience that particular agony again."

"What?" Mischa stole the cigarette out of Annika's mouth. "You mean you don't want to be dying from an infected bullet wound that

I had to pack full of gauze, suture shut in a trench, and then pray hadn't shredded any intestine?"

"Yes," Annika responded tartly. "That."

"No," Dimitri said, taking another bitter sip and tilting his head down onto Vasily's shoulder, tucking his nose against Vasily's throat and hiding his eyes in Vasily's hair. "None of us want that. I never wanted that for you. I didn't."

There was a hand on his, and then Vasily's fingers were intertwining with his own, anchoring him. A lump had lodged in his throat, and though he tried his best to breathe, the way his heart was pounding from the drugs and the way his head was spinning felt too much like panic for him to settle.

Annika cleared her throat. "I don't blame you, Dima. It wasn't your fault."

"Of course it was," he snapped back, raising his head and looking at her guilt-stricken face. "Anna, it was precisely my fault. Because you came to pull me off the battlefield at Vysoka when I stood there like a lovesick idiot, rooted in place because I had seen my husband for the first time in two months, and I *couldn't shoot him.*"

Vasily flinched beside him, and Dimitri almost jerked away, but Vasily just held his hand tighter.

"Your tactical failure at Vysoka and your insistence on continuing the fight likely had a role in losing the war for us, Dima," Ladushka said, slipping over the words. "But it was hardly the reason Anna was shot. That was entirely due to her failure to find cover and utilize the tactics of concealment."

Annika snorted. "I'd like to see you try to cover and conceal yourself in the middle of artillery fire while dragging a full-grown man behind you."

"Stop, Anna," Vasily said rather harshly, pulling Dimitri back into his side. Of all of them, he was the only one who sounded sober. "Stop, all of you. We're alive. No one died. We're all here."

No one had a rejoinder to that, but everyone stopped talking. Mischa broke the silence by splashing more of the green alcohol into their glasses, ruining the mix of the drink. It tasted like licorice when Dimitri raised it to his lips. He coughed on it as they passed around the snuffbox again, and this time, when he inhaled, he took enough that he was floating in a haze.

"We're all here," Vasily said again, brokenly this time. Dimitri tipped his chin up to look at Vasily, who had tears rimming his lower lashes. "We're all here, and we're alive, and I want us to celebrate. All right? I want us to celebrate."

He pulled his cards out of his pocket to shuffle, dropping Dimitri's hand. Dimitri was close enough to the cards that he could see more of the drawings on them than he ever had before, but his vision was too blurred to make out much.

They passed around the snuffbox again when the buzz started to wear down, fear creeping in around the edges of the drug-induced haze, and ended up sprawled in the parlor, playing a halfhearted game of cards where Annika kept trying to make up new rules to prevent herself from losing and Ladushka kept correcting her by remembering what Annika had outlined at the start of the game. Mischa also kept topping up all their glasses, with whiskey now instead of what they'd identified as absinthe, and they were eventually all so spectacularly drunk and high that it didn't even feel like Vasily would ever leave them.

The only time the illusion shattered was when Annika slurred her way through inviting Vasily to play, and he'd demurred. Dimitri's head was resting in Vasily's lap, Vasily's right hand threading through his hair while his left held his glass, perched on Dimitri's ribs.

"I don't want to do anything else with my hands but this," he'd said petulantly.

"Tomorrow, then," Annika had said blithely, and then paused, because while they were all wasted on alcohol and cocaine, they still knew that they were doing this because Vasily was leaving, Vasily might never come back, this might be their last night together, and none of them could face the thought of that sober.

Ladushka started tearing up, saying she didn't want to waste what time they had left, and then Mischa started sobbing too, and Annika put her arms around her legs and rested her chin on her knees and started to cry.

Then they all huddled together, in the middle of the room, holding each other, the fire burning low. They toasted one more time, Vasily raising his glass. "If I die first," he began, and for the first time, no one could answer, no one could say anything.

Vasily gathered Dimitri up in his arms after that, cradling him close to his chest, and took him upstairs to bed, Dimitri praying all the while that this wouldn't be the very last time, but fearing that it very well might be.

✳

Dimitri let Vasily hold him all night, dozing in blankets piled on the floor, and wondered in the darkness if he was measuring out the final, fleeting beats of Vasily's heart, pounding back against his own.

✳

Dimitri woke alone, sunlight pouring through the curtains, his head throbbing with an uncharacteristic hangover. There was a note tucked in between his fingertips. It was sealed with wax, and on the outside Vasily had written *Not Yet.* And behind the note was a single playing card. The joker. When he looked at it, he realized that Vasily had sketched over the illustration, replacing it with his own features.

The entirety of him revolted. He dropped the note and the card on the ground.

Tears pricked at Dimitri's eyes at the thought that he hadn't had the chance to say goodbye one last time. But then he realized it might have been better that way, because he wouldn't have known what to say, and maybe Vasily had anticipated that and taken pity on him.

Dimitri stood on shaking legs. He shoved a pill from Mischa's bottle into his mouth, wincing at the bitterness, then took a shot of vodka, then another, then another, and then when the decanter on his bureau was empty, he crawled into bed and pulled the furs up and over his shoulders.

For a while, he just lay there, wondering what he had done in life to deserve this, constantly lying in bed while waiting to see if people he cared about would come back to him, his heart throbbing with pain the whole time. He could still feel the phantom sensation of the note between his fingers, the awareness of coming back into consciousness holding something that hadn't been there before, something that shredded his heart, and bile rose up in his throat. He tried to flex his hand to get rid of the sensation, but even the pleasant numbness from Mischa's medication and the alcohol didn't stop the way that his body reacted, his mind being forcibly thrown back into the past.

The weight of all his grief crushed him. The memories of another night, his hands slick with blood, came for him. Memories that he had tried too hard to hide from, because reliving them would surely break him.

And all of a sudden, the tears started and they wouldn't stop, first a trickle and then a flood. Dimitri burrowed into the bed, his breath coming in gasps, his sides shuddering with the force of his sobs. He pulled his knees to his chest and let out every scrap of grief he'd tried to keep hidden, tried to keep buried.

He finally let himself go back to that night.

★

On the last night of Alexey's mortal life, they'd had one of their worst arguments.

"You're too weak to see the power you could claim," Alexey snarled. "You have to do this to protect the empire, Dima. We will never have true-born children, and with the rest of your family dead, we have no full-blood heirs. If you die like your parents, the empire will be in crisis."

"I *know*," Dimitri yelled, his throat raw, his eyes full of angry tears he couldn't control. "Do you think I want to leave you? Do you think I want to be blown up during a parade? Do you think I want my rib cage torn open and my organs flung over a crowd of people? Do you think I want to be ripped limb from limb? *Really*, Lyosha?"

"I think you're too scared to do what you must to rule," Alexey growled, advancing on him, pinning Dimitri to the wall in the cage of his arms. "I am begging you. Do this for me. Do this for Novo-Svitsevo. You must, Dima. You must."

Dimitri pulled him in for a kiss, rough and bruising, because he could not stand that he was making Alexey upset, even though Alexey had started it, even though Alexey always started it, and Dimitri needed to make it better.

He needed to make this stop. He needed to fix this too.

When Alexey gave in, Dimitri thought he had escaped the argument for the rest of the night, thought he had patched up the wounds he had made by refusing. Alexey undressed him hastily, and Dimitri dropped to his knees, reflex taking over, leaning his head into the hands that Alexey threaded through his hair, apologizing by taking Alexey in completely. When Alexey pulled him off, he lifted Dimitri up and pressed him against the wall, thrusting into him roughly, biting at his neck, Dimitri panting for more. Dimitri wrapped his body around his husband, releasing himself to the freedom of being small in Alexey's arms. And when they finished, he smiled sweetly at Alexey and asked him if they could head to bed.

He thought, like always, that he'd been forgiven. That he had given Alexey enough to be forgiven.

"Do you think," Alexey said slowly, crossing his arms, "that a good fuck would make me forget what we were talking about?" He arched a brow and divested himself of his soiled clothes, pulling on the black velvet dressing gown that he always wore to bed. "You'll undergo the experiment, Dima."

Dimitri leaned against the wall, his lips swollen from kissing, the core of him aching with every shifting movement, his body limp. He stared at Alexey, who had decided for him that he would do this blasphemous thing, risking his righteousness and his place in heaven for immortality, which was meant only for God. That he would trust his life and his soul to this mysticism that Alexey had fallen prey to, that had consumed him whole. That he would leave his empire in Alexey's hands, when he knew how cruel Alexey could be to those under his command.

The apology hadn't worked. Maybe it never would have worked, not for this.

And so, for the first time since they'd met, Dimitri looked his husband in the eye and said no.

Alexey's eyes went dark. "You would defy me?" Alexey turned his back to Dimitri and stared into the fire. "You *dare* defy me? You doubt my wisdom when you know that I am the one who taught you to rule?"

"You are not always right," Dimitri said, his voice shaking with anger.

"But in this case, I *am*," Alexey retorted, his voice rising in pitch.

There was a lump in Dimitri's throat as he snatched his nightshirt from the floor and pulled it back on angrily. "I can't fucking believe you," he screamed, and then Alexey grabbed him by his arm hard enough to bruise and said, "Don't be such an insufferable coward, Dima. A leader needs more backbone. You know how to take it, I'll give you that, but you don't know how to *give*."

Dimitri shoved him away as he started to cry, backing up towards the wall. "I may not be ruling the way you would," he yelled, "with fear and violence, and yet Novo-Svitsevo is doing *just fine*."

"For now," Alexey said icily, his arms crossed. And then Dimitri picked up a crystal decanter from the sideboard and threw it at Alexey's head, just barely missing him. The vessel exploded against the wall.

For a moment, there was stunned silence in the room. Then wrath consumed Alexey's features, and he stepped forward and slapped Dimitri across the face so hard that his neck ached. "How *dare* you," Alexey hissed, and then Dimitri slapped him right back, leaving a red streak across his cheek.

And then they were in a full-fledged fistfight.

Alexey pinned him down with a hand on his throat and a knee on his chest, and then Dimitri went for Alexey's face, raking nails down his cheek. All the while, they were screaming at each other so loudly that the entire palace must have heard them.

They fought, and when they had finally exhausted themselves from screaming, they sat sullenly on the carpet, breathing hard. Then, when he'd caught his breath, Alexey pinned him to the floor and took him again, so roughly this time that Dimitri's hands were scrabbling at the carpet for purchase, tears leaking from the corners of his eyes with the force of the pain and pleasure. Dimitri was relieved that they had made it to the part of the fight where they were fucking out their anger, as opposed to using fists and words, and when he came his body sagged, all the tension fleeing out of him.

When Alexey finished, he let his forehead tip forward until it was touching Dimitri's and said, "Dima, I will always love you."

And then he stood up and got into bed without another word.

Dimitri cleaned himself up in the bathing chamber, taking a long soak in the claw-foot tub, his toes curling around the copper rim. He washed the blood off the cuts speckled across his arms and legs, and picked bits of glass out of the back of his heel where he must have stepped on remnants of the shattered decanter without noticing. He put salve on the skin that he knew would bruise, and took stock of which of the old and new wounds would need to be cleverly covered with clothing come morning. Then he crawled into bed next to his husband and fell asleep. He was relieved that the second time, the apology had been enough. Maybe his refusal had gotten through to Alexey because he'd never done it before.

Then, in the middle of the night, he was stirred by something moving his hand. He was disoriented, and it was dark, the curtains drawn. He was grasping something hard, and there were fingers around his hand, pulling it . . .

He fully woke up just in time to watch Alexey plunge a blade into his own chest, Dimitri's hand wrapped around the hilt. There was blood everywhere, hot on his hands, gushing out of the wound in Alexey's chest with each beat of his heart. Dimitri tried to pull the blade out, but Alexey just looked him in the eyes, blood bubbling up from his lips, and forced the blade in further.

"Alexey," Dimitri gasped, his body cold with shock, tears clouding his vision. "What have you done?" He pulled again and the blade came free with a sick sucking sound that made him gag. He pulled Alexey's nightshirt up, sodden with blood, only to reveal his husband's chest caving in with every breath, blood foaming pink around the edges of the wound. Alexey's face was growing pale, his breath labored like every inhale cost him.

Dimitri, too, could not breathe. Could not think or comprehend what was before him. His hands were coated in Alexey's blood, slick and crimson, filling the air with a metallic tang that rested heavily on the back of his tongue and made him retch. He grabbed the sheets and wadded them up, pressing them against the wound, hoping to stanch the bleeding. But they soaked through, and Alexey just looked at him and mouthed *no* with bloodstained lips.

Everything in Dimitri went numb. Cold. His heart pounded harder even as Alexey's slowed.

Dimitri reached down and cradled Alexey's head in his hands, somehow knowing that even if Alexey could be saved, that wasn't what his husband intended. Alexey's cheek rested against Dimitri's arm, and he was already growing cold, his breaths coming in shallow gasps.

"You left me . . . no choice," Alexey panted. "This is the only way to protect the country, since you are too weak to." He coughed, spraying Dimitri's bare chest with blood.

"No, no," Dimitri was pleading. "Don't die, please don't die. Don't leave me alone. Let me get Mischka, hold on—"

Alexey shook his head. "I won't die," he whispered. "Not if you do exactly as I say." He coughed again, his breath rattling. "Instructions on the table. Work quickly. Do not fail me, Dima."

And then, the light fading from his eyes, his body growing still, his hand gently let go of Dimitri's wrist, falling limply to the sheets.

Alexey died as Dimitri clung to him and begged him not to.

Dimitri thought he might be screaming for help, but perhaps he hadn't been, because no one came. Or the servants were so used to their door being barred, to the screaming and the fighting that had become commonplace over the last months, that no one came to see what was going on.

Dimitri was left kneeling on the bed, covered in blood, sobbing, looking down at his husband's corpse. He turned to the bedside table—almost knocking over the candle still burning there—to reach for the pile of parchment that Alexey had put under the corner of a vase of roses. He flipped through the pages with shaking, blood-stained hands. It was instructions for the experiment that Alexey had wanted Dimitri to undergo, written in Alexey's meticulous script.

Dimitri could not disobey this last command of Alexey's. And Dimitri could not bear to never see Alexey smile again, laugh again, cry again, scream at him again.

And so he had gotten up, washed himself clean, dressed, and dragged his husband's cooling corpse down to the basement experimentation chamber, where he proceeded to sin against the Lord his God. All because he had been too weak to disobey Alexey.

All because he had been too weak to be alone.

*

After what might have been minutes or what might have been hours, the sobs slowed enough for Dimitri to catch his breath. And that's when he heard the pounding at his bedroom door.

He got up on shaking legs, opening the door as his hand trembled. Annika was poised with her hand raised to knock again, with Ladushka and Mischa fanned out behind her.

He stood there, looking at their concerned faces, their shocked expressions and open mouths, and let them see all of him. The tears, and the raggedness of his breathing, and the hunch of his shoulders.

There was silence among them, filling the small room. And then Annika stepped forward and put her hands on his shoulders, touching her forehead to his.

"He's gone," Dimitri finally breathed out, and he wasn't sure if he was talking about Vasily, or Alexey, or both of them.

Annika seemed to understand. "I know. You let him go. You've let them *both* go. And now you've finally begun to wash yourself clean of the Pretender. You've finally let yourself truly begin to grieve him. And what he did to you. What he forced upon you."

Dimitri was empty and hollow. His grief had poured out of him, and now he was a vessel left to fill. With anger, with revenge, with the fortitude he'd need to take his country back. To make Vasily's gamble worth it. His friends—his family—clustered around him, embracing him, and he took their comfort and their strength, letting it gird him.

Finally, there was nothing more of him to break. The entirety of him had been shattered, and now the only thing left to do was build himself back up.

SEVENTEEN

ALEXEY

The piercing, soundless ringing that always accompanied a merging of the middle world with his own, coupled with the strong smell of sulfur from opening the rift to swallow his creations back up, had set Alexey on edge enough to want to snap his own neck.

He grabbed a beaker from the table next to him and flung it at the wall with a wordless scream of frustration, hard enough that it cracked the stone before clattering to the ground. He grabbed at his hair with both hands, pacing around the room.

In the last week, he had created thirty-six *zemonyii* from the Leyvin who had come to the palace. All of them, now, were used up. Each had survived the transition from human to *zemonyii*, and yet none of them had been controllable. That surprised him; he had been able to control smaller demons, the ones without much physical potency here in the lower world, but these *zemonyii* were too wild, or too headstrong, or too powerful to obey him.

Alexey had tried coaxing them out of their feral nature with kindness. He had tried feeding them bits of meat to gain their trust, striking them to gain their obedience, torturing them to gain their fear.

None of it had worked.

As soon as the *zemonyii* were released from their bindings, they would attack anyone who was near. Alexey had learned to keep the darkness within him at hand, so he could quickly reopen the void and banish his creations back into the middle world. Ripping out the throats of the creatures was satisfying, yet took far too much effort with how stiff his hands were.

They could not serve as commanders of his army to come if they would not obey him.

The cries of the Leyvin who had died rang in his ears as he paced the chamber, circling around the chair he chained them to before the experiment began. They all fought, before the transformation. They pleaded, cried, or raged at him, even though he was offering them power beyond their wildest dreams. Even though he was giving them a place of pride in the army that would rule the world. They all cried out for their families, begged him to let them go, prayed to God, as if Alexey Balakin, God's finest creation, was not standing in front of them, offering to be their family, giving them a chance to protect the empire from any of the monstrosities that would stand against it.

None of them loved Novo-Svitsevo like he did. None of them was as strong as he was. They were depressingly weak, insects he could crush under his heel.

None of them had the core of strength, the spine of iron, that Dimitri had possessed. He breathed in deeply, and swore he caught a hint of the tobacco and patchouli scent of Dimitri's skin.

Alexey paused in his pacing, scrubbing at his eyes, banishing Dimitri's ghost to the far reaches of his mind, where it could haunt him no longer.

He needed to clear his head, and he needed to speak to God. Alexey yanked open the door of the experimentation chamber and took the steps two at a time, emerging through the hidden door set into one of the palace corridors. He brushed off noble after noble who tried to cling to him as he headed for his council chamber.

He found the man he was looking for arranging the papers on his desk, preparing for that evening's meeting of the council. "Ivan, come," he snapped.

The boy sprang to attention and followed Alexey to his bedchamber like a puppy trailing its master. When they were inside and the servants had been dismissed, Alexey stripped and ordered Ivan to do the same. The mystics had known there were three ways to quickly commune with God—drugs, ecstatic dance, and sex. Drugs no longer worked to alter his mind after his rebirth, and ever since Dimitri had left, Alexey had not felt like dancing.

He could take the time to meditate and pray, but using Ivan was easier.

"You will help me speak with God," Alexey ordered, ignoring the fervor shining in Ivan's eyes as the boy backed up until his thighs touched the sheets. He grinned as he splayed himself out on the bed.

Alexey took what was offered. It was always easiest for him to reach the realm of God when united with another. He and Dimitri had spent hours in each other's arms, joining together, their bodies becoming one as Alexey's mind opened to the voice of God.

Alexey ignored the bitterness in the back of his mouth, the metallic taste of regret, as he ran his hands up Ivan's thighs, taking the vial of oil that Ivan pulled from underneath the pillow and engaging in just enough preparation for Ivan to accommodate him. He closed his eyes as he shifted his weight on top of the smaller man, pushing into Ivan's heat. It was easier when he didn't have to look. He ignored the rasp of Ivan's voice as he begged for more, tried to block out the sound of his moans, because it was all so much like Dimitri that it made something hollow within Alexey ache.

Eventually, when he couldn't take it anymore, he stuffed part of the silken sheet in Ivan's mouth, gagging him. Ivan stiffened even more against Alexey's stomach, and when Alexey thrust into him, Ivan's back arched.

Buried in Ivan, Alexey called out to God. He felt the void that lived within him widen, and open, and the Divine came forth to answer the question in his mind.

Listen, my child, God said to him. *You will be their god. They must worship you. They must love you for you to wield them.*

I will control them with . . . love? Alexey did not mean to question God, but his doubt slipped out before he could rein it in.

Love is what controls you all, my child, God replied. *It is love that binds you all to me, and to each other. It is love that makes you holy. It is in love that you become righteous.*

Tears gathered in Alexey's eyes as he thought of the love that had transformed him.

Alexey gasped as he came, and the void within him shrunk and God left his mind. He pulled out of Ivan's body, leaving Ivan panting on the sweat-soaked sheets, and smoothed back the hair from Ivan's brow.

"Do you love me?" He looked into Ivan's eyes, and it was Dimitri who was lying there, Dimitri who replied, "Yes, *Moy Tzar.*" It was Dimitri who he leaned down and kissed, Dimitri who he gathered up close and held to his chest and leaned into, as if this was where he would find his salvation.

*

The council chamber was crowded with his lords and ladies, the ones who were not so terrified of him that they scurried off to their regional holdings. Still, they shuffled like sheep being circled by a wolf. Alexey leaned back in his chair, resting his head against the ornately carved back.

"Those numbers are incorrect, Lady Dumkoffa. You will check the reports of the last harvest, and next council session, you will not display such staggering incompetence." Alexey waved off the noble in charge of his agricultural taxation. The idiot could not even realize that the numbers she just gave him added up to less than they should.

The woman quivered, but nodded, backing away to the edges of the room so that she was ensconced in shadow.

"Lady Zakharova," he said, beckoning her forward with a finger. "You will report on the security of the empire."

His minister of defense bowed shallowly before she began her report. "We have fixed the supply lines for your army that is gathering to the south, *Moy Tzar*," she said.

"Excellent." Alexey sometimes wished he did not have to personally attend to the details of running the empire, yet that was the only way he could ensure things happened as they should.

"And, *Moy Tzar*, there have been skirmishes on the border with Urushka." Her throat bobbed and she paused. "Our intelligence from the east is indicating that there may soon be an attack. How would you like us to prepare?"

Of course the east was restless. Novo-Svitsevo was a resource-rich empire, ripe for the taking, with a new and untested Tzar and an army devastated by a brutal civil war. If he was a ruler of one of the eastern states, he would be plotting an invasion too, removing a threat and gaining a country at the same time.

Still, Novo-Svitsevo had nothing to fear. Not that his lords or ladies knew that. Not that anyone in Novo-Svitsevo knew that but him.

"They will not oppose us." He folded his hands in front of him, resting them on his stomach.

"*Moy Tzar*," Lady Zakharova said, shifting on her feet. "I do not mean to argue, but I do not believe that view is correct. Our intelligence says—"

"Do you *dare* defy me?" Alexey stood up out of his chair and pushed it back, stalking around his desk. At the flare of his anger, he felt the void answer his call, felt the greedy hands reaching up and through him as he grasped Zakharova's throat, crushing her windpipe, squeezing hard enough that she started choking.

The rest of the council fell silent as she scrabbled at his wrist, bucking against him as he lifted his hand and took her body with it, her feet dangling off the floor. After a moment, when she'd started to go limp, he released her and let her fall to the floor, gasping.

Watching the horrified expressions of his lords and ladies was satisfying beyond measure.

"If you oppose me," Alexey said into the dead quiet, gazing at Zakharova crumpled on the ground, "that is what will happen to you. If you dare defy me, that is where you will end up. Nearly dead, at my feet. Alive only because of my mercy."

No one moved. No one even breathed. The room was full of frozen nobles, each a trembling pillar of fear so vivid and profound that he could sense it coming off them in waves.

Alexey schooled his features into a mask of indifference. "Do you all swear your loyalty to me?" He stalked forward into the crowd of nobles, staring into widened eyes, meeting terrified gazes. "Do you swear to follow my every command, or would you rather die?"

Morozov met his eyes, and Alexey drew satisfaction from the devotion there. "*Moy Tzar*, I swear by soul and by body that I will obey you." He dropped to his knees before Alexey and bent down to kiss his feet, the golden red of his hair shining in the candlelight.

Alexey looked around the room, stone-faced, and one by one the other lords and ladies knelt before him, a mass of trembling hands and whispered prayers, fingers clutching amulets, eyes downcast, no one even daring to meet his gaze.

"Those who obey me will be blessed, for you serve the Lord my God Himself," Alexey said into the quiet. He raised his hands over the heads of his trembling court, his fingers split, and intoned a blessing. "You are my children, and I will care for you. All I ask for is your perfect obedience."

He walked out of the council chamber and left the lords and ladies where they should be, bowing to his power.

EIGHTEEN

VASILY

He learned quickly that he had to keep moving, to avoid the ghosts of the past.

Everywhere that Vasily stopped bore the scars of the war. He looked out the window of the carriage he'd rented once he'd made his way to the border village of Livsky on foot, and saw acres of burned land, villages that had been decimated by artillery fire or Alexey's campaign of arson or both. Every time he saw a peasant walking by the side of the road with an eye gouged out, a limb missing, burns or scars covering their body in places they couldn't hide, Vasily had to fight to keep from retching.

The worst were the people, especially the women and the children, whose bodies looked whole but whose eyes were dead. Vasily knew what had happened to them. He felt it in his gut, his body clenching up in sympathetic response, his eyes burning with the effort of holding his emotions in.

This was what his failure had wrought, not a homeland where the sky was a vast, clear expanse of blue the color of Dimitri's eyes, but where the land was dead and the people were deader. Not for the first time, Vasily hated himself for not stopping Alexey when he'd had the chance. Instead, like a fool, he'd held Dimitri's hand as he'd prayed over Alexey's body, then snuck back off when Alexey returned to life.

He'd been a fucking idiot of the highest order.

Now people were suffering because of what they'd done. People across Novo-Svitsevo felt like Vasily had felt all his life—powerless and used and spit out and alone. Except this time, it was because of him.

When he'd hired the carriage to Rav-Mikhailburg, he'd told the driver he'd be stopping each night at an inn. Vasily regretted the decision almost immediately when, on the first night, he'd sat down to dinner in his austere rented room, tasted one spoonful of the soup sent up by the kitchen, and started to sob. Because it was too hard to have Novo-Svitsevo back when it didn't yet belong to them.

He was almost glad when he lay down in the too-hard bed and pulled up the thin sheet, sleep fast to claim him.

✳

It had to be a dream he awakened within, because he was weightless and too heavy at the same time.

Once he got over the shock, the first thing Vasily noticed was the disorientation—of falling asleep only to immediately wake up again, but in a different place. The second thing he noticed was that he was gazing at a fuzzy-looking Dimitri from behind, hunched over something on the ground, his sides shaking.

The third thing he noticed was that, in his distress about being in the country he'd longed so badly for over the last year, he'd forgotten something crucial. He'd forgotten to take one of Mischa's pills.

"Oh, fuck." The curse slipped from his lips, and he wasn't sure if he was speaking or thinking. But it didn't matter, because suddenly there was a hand on his forearm, grabbing him and spinning him around. Vasily brought up his elbow on instinct, trying to jam it into the person's chest to propel them back, but the person dodged.

"You're not supposed to be here." There was a second Dimitri, in the dream. This Dimitri was pale, his brow covered in a sheen of sweat. He looked like he was about to be sick, his skin tinged green around his mouth. He looked older and more solid than the Dimitri crouching on the ground, his face thinner and the circles around his eyes heavier, dressed in that black dressing gown again. This was *his* Dimitri, aged by the war and everything that came before and after, which meant the one on the ground, that Dimitri was . . .

"You're not supposed to be here, Vasya. Not yet. It takes four days to get to Rav-Mikhailburg by carriage."

"I'm in your dream, aren't I?" Vasily took in Dimitri's demeanor and the way he was clenching his jaw, the way he was gripping Vasily's arm hard enough to bruise. "This is from when Alexey—"

Dimitri's voice was pleading as he interrupted Vasily. "I don't want you to see what I did."

But Vasily ignored him and turned around to look at the dream's setting. He knew this room, its dark walls and its iron furnishings. It was Alexey's laboratory, the place where he claimed to be working the Holy Science. In reality, it was the place where he had indulged his apparent proclivity for increasingly disgusting forms of murder.

Vasily looked at the other Dimitri in the dream, the one kneeling on the stone floor, a drain set into it. He had a ring of bruises decorating the hollow of his throat, where a blue silk dressing gown was gaping open, the sleeves stained with blood.

He moved with the efficiency of someone who'd butchered more than his fair share of game after a successful hunt, digging the knife in around the joints. But his hands were shaking so badly that Vasily could hear the clatter of the blade against the bone. Every time a bit of tendon was severed, Dimitri shook harder. Blood was pooling on the floor, and when finally the leg he'd been working on had been mostly separated, Dimitri pulled it from the body and set it aside like it was something precious. He was praying, but Vasily couldn't hear what for. Tears were streaming down Dimitri's face, and he went to wipe them off, smearing blood across his cheeks.

Vasily was glad that this was a dream and apparently he couldn't vomit, because he would have.

There was a pile of parchment lying on the table next to them, so white it was almost glowing in the dark. Vasily picked it up with shaking hands.

It was all there, written in Alexey's meticulous script, pages and pages of confessions and instructions. Vasily wanted to die as he started thumbing through it, horror clouding his vision as he read.

Alexey had forced Dimitri to murder him.

Alexey had instructed Dimitri, in exacting detail, to take his dead body and sever his arms, legs, and head, quarter the torso of his corpse, and enclose the pieces in a dome that he had engineered before his death. Vasily glanced up, seeing the dome in the corner of the room, open now. Waiting.

Alexey had wanted Dimitri to pray over his corpse, invoke angels, and use chemicals he said mimicked the sap from the tree of life to regenerate his body.

Alexey had wanted Dimitri to believe that this would work, and that after nine months of being watched over, Alexey would emerge from the dome, not just whole and alive but immortal and indestructible.

Vasily had never asked Dimitri what had happened between Alexey's death and Alexey's encasement in the dome, the glass too clouded to see through and the edges sealed meticulously with lead. He'd never wanted to. Maybe he'd been scared to.

But now he knew exactly what had happened, because he was watching Dimitri kneel over the nude corpse of his husband, sobbing now as he started severing the other leg.

"Oh, Dima." Vasily's jaw worked open, and he wasn't sure what else to say. His hands balled up into fists, and Vasily wondered how he was going to keep from punching Alexey Balakin square in the jaw when he saw him in the palace in a few days' time, for the way he had so thoroughly tortured his husband, even from the grave.

"Everyone thinks the war broke me," Dimitri said, his voice cracking. "But I think I was broken long before that."

"Shh." Vasily gathered Dimitri to him and pulled Dimitri's head into the hollow of his throat. Vasily's chest was so tight it felt like he was being crushed to death. He tucked his face into Dimitri's hair and ignored the studious sounds of sawing coming from their right. "You're not . . . you're not a bad person, Dima. I know bad people. You aren't one of them. Your hand was forced. He used you. He knew he could."

Dimitri tensed briefly, and Vasily felt Dimitri's fear for a moment as if it were his own. Vasily's hands were steady, and yet they felt like they were shaking. He realized Dimitri must be worried that he would condemn him as a murderer, as a blasphemer, but Vasily knew deep in the core of himself that he could never abandon Dimitri as long as he lived, because he didn't abandon those he cared for, no matter what they had done.

And then, as Dimitri relaxed and sagged into his chest, a feeling of *safety* washing over them both, Vasily realized that if he could feel Dimitri's fear and then relief, then Dimitri could feel his emotions too. This had to be part of the magic, part of the exchange, their emotions open to each other as they met in dreams. Panic started to rise up in his throat, like it had when they'd first discovered the spell had worked. But before he could explain, his vision began to darken at the edges, and Dimitri dissolved in his arms like smoke.

And then Vasily woke up.

*

Vasily took the pills Mischa had tucked into his bag after that, slipping into dreamless sleep for the next three nights, at the next three inns. Not because he didn't want to see Dimitri's nightmares—on the contrary, he wanted to be there to comfort the other man through them. It suddenly made sense why the circles under Dimitri's eyes had never left.

No, it was because Vasily didn't want Dimitri to end up in *his* nightmares. Those would reveal far more about himself than he cared to admit. Even the friends he trusted with his life didn't need to know where he had come from and what had happened to him to set him on this path of his. They didn't need to know why he flirted as though his life depended on it, why he couldn't sleep with the door unlocked, why he had to have the upper hand in every one of his increasingly numerous sexual encounters.

Some secrets were meant for keeping.

Vasily was relieved when they finally reached the outskirts of the capital. The wheels of the carriage bounced across the cobblestones of Rav-Mikhailburg, and Vasily fought back a wave of nostalgia. He flipped through his cards again and again, desperate for something to do with his hands. Fifty-one of them, now. Short of a deck.

It was the middle of the afternoon, and his carriage pushed through throngs of people bustling around—men in suits, women ushering crowds of children around, people with boxes in their arms or stacks of files tucked close to their chest. This was the city that Dimitri had ruled from, and as such it showcased the potential of Novo-Svitsevo with its art and its commerce. The buildings were in the old style, their ornate facades painted all manner of pastel colors, gleaming in the sunlight, with windows offering peeks into lavishly decorated rooms full of paintings and silk drapes and gold chandeliers.

They passed Vasily's favorite bakery, with loaves of braided bread piled high in the window. He could almost taste it through the pang of wistful longing that went through his chest.

The palace was visible from any point in Rav-Mikhailburg, perched on the hill at the city's center. It was massive, and Vasily had to bite his tongue to keep from instructing the driver on how to best reach the gate, because he was supposed to be new to this city. When they reached the entrance, there was a sullen-looking palace guard standing out front, his rifle tucked at his side, his shoulders squared.

Vasily retrieved his bag from the back of the carriage, paid his driver the final amount he'd promised, and waved the carriage off before turning to the guard. He tucked his hands into the pants of the rough-spun trousers he'd acquired in a secondhand shop along the way, the loose tunic he was wearing underneath a heavy sheepskin coat already starting to get damp with his nervous sweat. He wished he hadn't needed to get rid of his suits. He'd feel far more comfortable if he was dressed like himself, instead of like a peasant.

But then again, this entire exercise was going to be one exquisitely long string of discomforts, so he might as well get used to it now.

"I'm here to see the Tzar." He cleared his throat before speaking again, his voice scratchy from days of silence. "He had an advertisement in the paper." He hoped the regional accent he'd been rehearsing in his head was accurate.

He pulled the crumpled piece of newsprint from his breast pocket and held it out for the guard, who just stared at it, his lip curling. "One moment."

He banged on the side of the guardhouse with a fist. Another guard poked her head out of the door, gazing at Vasily sharply as if assessing a threat. Vasily was irrationally glad to see that palace security was still in place—at least they weren't just waving him inside.

The guards glanced at each other, and then the woman turned to Vasily. "I will need your name and your place of birth."

"Mikhail Haleyvin. I was born in Voloski." A chill worked its way up his spine, and his palms grew slick with anticipation. If stealing a dead man's identity to slip into the palace didn't work, Vasily hoped he could run fast enough to evade the guards.

When she had written his information down on a scrap of paper, the woman disappeared and the other guard went back to ignoring him in favor of scanning the street.

Vasily's muscles were locked with tension by the time the female guard reappeared and unlocked the gate. She nodded at Vasily, whose shoulders sagged with relief. "Welcome to the palace of the Tzar, Mikhail Haleyvin. We are honored to make your acquaintance." Her voice was flat and bored, and she barely gave Vasily a second glance as she let him into the courtyard.

Grigori Morozov was waiting for him, wearing a richly embroidered jacket, the planes of his face still unfairly perfect. There was no spark of recognition in Morozov's expression, and Vasily thanked God that he had never had occasion to speak to the man before now and had just had the displeasure of observing Morozov from afar as he scurried around, helping Alexey fuck the empire. Vasily wondered idly if he'd achieved his life's ambition of sucking Alexey's cock yet.

Or better yet, Vasily hoped for one vicious moment that they *had* slept together, and Morozov had given Alexey syphilis and both their asses were covered in bleeding sores. But then he remembered that Alexey couldn't get syphilis, because he was dead.

Morozov bowed. "I am Chancellor Morozov, who serves at the pleasure of the Tzar."

Vasily swallowed how much he hated the man and bowed back, pushing enthusiasm into his voice as he replied with thanks, stretching a broad smile across his face.

Before Morozov led him inside, Vasily craned his neck to look up at the palace, looming before him in an expanse of creamy white stone, pastel blue paint, and carved marble, its hundreds of windows reflecting the sunlight. Gold accents glittered at the tops of the windows and columns, nearly blinding him. The ache inside his chest came back at the sight of the building that had been his home for several perfect years.

They walked through the massive palace doors and into the enormous entryway filled with art, the ceiling frescoed and the walls lined with gilded tables upon which statues and clocks were perched. Vasily made himself pause and gape, pretending to be a man from the provinces who had never seen such wealth. He looked at a vase he'd always particularly hated like God had sent it down from heaven just for him.

Morozov chuckled and put a hand on Vasily's shoulder. "Come. The entire palace is beautiful, and you will be able to explore it all. Let me show you to your rooms."

He was ushered up the grand staircase and through a series of winding corridors, through the extravagant southern ballroom with its patterned floor of inlaid stone, and then down a hallway. Finally, they arrived at a door in the wing of the palace reserved for guests, which the chancellor opened.

"Your rooms, Mr. Haleyvin," he said. "Your maids will be here shortly, as well as a steward to attend to any needs you have. Food will be brought up from the kitchens if you desire a meal. And then you may rest until the Tzar is ready to greet you personally."

He bowed, and walked down the corridor, leaving Vasily pretending to gape even more like a fish out of water for the benefit of the guards stationed down the hall. He walked into the room and dropped his things, the carpet so plush that his heavy bag barely even made a thud. There was an ornately carved writing desk posed in front of an enormous window draped in dark-blue silk fringed with gold, which looked out onto a garden that was manicured and green despite the season. It was much like his old room, two floors down and in the western wing, where the rest of the nobility permanently resided in the palace, closer to where Dimitri and Alexey slept.

Servants bustled in to show him to the attached bathing chamber, running a bath for him. He undressed and let himself be scrubbed, luxuriating for the briefest moment in the kind of service he'd missed since their exile. He eyed the servants, but as he suspected, Alexey had had all of Dimitri's replaced, so he didn't have to worry about being recognized—not that he'd been important enough for any servant to memorize his face.

When he'd been cleaned thoroughly enough to appease the servants, he was confronted by two others holding out sets of court clothes: tight breeches and high leather boots, silky white shirts and stiff jackets made of velvet.

"The blue, do you think?" one of the women said to the other.

"No," Vasily said, shuddering. "The gold."

It would set off his skin, and the way the jacket was cut would make him look more slender. Both were things that would help him if he was going to try to seduce Alexey.

Even though he hated it with every fiber of his being—he knew what would catch Alexey's eye. And he was here to do just that.

So as much as it made Vasily's skin crawl, he knew he'd better play the fucking part.

✴

He wondered how long he'd have to wait before he saw Alexey, but the answer turned out to be not long at all. Morozov reappeared as soon as Vasily was fully dressed.

"The Tzar will see you now," he said.

Vasily had made a living courting danger in the palace, and then he'd fought in a war despite not being a soldier, and then he'd orchestrated an escape for five people out of a collapsing country where they were being hunted like animals. He was friendly with fear, and good at quashing it. But even he couldn't stop the tremble in his hands as Morozov led him down hallways he pretended not to recognize, straight to the door of Alexey's study.

He tried to breathe in deeply to calm himself, but his breath hitched in his throat. So he gave in to his nerves, because Mikhail

Haleyvin was a butcher's son who would likely be quaking in the presence of royalty. He let himself go pale, biting his lip, twisting his hands together in front of him.

Vasily's heart was in his throat as Morozov pushed open the door.

Alexey's study was almost exactly as Vasily remembered it from the last time he'd broken in to sneak around, almost two and a half years ago. The room was small and dark, crowded with leather furniture next to a roaring fire, with books lining the walls in their walnut shelves. The only difference was a birdcage on a stand in the corner, conspicuously empty. Vasily wondered if Alexey had eaten its inhabitants. It would be so like the man.

And then Vasily felt like he might pass out, because for a heartbeat he thought Dimitri was sprawled on the bearskin rug before the hearth, barely dressed, reading a book.

But Dimitri was back home in Wilnetzk, so he blinked to clear his vision. Alexey kept the room wreathed in shadow, and it was difficult to see. The curtains were drawn, and while there was a lit candelabra on the desk, and one in the corner, the rest of the room was only illuminated by the light cast from the fire. When his gaze refocused, Vasily analyzed the planes of the man's face, his height, and his wide-eyed expression as he turned to face the doorway.

Ah. It took a moment for Vasily to place the man as Ivan, one of the former Tzar's bastard sons. Vasily's mouth sank into a frown before he could smooth it out. Ivan was young, twenty-three years old if Vasily remembered his birth year correctly. He'd paid special attention to the boy because, out of all the former Tzar's bastard sons, Ivan had looked the most like Dimitri, even as a youth. He'd half expected Ivan to use his looks to get into trouble, but Vasily had never once had to pull the boy out of one of the tearooms that ringed the palace and convince the proprietor that *No, this wasn't actually the Tzar of Novo-Svitsevo, this was just an anonymous boy, don't let him use Dimitri's tab.*

He'd never even heard Ivan speak before. Ivan had been terminally shy, keeping his head down and working at whatever job he'd been assigned to. The single interesting detail he knew about Ivan's private life was that he sent each one of his siblings, Dimitri included, handmade cards for every holiday, which were apparently exquisite examples of papercraft.

And now he was lying sprawled in front of Alexey's fire, reading what looked like a romance novel, of all things, wearing only an oversized shirt that Vasily was sure was Alexey's.

Which brought him to the man sitting behind the desk.

"Leave us, Ivan." Alexey's voice was low and smooth as silk as he raked his eyes up and down Vasily's form.

Something in Vasily's chest constricted as he looked at Alexey. He was struck by the strangest compulsion to make sure that Alexey was all right, which was odd because he didn't give a rat's ass about the man.

Shh, he whispered to the part of Dimitri that he carried within himself. *Not now.* Because that was certainly Dimitri's love he was feeling, pounding next to his heart. Something within him stilled, then pervaded him with such a sense of longing that he almost put a hand to his chest.

He was rescued by Ivan rising up from the rug, the shirt slipping off one narrow shoulder, his arms hugging the book to his chest. Ivan nodded politely at Vasily, then crossed the room on bare feet to offer himself up to Alexey for a kiss. He was limping slightly, and Vasily hated to think of why. He'd seen that same hitching walk on Dimitri one too many times for him not to know the cause.

Alexey obliged, but his eyes flicked to Vasily as his lips met Ivan's.

"I'll be waiting in bed, *Moy Tzar*," Ivan said softly, and the way he looked at Alexey, all doe-eyed and pleading, made Vasily want to scream. "Should you want me."

Ivan brushed by Vasily's shoulder as he made his way out the door.

The contact made Vasily refocus, and when he steadied himself, he dropped into a deliberately artless bow.

"So you are Mikhail Haleyvin of Voloski." There was a scrape of wood against wood as the chair was pushed back from the desk, and then Alexey was standing in front of him. Vasily stayed in his bow, staring at Alexey's immaculately shined boots, until Alexey reached out a hand and cupped his chin, pulling him upwards.

Vasily shuddered at how cold his skin was, and felt Alexey draw the tiniest bit back before tightening his grip enough to hurt.

"Yes, *Moy Tzar*," Vasily replied. "I've come because you called for Leyvin." It burned the back of his throat, calling Alexey the Tzar. It was the first time he'd done it. But he swallowed it down. And as much as he felt, in the part of him that was still an animal, that something was deeply wrong with the man in front of him, Vasily forced himself to lean into Alexey's touch.

Alexey had always, always wanted to be loved. And obeyed.

Alexey's breath hitched.

"You honor me by coming to my palace." Alexey's thumb stroked the side of Vasily's jaw. "And I wish to honor you. Tomorrow night you will dine with me. Explore the palace if you wish, and if there is anything you need, it will be procured for you."

Alexey licked his lips, and Vasily prayed to God that Ivan was satisfying in bed, because while he would bury every fear and instinct of his and let Alexey fuck him for days if that would save Dimitri and Novo-Svitsevo, he'd really rather not.

Vasily cleared his throat and forced himself to break away from Alexey's stare. He blinked, slowly and deliberately, then lowered his eyes like he was awed by the presence of the Tzar. "The newspaper, it said you wanted to pray with the Leyvin. When do you wish to pray, *Moy Tzar*?"

Alexey chuckled darkly. "Soon enough. But first, you must make yourself at home." He snapped his fingers, and the door opened again,

Morozov stepping back into the room. "I bid you good night, Mikhail Haleyvin. You have had a long journey, and you must rest."

✳

Vasily ate the food that was delivered to him, and then went to bed as early as he could manage, shutting his eyes and praying that he found sleep quickly so he could speak with Dimitri.

But when he opened his eyes again, he felt sick. He had known they wouldn't always be visiting Dimitri's dreams.

It was the same nightmare as always. He was seated next to a younger version of himself, who had curled up tightly into a ball on a narrow bed, just like he had every night when he was eight or ten or twelve years old, and he knew that pieces of him were about to be taken, pieces that he wasn't ready or willing to give. That was how this went, over and over, his unconscious mind unwilling to forget the secret he had buried so deeply.

But no—for once, he wasn't alone, because Dimitri was sitting in front of the door like he was guarding it, his knees bunched up to his chest, a cigarette dangling from his lips. The smoke masked the smell of vodka and stale sweat that usually permeated this memory.

There was a long, long silence. Vasily couldn't stand to meet Dimitri's gaze.

"Vasya." Dimitri bit his lip. "What's outside the door?"

A chill crept down Vasily's spine. Dimitri knew. Because of course he knew—he could feel the fear and the pain that invaded this dream as if it were his own, the same way that Vasily had felt everything Dimitri had the last time.

He swallowed. "A monster."

For a moment Dimitri was silent, and Vasily thought he might let it go, but he was Dimitri, and so of course he didn't.

"Who?" The way Dimitri looked at him was the way Vasily never wanted to be looked at by anyone, ever. With pity, like he had been ruined.

"A monster," Vasily repeated, but Dimitri kept staring at him, so he took a breath and continued. "Someone you don't even know, someone I haven't seen in years. You got me away from him, finally, wouldn't you know it." He choked on a laugh. "And I just . . . every time I think about it, I just . . ."

Dimitri got up and sat next to him on the bed, grabbing Vasily's hand and holding it. The warmth anchored him. "I never want Novo-Svitsevo to suffer the way I did. I have to repay the debt, to her, for saving me." Vasily forced the words out through the impossible tightness in his throat, trying to put into words how years and years of hatred and anger and fear burned inside of him, and somehow the only way to let it out was by fixing this.

He looked down at Dimitri's hand in his. It had gone white with the way he was squeezing it, and yet Dimitri hadn't complained, hadn't flinched.

Vasily made himself ease his grip, letting out a shuddering breath.

Dimitri brought his forehead to Vasily's, picking up his other hand and squeezing that one too. "What would you do now, to him, if you could?"

Vasily had thought about it often, so the answer sprang to his lips before he could even debate the wisdom of telling this to Dimitri. "I'd kill him slowly and then use his cock as a paperweight."

Dimitri chuckled. "Good choice." He pulled back. "Do you have news?"

Vasily sagged with relief that Dimitri was done questioning him. He imagined his mind as a safe and locked all the feelings away. Dimitri flinched, which Vasily hoped meant he'd succeeded in blocking his emotions from Dimitri, had succeeded in being less of an open book.

"He just said to make myself at home." Vasily dropped one of Dimitri's hands and picked at the threadbare blanket. His feet were bare and freezing against the flagstones on the floor.

"Anything else?" Dimitri cocked his head.

It struck Vasily that no, there was nothing else. He'd learned nothing else. He hadn't needed to see Dimitri.

No, he'd just *wanted* to. Because he missed him, because he wanted to make sure he was safe. Because he didn't want to feel so alone.

"He scares the fuck out of me." Vasily couldn't help but admit it.

Dimitri lowered his head onto Vasily's shoulder and breathed in deeply. "I've never told this to anyone, but at the end, even as I loved him, I was scared of him too."

As the door started to creak open, Vasily woke up.

NINETEEN

DIMITRI

The next morning, Dimitri lay in bed, staring at the ceiling, wishing he hadn't woken up to a house with one fewer occupant. He twisted the sheet in between his fingers, desperate for Vasily to be there so that he could soothe away the terror that had seeped from the other man in last night's dream. Finally, when he couldn't ignore the rumbling of his stomach, he dressed and went down to breakfast.

Ladushka and Mischa were fighting over the last piece of toast on a plate, while Annika was surgically cutting into a large stack of waffles drenched in golden syrup. Vasily's place at the table was conspicuously vacant. Dimitri could almost imagine him sitting at the table and reading a newspaper, a cup of strong coffee in one hand.

He swallowed hard as everyone looked up.

"How are you doing?" Annika asked quietly, her eyes round and large.

"Probably fucking awful," Mischa grumbled. "Vasya, of all people, just left on a mission that could end in his death, and it's been days of silence. How would you be?"

"What's that supposed to mean?" Dimitri asked, something uncomfortable shifting in his chest, but he was distracted by Mischa grabbing Ladushka's toast while she scowled.

Mischa licked the entire length of it before popping the corner into their mouth, and Ladushka frowned. "You could not have let me share?"

"No," Mischa said prissily as Annika chuckled. "I could not. I am a growing person. I need my toast."

"Mischka, you're thirty-two. It has truly been decades since you grew an inch." Dimitri pulled out a chair, rolling his eyes at the way Annika got up to put more bread on the stove. "Anna, Lada can do that herself if she wants food. You don't have to be the mother hen."

He was secretly glad for the bickering and the distraction, because otherwise they would all notice that something else was amiss. The dreams he had shared with Vasily were for the two of them alone. His gut churned at the thought of telling the rest of them what he had learned last night—or what he had revealed to Vasily a few nights prior.

These dreams were for them alone. Private. Sacred, somehow.

"She likes being the mother hen." Mischa stole a bite of Annika's waffles while her back was turned.

"More importantly, now that Dima has gotten out of bed, we need to discuss the true issue at hand." Ladushka folded her hands in front of her on the table, her back ramrod straight, food forgotten. "Dima, I know that no one else will say this, because they are worried for the state of your mind, but I am your political adviser, so I must advise you that there is only one ultimate solution to the problem of the coup launched against you. We must figure out what to do with Alexey so that Vasya's information can be put to use. There is only one conclusion."

Dimitri's stomach lurched. "Go on."

"We must find a way to kill Alexey Balakin." Ladushka eyed him levelly. "Because as long as he lives, he will be a threat to you."

Dimitri started to gag, the motion reflexive as nausea rushed through him at her words. He made it to the sink before he threw up bile. Annika was there, rubbing his back, as he spat a few times into the sink, then ran the water and splashed it over his face, shuddering.

"I'm going to pretend that's from you drinking last night and not from some kind of objection," Mischa said around a mouthful of toast when Dimitri turned around and sat, shakily, at the table.

Dimitri didn't say anything. He couldn't.

"It is going to be hard to kill an unkillable man." Ladushka wiped the crumbs Mischa had spewed off her arm coolly. "It is going to take a significant amount of effort to untangle this puzzle."

Dimitri took a deep breath and tried to ignore the twisting in his gut. As much as he didn't want to admit it, he knew, deep in his soul, that Ladushka was right. Alexey was an abomination, and that abomination had to die.

"How do you end an immortal life?" Ladushka steepled her fingers.

"As much as I hate to say it," Annika said, returning to the table with a new stack of toast, "I think that creepy library might have some clue." She grimaced.

"It had the answer to our communication problem," Mischa mused. "So maybe it contains the answer as to how to kill Alexey."

"Let's visit it, then." Annika cocked her head. "But first, *Moy Tzar*, you will eat breakfast. No one should plot murder on an empty stomach."

*

Two hours later, they were standing out front of Aleksandr's door, Ladushka pounding on the wood as Dimitri tried not to look at any of the skulls in the garden. Mischa nudged one with a foot, and Annika slapped their arm. "Respect the dead," she hissed.

"You're back?" The old man pulled open the door, releasing a cloud of foul-smelling smoke that they all promptly started choking on. "How much reading could you possibly want to do in one week?"

"It isn't any of your business," Dimitri countered. "Are you going to let us in, or not?"

"Knowledge isn't free," Aleksandr said, holding out a palm petulantly.

They'd fought in the carriage over who would give up what next, but Dimitri had stayed out of it, staring out the carriage window, burrowing into his scarf, letting his hat shield his eyes. In the end, Ladushka had won, and she pulled out the worn bookmark that she always used.

"This is from the personal collection of Khanna Ferreiranovich. It was given to me by her daughter after her death, and every time I read, I use it. It reminds me of her, and the hours she spent teaching me to write with clarity and emotion."

Aleksandr accepted the bookmark, curling it up in his palm before biting the edge. "This will do." He threw it over his shoulder, and it never hit the ground. Dimitri blinked several times, but it didn't reappear.

"*Moy Tzar* is also a very generous man," Mischa said snarkily, pulling a silver gir out of their suit pocket and flicking it at Aleksandr, who caught it deftly. "He would also like to make a donation to your clothing fund. Perhaps next time you could try some pants?"

Dimitri studiously avoided looking down at the half of Aleksandr that was fully nude, concealed only partially by the hem of a ragged old shirt.

"These are my experimentation clothes," Aleksandr huffed. "You came unannounced. Be grateful that I'm letting you in at all. This library runs by appointment only."

"We thank you, sir," Annika said sweetly, giving the librarian a slight half bow, even though her face looked like she was sucking on a lemon. "We apologize for coming without letting you know first."

"Ah, an apology from the angry one." Aleksandr smirked. "I suppose I could let you in."

They all shuffled into Aleksandr's house, wincing against the acrid fog that hung in the air. "You know the way," he said, and promptly vanished into the cloud of smoke.

✳

"This is awful," Mischa moaned, their head in their hands. "There must be a thousand books here."

"It is never easy to acquire knowledge," Ladushka murmured, her nose deep in a book. "It requires patience and persistence. You should know, from medical school."

"I read fewer books to learn how to treat every ailment of the human body." Mischa sneezed, jarring a stack of books and causing a cloud of dust to rise up around the table. Then they all started coughing.

Dimitri turned the page of the book in front of him, full of gruesome diagrams of dissected human remains. They'd been searching for what felt like hours, but no one had found anything on how to kill an unkillable man.

"Remember, it isn't going to be something obvious," Annika muttered. "It's unlikely we're going to find a book that specific. We'll have to be creative. Look for how to break a curse or unresurrect something."

"Like that's a thing," Mischa snorted. "Unresurrection."

"Focus," Ladushka hissed.

Dimitri flipped through the pages of the book in his hands, his vision blurring. Maybe it wasn't possible to kill Alexey. Maybe they'd have to live with the monster he'd created forever.

Dimitri was vaguely aware that, over the last hour, he'd started sweating, and that his vision was gradually blurring around the edges. His fingers shook as he turned another page, and suddenly he was looking at a drawing of a long, ornate knife dripping with blood.

He swayed in his seat.

"I'm taking you home." Annika's hands were firm on his shoulders, helping him up. "The rest of you can come or not. But Dima and I are done for today."

He hated feeling weak, hated that he couldn't do this, but he was so grateful as she guided him out of the house and into a carriage that he could have kissed her.

When they arrived back at the house, Dimitri dragged himself up the stairs and into his room, letting the door swing shut behind him. He was drained from trying to find a way to kill Alexey, from the knowledge that such a thing might be impossible. He felt sick, and sad, and angry that there was an entire library devoted to helping people do what Alexey had done, to spit in the face of God and create monsters and turn themselves into horrors. No one should know what he now knew, after just a few hours of halfheartedly reading through books.

He was never going to be able to feel clean again after one single afternoon. Alexey had studied the Holy Science for years.

Alexey was still so much a part of him, still controlling him, still leaving him crippled with guilt and with grief. He was nothing more than a boy living in the past, wishing that there was some way to undo his sins so he didn't have to grapple with the consequences in the present.

★

For the next week, Dimitri and his court spent their days in Aleksandr's library, shifting through increasingly disturbing books that all had a suspicious amount of information about necromancy, trying to find a way to kill Alexey.

"This is futile," Dimitri said on the morning of the seventh day. They'd given up two of Annika's knives, Dimitri's grandmother's rolling pin and a letter from his youngest half sister, Mischa's pocket watch and a vial containing some kind of liquid they refused to name, and still they'd found nothing. His eyes were burning, and he fought the urge to sneeze from the dust swirling around the room.

"The pursuit of knowledge is never futile," Ladushka said sharply, her nose so close to the book she was reading that it was almost touching the page.

"Dima," Annika said gently. "Are you sure there's nothing *you* know about how to . . . end this? Anything you heard, or anything you were told?"

Dimitri got up, his chair screeching on the wood of the floor, to pace around the room. He ground his teeth and hit his hand on the side of a bookcase, which shook precariously, then he let out a wordless scream of frustration. He whirled on his court, who were suddenly watching him with rapt attention. Mischa was gripping the table, white-knuckled, as if they were a heartbeat away from springing up and restraining him.

"Do you think," he said, his anger barely leashed, "that Alexey would have forced me into this and then told me how to kill him?" His sides were heaving, and he shoved his hair out of his eyes. "Do you truly think that if I had that knowledge, that I would be hiding it from you? Do you think so little of me, even now?"

He looked each one of them in the eye. Ladushka was impassive, as always. Annika was biting her lip, her eyes wet. Only Mischa was leaning forward, their fascination evident.

"Good," Mischa said, satisfaction lighting up their face. "You're finally getting angry again. You're healing, Dima."

"Fuck you," Dimitri spat back, although there was no heat in it. In truth, he wasn't mad at his friends. He was mad at himself, and mad that there were no easy answers. He slumped back down into the chair he had abandoned, tensing up as it creaked ominously.

He debated for a second before pointing to the one book he'd put aside that morning, the only one with some scrap of information they could use. "There might be a way to find an answer in there."

"Why did you not say so?" Ladushka huffed, still sour from the loss of her favorite fountain pen that morning, then lunged across the table to snatch the book up, turning to the page that Dimitri had marked with a scrap of paper. "Oh, I see."

Annika groaned. "Do I even want to know?"

"*I* want to know." Mischa sneezed. "I need to get out of this room. You'd think the librarian never dusts."

"No doubt he does not," Dimitri said, sagging further into his chair. "It's instructions for summoning a demon. A small one, mostly nocturnal. They're easily bribed, apparently, into telling secrets."

A small part of him wished that the answer a demon would give was *Nothing, there is nothing you can do to kill him, so let him live.* But a bigger piece of him hoped that one of the creatures that dwelled in the middle world would have some answers for them, some way to rid them of Alexey forever.

Annika gagged audibly. "You want us to summon a *demon*, Dima?"

Mischa merely shrugged, looking unperturbed. "We could keep looking here forever and maybe find nothing, or we could try this. Knowledge can be found in all sorts of places."

"Yes," Ladushka said, her eyes shining with the fervor of learning, her head still bent towards the book. "I agree. This is so interesting, and the instructions are so detailed . . ."

Annika pried the book out of her hands and tucked it into her satchel. "I think we have what we need. We should go." She shuddered. "I don't want to spend a minute longer here than we need to."

They shuffled out of the library and out the front door. Dimitri didn't miss the way that Annika spat on the ground three times as soon as they crossed the threshold, Mischa imitating her. After a moment's pause, Dimitri let the rest of his court walk on ahead, then copied her too.

*

Dimitri curled up on the sofa on their return, where he passed the afternoon reading an admittedly compelling romance novel to try and purge all thoughts of demons and Alexey from his mind.

He was also doing his best to forget what he'd seen in Vasily's nightmare, otherwise he'd burn up in a fit of incandescent rage and head back to Novo-Svitsevo, danger be damned, to do a bit of hunting for monsters.

Still, those few hours had almost been pleasant, the afternoon light coming in through the window, the fire warming the parlor, and he hadn't minded when Ladushka had walked around muttering to herself, then sent Mischa away on some errand.

Annika was knitting a sock, her tongue between her lips, occasionally stretching Dimitri's leg out so she could measure it against his foot. "Why are your feet so big?" She scowled and picked at a stitch.

"It's true, you know, what they say about feet," he mumbled, thumbing through another page. He ignored her snort of laughter, though, because just then the front door creaked and a distinctly animalistic smell wafted in.

"Mischka," Dimitri said, his eyebrows almost at his hairline as Mischa walked into the parlor and shrugged off their coat. "What the fuck is *that*?"

Mischa bent down to cover the ears of their newest charge. "Don't be a cock," they hissed. They straightened up. "This is Piotyr, our honored guest."

Dimitri tried to keep his voice even but failed. "Why is there a *goat* in my home?" The goat walked forward, pulling on the rope that Mischa had looped around its neck like a leash, and nudged Dimitri's hand with its velvety nose.

He pulled back as a memory of Alexey sleeping on the sofa in the library with their cat on his chest and a dog at his feet flitted across his mind. Alexey had always loved animals, and they had always loved him.

Dimitri wondered if animals could still stand to be around Alexey, now that he was an abomination.

The goat looked at him with its slitted eyes and bleated ominously, like it knew who he was thinking of. Dimitri dropped his book, grabbed a half-empty glass from the sideboard, and took a large swig of vodka to wash away thoughts of Alexey. He grimaced at the goat, which bleated again, but in a far meaner manner this time, like it was judging him for his alcohol dependence.

Annika put aside her knitting and slid off the sofa, kneeling on the floor, petting the goat after Dimitri had pulled away. "How are you?" she crooned, and the goat butted its head into her chest affectionately.

The floorboards creaked as Ladushka rounded the corner into the parlor. "Oh, thank the Lord," she said to Mischa. "It took you long enough."

Dimitri pinched the bridge of his nose. "Why is there a goat in my parlor, Lada?"

Ladushka looked at Dimitri in that withering way of hers that made him feel like an imbecile. "You wanted to find a demon. Did you not read the instructions in the book you yourself found?"

Dimitri flushed with embarrassment. "Not all of them, clearly."

Ladushka clicked her tongue disapprovingly. "Animals can see demons. The goat will take us to the demon."

"Piotyr," Mischa said reverently, tilting their hands and chin up to the heavens. "The demon hunter that will save Novo-Svitsevo. I, er, borrowed him from a farm on the outskirts of the city. I'll return him when we're done."

Dimitri shook his head in disbelief. They were truly doing this, truly stooping to the level of relying on demons to guide their way.

"We need food to bribe the demon with," Ladushka said, impervious to the fact that the goat was now chewing on the edge of the parlor rug. "Or money. Perhaps both." She stared off into the distance. "I wonder how much money a demon considers to be a good bribe."

"Can you stop being so academic for a second?" Annika insisted, frowning. "This is dangerous stuff. What if one of us gets possessed?"

"We will wear amulets," Ladushka countered. "It is quite safe, you know. If the demon comes near you, just spit on the ground. You do that all the time as it is, Anna."

"May the Lord protect us," Annika murmured.

Dimitri's gut was churning, and he couldn't tell if it was because of the goat's musky smell or of getting closer to the knowledge of how to kill Alexey. Something inside him still hoped that if they never discovered how to kill Alexey, they could just keep on living their pathetic lives until they died. That Alexey would never find them, that he'd never have to face his husband again, never have to confront his failure.

But that would make the danger that Vasily was in worthless, so he forced himself to push away the impulse.

Dimitri got up, turned towards the window and shoved his hands into his pockets. He swallowed hard, a chill winding its way through his core. "How does this end?"

"The goat?" Mischa laughed, but the sound was forced. "Hopefully with a cuddle."

"Shut up," Annika said, her voice low. Dimitri closed his eyes and turned away, tilting his forehead against the glass of the window.

"It ends with you killing Alexey Balakin," Ladushka said. "He should have been killed months ago."

He hated the accusatory edge in her voice. He knew that, deep down, she blamed him for stymieing their efforts to kill Alexey at every turn during the war.

He just hadn't been able to do it. He'd hoped that they'd win, and that, in his victory, he could have found some way to undo the experiment that Alexey had undergone. Found some way to turn him back into the man he'd loved for so much of his life, from the monster he'd become.

Instead, he'd stared at Alexey on the battlefield at Vysoka, two hundred paces away. And he'd lowered his pistol, let Alexey walk away sneering. Because he'd always been too weak to do what needed to be done. Because he'd been too weak to kill the man who'd made him.

He'd spent the last year wondering if Alexey had been right, if he'd been too weak to be the Tzar that Novo-Svitsevo needed. He still heard the echo of every one of Alexey's scornful remarks over and over, every time he was alone.

You give power away too easily. You let others rule you when you should rule them. You are crippled by kindness, blinded by mercy. You are weak, Dima. The only way you will ever be strong is to let me guide you, perfect you.

Maybe he was right. For a long time, Dimitri had believed he was. But now, whether it was Mischa's tonic or the clarity of time or the slow process of healing his own soul, something within him had shifted. And while he grieved the end of his relationship with Alexey, he wondered if perhaps he was not the only one at fault.

When Alexey had finally been reborn, he'd looked at Dimitri with his coal-black eyes and caressed his hair with fingers as cold as the grave. *My beloved*, he'd said. *Now I am your strength. Now I am the empire's strength. You sit on the throne. But I am the one who rules.*

Alexey could have stopped the war before it began, if only he had known his place, if only he had not reached for more. Instead, Alexey had given up on him and taken power for himself, had forced Dimitri to make choices no man should ever have to make.

Alexey had never asked. He had never listened. He had just taken, and taken, and taken from Dimitri and from Novo-Svitsevo until there was nothing left.

Dimitri opened his eyes and turned to look at his court, the people who had always been there for him, through every failure, through every bad night.

"You're right. This is what must be done," he rasped, making a final decision. It would be his friends who would save him, not Alexey. Not anymore. "Let me get my coat."

✳

They made it out onto the street with the goat and walked barely a block before it stopped dead. Despite Mischa's pleading and tugging on the leash, it refused to budge.

"Dima," Annika said, crouching down to the goat's level. "I think he wants you to carry him."

Ladushka rolled her eyes. Mischa tried to scoop the goat up, crooning, but it danced away from them. Eventually, they gave up, shrugging. "Just do it, Dima. If Anna the Goat Whisperer thinks you need to carry the goat, just do it."

Dimitri cringed, but hefted the goat's furry body up under his arm. To his dismay, the goat immediately stopped bleating and raised its nose up to sniff at his chin, mouthing at the scarf wound around his face.

"See," Annika said. "I knew what it wanted." She ruffled the fur on its head, then paused. "My parents' estate has goats. The kids like to be carried when they're born. My brothers and I spent every spring with them in our arms."

She turned on her heel and kept walking, her shoulders squared. Dimitri exchanged looks with Mischa, who bit their lip. Annika almost never spoke of her family. They had been on the wrong side of the war.

Annika showed more loyalty to him than he had any right to command.

"Where are we going?" The goat's tiny body was warm against his, and he hated how carrying it relaxed his shoulders minutely. He pulled his hat lower over his eyes and drew his wool coat tighter across his chest.

"The park." Ladushka tilted her head up, examining the sky. "Good, it is almost dark."

They walked, heads down, clustered together. Ladushka led them to the park at the edge of their neighborhood. Dimitri had never been—he'd had no use for lounging or strolling among the fashionable rich of Wilnetzk. But Ladushka must have, because she wound them through the hedge-lined paths, devoid of others now that it was dark, until they came to a clearing.

"Put Piotyr down," Ladushka said. "And let him find us a demon."

Dimitri complied. The goat leaned against his leg and started to bleat. He stared blankly at Ladushka. "I don't see Piotyr finding us a demon."

"Ask him nicely." Mischa crouched down and took the goat's face in their hands. "Find us a demon, blessed Piotyr, so we may praise you." Ladushka rolled her eyes, and Annika put a hand over her mouth, stifling a laugh.

"Go on, Piotyr," Annika urged.

The goat tilted its head at them, then looked up to Dimitri. Curse it all, that the one thing that would respect his authority would be an infant goat. "Go on," he said gruffly.

The goat bleated once and trotted off happily, its leash trailing behind it. Annika dashed forward to grab the trailing rope, and they all followed the goat, which was marching towards a crumbling fountain on the edge of the park with a suspicious amount of intent.

They came to the fountain, overhung by a large willow tree. The goat stopped moving and sniffed at the air, then bleated once and returned to Dimitri's side. He picked it up again without a conscious thought and tucked it to his chest.

Annika huddled up to his right, and Mischa to his left. He hoped his friends were as terrified as he was. There was something unnatural about this corner of the park, the air too cold, the bite of the wind too menacing. Annika was praying under her breath and fingering the amulet she wore around her neck.

There was a shimmering patch of air on the side of the fountain. "Would you reveal yourself to us?" Ladushka stepped forward, pulling a shallow dish and a bottle of cream out of her coat. She alone appeared to be unafraid. She uncapped the bottle and set the dish down on the ground, then poured the cream in. "We wish to speak. We bring offerings in exchange for your knowledge."

Nothing happened.

"Now we need to say the spell," Ladushka said. "To make it visible." She pulled a piece of paper out of her pocket and passed it to Dimitri. "Read it," she ordered.

"The Lord our God," Dimitri started to read, then had to stop to clear his throat and steady himself. "The Lord our God," he continued, "I proclaim your splendor and your majesty, so as to command all the formless spirits, angels of destruction, and demons to reveal themselves to us, so they may no longer walk unseen."

He shoved the paper into his coat pocket when he finished, feeling foolish. Still, nothing happened. They all stared at the fountain. Dimitri increasingly felt like an idiot, allowing himself to be led to a park by a goat, of all things, and then stand there witless.

"Let's go," he said after a minute, the back of his neck prickling. "It's not working." Ladushka frowned, but Mischa and Annika sagged with relief.

Annika took his hand and started to pull him away.

But then the dish tipped, rattling against the flagstones. Dimitri whirled around to see something lapping at the milk like a cat, splashing droplets everywhere. Gradually, a form came into view—small and furred, with wings like a bat's and feet like a chicken's. Its face was vaguely human, and Dimitri recoiled, bumping into Mischa's chest. Mischa's breaths were coming faster, their heart pounding hard enough for Dimitri to feel it. Annika gasped, and Ladushka went perfectly still.

"A *mazzikin*," Ladushka breathed. "Hello, you."

"You wish for knowledge?" Its voice was soft and melodic, a song in the night, so different from the hellishness of its body.

Ladushka turned to Dimitri, raising an eyebrow. He tried to speak, but the words lodged in his throat. He shook his head minutely.

Ladushka sighed, but spoke instead. "There is an aberration. A soul stolen from God. We believe that the man Alexey Balakin has become immortal and wish to know how to kill him. The middle world of demons may have the answers." She crouched down, refilling the dish with more cream. "Would you tell us?"

"Something has been taken from us." The demon paused to lap up more cream. "That I can tell you. We all felt it, those of us who dwell in the middle world. We feel it still."

Ladushka emptied the rest of the cream into the bowl. "Tell me more about this."

"The middle world is unsettled." The demon sprang backwards, its birdlike feet gripping the ledge of the fountain as its wings flared for balance. "There is a disturbance. Something is calling out to us, and it feels like the protection of a father. Many are drawn to it. Many wish to go, despite the admonition of the princes of the realm."

Dimitri's mouth was dry, fear making it hard to swallow. "Have any gone?" His voice came out as little more than a whisper.

The *mazzikin* bobbed its head. "One did, long ago. Samael. A voice called in the darkness, and Samael answered. He fell to the seduction of the voice, and he joined his strength with it."

"How long ago?" Dimitri hugged the goat tighter to him. "How long ago did the demon answer the call?"

"Two years, in the time of men."

Mischa shifted closer to Dimitri, and Dimitri's mouth flattened into a line. Annika took his hand again, curling it tightly with hers. "Does the voice still speak to the demons?" Dimitri prayed to God that the answer was no. But he knew that was a prayer that would never be answered.

"They speak of a void," the demon said. It hopped up to the tree, the branch bobbing under its weight as it perched eye level with Ladushka. "It calls to them. Some answer, and they return with tales of power. The voice allows them to take life from the Lord's creatures. It promises them things, in the dark of the night. That they will be able to walk the world of men, even under the light of the sun."

"It's Alexey," Dimitri whispered, horror unfurling within him. "He's the one calling to them."

"We need to know how to kill him," Ladushka said. She pulled a coin out of her pocket, and the *mazzikin* grabbed it out of Ladushka's fingers and pressed it to its small chest.

"The voice has two makers." The *mazzikin* licked cream from around its lips. "The Lord our God, and its beloved. The voice calls out for the beloved in the dark too. The beloved can kill the voice."

Dimitri's heart had surely never been so heavy. His existence had never weighed on him quite so much as it did now.

"Can anyone else harm the voice?" Ladushka brandished another coin, and the *mazzikin* reached out and snatched it.

"They can harm the voice, but they cannot kill it. The beloved can kill the voice, the beloved alone."

Ladushka straightened up. "Thank you," she said, ever courteous. "You have been a great help."

"Let's go," Annika whispered. "Let's go home."

Dimitri was vaguely aware of Mischa's arm being slung around his shoulder, Ladushka and Annika whispering behind them. His eyes stung and his chest was hollow. Somehow, he had known this, but had never been able to admit it to himself.

He'd have to be the one to kill Alexey.

There was clarity in the pain, comfort in the knowledge. He would have to end what he started, and he would do it, even if it broke him. Because the demon confirmed what he had always known. That Alexey Balakin loved power and would stop at nothing to gain it, even if that power was pulled from death itself. That he was going to do something horrible, unforgivable, so far was he from God's light and the rationality of man.

This was the last and most final act of love that Dimitri could offer to Alexey, before he sinned so gravely that his eternal rest would be forsaken for damnation.

He would kill his husband before Alexey destroyed himself, and Novo-Svitsevo along with him.

TWENTY

ALEXEY

The man was perfect, so perfect that Alexey could not help the thrill that went through him at the thought of making Mikhail his to command, the first soldier in his new army. The custodian of his power, the conduit between him and the dark of the middle world.

He was of the line of Leyvin, and the supplication in his eyes had been enticing yet had hidden a secret fire. There was something about him, after the perfect subservience that Ivan offered, that reminded him of Dimitri. Mikhail Haleyvin was how Dimitri had once been, bold and unafraid. When he reached out and touched Mikhail, Alexey could swear he was touching his husband, just like on that first night when Dimitri had been leaning against a windowsill on his estate, Dimitri's hair ruffled by a summer breeze, proud and full of longing.

And yet he was better than Dimitri had been, because Mikhail had looked at him and not flinched at what he was. Mikhail's mind had recognized the need to master the base instincts of his body, and though he had shuddered at Alexey's touch, he had not looked away.

He was the one Alexey would make his foremost general.

Alexey grasped the edges of the immersion pool and submersed himself again. If he was to follow the word of God and make Mikhail Haleyvin love him, he needed to be pure before he went to him.

You do well, my son, God told him. *You have chosen well. He is perfect for us.*

Alexey closed his eyes as the void within him grew at the closeness of the Divine. God reached out to him, and he reached back.

Thank you, the Lord my God, Alexey said back fervently. *I honor you, in all I do.*

Do not rush him, God commanded. *It is an important task, what you seek to do. He must be treasured.* Ani l'dodi v'dodi li.

Alexey sighed, letting his hands float on the surface of the water. *I am my beloved's, and my beloved is mine*, he echoed back to God. A memory flashed before him, of Dimitri in a crown and gilded jacket, his cape trimmed with the finest fur, circling Alexey seven times with seduction in his eyes, saying those words during their royal wedding ceremony, so different than when they'd married in private before leaving Chernitzy, just the two of them under the stars.

The presence of God retreated from Alexey's consciousness, and he rose out of the pool, letting the waiting servants dry and dress him, this time in a black suit, the vest embroidered with black thread, the bone-white of his shirt the only color that Alexey conceded to wear. "Bring Mikhail Haleyvin to me," he commanded. "In the western dining room. Have food sent for us."

Alexey returned to his study and paced the confines of the room, plotting how to inspire love in Mikhail. First, he decided, he needed to understand him.

When Ivan came to fetch him and guide him to the midday meal, he didn't miss the disappointment etched on the younger man's face. Alexey paused before the dining room doors and drew Ivan to him, ignoring the way it caught the attention of the guards and servants lining the hall. He nipped at Ivan's ear and brushed a kiss against his lips. "You will wait for me, tonight, in my rooms?"

Ivan's cheeks flushed as his eyes brightened, and he ducked his head, leaning into Alexey's chest. "Yes, *Moy Tzar*. As you command. It will be my delight." Ivan bowed, then turned and sauntered back down the hall, Alexey's eyes following the sway of his hips.

Alexey pushed down any thoughts of arousal. Now was not the time to lose himself in thoughts of another. He had to be fully present, fully *here* in order to bring Mikhail into the fold. He nodded to the guards on either side of the threshold, and they pushed the doors open.

The western dining room had been Dimitri's favorite, a tiny jewel box of a room that looked out over one of the expansive palace gardens. The walls were ornately frescoed and gilded, and a small table of inlaid wood was surrounded by comfortable armchairs upholstered in silk. It was where Dimitri had held meetings over caviar and blinis with his closest lords and ladies, and Alexey had upheld the same tradition.

Humans, he found, were creatures comforted by habit.

Mikhail was sitting stiffly in one of the chairs, his arms gripping the sides as if he was about to be seized by some unknown force and carried off. Alexey chuckled when Mikhail relaxed marginally at his arrival, his shoulders lowering and the furrow between his eyebrows smoothing out.

"*Moy Tzar*." Mikhail dipped his head, and then looked up through his eyelashes, his eyes dark, a hunger lurking there. Alexey took a moment to appreciate the man's beauty, the way the early-winter sun streaming in through the windows highlighted the lustrous gold of his skin, but it did nothing for him. He should have admired the way that the suit the palace dressers had found for him, a green so dark it was almost black, set off the strength of his thighs and the breadth of his chest and the hazel of his eyes. But no, there was nothing still.

"Good morning," Alexey said, the pleasantry sticking briefly in his throat. He had not truly been attracted to anyone since Dimitri left and Ivan had taken his place. He cleared a small space in his mind, slipping into a moment of meditation, making room for a brief brush of contact with the Lord. He sought out reassurance that this was not a failing of his that would doom Novo-Svitsevo.

Perhaps there is another way to make the Leyvin love you, God suggested to him, the divine voice low and seductive in his ear.

A shudder went through Alexey. *In time.*

He walked across the room to Mikhail, then offered up his hand. When Mikhail took it and kissed the back of his palm, the other man's fingers were steady, the warmth leeching into Alexey's stiff fingers.

Here was someone with the backbone to lead his armies, someone who wasn't afraid of him and wouldn't be afraid of the soldiers that would be his to command. One of God's chosen Leyvin, who had strength at his core, all at Alexey's disposal. He sat down across from Mikhail and folded his hands on the table.

"I wish to know more about you, Mikhail Haleyvin of Voloski," he said as servants began carrying in trays of smoked fish, tureens of soup, delicate pastries stuffed with spiced meat, and a large and ornate samovar. "Tell me of your life."

Mikhail pulled a pastry onto his plate, then took a small bite after sniffing it suspiciously, like it might not be to his tastes. He licked his lips, and something in Alexey heated. "This is very good, *Moy Tzar.*" He regarded Alexey's empty place setting warily. "Will you not have any?"

"I no longer require food to sustain me." Alexey arched an eyebrow. "It is a benefit of my rebirth, thanks be to the Lord my God and His Holy Science."

Mikhail's eyes widened. "I've heard of the Holy Science, in the shul in Wilnetzk that I attended. The marvels it can do. Would you tell me of it?"

Alexey stifled a pleased smile. If Mikhail was already interested in the Holy Science and its miracles, it would be far easier to turn him to his plan. "It would be my pleasure. But first, tell me of yourself. I like to know my guests."

Mikhail paused for a moment, the shadow of grief flitting over his features, then took a long drink of tea. "I grew up in Voloski. My family has been butchers for generations."

Alexey noted the stillness of the other man's body, the way his fingers clenched into a fist. "And what of your family, now?"

Mikhail looked up. His eyes were glassy, tears clinging to the lower lashes. "They died, in the war. I was the only one who was spared."

Alexey knew what he was not saying, and who had ruined most of the villages to the south of Rav-Mikhailburg.

The troops he had commanded had shown a remarkable lack of decorum at times, but Alexey supposed that was just what happened when dealing with the common people, unable to control their base instincts. He had heard reports of looting and rape and brutality but had brushed them aside and delegated the issue to his generals. He had no idea if they had dealt with that or not—his concern was to win the war against Dimitri.

Here was one of the victims.

"May their memories be blessings," Alexey said as gently as he could. "Were you spared because you served?" He hoped that the man had no lingering loyalties to Dimitri—that would make Alexey's job all the harder. But such a thing was unlikely, he consoled himself, when the man had delivered himself to Alexey's doorstep.

"No." Mikhail's throat bobbed. His eyes were downcast. "I have an illness. It pains me sometimes, in my joints. I was unfit to serve when officers came to my village." He took another long drink of tea. "It shames me that I was not able to serve you."

Alexey fought back the grin of triumph that almost spread across his features. "It is no matter." After a second's pause, he reached across the small table and cupped Mikhail's chin in his hand, tilting the other man's eyes to meet his own. "You can serve me now."

A bolt of heat should have gone through his core as Mikhail's eyes immediately dropped to his belt, but once again, there was nothing.

"*Moy Tzar*," Mikhail rasped, his cheeks flushing. "It would be my pleasure."

Alexey made himself chuckle, then dropped his hand. Perhaps later, his body would respond. If it didn't, he could look to his snuff-box for chemical assistance. "I want you to join me in prayer, here. The Holy Science commands that I honor the Leyvin, the bloodline of old."

Mikhail nodded, his flush ebbing away, his eyes sharpening. "It would be my deepest honor to join you, *Moy Tzar*. Where are the others?"

"Pardon?" Alexey tilted his head.

"Where are the rest of the Leyvin?" Mikhail was studying him too keenly, and Alexey ground his teeth at how quickly the other man had put him on the defensive, where just a heartbeat ago he had held him in the palm of his hand.

Still, it was a good quality in a general, the ability to unbalance a game.

"Few have taken me up on my offer," he replied smoothly. "And those who have come to pray with me have honored me with their presence, but then returned to their families."

"Ah," Mikhail said darkly. "What a shame, *Moy Tzar*, that all the rest have left you."

"Mikhail," Alexey drawled, "I was not as interested in any of them as I am in you." He forced his eyes to rove over the span of the other man's shoulders, the broadness of his chest, the way his thighs strained against the fabric of his suit pants. "None of them had your charm."

Mikhail blushed furiously and ducked his head. This would be easier than Alexey had ever anticipated. One, perhaps two visits to his bedchamber at night if Alexey could bear it, a few flattering dinners, some instruction in the Holy Science, and then Mikhail would be entirely his, ready for his transformation.

"I wish to learn more about the Holy Science," Mikhail said, breaking the silence.

Alexey nodded. "It is a gift from the Lord my God. A way for us to access the secrets of the heavens while we walk the earth. With its understanding, we can call on the angels, we can control life and death, we can work miracles and perform magic. God did not intend for us to be helpless creatures, Mikhail Haleyvin. God made us in His image, and that means that we, too, are creators." The void within him echoed its assent, the way it always did when he spoke of the Holy Science with reverence.

"What are these miracles you can do? What can you create?" Mikhail cocked his head.

Alexey toyed with the embossed silver knife next to his plate, then picked it up and dug it into the wood of the table, making a scar. "I can create things that no man has ever seen," he said quietly. "I can use the power that God gave me in my rebirth to give life to others."

"I would like to see this," Mikhail breathed.

"All in good time." Alexey stood up and offered him a hand. Without hesitation, Mikhail took it and rose. "All in good time."

✳

"He seems very receptive." Alexey paced the confines of his study, circling Morozov, who sat at a table marking up notes. "I think that the best way to proceed is to complete the ritual preparations for opening the permanent rift between this world and the middle world, and then perform his transformation. I will need my strength."

Morozov nodded. "If the Lord our God says he must love you in order to be a loyal *zemonyii*, we must ensure that he is yours, heart and soul, before the experiment."

Alexey paced faster, his heart thudding against his ribs with anticipation. "I can almost taste it, Morozov, the pieces of my plan falling into place with the guidance of God."

"It will be a great and terrible thing you will do, *Moy Tzar*." Morozov pressed a hand to his chest. "I am honored to be a part of it, however inconsequential. I have found the ingredients you requested as well. They wait for you in the smaller experimentation chamber."

"What happened to the magician you got them from?" Alexey looked at Morozov sharply.

"She is no longer here to speak of what we discussed," Morozov said with a wicked grin. "A few bullets ensured it."

"So you have it all then?" Alexey drew in a shuddering breath. He could not believe that it was drawing so close, the moment where he could enact the feat that he had needed the strength of immortality to achieve.

"I do, *Moy Tzar*. The only question is how we will assemble the court and encourage their prayers. The magician was quite clear that an ordinary gathering of the righteous is not enough." Morozov stroked his chin. "And she warned that the procedure to open the permanent rift might claim the lives of those who are too weak to withstand the face of God."

"I will find a way," Alexey muttered. "It is too important for us to fail this. If it requires the lives of some of my lords or ladies, that is the tithe God requires for power, and we will pay it gladly."

Morozov's hand stilled on his throat. "Will it truly work, *Moy Tzar*? Will we truly be able to merge the world we walk with the middle world of demonkind?"

"Of course it will work," Alexey spat, whirling on him. "I remade my body and claimed immortality. Everyone doubted me, even my own husband. They accused me of insanity, until I was returned to them, and now they are bowing at my feet." He drew his shoulders back. "I will rend the world apart, Morozov. Me and my *zemonyii* will call forth the demons that God has created for us to use. We will command the strongest army the world has ever seen, humans and demons both, then cleanse the earth with guns and magic and our righteous faith." He slammed a hand into the wood of the table, sending a crack spiraling down its leg. "No one will dare to harm Novo-Svitsevo when they see what we do to our enemies. No one will stand before us. They will all fall at our feet and beg to join us, beg for the protection of our power and the love of God."

He would be the true father of his nation, then, having made Novo-Svitsevo the most powerful empire on earth. He would have the satisfaction of sitting securely on his throne, not having to worry about scheming nobles and restless neighbors, not when he was the right hand of God, commanding an army that no mortals could match on the battlefield.

Morozov fell out of his chair onto his knees and bent forward to kiss Alexey's boot. "*Moy Tzar*, it is the honor of my life to serve you and see your plan fulfilled. No one has the strength to protect our country the way you do. Only you can make it safe."

Alexey looked down at the man at his feet, convinced by the declaration of his faith. But instead of being contented with Morozov's loyalty, Alexey just wished it was a different man standing with him at the dawn of a new world.

✳

After an inspection of the sacrificial tools that Morozov had procured, Alexey retired to his chambers. He had barely shut the door behind him and unclasped his cloak when Ivan emerged from under the furs on the bed, his hair tousled from sleep.

"I didn't think you were coming," Ivan murmured, rubbing his eyes. "I apologize, *Moy Tzar*. I was so tired."

Alexey advanced on the bed, pulling off his jacket and letting it fall to the carpet, then kicking off his boots.

"I had something to attend to," Alexey said. "Being the Tzar is busy work."

"You mean some*one*," Ivan countered sulkily, so unlike him. "That man, Mikhail. Your eyes haven't left him, even when I'm in the room."

"He is a tool, Ivan, and nothing more," Alexey snapped. "Jealousy is unbecoming."

Ivan pouted from the bed, and Alexey cringed. Dimitri had frequently used that pout to manipulate him, to bend him to his will. It was no less effective from Ivan. Alexey felt his heart soften, and he sat down on the edge of the bed, drawing Ivan to him. "He is not the one sharing my bed tonight, or any night." Alexey could afford such a small lie. He planted a kiss on Ivan's head. "You are precious to me."

Ivan sighed and relaxed into Alexey's chest. "Not just because I look like my brother, *Moy Tzar*?"

Alexey stilled. And something tender within him compelled him to lie again. "Not at all, my love. You are special in your own right."

As he crawled into bed and let himself be warmed by the heat coming off Ivan's skin, pulling the smaller man underneath him with firm hands on both of his wrists, Alexey closed his eyes and breathed. Everything was drawing into place. He was doing the work of God, and doing it well.

So he could not understand why God had not answered his final and most fervent prayer, to have Dimitri Alexeyev struck from his heart.

TWENTY-ONE

VASILY

Vasily was glad that over the course of his life, he had gotten used to living in constant terror, looking over his shoulder, fighting the urge to jump at noises. He would be a piss-poor spymaster if he let something like fear get in the way of doing his job and doing it well—but nothing, not even his childhood, not even sitting in a trench under constant artillery fire, came close to being as nerve-wracking as being in the presence of the piece of shit currently in charge of his beloved country.

Though Alexey's fanaticism gave Vasily an advantage—Alexey was doing next to nothing to make sure "Mikhail" was who he said he was. There were no drugs in his food that would loosen his tongue or spies listening in on him in his room. No one was even going through his things. The only threat was Ivan, who was paying him an inordinate amount of attention and kept trying to catch him alone. It was taxing, trying to avoid him, but Vasily wasn't about to get himself shot for being unattended with the Tzar's plaything.

His current lunch in the parlor with Alexey was, therefore, awkward, since Ivan was in attendance. The boy looked like he was trying to catch Vasily's attention, with half-aborted hand gestures behind Alexey's back. When the meal ended, Alexey swept out of the room without a second glance at Ivan, who had taken on the look of a kicked puppy still desperate for its master's approval.

Vasily truly wondered how Alexey managed to keep getting boys to give him that look.

He stood up, but the room was suddenly devoid of other servants, and Ivan was standing in front of the doors, which he hastily shut. His hands were shaking so badly that Vasily could see it from across the room.

"Do you need something?" Vasily arched an eyebrow, not even sure that he should be talking to Alexey's pet. His eyes wandered to the cuffs of Ivan's suit jacket, where the pale skin of his wrists was marred with yellowing bruises in the shape of fingerprints.

"Mr. Haleyvin, I, er . . ." Ivan looked at him, swallowed, and flushed, clearing his throat awkwardly.

"I, um . . ." Ivan flushed even deeper. Vasily thanked God that Dimitri didn't blush like this, because if he did, Vasily would never get any work done. He'd just spend hours every day finding increasingly clever ways to make Dimitri turn pink.

Vasily didn't want to scare Ivan, but he also didn't want to be caught here, in what could look like a compromising situation. He made his way to the door and reached around Ivan's body for the knob.

"No, please." Ivan's eyes were wide. "I just have a—I just want to ask you a question. Nothing untoward, I promise."

Vasily stopped, his hand on the doorknob, his expression softening at the terrified look on Ivan's face. It was going to be the death of him, this protective instinct of his. "All right."

"Am I doing something wrong?" Ivan looked up at him and blinked rapidly, the way that Dimitri did when he was trying not to cry. "You're a butcher's son, and you only just arrived at the palace, but his eyes haven't left you since. He follows you everywhere, he can hardly look away. He hasn't—" The boy sniffed, and Vasily reeled. "I don't know if you know, but I'm his consort. I have his heart."

It should have been a fact, simply stated, but Ivan ended it like a question. Like he wasn't sure.

"He hasn't been as attentive since you got here," Ivan continued on. "I thought you might be able to tell me what I'm doing wrong, what you're doing right, because you seem to capture his attention so effortlessly, and I just want to be *good* for him, that's all I want."

He was a boy, Vasily realized, terrified of being alone, not knowing what he was asking for.

Ivan brushed away a tear that had started tracing its way down his cheek with the back of his hand. "And I love him. I love him with all my being. People see the iron ruler, but they don't see the Tzar who is tender in the darkness, who wants with all his heart to be loved and obeyed. And he loves me back. At least, I thought so, before you . . ."

Oh, Ivan, Vasily wanted to say. *Loving someone and possessing them are so alike, and yet worlds apart.*

"Just tell me what to do," Ivan whimpered, his voice no more than a whisper. "Please."

Vasily swallowed hard, because it could have been Dimitri standing there. Dimitri, who was traded for a fortune at twenty years old, who had probably looked even younger and more lost than this, who had been left all alone with Alexey Balakin in an unfamiliar place, who couldn't have known what to do because he had never been with anyone before.

They'd managed to save Dimitri by the grace of God. There was no one coming for Ivan.

Leave, Vasily wanted to say. *You need to leave.*

"Try being a little more confident in yourself," Vasily instead offered weakly. "I don't know. I haven't noticed the Tzar—I'm not here for that. I'm here to pray with him, that's all. I'm sorry, I don't have advice for you."

Ivan shook his head, wrapping his arms around his narrow chest. "I'm never going to be good enough for him. He's going to leave me, isn't he?"

You should pray to the Lord our God that he does, Vasily thought bitterly. *You should pray he kicks you out of the palace and never touches you again.*

But instead of saying that, he just reached up slowly, like he was trying to capture a spooked horse, and put an arm around Ivan's shoulders, the way a brother would. Ivan winced, like Vasily had accidentally touched a hidden bruise. It made bile rise up in Vasily's throat, and he lightened his touch so as not to aggravate whatever injury Alexey had caused him. "Come. Let's get you some tea." His heart broke for the boy, who had clearly fallen for a warped version of Alexey's charms. Or maybe Ivan had, like so many others, fallen in love with the promise of safety and security, and confused that for loving the man who abused him.

"I can't." Ivan shook his head. "I—I need to go. The Tzar's laboratory needs to be cleaned again, and the other servants don't put everything back exactly the way the Tzar likes it."

Vasily stilled, his arm dropping to his side. He hadn't thought to pull information out of Ivan, and he cursed himself for missing the opportunity. Of course Ivan would have seen more than anyone else in the palace save Morozov. "What's he doing there? I know he has some very interesting experiments."

"Oh!" Ivan brightened. And then he started talking, and Vasily's world fell to pieces.

✳

"I know what he's doing to them. To the Leyvin." He and Dimitri were on a wooden barge, in the middle of an enormous lake. The smell of summer honeysuckle wafted through the air in the dream, and the sun was warm on Vasily's face. A huge house—more like a small palace, really—crouched on the horizon.

It was disturbing, how pleasant it was. Vasily tensed, waiting for the horror to come.

Dimitri was hunched in on himself, seated on a cushion on the barge's deck. He was studiously averting his eyes from the shore. Vasily turned and looked towards the edge of the lake.

Alexey was standing there, his hand on the collar of a hunting dog, its tail wagging playfully. His face was unlined and carefree, and a smile played on his lips. It would have been an attractive picture, if the front of his white tunic wasn't drenched in blood, the handle of a knife sticking out from between his ribs.

Ah. So there it was, the nightmare within the gilded dream. Vasily looked away.

Dimitri sighed. "You do?"

"Yes." Vasily paused, wondering how to soften the blow. "Dima. I—" He paused, then swallowed, his saliva thick in his mouth.

There was no way this wasn't going to hurt. Better to get it over with.

"I learned something today." Vasily sighed, thankful that in dreams, his hands were steady, hiding the tremor that had taken up residence there. He grasped for Dimitri's hand, smoothing his thumb over the back of Dimitri's palm.

Dimitri closed his eyes, the veins showing blue through his lids, his face creased with pain. "Just tell me how bad it is."

"Alexey wants to create a better form of humanity." Vasily's voice was nothing more than a whisper. "A different kind of soldier. From what I've gathered, Alexey thinks that the Leyvin are the ones who can be made into this . . . creature. He's calling them *zemonyii*." Vasily inhaled raggedly. "Some mystic freak hundreds of years ago claimed to make these creatures that could control demons, being half demon themselves."

Dimitri's face had gone stark white. The tendons in his hand twitched under Vasily's thumb. "He's making more of himself."

"I don't think so." Vasily shook his head. "I think this is a kind of creature that can wield less power than Alexey can. More of a conduit, if you will, than a source of power in their own right." Vasily stole another glance at the dream-Alexey standing on the bank of the lake and shuddered. Even if he would have traded being trapped in his uncle's manor by propriety and lack of opportunity for nearly anything, Vasily knew that Dimitri had had it no easier. Dimitri had been twenty years old and a possession, his childhood a prison whose confines merely hadn't been revealed yet. His parents had raised him to be sold to Alexey Balakin, or if not Alexey, then to another person who could have been just as bad, or somehow even worse. No, Vasily wasn't sure he would trade places with Dimitri at all, even if it allowed him to swap his uncle's crueler forms of abuse for true luxury. "He sees himself as the commander of a new army, and these creatures are his generals. He breathes a bit of his power into them, and they transform into these half-human, half-demon beasts. He hasn't gotten one of them to actually listen to him yet, though. They appear to be feral."

"Thank the Lord our God," Dimitri breathed.

Vasily's breath hitched. "Do you know he thinks God is speaking directly to him? He talks about it."

"Oh." Dimitri opened his eyes and barked a humorless laugh, his eyes hard as flint. "Yes. I did. Except listen to this—it's not God. It's a demon whose name is Samael."

"What the fuck?" Vasily jerked back, but Dimitri's hand tightened in his. "How did you learn that?"

"Lada bribed a demon, which we found with a goat Mischka supposedly borrowed from a farm. But don't worry, Anna protected us with her spit." Dimitri's mouth quirked up, and Vasily's chest split through with longing as Dimitri described the entire ordeal, making Vasily laugh for what felt like the first time in years.

"We miss you too," Dimitri whispered when he was done, squeezing Vasily's hand.

Vasily fought back the urge to say, *Not in the way I miss you.*

Instead, he denied his feelings one more time and cleared his throat, continuing on with his report. "Alexey was looking at me like I was a piece of meat, even as your half-brother was hanging all over him."

Dimitri snorted. "Which one? Ivan?"

"How miraculous that you only needed one guess." Vasily rolled his eyes and smiled despite himself. "He clearly has a type."

"No, he clearly has a hatred of losing his possessions." Dimitri bit his lip, turning his face into the sun. Vasily's heart tightened at the way the light played over the planes of Dimitri's jaw. "He's doing it again, to someone who is just a boy. Ivan was always so sweet. He's not—he's not going to be able to withstand this. Please watch out for him, for me. He's going to get hurt. He wouldn't know how to guard himself against a monster."

Vasily fought back the urge to say, *You were just a boy too.*

Instead, he reached out and brushed back a stray lock of Dimitri's hair. Dimitri reached up and caught Vasily's palm, pressing it against his cheek, letting out a breath.

"I was so stupid." Dimitri's voice was hitching in the way it did when he was trying not to cry. "What a monumental cock-up I was, to think that Alexey ever loved me more than he loved power. What an idiot I was, such a fucking lovesick idiot, to think that I could ever trust him, that I would ever be *enough* for him. Because I clearly meant nothing to him at all."

Vasily couldn't help himself. "It's Alexey who was the idiot," he said quietly, "to not know what he had. He was a man holding a diamond in his hand, ignoring the way that it sparkled in the light, thinking it was nothing more than glass."

Just for a moment, he loosened his hold on his emotions and let a tiny bit of yearning leak through, because he could not bear to see

Dimitri sad, because he could not stand Dimitri feeling less than worthy because someone like Alexey had mistreated him.

Dimitri turned to him, eyes wide, tentative, his tongue darting out to lick his lips.

"Vasya—" he began at the same time as Vasily said, "Dima, I—"

And then Vasily woke up, tears in his eyes and a vise around his heart.

TWENTY-TWO

DIMITRI

Waking up brought with it a horrific sense of loss.

Dimitri let himself cry it out, hugging his pillow and wishing he knew what Vasily had been about to say. It was far too early, the sun not yet risen, and when he had exhausted himself and his heart hurt from longing, he made his way out of bed because he couldn't stay there.

The house was still quiet, and he made his way down the stairs. The only sound was a muffled, repetitive *thump* coming from the dining room. He walked in to find Annika in the middle of training, her brown skin slick with sweat, her cotton shirt damp around the collar. The muscles in her forearms stood out as she hurled the last knife from her belt into the target tacked to the wall, where it clustered with the others right around the bull's-eye.

She didn't comment on his puffy eyes or the way his breaths were still hitching as he walked into the room to stand next to her, not even sure what he wanted except to not be alone anymore.

He was relieved when she just gave him a tired half smile and went to collect the knives from the target, sticking them into her belt, save one.

"Here, you try." She flipped the blade in her hand, offering him the hilt. He took it, the weight familiar in his hand even though he hadn't trained with her in months.

He took a breath, steadying himself, remembering how to throw a blade. When he released it, the knife thudded into the target, two inches from the center.

"Again," Annika said, repositioning his hips with a light touch of her fingers. "Release it delicately, not like you're throwing an ax." She handed him another knife.

Dimitri did, and the knife struck center. He shook off the burn in his arm, his body far weaker than it had been by the end of the war.

"Good," Annika said. "Now hand-to-hand." She swung at him without warning, catching him in the cheek and making stars explode across his vision. He swallowed down the blood that spilled out of the cut his teeth had made on the inside of his cheek.

He advanced on her, and she grinned, her hair bobbing behind her where she had tied it back. "Come on, then."

He feinted right with a fist and managed to catch her low in the kidneys with his left hand when she turned. But she whirled around and jabbed an elbow into his throat, making him double over, choking. He took advantage of his moment of weakness—and her momentary distraction—to headbutt her in the ribs, and when she stumbled back, he followed it with a punch to the gut.

The sound she let out, a soft whoosh of breath, made his heart seize. "Are you all right?"

"I am. You just hit me in the wrong spot." She rubbed the place on her stomach where the bullet had gotten her, and his stomach churned in sympathy. But she grinned at him, her eyes bright. "See? Your body doesn't forget. We just need to build it back up."

"I appreciate your confidence, Anna." Dimitri used the sleeve of his shirt to wipe the blood from his lips, forcing his breathing to slow down, feeling his heart calm. She was all right. She was alive. They were all right.

He walked to the wall of the dining-room-turned-training-room and slid down it, looking at the portrait of his mother and his siblings that hung there. Looking at himself, young and innocent, immortalized in paint, stung in ways he didn't care to interrogate. And seeing the faces of his dead mother and siblings—it made this breath catch in his throat. He'd have to have one of his court remove the painting and hide it somewhere.

Annika joined him, letting her head fall to his shoulder even though his shirt was soaked through with sweat. "What are you thinking?" Her voice was gentle. "What's got you up so early?"

"A dream. With Vasya." He didn't want to share what Vasily had told him, not yet. He didn't want to have to repeat it twice, telling Annika only to have to tell the others too.

But there was something haunting his mind that only Annika would understand.

"I'm thinking about what it would be like to go back," Dimitri admitted. "To go home." He toyed with the edge of his sleeve. "Anna, I'm thinking about what it would be like to kill him."

"It would be a blessing to go home." Annika took a deep breath. "I never thought we would, not really. And I'm still not sure we'll be able to. We don't know how to get back into the country and into the palace. And then it's up to God if we can get you close enough to the bastard to kill him. But if you do kill him, it will hurt." She paused. "When I told my family I would never speak to them again if they went against us in the war, it was like ripping out my own heart. But I meant every word of it."

Dimitri didn't move a muscle. Annika so rarely spoke of the family she had forsaken that he didn't want to stop her from talking.

"I meant it because to people like you, to people like me, there's more to our lives than family, than friends, than love," Annika continued.

"There is duty, and loyalty to one's country, and the knowledge that we will do what we must to protect our people. And we failed the people of Novo-Svitsevo. We owe penance for that." She twirled a strand of hair around one blood-encrusted finger. "And maybe we'll pay with our lives. Maybe that would be for the best. Because even if we win, I'm afraid the country might be too broken to repair."

"It's not your fault, Anna." He turned to look her in the eye. "I know you blame yourself for us losing the war, but it's not your fault."

She huffed a grim laugh. "It may not be entirely my fault—he was so willing to stoop below the laws of war, below honor, that we couldn't have predicted what he would do. How could we have known that he would use peasant children as human shields at Vysoka? How could we have predicted that he'd sneak his diseased soldiers into our camps, spreading sickness? How could we have known, Dima, that he would order his soldiers to kill every innocent civilian they saw who didn't pledge allegiance to him?"

Dimitri's stomach churned at the recitation of all his husband's sins, the horror he had brought upon Novo-Svitsevo during the war.

"But it's my fault that I didn't tell you to stoop low enough to meet him," Annika said roughly. "I should have counseled you differently."

"I'm grateful," Dimitri said quietly, grasping her hand in his, "that you kept me honorable. That you kept me above the level he sank to. I wouldn't have been able to live with myself otherwise, even if we had won."

"So now we pay for the sin of honor," Annika said. "Now we put you in danger to see if we can fix our mistakes."

"I'd rather it be me in harm's way than any of you," he admitted. "My worst fear is being left alone to face what's coming. I couldn't do it by myself."

"You're the Tzar, Dima," Annika said, tilting her forehead to his. "You are the righteous hand of the Lord our God. You are doing what you must. God will protect us."

Dimitri closed his eyes and let his friend's warmth and surety sink into him. And he prayed to God that the price of winning this war wouldn't be Vasily's life. He prayed that he wouldn't have to endure another sacrifice for Novo-Svitsevo. Because deep down, in a quiet place next to his heart, where Vasily's awareness sat, he knew this would be the loss that broke him.

✱

Dimitri went back to his room to bathe and change, and then made his way to where the others were eating. Annika sat down next to him, freshly clean and frowning.

It hurt less than he thought it would, recounting what he had learned from Vasily. Knowing the three of them were there for him helped to soothe away some of the fear and to brace himself against the disgust.

"That's . . . horrifying." Mischa's mouth hung open, their hands clutching a mug of tea. "What does that even mean?"

Dimitri swallowed the eggs he'd shoveled into his mouth from the plate that Ladushka had slid in front of him as soon as he sat down. His appetite had finally returned, and he was constantly starving. "Vasya said Alexey thinks that God has commanded him to create some kind of half-demon soldier, so that he could do fuck knows what." He chased the food with a long drink of bitter black tea, grimacing at the fact that someone had added too much lemon. Ladushka, sitting next to him, poured him another cup and patted him on the back.

"And Vasya thinks he's experimenting on humans?" Mischa slid him a piece of toast, and he started chewing gamely. Their brow was furrowed.

"Why would we doubt that?" Dimitri said archly, raising an eyebrow. "Alexey's comfortable experimenting on humans. He's done it before, to himself."

"Did Vasya think they were volunteers?" Annika twirled a fork in her fingers, frowning. "I mean, not that that would make it better."

No one answered. Dimitri doubted that Alexey was asking people nicely if they would be the subjects of his horrific experiments.

"It is connected," Ladushka said, her eyes closed in concentration. She was touching her fingertips to her temples, the way she did when she was making connections between scraps of information. "This is connected to the supply lines. I just—"

Annika dropped the fork she was toying with, and Dimitri's stomach curdled. "Explain what you're thinking," he ordered.

Ladushka opened her eyes. "Weeks ago, Alexey Balakin started calling for soldiers. He is grouping them in the countryside. But you do not form an army without a reason, yes?" She looked to Annika.

Annika nodded, her hands gripping the side of the table so hard her knuckle bones showed through the skin.

"We know Alexey is calling for Leyvin to come to him. But Alexey did not want to pray with them. He wanted to prey *on* them. He is experimenting on the Leyvin. And now we know he is forming some kind of new demonic soldier, through experiments with the Holy Science. He is forming an army. And . . ."

She trailed off, looking stricken. "Only part of that army will be human," she eventually choked out. "And the supply lines, they all lead . . . everywhere. Here, to the east . . . We thought it was a feint. But it was not. If he had an army with the power of demons behind it, he could take on every nation in the world. And win. If Alexey is not stopped, it is not just us who will suffer. It is everyone, across the whole world."

"You think Alexey is making a fucking demon army," Mischa deadpanned. They squeezed their eyes shut, shaking their head. "He's making a fucking demon army, and he's going to try to take over the fucking world with it. That's his plan. To become Tzar of the world by using demons and bombs and fuck knows what else."

"He would be unstoppable," Ladushka said thinly. "He beat us the first time. This would be worse."

Dimitri's fingers dug into his skin as he gripped his thighs. "And we still don't know how to stop him."

"Also, how do we know if the demon was telling the truth about you having to be the one to kill him?" Annika bit her lip and fingered her amulet.

Dimitri shrugged. "Why would it lie?"

"Forgive me if I sound overly rational, but I personally watched Alexey Balakin take a saber through the stomach and stand up and pull it out." Mischa ticked off on their fingers. "Also, I saw him shot roughly fifteen times at Domachëvo and care not at all, have most of his body engulfed in fire during an explosion at Lobaski, and I personally shot him in the head at Klyasovo that one battle." They paused. "I know I'm not a crack shot, but when you shoot a man in the head and his skull just knits back together, it seems odd that Dima is going to find a way to kill him for good."

"Also consider, Dima," Ladushka said, her hands back on her temples, "if you get close to him and try to kill him somehow, and he does not die, I do not think you are going to survive it. His body is indestructible, and after watching him lift that horse off his own legs at the battle of Sotnikovo, I am fairly sure he is roughly twenty times stronger than the average man."

"I remember all of this," Dimitri said bitterly. "You don't need to remind me. If we're going to kill him, we only have one chance." He looked around at his court. "So we need to find a way to weaken him first. I would say we should go back to the library, but I don't think we're going to find the answers we need quickly enough, searching through all those books." He shook his head. "I think maybe we should ask the librarian himself."

"Fine." Annika bit her lip. "But if Alexey is turning the Leyvin into demon-creatures—or trying to, anyway—isn't Vasya in danger? Shouldn't you tell him to sneak out?"

Shouldn't I? Dimitri thought, the fuzzy memory of Vasily sharing something with him, an emotion he couldn't quite place, coming back to him from last night's dream. All he wanted to do was beg Vasily to come back. All he wanted to do was spend another night in his arms. It was as if something within him had cracked, Vasily filling the fissures that Alexey had left behind. He had woken up crying, feeling like he had been robbed of something he'd never known he'd had. But he'd buried it deep down within himself before he came down to see the others, because if he thought about putting a name to what he and Vasily shared, right now, while the other man was in danger, he didn't know if he'd survive the realization.

Yes, he wanted nothing more than to tell Vasily to come back to him.

But Dimitri looked at Annika, at the worry etched in the lines around her mouth, and remembered what it was like to be Tzar. "No," he said, watching her shoulders sag at the same time Ladushka smiled grimly and Mischa's eyes burned with pride. "He stays, for as long as possible. Vasya said Alexey hasn't mentioned experimenting on him directly yet. He can protect himself. He knows what he's doing."

A grim silence followed, but no dissent. Dimitri's shoulders relaxed marginally when he realized they weren't going to challenge him.

Annika raised her teacup, and Mischa and Ladushka followed suit. "If I die first," Annika said.

"I'll tell you the secrets of heaven," Dimitri finished, and drank. "Because you are my court, and my friends, and my family. Because you are the ones who never wavered, who pulled me back from the brink even when I was trying to gather up the courage to fling myself off the damned roof." He drained the last of his tea. "And for that, I will always be grateful."

✳

Dimitri himself was the one to pound on Aleksandr's door this time. It was jerked open with such force that he almost fell into the magician, who was covered in some kind of oily liquid that gave off the smell of rotting fish.

"You always interrupt my experiments," Aleksandr grumbled. "The head said you'd be by today. You couldn't have come half an hour later?"

"No," Dimitri said. "We need information again." He fingered what he'd put into the pocket of his coat before they left. If they were going to get the magician to tell them what they needed to know, Dimitri had a feeling that they'd have to give up something far more important than some trinkets.

"Come in, then." Aleksandr stepped aside.

Dimitri and his court ducked past the magician into the hall and retraced the path they had taken on their first visit. Aleksandr ambled into the living room behind them, grumbling. "I suppose you won't go away until you've got what you came for?"

"Precisely," Dimitri said coolly. He cocked his head, looking at the librarian. He had to frame his query in such a way that it wouldn't immediately be apparent that he was trying to go after Alexey. "If I wanted to live as long as I could," he said slowly, "I would know how to do that from your library." He licked his lips. "But what I'm concerned about are the ways in which my enemies might still find vulnerabilities to exploit. The gaps in the armor of immortality, if you will."

Aleksandr shrugged, and Dimitri's heart sank. "Not my area of expertise."

Dimitri quietly took the ring out of his pocket and held it aloft. It felt like it weighed a hundred pounds, and his hand shook. "Do you know what this is?"

Aleksandr's eyebrows shot up his forehead, and he reached out for the ring. Dimitri bit his lip and had to keep from snatching it back as he watched Aleksandr turning it over in his hand.

"You said you threw it in the Nevka," Annika whispered from behind him. "You said you got rid of it, Dima."

"Well, I lied," he hissed through gritted teeth. "And it's a good thing I kept it."

Mischa rescued him by shushing Annika and putting a hand on Dimitri's shoulder, anchoring him.

"For a Tzar's wedding ring, for the vise around his heart, I can tell you that the angel Gavril might know something. I've called upon him once or twice." Aleksandr pocketed the ring, and Dimitri could have cried, watching it vanish. "Or rather, I've tried to. If he doesn't find you righteous, he won't come, he'll just give you the worst head-ache of your life. I've heard the best time to petition him is *havdalah*."

It was an unsatisfying answer, but at least it was something. And it wouldn't do to spend yet another futile day in the library, wasting time. Dimitri motioned to his court and brushed past Aleksandr. But he was stopped by a rustling. He paused and swiveled around. The head set into the small mahogany table was shaking off its cover, blinking slowly at him.

"You are going to suffer," the head said, its voice echoing strangely around the room. "You are going to suffer, more than any living man has suffered. The pain will almost break you. But you cannot allow it to. You cannot give in."

Dimitri shivered, his sudden spike of fear making the room spin. And without another word, he turned on his heel and left, his friends at his back.

TWENTY-THREE

ALEXEY

Alexey was only half listening to the report by his court physician on the cases of dysentery plaguing the countryside, which the woman was saying had claimed tens of thousands of lives.

Ordinarily, he would have cared. Ordinarily, he would have sent his civil engineers to the affected areas and made sure that the peasants' drinking water was routed from the nearest safe stream, that they had clear wells uncontaminated by the dead. Ordinarily, he might have even ordered that the villages be fitted with indoor plumbing, as a show of his generosity. He'd found that nothing made loyal subjects like water that came out of a tap.

Usually, when he held court, nothing evaded his notice. There was no detail too insignificant to matter in the exercise of power, because empires were held together by the smallest of things.

But now, he was consumed with thoughts of the world that was to come. Excitement was building in his chest, along with hope and trepidation. So much rested on the next crucial phase of his experiments. So much was dependent on his ability to craft generals who could help him hold back the tide of power from the middle world.

He was only one man, and he could not control all of God's demons alone.

Finally, the woman stopped talking, and he muttered something to Morozov about dealing with the situation. He signed the stack of orders and proclamations that Ivan laid out in front of him, his eyes barely skimming the words. And when at last his advisers had stopped prattling on about the running of the empire and filed out of the council chamber, he stood and flexed his stiff fingers. He called for a palace steward, who snapped to attention in front of him.

"Take me to him," he commanded. The steward nodded and led Alexey to Mikhail.

He was sitting in one of the palace parlors, a book open on his lap, staring out of the window to the city beyond. His suit was gray this time, and Mikhail had forgone a tie, his collar gaping open at the throat. He was perfectly still, tense, a deer with its ears pricked in the forest, waiting for the next crack of a branch that signaled a hunter was near.

"Hello, Mikhail," he said smoothly, noting the way the man first jumped, then settled and relaxed when he turned and saw it was Alexey.

Good. Alexey was pleased to see Mikhail's trust in him growing.

"What is on your mind?" He crossed the room to Mikhail, his footsteps soft on the carpet. This parlor was decorated all in delicate pinks, from the rug to the paper on the walls to the silk curtains framing the windows. The color cheered him. It had been one of his favorites, before he'd discarded his wardrobe for the black garments he had come to favor. He flexed his hands, hoping the warmth of this parlor's two fires would work motion back into them after hours of holding a pen.

"Your joints, do they hurt?" Mikhail gazed at him, and Alexey quickly used the folds of his cloak to conceal the evidence of his weakness.

"No," he said brusquely.

"I told you that mine did, *Moy Tzar.*" Mikhail dipped a chin at him. "I can see it in the way you stand. You favor your right side."

For the first time since his rebirth, Alexey felt himself flush with embarrassment. Mikhail could truly unbalance him.

"I do," he admitted. "When I was reborn, I did not anticipate the way it would change my body. The Lord my God blessed me with strength and speed, and my body heals faster than any man's could without the grace of God." He pulled out a knife from his belt and slashed his palm, studying the blood that welled there. "But the one thing I did not anticipate was that I would come back to the realm of the living with blood that was cold." He turned his hand over to show Mikhail that, in moments, the cut had become nothing more than a shiny pink scar. "So yes, my joints are often stiff, especially in the mornings, when I write for a long period of time. Without warmth, my body suffers."

"Take a cloth bag," Mikhail said, fascination written on his face. "Fill it with barley husks and lavender flowers, and the leaves too. Put it by the fire, and when it warms up you can put it on anything that ails you. The weight and the heat will help."

He reached out for Alexey, almost as if he could not stop himself. Alexey let him caress a finger with trembling hands, the heat of Mikhail's skin almost unbearable.

Mikhail looked him directly in the eye, a challenge.

Alexey sucked in a breath. He flipped his palm and grabbed the other man's hand, pulling him up to standing, the book on Mikhail's lap thudding onto the floor between them so loudly that Alexey was surprised the whole palace did not come running.

They were almost of a height. Mikhail's eyes were flecked with gold, his cheeks flushing a deep bronze. His pulse pounded in his wrist, resting against Alexey's.

Alexey leaned forward a hair's breadth, cupped the back of Mikhail's head, and brought their lips to touch.

There was nothing in the kiss, no passion, no heat, no desire. But Mikhail must have felt *something* because his body melted against Alexey's, his lips parting. Alexey fought back a gag at how wrong it felt, someone without Dimitri's delicate form kissing him.

For the first time, it felt the smallest bit like he was being disloyal to his husband.

Alexey drew back hastily but had the good sense to lick his lips suggestively, then shake his head as if he was mastering himself. Mikhail was panting slightly. But he couldn't continue, so he'd have to change tack.

Alexey turned and sat down in an armchair by the fire. "I need something," he said, leaning back in the chair, crossing a foot over his knee, affecting nonchalance since he wasn't sure he could keep faking interest.

Mikhail bit his lip, then sat down opposite Alexey.

"What do you need?" Mikhail raised his eyebrows.

Alexey decided now was as good a time as any to tell the truth. "I am looking to create generals who will share a piece of my power. Soldiers who are able to whisper to God the way I can. I share a piece of my soul with them, and they are inexorably linked to me. They will help me rule the new world."

He paused, and then stood, crossing over to where Mikhail sat.

"I have not known you long, but I sense you are just the person I have been searching for. Someone who can bolster me. Someone with a spine of steel, a fearless heart, and above all a love for Novo-Svitsevo and its people." His knees touched Mikhail's, and he reached down to cup the other man's chin in his hand. "Mikhail Haleyvin, I wish for you to join me as a general in my army."

The man's lips parted. "But I don't . . . I mean, I didn't serve in the army, I don't know anything about war. How can I be a general? I'm just a peasant. I'm just a butcher's son."

"This is a different kind of war." Alexey chuckled. "And a different kind of army. You would need to accept my power within you, to become a *zemonyii*, in order to serve."

"A . . . what?" Mikhail was staring at Alexey, transfixed.

"A *zemonyii*," Alexey explained. "Something more than a man. Someone who has accepted the Holy Science into them, and allowed it to transform them."

"I . . ." Mikhail's brow creased, and a spark of worry burst to life within Alexey, the fear that he had miscalculated with Mikhail, misunderstood his desires. Alexey's muscles bunched, ready to break the other man's neck if he tried to escape, the way so many of the others had, the ones he had neglected to restrain before he offered them a chance at glory.

Mikhail licked his lips. "Would it hurt?"

Ah. A normal question, for a human who feared pain and the unknown. A part of him envied Mikhail's innocence.

"I can show you one of the experiments, if you like," he offered gently. He ignored the fact that there were no Leyvin left to experiment with. He sank to his knees and bracketed Mikhail's body with his arms, resting his hands on the chair's armrests. "When I underwent my own experiment, there was no pain. Only the bliss of communing with the Lord my God."

Mikhail nodded, his eyes wide and dark. "And what would happen to me . . . after?"

Alexey reached out to tuck a stray curl of hair away from Mikhail's forehead, trying to imbue the gesture with tenderness. All he could see in his mind's eye was Dimitri's hair, mussed with sleep, falling into his eyes. "You would stand beside me as we faced down the enemies of our country one by one. You would have access to power beyond your wildest reckoning. You would be able to protect the ones you love."

"I have none of those left." Mikhail's tone was bitter, and his eyes went hard. "They all died in the war."

"Then avenge them." Alexey moved his hands to grip the other man's knees, feeling the strength of the corded muscle there. "Use your pain as the country's protection, Mikhail. Make sure your agony is never shared by another Novo-Svitsevan."

Mikhail drew in a shuddering breath and met Alexey's eyes. "Okay," he said, nodding. "When do we start?"

Alexey made sure none of his satisfaction showed on his face and stood. "Soon. But for now, I must pray, and you must continue to enjoy yourself."

He left Mikhail as he had found him, staring out the window, as he went to seek communion with God.

*

Alexey sent away his servants, barred the door to his chambers, and spent the afternoon in prayer.

He no longer begged and pleaded with God to answer his calls. He knew that God would, because God always whispered in his ear that Alexey was His chosen son.

Because you are. God caressed his heart, and his mind, with a sensuous touch. *Because you were the only one who dared to use my Holy Science to make yourself anew.*

I showed you who I was, Alexey reminded God. *I showed you my worth.*

And that is the difference between you and the rest of man, God said. *It is why only you can be their master, their father, their Tzar.*

Alexey reached for the void, held in the safety of God's arms. It was responding to his touch more now, its power awakening when he asked for it, instead of pushing out towards the edges of him when he lost control. A hand reached through, and he grasped it, pulling. A curl of power emerged from his mouth, ghosting along the floorboards in a hint of shadow. A beetle was crawling along the floorboards, and at the shadow's touch it curled into itself, convulsed, and stopped moving.

What is it, truly? Alexey asked the question that his study had not answered. *What is the power that lives inside of me, the Lord my God?*

That, my son, said God, *is death. It is with death you create, and it is with death that you spread oblivion.*

Alexey's heart stilled at the truth of it, the way it echoed in his bones. But then his head snapped up, his connection to God broken by the sudden pounding on his door.

He got up from his knees, pulling off his prayer shawl and folding it with agitated hands, his teeth grinding together. He and God had so much to discover, and he was never going to be able to master the mysteries of the Divine if people kept interrupting him.

The pounding got louder as Alexey yanked the door open with a snarl. "I told you to leave me alone."

"*Moy Tzar,*" Morozov said, his eyes wild and his cheeks flushed. "This simply could not wait." He was clutching a book, one of the registers of the Leyvin bloodline from the inscription on the cover. "I have news. Wonderful news. My research has borne fruit at last."

Alexey sighed, but let him in. "What research do you speak of?"

Morozov put the book down on Alexey's writing desk and flipped it open to a page he had marked with a strip of leather, pointing eagerly at one of the entries. "*Moy Tzar*, you know how eager I am to serve you, in every way. And so, in my personal time, I have been poring through my family tree, trying to link my heritage with the blood of the Leyvin. And for weeks I have been disappointed, because none in my father's line bore the right blood to render me useful to you. But now, I have traced my mother's line. And here, you can see, back in my heritage, my great-great-great-grandmother married a Leyvin." He bowed deeply. "*Moy Tzar*, I beg of you, use me for your general. There are none more devoted to you than I."

Ah. Perhaps this was a welcome interruption indeed.

Alexey smiled at Morozov's devotion, at his desire to serve, and he grasped his chancellor by the shoulders, peering into his eyes. "You have done well, Chancellor Morozov. Very well. I accept your offer, because you are right—I have no servant more loyal than you."

"When can we perform the experiment?" Morozov was shaking with anticipation under Alexey's hands, his eyes gleaming.

Alexey thanked God for putting the opportunity he needed before him to find not one, but two perfect generals for his army. To offer Mikhail Haleyvin a chance to see the power that awaited him. Alexey swallowed hard. "We do it tonight."

✶

"Are you ready?" Alexey offered a hand to Mikhail, who had set down his fork and knife on his now-clean plate.

He had watched Mikhail eat and engaged in a discussion of what the Holy Science said on the topic of resurrection. Alexey had forgotten how much he enjoyed teaching others, how satisfying it was. Mikhail sometimes had trouble understanding the language of science, but that was not surprising of a butcher's son with little formal education. What was more encouraging was that Mikhail had asked a multitude of questions—about the Holy Science, about his plans for the future of Novo-Svitsevo, even about his own resurrection—and had listened attentively when he'd explained the mechanics of the resurrection dome, the intricacies of the process, the way he had drifted and communed with *Malakh ha-mavet*, the angel of death, bargaining to come back to his body and return to life.

Mikhail grasped his hand and rose. "Yes, I am." His gaze searched Alexey's face. "You will be turning someone into a . . ."

"*Zemonyii*," Alexey supplied. "Yes. My chancellor, Morozov, one of my most loyal supporters. He wishes for the transformation to occur tonight, so that you might be able to witness it and be inspired." He threaded Mikhail's hand through his arm and steered him out of the dining room.

The other man opened his mouth, then closed it. His hand tightened on Alexey's arm as they walked down the palace hallway.

"I was nervous too, when I decided to become something more." It was important to confide in Mikhail, to soothe his fears. "But it was worth it, in the end. To serve my country. You understand."

He nodded tightly. "I do."

Mikhail didn't say anything else for the rest of the walk to the experimentation chamber. When Alexey guided him down the stone stairs and into the small space, Mikhail seemed to shrink into himself. Alexey patted the man's arm to comfort him, and then steered him to a chair in the corner.

"Don't move," he said, sitting Mikhail down with a firm hand on his shoulder. "No matter what you see. I wouldn't want you to be harmed."

Morozov was already waiting for him, stripped to the waist. He'd bound his own ankles to the chair, and one of his wrists. Alexey bent over to fasten the other one. "Are you sure?" He leveled Morozov with an assessing glance.

"Absolutely," Morozov replied, certainty written into the set of his mouth and the square of his shoulders. "It is my most fervent wish to serve you, *Moy Tzar*."

Alexey withdrew. "Then we begin."

As he had with the rest of the Leyvin, Alexey knelt down and wrapped himself in a prayer shawl, kissing the fringes before beginning to pray. He took a knife from the table next to them and sliced open the pad of his thumb, drawing the ritual symbols on Morozov's chest with his own blood, then closed his eyes.

This time, the shadow that emerged from him felt different. The darkness was not the cold of death, but the comfort of a night spent in Dimitri's embrace. He felt, rather than saw, when it connected with Morozov's chest and pierced his heart. Alexey's power vibrated between them like a tether, like a living thing, before fading away as Morozov absorbed it completely.

For a second, nothing happened. Alexey stayed still on the floor, the stone bruising his knees, praying silently to God to fulfill his desire, to make Morozov into the perfect servant. There was no motion in the room as the last of his power entered Morozov, no sound, no indication that the experiment had been anything other than a failure.

He drew in a deep, steadying breath, fighting the way his limbs wanted to shake with the tension of the moment.

Alexey opened his eyes. Morozov had not screamed. Alexey knew then that he had not fought the transition, had accepted it as completely as Alexey had accepted his rebirth.

Morozov looked at Alexey with black eyes that shone with intelligence. He looked down at his hands, which now ended in scaled fingers tipped with claws, the skin mottled with stark black veins. Alexey gazed at them in wonder.

This was no raving creature. This was the general he had hoped to create.

Blessed be you, the Lord my God, Alexey prayed, gratitude welling up from the depths of his soul.

"*Moy Tzar*," said the thing that had been Morozov, his tongue darting out to lick blackened lips. "I feel . . ."

"Like you are finally whole," Alexey said, reaching out to unbuckle the straps. He felt none of the fatigue that had plagued him with the other transformations. Instead, he felt invigorated. Like he had just brought a child into the world, instead of having fought a monster. This power of creation was precious, not a chore.

"We must test if it worked," Morozov said, standing on his newly avian feet, his talons scratching against the stone of the floor. "*Moy Tzar*, please, I must know if I can serve you."

"Of course." Alexey called on the void within him and tore a rift in the fabric of the world with one hand. The rip was the purest black, revealing nothing of what was beyond, thrumming with power and warping the room around the edges where it touched the material plane. A demon shuddered out of it and into awareness, its spirit rebelling against the call to the lower world. This one was small, winged, with a hunched back and a snarling face, slashed by a mouth glimmering with needle-sharp teeth. It screeched, a grating sound not meant for human ears, and started to lunge for Alexey, wanting to punish the one who summoned it forth from the comforts of the middle world.

It was always this way when he called forth whole demons, powerful demons, creatures that could think and feel and disobey, instead of just the obedient, powerless demons like the one in his study. These fought him, and yet he needed them for the war he was to fight. His power alone was not enough.

Alexey flexed his fingers, ready to return the demon to the middle world if he needed to, but then Morozov held out a hand and the demon stilled.

"Come," Morozov grated, and the demon went.

It sat by his side, still, like a hound attending to its master.

Morozov looked at Alexey, with eyes that were now black like Alexey's own, and grinned wolfishly. "They answer to me."

"Because you are one of them," Alexey said. "You are not a master, or a father, as I am, someone they rage against for their captivity. You are a spirit that comforts them, because you are alike."

The *zemonyii* that had been Morozov knelt and kissed the hem of his cape. "I thank you, *Moy Tzar*, for this gift of power. I will use it to serve you and to protect our country."

Alexey turned back to Mikhail, who was still in the corner. His body was rigid, his hands gripping the arms of the chair, his mouth hanging open.

"Do you see the power of God, now?" Alexey went to him and caressed his cheek. "Do you see what the Holy Science can do for us? For Novo-Svitsevo?"

Mikhail didn't speak, but nodded. There were tears gathering in the edges of his eyes. Alexey could understand being so overwhelmed by awe, by reverence in the face of God's power, that words escaped him. It was how he'd felt when he'd first discovered the experiment that led him to eternal life.

"Come," he said gently. "Let's take you to bed."

*

When he had guided Mikhail back to his guest rooms, and then instructed Morozov to remain secreted in his chambers until his transformation was announced to the court, there was one last thing Alexey needed to do. He rubbed his hands together, striding down the corridor with determination. Everything was going right. Soon he would have the power to unify the fractured court, to repair this shattered country. To defend it from all the enemies that would seek to destroy it.

He just needed one more thing to bolster his power over Novo-Svitsevo.

Alexey found Ivan playing cards with several of the other Abramovich bastard children in one of the disused parlors. "Ivan, come," he said. "We have something to celebrate."

Ivan abandoned the cards in his hand and stood up as the others rose and bowed. "*Moy Tzar*," he said, dipping his head in greeting and then blushing furiously. "I am always happy to celebrate with you—it is far more thrilling than even our monthly poker night."

Alexey put a hand on the small of Ivan's back as Ivan called out his goodbyes and steered him towards the royal bedchambers. "I performed the transformation on Morozov tonight," he said, once they were safely ensconced behind closed doors.

He didn't miss the flash of hurt that crossed Ivan's face before the boy smoothed it away. "And?"

"It worked, Ivan," he breathed. "It worked. Soon, so soon, we will be able to stand strong against the Free States, against the western provinces, against Urushka, against anyone who seeks to defy us. Once they see what we can do, no one will dare."

He reached down to kiss Ivan, but Ivan pulled away. "Are you sure you will not allow me the honor, *Moy Tzar*?" Ivan paused and looked at him through the fringe of his lashes.

Alexey disregarded the plea. "Not you, Ivan," he said. He pointed to the bed, and Ivan obediently sat on it. "Never you. I have a role far more important for you than becoming a *zemonyii*." He paused, ignoring the tiny piece of him that whispered that this was a betrayal. "It is time that I have someone to rule by my side."

He crossed over to his desk and slid open a drawer, pulling out the proclamation he had drawn up and signed a week earlier, the conclusion of the plan he'd formed when he'd first brought Ivan to his side.

"No small part of this country still feels loyalty to your family's house." A pang went through his chest at the admission.

He swallowed and took out the small box that had been lying underneath the document, tucking it into the pocket of his cloak.

"Of course, your father's house has been decimated. But not entirely." He turned and handed the proclamation to Ivan, who scanned it, brow furrowed. "It is so fortunate that the former Tzar Abram saw fit to legitimize his favorite bastard son before his death."

Ivan looked up at him, his mouth open. "This . . . this is not real. My father never acknowledged me before his death." He bit his lip, but his eyes were glassy. "Not in that way. I don't even carry his name."

"What does it mean for something to be real?" Alexey raised an eyebrow and smirked. "If the former Tzar Abram hadn't wanted me to forge his signature, he shouldn't have left so many samples of his handwriting lying around the palace."

Ivan put a hand to his mouth, stifling a sob. Alexey came to sit beside him, wrapping an arm around his lover. "Ivan *Abramovich*," he said gently, feeling the shudder that wracked Ivan's smaller form. "Your role is to take up your brother's mantle and rule beside me. Your role is to unite this country, to show them that the house of Balakin is joined with your brother's house, and that to support me is to support the former regime."

"Are you—" Ivan's eyes were wet with tears, but were shining with hope and love.

"I am." Alexey pulled the box from his cloak pocket, opening the lid and withdrawing the ring he'd had commissioned, a solid circle of garnet, the deep red of blood. "I am taking your hand in marriage, Lord Ivan Abramovich, sole heir to the house of Abramovich, ruler of the province of Nizhniy Karevskiy, ancestral home of the Tzar. I bestow upon you all of your brother's lands and fortunes. When we marry, you will be styled Tzar Consort Ivan Alexeyev, Lord of Nizhniy Karevskiy."

He slid the ring onto Ivan's finger and ignored how, this time, this second time, he felt nothing but a vague sense of guilt and satisfaction that his plotting was coming to fruition. He'd known that Ivan wouldn't be able to resist saying yes, not when the only thing the boy wanted in life was his love.

"Would you—" Ivan was truly crying now, and Alexey deigned to wipe away his tears. "Would you be doing this if I wasn't my father's son?"

No, Alexey thought. "Yes, of course. Don't be ridiculous."

Ivan turned to him at that and kissed his hand, then claimed his mouth, his hands scrabbling against the buttons of Alexey's coat. Alexey grinned and pushed the other man down, pinning him to the bed while he divested himself of his clothing.

"There have been so many victories tonight," Alexey purred, stripping off Ivan's pants. "But there's still one last thing for me to conquer." And he proceeded to lose himself in the body of his second husband-to-be and banished all memories of Dimitri to where they belonged. In the past, along with all of Alexey's weaknesses.

TWENTY-FOUR

VASILY

"Watching him do it was disgusting. Really fucking disturbing, in truth. If I had any doubt about his competence with his Holy Science, I don't now." Vasily sat on the ledge of the second story of the Great Shul of Rav-Mikhailburg, looking down into the congregation. It was a new vantage point for this dream, and he watched the edges of the scene blur and warp as dream-Dimitri, below him, made his way down the aisle.

"I never did. Not for a second." His Dimitri swung his legs like a child, peering down to the first level. "Those clothes were so covered in gold thread that I could barely bend my legs to walk. The first wedding was better, the one where it was just him and me."

Vasily snorted. "That's what you get, for being royal. Try being a part of the impoverished nobility, where we'd sell our souls for enough money to fix our leaky roofs."

Dimitri scowled. "Splendor has a price," he snapped. "Try relieving yourself in that getup. Near impossible."

"I could have relieved you." Vasily did his best leer and made an obscene hand gesture. Dimitri smacked him on the arm.

The contact sobered Vasily. Touching Dimitri, even in dreams, made him ache. He hadn't been away from Dimitri for this long since they'd met, and his heart hurt at the loss, almost like it needed Dimitri nearby to keep on beating. "I didn't know this was your second wedding."

"It was," Dimitri said softly. "We were married two days after my parents died, the night before we set out for Rav-Mikhailburg. It was when I took his name, even though by right, he should have taken mine. I went from Dimitri Abramovich to Dimitri Alexeyev." He snorted. "I was such a hopeless romantic, then. But I was sad, and he was there, and in the moment it felt right."

The way he said it sent something stuttering in Vasily's chest. The way it sounded almost like *regret.*

And then, because he was an asshole of the highest order, and because he might very well die soon anyway if Alexey found him out, and also because something in him wouldn't rest until he knew, he turned to Dimitri and asked, "Would you do it again? A third time?"

"Do what?" Dimitri hadn't taken his eyes off his dream-self, still making its way down the aisle to where Alexey Balakin stood, an ermine cape around his shoulders, a grin playing around the edges of his mouth.

"Marry him." The words tasted like ash on Vasily's tongue as he gestured down to the scene below. "Knowing what you know now."

He'd always told himself that he was at peace with the fact that Dimitri still clearly loved Alexey, even after all the other man had put him through. The abuse, the manipulation, the lies, the war. Except that wasn't true, because honestly, Vasily had never understood it— the way Dimitri, a good man, could waste his heart on someone so obviously unworthy. Someone who looked at his sharp edges and wanted to grind them down, instead of helping him hone himself into a blade. Someone who wanted to mold Dimitri into a different person, instead of treasuring him for who he already was.

"I was never free to choose." Dimitri's voice was low, and thick, and the way he said it made Vasily's throat tighten. "But if I had been,

I think . . ." He trailed off, biting his lip, looking downwards again. A pang of sympathy went through Vasily's chest, because he had also never been free to choose, and he reached out and grabbed Dimitri's hand, intertwining their fingers on the cold surface of the marble, Dimitri's skin burning hot even in Vasily's dream.

"I think," Dimitri tried again after breathing in, then out, "that maybe, if I had been free to choose, I would have chosen a man like you."

Vasily jerked his head around in surprise. Dimitri's eyes were rimmed with tears. Vasily reached out to brush them away with a thumb, but the dream was fading at the edges and by the time he touched Dimitri's skin, the other man was gone.

✴

It was cruel, that instead of Dimitri, Vasily got Alexey instead.

He was even more desperate now to determine what Alexey was doing, so that he could go home to Dimitri. So that they could talk about what Dimitri had meant, and not in a fucking dream that would dissolve like smoke right at the most important part.

Vasily dressed in burgundy, the color deliberately alluring against his skin, and left the first few buttons of his shirt open. Then he threw a heavy coat over his shoulders and went to go hunt down a monster.

The gardens of the palace at Rav-Mikhailburg were luxurious, even in the approach of winter. Long lines of neatly clipped box hedges enclosed the paths, opening to reveal small clearings framed by sculptures, fountains in their centers. Even though the plants had been mostly covered over to protect them against the frost, Vasily could swear he smelled a faint hint of the roses that would normally fill the gardens with a riot of color.

He closed his eyes and let the icy air scour his cheeks, washing away some of the disgust over what he was about to do. Then Vasily set off for the southern arbor, where he knew Alexey had a habit of lurking early in the morning. After what he'd seen last night, watching a man turn into something else, something dangerous, he needed to understand exactly what Alexey had in mind for Novo-Svitsevo. But Alexey wasn't the kind of person to simply tell his plans to anyone—he'd need to be sure that Vasily was on his side.

Which wouldn't be a problem, because Mikhail Haleyvin was obsessed with Alexey and greedy for the chance to serve him. And if Vasily could do anything, it was play a part.

"The gardens are usually nicer," Alexey said, without turning around as Vasily snuck up behind him. "I hope you will have a chance to see them come spring."

As if demons would stop to appreciate the flowers, Vasily thought, fighting not to roll his eyes. *Or care one fucking bit about a garden.*

When Alexey turned around, his cheeks were tinged with blue, not the healthy pink that would normally signal a flush of blood given the cold. There was tension in the set of his shoulders and around his mouth that made Vasily think he was nervous. Vasily dipped his head. "If you would have me, *Moy Tzar*, it would be my honor."

He flicked his eyes up through his lashes, throwing a heated gaze Alexey's way. He hoped Alexey never realized that he was simply copying every small action that Dimitri made when he was aroused.

It worked. Alexey's lips parted, and his tongue flicked out to lick them. "I would have you," he replied, his voice husky. But then the tension returned to his face. "Have you thought on what you saw last night?"

Ah. Alexey was nervous that he—Mikhail—would refuse his offer.

"You must be truly blessed by God, to be able to create in such a way." Vasily picked his gaze up, looking into Alexey's eyes and arching his neck, baring his throat. A subconscious sign of trust in the presence of a predator.

"You approve, then," he said, looking at the smooth arc of skin Vasily had bared. "Of my . . . methods."

Fuck no. "*Moy Tzar* is blessed by God." Vasily forced himself to take three steps closer, until he could reach out and touch Alexey. "Of course I approve of your methods."

Alexey stilled and studied him for a moment. Eventually, he offered Vasily his arm. "Walk with me."

Vasily wound his hand through the crook of Alexey's arm, resting his fingers on the iron-hard muscle there, wishing he'd been given gloves so that he didn't have to ruin the innocence of his poor fingers by actually touching Alexey's bicep.

Alexey led them down the garden path, into the open section before the hedge maze. The wind was fiercer here, and Alexey flipped the edge of his cloak around Vasily's shoulders. He had no body heat to warm them with, but the cape did cut the bitterness of the air, and Vasily forced himself to melt into Alexey's side, the way Dimitri did when he was cold and wanted comfort.

"I do not just want generals," he said after long moments of silence, the only noise the crunching of the gravel under their boots, steering them into the hedge maze. "I want leaders."

Vasily ignored the instinctive panic growing in his gut at being led into a secluded area with Alexey Balakin. He forced himself to breathe in through his nose and out through his mouth, then quirked an eyebrow up, the way Dimitri would have done. He opened his mouth, but feinted at the last minute, like he was demurring.

Alexey chuckled. "You want to know why."

"Yes, *Moy Tzar*." Vasily wondered if Alexey knew how easy he was to manipulate with a few stolen glances. Likely he did not. Habitual manipulators always thought they were above the influences of others.

Alexey stopped them and pivoted, forcing Vasily to drop his arm. He backed Vasily up until the hedges were pricking the back of his neck. They were almost of a height, and so as Alexey took his hands and gripped them, hard, Vasily had no choice but to look directly into his eyes.

They weren't black, he realized, not up close. They were the deepest red that Vasily had ever seen, the color of pooled blood. Like the vessels had burst, leaving the irises of Alexey's eyes flooded.

Vasily did not flinch. Instead he sighed, letting the lids of his eyes flutter shut, just a man ecstatic to be shown sexual favor and attention by the most powerful person in Novo-Svitsevo. His heartbeat picked up when Alexey pressed a tender kiss to the curve of his jaw, but that was good too. Alexey would misread it and think it was from arousal, not revulsion.

"I want to make us strong," Alexey whispered when he pulled back. He was panting. "And I need men like you to do it."

Vasily almost returned the kiss, but Dimitri never would have initiated. Instead, he stepped forward, bringing them even closer, although not before subtly shifting his coat to block Alexey from realizing that his cock was about as interested in this encounter as in being cut right off.

Vasily rested his head on Alexey's shoulder, tilting his gaze up to catch Alexey's. "You are already so strong," he whispered.

Alexey looked vaguely horrified for a flash of a second, and Vasily almost backed up, but then Alexey pasted a smirk on his face.

Interesting. So Alexey wasn't truly interested either, merely playing yet another part. Vasily felt his shoulders relax marginally. Maybe he could avoid having to consummate his ruse in the royal bedchamber.

Alexey dropped his hands and instead picked up Vasily's chin, tilting his head back up, brushing a stone-cold thumb against Vasily's studiously clean-shaven jaw. Neither Dimitri nor Ivan ever let stubble grow, and so Vasily had been shaving his off every morning. Now he was glad. He closed his eyes, leaning into the touch. He didn't know how Dimitri had done it, sleeping with a corpse for months and months after Alexey's resurrection. Vasily wouldn't have been able to bear it.

"My goal has always been to protect the country," Alexey said slowly. "To see its people safe from harm." He paused, and Vasily opened his eyes to watch Alexey's throat bob as he swallowed, a look of what Vasily would have sworn was regret crossing Alexey's face. "The war was unfortunate. It truly was. But Dimitri Alexeyev was too weak to confront the threats we face. From the Urushkins, who want our resources. From the nobility of the western provinces, who can rebel and leave us without access to trade. From the anarchists within our borders, who get help from the governments of the Free States. From the enemies we don't yet know, from the enemies that haven't yet been born."

Vasily swallowed what he wanted to say, which was *You're a paranoid fuckwit, you cockslit of a dirtbag*, and instead just nodded encouragingly.

"I am going to do the impossible." He paused, then lowered both of his hands to grasp Vasily's upper arms, like he was afraid Vasily would bolt. "I am going to merge our world—the lower world—with the middle world of demonkind. There is an entire realm of power that the Lord my God created, that we can harness, if only we dare to."

Thank fucking God he was being held in place, because Vasily's knees buckled without his permission. Alexey took his weight, frowning. "Are you all right?"

"I am awed," Vasily managed to choke out, "by your plan. Tell me more of it." He prayed that he sounded sincere. Or at least overcome with emotion, of a good kind.

Terror was flooding through him like ice. Alexey was going to tear the fucking world apart and doom them all.

Alexey smiled, and it was chilling. "It means that I will open a permanent rift between our world and theirs, and allow them to come through that rift to serve me."

"Is that . . . safe?" Vasily replied like an idiot, and not like a spy trying to tease out as much information as he could.

But Alexey just chuckled and tapped Vasily's nose, like he was some kind of disobedient child. "Of course it will be, unless I lose control. Which I will not."

Vasily's mind raced. If Alexey let an *army* of demons—an untold number of actual *demons*—into the world and he was the only one who could control them . . . no one would ever be able to kill him. He would be the only thing standing between humanity and whatever countless horrors lurked in the middle world. If he could even be that.

Every scary bedtime story about demons Vasily had ever heard came back to him in a rush. None of them were about how demons were good, kind and lovely dining companions. Everyone in the world was liable to wake up the morning after Alexey's experiment with their livers devoured and their eyeballs plucked out.

"Of course you will control them," Vasily got out. He took one of Alexey's hands in his and kissed the back of it. "You're the Tzar of Novo-Svitsevo." *For now*, he added in his head.

Because if he had been waiting for a sign from God that Alexey Balakin absolutely had to die, this was it.

"I can control them through the Holy Science, not my position as Tzar," Alexey said. "The details are not of your concern. But you and Morozov, and the other generals I create—you will be the ones to lead my new army. Humans and demons, their power combined, will make Novo-Svitsevo the most powerful country the world has ever seen."

Right. Vasily had almost forgotten, in his panic, that he was apparently part of this so-called plan.

"Oh," Vasily managed weakly. "Yes." He prayed that Alexey didn't notice the sweat gathering on his palms despite the chill in the air.

"It's overwhelming." Alexey smirked. "I was astounded by it myself, the first time I uncovered God's mysteries." He opened his arms wide. "But this is Novo-Svitsevo, and if any country in the world should be protected by the wonders of God, it is this one. It's only unfortunate the sacrifice it will take."

"And what is that?" Vasily managed to choke out. "What is that sacrifice?"

Alexey had the good grace to look away, breaking his hold on Vasily's gaze. "I've had to assemble a sizable number of people to help feed this new army. My soldiers have been laying supply lines, so then, when the *zemonyii* and other demons arrive . . ."

"The conscripts," Vasily said flatly. It was all he could do with the horror washing over him in a wave. "The new conscripts."

"A regrettable sacrifice, but a noble one." Alexey met his eyes again. "Their memories will be a blessing to Novo-Svitsevo and us all."

He's evil, Vasily thought. *He's completely, utterly fucked up in the head.*

Dimitri had to know. This couldn't wait. So Vasily did the one thing that he gathered would get him out of this situation the fastest, and stepped forward to kiss Alexey, winding his arms around the other man's neck. As anticipated, Alexey's entire body seized up—he didn't truly want to touch Vasily, not like that.

Maybe, Vasily thought, *Ivan's finally made an honest man out of him.*

Alexey kissed him back briefly, then broke away, wiping his mouth in a gesture that must have been unconscious, because it was aborted halfway through, his hand falling rigidly to his side. "I am glad you are so . . . enthusiastic." Alexey grinned in a way that showed all his teeth and made Vasily shudder. "But I must be heading back now. Work awaits. Shall we?"

Vasily smiled and took Alexey's arm, and let himself be led back into the palace.

✳

Vasily forced himself to sleep through sheer force of will as soon as he was back in his rooms. The panic making his body as heavy as lead had helped.

He arrived in Dimitri's body with a start. *I thought you'd be dreaming too.*

He was looking around the parlor of the townhouse, out through Dimitri's eyes. Dimitri was holding a hand of cards, and there was a saucer of tea balanced on his thigh and a blanket around his shoulders, the weight warm and comforting. It was an echo of when they'd briefly shared one mind right after they'd been bonded to each other. Vasily was relieved it had worked.

Vasya? He felt a burst of anxiety from Dimitri. *Are you all right?*

The rest of the court was looking at him, Annika's face tight with concern, Mischa's with fascination. Ladushka sat primly in an armchair, her hands folded in her lap, observing impassively. Vasily's heart jumped at seeing his friends safe and well, but Dimitri's panic was too all-encompassing for him to truly feel joy at the sight.

Not in the fucking least. Alexey's going to open some kind of permanent rift between here and where demons live, and let them through, and he's going to use these zemonyii *he's creating as his generals. Once he does, no one will ever be able to kill him, because if they did, they'd be condemning the entire world to being overrun by the horrors he's controlling. And to feed these demon soldiers, he's going to turn the conscripts he's gathered into* food *for them.* Vasily would have vomited on his own shoes if he'd had a stomach to empty. *He's literally going to sacrifice tens of thousands of people who have no choice but to be there, and what happens when they're all dead? Who's going to feed those demons after that? Who are they going to consume?*

Vasily could feel the way that Dimitri's form stilled, the way his mouth went dry and his heart started pounding.

"Dima," Annika said slowly. "What's going on?"

Vasily's—Dimitri's—vision blurred around the edges. *Breathe,* Vasily ordered him, and he did.

"We were wrong," Dimitri rasped out. "Vasya's . . . here." Vasily felt him lift a hand and point to his own head. "Alexey is going to create these . . . generals that Vasya described last night, and then use them to command an army of demons when he rips open our world. And he's going to feed them using the conscripts he's gathered. They're not soldiers. They're a meal."

"He fucking what," Mischa deadpanned.

"I was only half-wrong." Ladushka put a hand to her mouth. "He is using the supply lines, but not to prepare for war. They are to feed the soldiers, who in turn will feed this demonic army . . ."

Mischa blanched. "This is fucking bad."

"Yes." Dimitri let a breath out through his pursed lips, gripping his own thighs, steadying himself. "So we need to kill him before this happens. Which means we need to get close to him."

"What does Vasya think?" Annika asked, biting her lip.

That this is a shitty hand we've been dealt, Vasily said, wishing he could tuck her into his chest and give her a hug. He hoped this wouldn't be the last time he saw all of them, his friends, his family. *And since you said you're the one who has to kill Alexey, you need to find out* how *as soon as you can.*

"And then we'll need to find a way to get to the palace." Dimitri took a shuddering breath. "But the only way . . ." He paused, a realization rocking through him so hard that even Vasily felt it. "The only way Alexey would let us back into the palace is in chains."

"Ah." Ladushka leaned forward. "How clever."

Vasily hated the sound of that suggestion. *What do you mean?*

"I'm proposing that Vasya leave the palace under the pretense of hunting us down, as a show of loyalty to Alexey. And then we simply walk right into the palace, albeit as captives."

Annika and Mischa looked horrified, but Ladushka nodded. "A sound plan. It should work."

Can you do this? Dimitri's heart was pounding. Vasily wanted to reach down and soothe it, even as he wanted to vomit at Dimitri's idea.

I'll appeal to his vanity, Vasily replied. *Maybe claim that God sent me a dream, or some kind of portent, to aid him. That God intended for me to be used as Alexey's vessel to accomplish this special mission and capture you. Would Alexey believe me?*

You could tell someone the sky was purple and they would believe you, Vasya. Dimitri's mouth moved up in the faintest grin.

Are you sure you want me to suggest this? Vasily wished he could kill Alexey himself, to spare Dimitri the danger. But nothing in life was fair, and in this he was useless.

Yes. Dimitri sounded more resolute than he'd been in months. *Do whatever you have to do to convince him that—*

But then, all of a sudden, Vasily was jerked awake, back in his own body. There was a maid bending over him. "You were asleep," the woman said, "and the Tzar requested your presence for lunch."

Vasily shook his head, clearing any hint of a guilty expression off his face. "I'm sorry," he said, affecting a yawn. "I had a headache. But that would be delightful. Take me to him."

He let the woman smooth out the wrinkles in his clothes and rearrange his hair, and went to go convince the Tzar of Novo-Svitsevo it was his God-appointed duty to hunt down Dimitri. Just not for the reason Alexey would think.

TWENTY-FIVE

DIMITRI

Aleksandr's instructions had been simple. They were to call on Gavril, the archangel of God, at the conclusion of the sabbath. If the archangel found them worthy, he would answer their question.

A day after Vasily's sudden appearance in Dimitri's mind, they were all gathered in the kitchen, picking at the food Annika had laid out for a late lunch. Maybe it was what Vasily had said through him that was unsettling them all, or maybe it was the tension of not knowing if they would get this last piece that they needed to fell Alexey, but none of them appeared to have an appetite. Dimitri certainly didn't.

"I'm going to nap," Mischa said, standing from the table. Ladushka's head didn't even rise from the book she was reading, but Annika frowned. "At least for a few hours. I can't stand this waiting. It's getting on my nerves. Wake me at sunset." They walked briskly out of the kitchen.

Annika sighed, looking at Dimitri's mostly untouched plate, then her own. "I suppose I'll spend a few hours sharpening blades." She cocked her head at Ladushka. "Care to join?"

"Fine." Ladushka stood but kept on reading. "Let us go, Anna."

Left alone in the kitchen, Dimitri stared down at the chipped wood of the table. He had the faint scrap of a memory of rolling out the dough for braided bread here with his grandmother before she passed. She'd been one of the only comforting adults in his childhood who hadn't been paid to mind him. When he and his siblings had journeyed to Wilnetzk to see her, it was always a welcome reprieve from the stifling demands of court life and the coldness of his parents.

He wished he wasn't the one who had to make all the decisions, especially the ones that were liable to get his friends killed. Dimitri couldn't tell if the ruse he'd come up with would work, whether Alexey would believe that Vasily had actually found them—through the grace of God—but it needed to.

He got up, pushed the chair back, then made his way up the stairs to his room, where he draped himself in his prayer shawl, bowed his head, and started begging God with everything he had to let him set it all back to rights.

✷

Ladushka came knocking on his door as the sun began to set, and Dimitri gave up praying and turned his mind to their task.

They forwent dinner. None of them were hungry. Dimitri's nerves were frayed, and he repeated the same prayer over and over in his mind: *Please let this work. The Lord our God, if I have ever done anything good, anything right, please let this work.*

When night finally fell, Annika ushered them all to the parlor, shutting the curtains and flicking off the electric lights. Ladushka carried over the small table they used for the prayers at the conclusion of every sabbath, and Mischa brought over a bottle of wine, setting it on the table next to the silver cup and spice box they had laid out. Annika took a braided candle out of the cupboard against the parlor wall and placed it in the holder on the table, along with a match. Mischa pulled prayer shawls out of the cabinet, wrapping one around their own shoulders and tossing the other over Dimitri's.

"Are you ready?" Ladushka's eyes searched Dimitri's face.

Dimitri breathed in deeply, steeling himself. "Yes." He nodded. This would work. He needed it to. Novo-Svitsevo needed it to. He turned to the rest of his court, arraying themselves around the ritual objects, studying them in the dark. "No matter what happens, let me continue the ritual. No matter what you see. No matter what I say, or do, or whatever you hear, or even if it looks like I'm dying. I don't care."

Annika murmured her assent and pulled Dimitri under her arm. Dimitri nudged himself into her side and let Mischa pull him into their body too, an arm across his back. He took the comfort before they both dropped their arms, relieved that they remained standing close enough to touch. Ladushka completed the circle, until they were standing linked together, shoulder to shoulder around the small table.

He rolled up his sleeves, then picked up the kiddush cup, cradling the base in his palm. The engravings were rough against his thumb. He had been gifted this cup at his birth, drunk from it all his life, used it at both of his weddings, had carried it through the war, all the way to exile in Wilnetzk.

Every week, he had thought it a slap in the face that they were drinking from a bejeweled, gilded kiddush cup fit for a Tzar when he was nothing more than a failure. Now, watching the jewels glitter in the dim light from the window, he felt something that might have been hope.

He nodded to Mischa. They uncorked the bottle of wine, then poured it into the cup until it was overflowing, a symbol of abundance, the wine dripping down onto Dimitri's hand, down his arm, splashing onto the table below.

Annika lit the candle, a single flame in the dark.

He took a breath to steady himself as his friends began the prayer. Mischa started the *nigun*, Ladushka's ethereal voice joining in a register above. Annika started them swaying back and forth, and Dimitri closed his eyes, letting his friends' closeness and their song guide him to the quiet place within himself where he could speak to the Divine.

I will trust God and I will not be afraid.

Mischa's voice reverberated through him as they spoke the beginning of the prayer, the surety of the liturgy grounding him.

Dimitri joined his voice with Annika's, the melody slow and haunting. He raised the cup of wine aloft. *Barukh ata Adonai, Eloheinu Melekh ha'olam, borei p'ri hagafen.*

Mischa returned to their melody as Dimitri set the wine down and lifted the box of spices in his wine-soaked hand. He closed his eyes and sang again, pulling the words from the part of his soul that was yearning towards God, the part of him that was protesting his abandonment by the Divine. *Barukh ata Adonai, Eloheinu Melekh ha'olam, borei minei v'samim.*

He brought the box to his nose and inhaled, the scent of cloves and cinnamon sharpening his awareness, then passed it to Annika. She cupped the box in her hand and brought it to her nose, closing her eyes to inhale. She passed it to Mischa, who gave it to Ladushka, who returned the box to Dimitri. He set it down on the table.

Dimitri sang a final prayer. *Barukh ata Adonai, Eloheinu Melekh ha'olam, borei m'orei ha'eish.* He cupped his hands before him, reaching them out towards the candle, watching the light reflect off his nails, touching the edges of his fingertips to Annika's and Mischa's, all of their hands encircling the flame.

After a breath, they stopped their song, and Dimitri lifted the cup, drinking deeply, the wine bitter on his tongue. Then he placed it back down onto the table, lifted the candle with shaking hands, and dipped it into the remainder of the wine, plunging them into darkness.

He took a deep breath, ignored the way he was unsteady without Vasily's reassuring presence at his side, and licked his lips.

"The Archangel Gavril," Dimitri rasped into the night and the silence. "We are the righteous, and we call on you, during this last moment of sacred rest, before we re-enter the world of the profane."

For a heartbeat, nothing happened. Dimitri's breath turned ragged, and he fought to keep his calm and the state of meditation he had reached with the clarity of prayer and the closeness of his friends.

He dared to hope, dared to let warmth and certainty flare within him, reaching out to the Divine, connecting with the sense of righteous steadiness that he had always found inside himself before he prayed to God for guidance.

Then a flame sprang to life on the wine-soaked candle he had laid on the table. Slowly, it grew, until the entire table was on fire, yet there was no crack of burning wood snapping, no smell of smoke. He felt Mischa and Annika stiffen, their eyes growing as wide as his must have been. The flames licked out to touch their feet, and Dimitri tried to step backwards, but he was rooted to the spot. The flames were cold when they touched his skin, like the ice of the river he and his friends had once jumped into to fulfill a bet, laughing all the while.

And then he heard the voice.

It wasn't male or female, or old or young. It simply *was*, and it echoed through his head with the force of steel ringing against steel. His vision blackened, or maybe it was entirely consumed by flames— his senses were so disoriented that he could not tell.

Why do the righteous call on me?

Dimitri opened his mouth to speak, but no words came out. So he responded in his mind, and prayed the angel could hear. *We want to know how to weaken an immortal man, so that he may be killed.*

Why do you require this? The angel's voice reverberated through his chest, and his heart started to beat erratically.

To kill Alexey Balakin. Even Dimitri's mental voice sounded strained, breathless. *For he has sinned against the Lord our God, and he must be destroyed.*

A burst of fury tore through Dimitri, and he couldn't tell whose it was.

He is the one communing with the demon Samael. He is the one fighting the command of the Lord our God: that the world of demons and the world of men shall never meet. He angers Adonai, he profanes the Divine. The angel was furious, and Dimitri fought the urge to prostrate himself before the voice and beg for forgiveness, as though he were the one who had sinned. Because he had. Because he was the one who had helped Alexey defy God by bringing him back to life.

The Tzar of Novo-Svitsevo must die for this blasphemy against the Lord our God. I will lend His name to you so that you may weaken this sinner. He must be destroyed. You must insert the Name into his mouth, and he will be stripped of his power, bare before you.

How will I know the Name? Dimitri fought to be practical, even if the pain in his body was enough to drive him mad.

Just as your sins are written on your bones, the angel replied, *so will you bear the name of God.*

There was a searing flash of fire down Dimitri's left forearm, and as he blinked, his vision returned, then he collapsed to his knees. "Fuck," Dimitri said, clutching his head, which was hurting so terrifically it felt ready to split open. "Fucking fuck." He was soaked in sweat and, he realized with a start, a great deal of blood.

"This is why we don't fuck around with mysticism," Mischa growled as they ripped open Dimitri's shirt. His teeth were chattering, and for a second, he felt absolutely nothing, no sensation in his body. He closed his eyes. He wondered if he was about to die. "This is why we don't fucking convene with fucking angels during *havdalah* services."

They pried his hands away from his head. "Hold him down, Anna," Mischa ordered. "In case he has a seizure." They pressed a finger into the crease of his jaw, measuring his pulse, and then pried open an eyelid.

"Mischka," Dimitri protested weakly, trying to swat them away, but Annika was holding him too tightly against her chest. His entire body was shaking so violently that his muscles started to spasm in response, and he couldn't control the tears leaking out of his eyes. Ladushka rushed to turn on the lights, and when they flared to life, she took one look at him and vomited spectacularly all over the floor. Dimitri's terror grew, his heart struggling to pound against his ribs.

"Not on my *pants*," Mischa moaned as Dimitri's stomach churned and he followed suit, spilling the contents of his stomach all over Mischa's lap.

"Get me towels, Anna, *now*." Mischa was pulling his sleeve away from his arm, and Dimitri was crying in earnest now, because all of a sudden the pain came back, slamming into him like a punch to the jaw. It hurt like nothing he'd ever experienced before, like a thousand cuts were being made in his skin at once and then salted. His body convulsed involuntarily, curling around his arm in an animalistic urge to protect his wounded limb. Annika dragged him backwards, and then her warmth was exchanged for the back of the sofa, propping him up. The room spun around him.

"Fuck fuck *fuck*," Mischa muttered, like it was a prayer. "Lada, go get boiling water. And the closest sewing kit you can find. And a fucking pen and paper."

Laduskha vanished as Annika returned, falling to her knees next to him, depositing a stack of towels on the ground. She gasped, looking down at his left arm, and he went to follow her line of sight, but she grabbed him by the chin, her small hand gripping his jaw with surprising strength. "Look nowhere but right at me, Dima." He obeyed, but was left wondering if his arm was even still attached to his body, with the way the whole limb was one mass of fire and agony.

Mischa's hands were at his waist, undoing his belt buckle. "I really don't think now's the time," Dimitri slurred, his tongue thick in his mouth, his vision beginning to narrow at the edges. "I feel—"

He didn't get to finish, because he screamed instead, buckling forward as Mischa yanked the belt around his upper arm, so tight he felt like his arm *would* be severed. "Hold this," Mischa said to Annika, who took the end of the belt from them. Annika's eyes never left his, and Dimitri clung to her gaze like a lifeline.

"You're going to be okay," she murmured soothingly. "I think . . . I think this is one of the prophecies. *You are going to suffer, more than any living man has suffered. The pain will almost break you. But you cannot allow it to. You cannot give in.* You're going to get through this, everything is going to be okay, Dima, darling, you're going to be fine."

Ladushka skidded into the room, her arms laden with goods. "The water is on the stove."

"The pen and paper, please." Mischa held out one hand towards her, and it was so coated in blood that Dimitri's stomach turned again. He tried to move, but agony lanced through him.

"Here." Ladushka came to join Annika and Mischa on the ground, offering a scrap of paper and a pen.

"I can't even see it clearly," Mischa said, letting out a frustrated groan. "Anna, can you?"

Annika let go of Dimitri's chin as she bent forward, and he made the single worst mistake of his life—besides bringing Alexey back from the dead—and looked down.

His arm had been flayed open from the wrist to the elbow. The skin was hanging like sides of meat at a butcher shop, and his entire arm was coated in blood that splashed down his hand and onto his pants, soaking them through. He could see his own bone, marred with what looked like writing. His stomach revolted.

"No, no, no," Mischa growled as Dimitri listed forward and opened his mouth to vomit again. "Don't puke into your own open wound, you bastard, I'm trying to save your life and your arm over here, don't make it harder."

"Anna," Dimitri moaned. "Get me a fucking drink. I need fucking vodka." He turned his head. "Mischka, am I dying?"

"You will be if you don't shut up and let me work," Mischa muttered. "Your radial artery is severed." And then a decanter of vodka was being lifted to his lips and the glorious burn flattened some of the excruciating pain that was emanating from his left arm.

"I can't see it clearly either." Annika's head was hovering over his arm, blocking it blissfully from his sight. "There's too much blood on the bone."

"Dima." Mischa's face was in his, suddenly, and they were using the perfectly calm, very soothing voice that Dimitri knew from experience they used only with soldiers who were on the brink of death. "Do me a favor. Drink as much of that as you can in the next thirty seconds, all right? Lada, leave the room. Anna, you write it down."

Dimitri didn't pay much attention to what they said past *drink as much of that as you can.* He tilted the decanter back and started to chug, but didn't miss the glance that slid between Annika and Mischa.

Dimitri's head was growing light and the bottle was growing heavy in his hand, and the shaking was receding and the pain was going soft around the edges, and then Mischa was laying him on his back and the bottle was being taken from him and his arm was being moved in a fit of pain—and was that a wallet in between his teeth?

"Three," Mischa said, slowly. "Two."

Dimitri blacked out as soon as Mischa poured the rest of the decanter of vodka all over his flayed arm.

ALEXEY

"It is an interesting proposition." Alexey twisted his cloth napkin in between his fingertips. Mikhail Haleyvin sat before him, across the dining table, his eyes shining with fervor. "But how would you find him, a man who has remained hidden all this time?"

Alexey knew, in the recesses of his mind, that he should have sent his best spies and scouts out searching for Dimitri. He should not have designated his worst trackers to the task, and then ignored their increasingly desperate reports and requests for aid in favor of other, supposedly more pressing matters. He knew that Dimitri could threaten his throne.

He knew that everything in him should want to track Dimitri down and kill him.

But when Dimitri had looked at him from across the battlefield at Vysoka, as Alexey's army had decimated the last of his, he'd had a pistol raised to Alexey's heart, and he'd lowered it, a look of pure agony on his face before he'd retreated.

Alexey's stomach had always curdled at the thought of hunting him down, after that last act of love. And Dimitri had made not a single appearance in the time since.

Every day after that, Alexey had prayed that Dimitri made no trouble, because as long as he made no trouble, he could stay alive. The moment he began to make a move for the throne, he would have to die. There would be no way that Alexey could maintain control otherwise. So he hoped that Dimitri would never make that mistake.

It was easier than wondering if he had the heart to kill him.

"I told you, *Moy Tzar*, that the Lord blessed me with a dream, in which I brought the traitor to you in chains, throwing him at your feet. The Lord told me that He would reveal to you the location where I could find the traitor." He paused, his eyes searching Alexey's face. "If you prayed to the Lord our God, do you think He would reveal anything to you? Any sense of where the traitor might be?"

Alexey cocked his head at Mikhail. "Where would you go, if you were him?"

"Home." The other man looked down at his lap, biting his lip. "If I were him, I would want to go home. Somewhere comforting. Somewhere that felt safe."

Of course that was what he would want. Alexey knew Dimitri better than he knew himself, knew how much the man craved comfort.

Home. Alexey closed his eyes against the memory of the snug library in their estate at Chernitzy, he and Dimitri curled up by the fire, books in hand. Long, late nights full of laughter. The comforting weight of a hound by his side. Since his transformation, he had not felt that kind of calm, that contentment. Even his dogs could no longer stand to be near him, shying away and whining when he approached.

No matter. Alexey shook his head. There were things more important than feeling cosseted, like power and protecting his country.

He should be thankful to Mikhail Haleyvin for bringing this to his attention, for pushing him to action, as a good general should.

He turned to the steward standing at attention at the doors of the dining room and snapped his fingers. "Send a message to Chancellor Morozov's steward. Tell him that the chancellor should compile me a list of all the property owned by the former royal family." He paused. "Especially those abroad. The chancellor should have something to work on during his confinement."

Mikhail choked on the wine he was drinking. Alexey smiled at him reassuringly. "Never fear for the chancellor's health, Mikhail." He cleared his throat, casting his eyes around to the servants scattered at the edges of the room, waiting to refill their cups, their food, pull out their chairs. "I am sure that in good time, his condition will be resolved. But for now, isolation is best."

"From your mouth to God's ears," Mikhail said, a frown creasing his features.

"Enjoy your day." He rose from the lunch table and gave a courteous bow. "I have matters to attend to with Ivan, and then we will discuss your proposal further." He looked over Mikhail's shoulder at the man standing there, whom he had appointed Mikhail's temporary steward. "In two hours, in my private study."

The man nodded, and so did Mikhail. He left Mikhail fiddling with his fork, staring out the window. If he thought he could help find Dimitri, Alexey would have to let him try. Alexey knew better than to defy a command or vision from God. The void within him writhed with pleasure at the thought of capturing Dimitri, making him pay for what he had done.

Dimitri would be a threat to the stability of the country for as long as he lived, and Alexey had already given his life for Novo-Svitsevo. He was willing to give up the rest of his heart for it too.

✶

He found Ivan standing in front of a large mirror in their sitting room, being measured by the head tailor. Dimitri's old wardrobe had been laid out around the room, and a small army of tailors was bustling around, altering it to the head tailor's barked measurements. "No more cheap suits for you, my darling," Alexey purred, gratified at the way Ivan turned and blushed.

Dimitri's extensive collection of jewelry was arrayed on velvet trays being held by waiting servants. Alexey picked up a diamond and sapphire circlet that he had commissioned for Dimitri, back when he was dressing his husband for the royal court and using him as a way to show off the products of Chernitzy's mines. He crossed the room to Ivan, skirting tailors and heaps of cast-off fabric, and placed the circlet on Ivan's head.

"You'll have to learn how to wear a crown," he mused aloud, adjusting the circlet where it rested on top of Ivan's abundant waves of dark hair. Dimitri had always kept his hair closely cropped on the sides, longer on the top, and it constantly fell into his eyes as he worked. Ivan's hung past his ears, in a way that didn't suit his fine features.

"Anything you wish, *Moy Tzar*," Ivan said, his handsome face split wide in a smile.

Alexey tutted. "We're going to be wed. You'll have to call me by my name."

Ivan flushed, furiously red, and Alexey turned to the head tailor. "How long until he's fit to be presented to the public?"

"*Moy Tzar*, the better part of the wardrobe will be altered to fit by dawn tomorrow. They were substantially the same size, so it remains a matter of hemming. We are having shoes remade. For now, the ones we have will be stuffed at the toe."

"Make sure my future husband does not trip in front of his court." Alexey chuckled. "We will discuss a wedding suit at another time. Everyone, leave us please."

Tools were dropped, and servants fled from the room like insects desperate to avoid being crushed.

"Are you ready for tonight?" Alexey tipped Ivan's chin up with a fingertip.

"Yes—" Ivan paused. "Alexey." He bit his lip, and Alexey felt a small shiver go through him. He couldn't deny the thrill of it himself, hearing his given name from Ivan's lips for the first time.

"No matter what happens, no matter what you hear, you must remember that you are now the last member of the noble house that has ruled this country for fifteen generations." Alexey stared into Ivan's eyes, searching out any doubt, any weakness that might embarrass him. "You must remain regal at all times. If you are insulted, you do not flinch. If you hear whispers about your birth, you ignore them. You smile and you nod and you bow to no one, because next month you will sit beside me on the throne."

"Yes." Ivan nodded and threaded his fingers through Alexey's. "I will."

"Good." Alexey kissed him and turned away, hoping that he could better control Ivan than he'd been able to control Dimitri. He shouted for the tailors, who poured back into the room to resume their work. "Oh," Alexey said over his shoulder to no one in particular. "Cut his hair. Make it look like Dimitri Alexeyev's."

*

Alexey was waylaid by his finance minister, who evidently needed to urgently discuss the taxation situation in two of the northern regions. When he had solved the problem and sent the minister off to be useless elsewhere, he finally made his way to his study.

Mikhail was sitting in one of the corner armchairs, but he sprang up when the door opened. "My apologies." Alexey unclasped his cloak and tossed it over a chair, crossing over to the fire. He closed his eyes, imagining that the warmth that touched his skin pervaded his whole body. "The running of the empire sometimes distracts me at inconvenient times."

"I didn't mind." He nodded at the shelves. "I was admiring your books."

"I'll tell the steward that you are to be allowed in to read at any time." It wouldn't hurt to be gracious, to let the other man feel at home. Besides, the truly sensitive documents pertaining to Novo-Svitsevo were kept in the false drawer in his desk, which Mikhail would never think to look for, let alone know how to open. There was nothing here that Mikhail Haleyvin could not see, not if he was about to embrace Alexey's Holy Science with everything that he was.

"Thank you," Mikhail replied, his eyes trained on the carpet. "A man knocked, about an hour ago. He said that the chancellor had already had a list of such properties compiled for you, and sent it to you with his regrets that he could not deliver the letter in person."

Mikhail handed him a neatly folded parchment from a nearby table, and Alexey sat down to open it and scan the contents. Most of these holdings he knew of—they were the royal palaces scattered around the country, Dimitri's personal summer dacha, the now-abandoned homes that had been owned by Dimitri's siblings, all of which he'd already had searched.

But there was one property that caught his eye, the last on the list, the designation written in Morozov's precise script in fresh black ink that evinced recent research. 10 Prospekyii Avenue, Wilnetzk, Lietuva. Former home of the mother of Tzarina Liliya Abramovich.

Mikhail had said that he would go home. Go somewhere that made him feel safe. Where would Dimitri feel safe, after the war? Certainly not in a place that Alexey already knew of, someplace Alexey could easily track him down. Dimitri did not know that Alexey had planned to be merciful.

Is this where he resides? Alexey asked God, closing his eyes in a moment of meditative prayer, knowing that God would confirm the rightness of his guess.

Yes, my son, God answered. *That is where your general will find Dimitri Alexeyev and what remains of his court.*

Alexey tore off the bit of paper that contained the address, then threw the rest of the list into the fire, watching the edges curl and blacken. "I will give you a contingent of soldiers to guard you on your way. A coach, supplies, anything you require. This is your first test as my general—bring Dimitri Alexeyev back to me, alive."

Mikhail took the torn scrap of paper from him and studied the address, then tossed it into the fire as well. When he turned back to him, Mikhail's eyes were hard. "I will not fail you, *Moy Tzar.* I will show you that I am worthy. I will succeed, because I am guided by the hand of God."

"Good," Alexey said, studying the planes of the other man's face. Mikhail held his gaze, unflinching. "When you return, we will carry out your transformation. Until then, stay safe, Mikhail Haleyvin." He raised a hand over the other man's head in benediction. "May God bless you and keep you."

"Amen," Mikhail finished.

"Do not fail me," he said, standing to leave. It did not escape him, as he walked out of the room, that the last person he had said those words to were Dimitri Alexeyev, right before he died.

TWENTY-SEVEN

VASILY

When Vasily arrived in the palace courtyard so early the next morning that the sun had not yet fully risen, the escort of soldiers that he'd been assigned were standing around a large black coach, guarding it like it contained all the treasures of the state. The group was composed of ten men and ten women, all wearing bright-red guard uniforms, carrying rifles so polished he could see himself in them as they were held at attention. And they all bore packs so large that Vasily wondered if they had planned on leaving Novo-Svitsevo for a year.

Vasily bit back a groan.

Alexey had no fucking clue how to do anything by stealth. Traveling with this many people would put a target on their backs for the kinds of robbers who lurked on the side of the road, since it looked like they were guarding valuable cargo. And they would be—but only on the way back. And it wouldn't be jewels.

"I don't need all of you." Vasily turned to the nearest soldier, looking her up and down, assessing whether she'd be slow enough to not risk seriously injuring Dimitri and the rest of the court during their "arrest."

The soldier looked at Vasily askance, her eyebrows furrowing. "We were personally selected to accompany you on your journey by the Tzar. We are part of his personal guard, we have all served in the army, and we have undergone extensive training in protecting persons of importance. Do we displease you?"

Vasily fought the urge to roll his eyes. "No. But how many of you speak Lietuvan?"

The soldiers looked at each other, confused. One of them, a woman with copper hair, raised a hand stiffly. "I was born near the border. I am fluent in the language and several of its older dialects."

"Great," Vasily said, pointing at her. "You're coming. Anyone else?"

A surprisingly young-looking woman standing near the back of the coach raised her hand. She must have barely been an adult. "I studied Lietuvan at university."

He took a closer look at her and noticed the icy blue of her eyes, the dark brown, almost black of her hair, her narrow face graced with the same exquisite cheekbones he'd recognize anywhere. Another bastard of Dimitri's father then, one he had never met face to face, but certainly had a dossier on, detailing every aspect of her life and her personality. Vasily wished there had been portraits of the bastard Abramovich children, but it wasn't as if anyone paid good money to memorialize their indiscretions in paint.

Two guards, plus him and the two heavily armed carriage drivers already perched on the driver's bench, would be more than enough to fake the arrest of four people without drawing unnecessary attention on the road.

Plus, the fewer guards around him, the fewer to notice anything strange about the court's behavior when they were arrested.

Vasily waved his hands dismissively. "The rest of you can leave." He flicked his fingers at the guards, still standing ramrod straight around the carriage, several of them scowling dangerously. "Sorry you had to wake up so early."

"But . . ." The woman who had initially spoken was staring at him incredulously.

Vasily sighed. "But what?"

"The Tzar sent us *personally* to guard you." She gestured around at the group, many of whom bore similar expressions of disbelief. "You wish us to . . . leave?"

Vasily pinched the bridge of his nose. These guards might have been good at killing, but none of them were very bright—none of them had realized the obvious tactical problem. Dimitri's personal guard had been far superior and could have probably out-thought this bunch even while half-dead and drunk to boot. "I do. I'm going to hunt down Dimitri Alexeyev, who is currently in hiding. Do you think that if I showed up in Lietuva with twenty guards all wearing bright-red uniforms bearing the palace crest that he wouldn't hear about it as soon as we reached the border? We'd be a walking notice that the Tzar is coming for him."

"But the Tzar himself ordered us—" The woman continued to fight, a flush creeping across her cheeks.

Vasily cut her off with a raised hand. "The Tzar personally told me that I could have whoever I wished at my disposal and could send the rest on their way. You are only here so I have a variety of guards to choose from." He knew she'd never question Alexey personally and uncover the lie.

The woman gaped at him. "But—"

"Do you think," Vasily snapped, his patience wearing thin, "that Tzar Alexey Balakin would share his detailed plans with *you*, personally?"

The guard bit her lip but shook her head stiffly, frowning. Vasily held his breath until the woman turned on her heel and started marching back to the palace entrance. The rest of the guards followed suit, save the two that he'd pointed to.

"Good," he said when the rest of the soldiers had departed. "I suppose you two have normal clothes in those packs?" He snapped his fingers. "Go change."

The guards nodded and turned on their heels, disappearing into the guardhouse and then reappearing mere minutes later dressed in clothes plain enough that they wouldn't stick out like a sore thumb in Wilnetzk. Vasily gave the coachmen a once-over, but their overcoats hid their palace uniforms.

"We'll ride in the carriage together." Vasily nodded towards the door. "And then, once we're near Wilnetzk, we'll swap for something else. The carriage will be conspicuous."

The copper-haired guard cocked her head at him, and he realized belatedly that he was still supposed to be a butcher's son from a no-name village, not someone who thought about the tactics of sneaking up on a former Tzar, who gave orders like he was used to it. "The Tzar has informed me exactly what to do, down to the smallest detail."

There—now he was free to be as clever as he liked and none of them would question him.

The taller guard, the one with Dimitri's eyes, nodded. "The garrison at Domachëvo will send a prison wagon behind us for the captives." She jerked her chin at the carriage. "That's unlikely to hold them all. Let alone secure them."

Vasily breathed past the tension growing in his chest, hoping that Dimitri's ruse would work and that none of his friends were about to get accidentally shot in the process of faking their own arrest. "Good. That's perfect."

The taller guard cleared her throat. "I'm Ayla," she said, tucking a wisp of brown hair back into her severe braid. Vasily wondered how she felt about hunting down her half-brother. He could put some details to her now that he had her name. Dimitri had been fond of her, calling her kind and clever. He had written to her frequently when she'd been at school, the fees for which had come from Dimitri's personal accounts.

The shorter guard stuck out her hand and shook Vasily's roughly. "Viktoria." Her copper hair was glinting in the early morning light, and a smattering of freckles graced the bridge of her nose. Vasily would have found her beautiful, except he was fairly sure he'd never be able to summon arousal again until Alexey was dead and buried in the ground.

Vasily yanked open the door to the carriage and hoisted himself inside, depositing his pack on the floor. Ayla and Viktoria followed, and Viktoria pulled the door shut, then banged a fist on the roof.

They rolled out of the courtyard, and their journey to Wilnetzk began.

★

Vasily had promptly taken one of Mischa's pills and informed the two guards that he would be sleeping through as much of the journey as possible, due to how prone he was to a terrible case of sickness from the motion of the carriage. In reality, Vasily simply could not bear to spend the long, dull hours on the road thinking alternately about how Alexey might be about to kill everyone in the entire world and how Alexey might be about to kill Dimitri specifically.

He couldn't decide which was worse: them all dying together, or Dimitri being gone and Vasily having to live with it. So he decided to pass the fuck out instead for the four-day journey.

He'd woken up only when Ayla had shaken him on the shoulder. He realized that the carriage had stopped.

"Do you wish to eat lunch?" Ayla pointed out the carriage window. They had stopped in a small town, and there were people clustered around the carriage, gawking at them. They probably thought some noble or lord was about to appear, given that the axles on the carriage cost more than they'd see collectively in a year. "This is a decent inn."

During the war, Vasily had learned to never pass up a meal, even if he wasn't hungry. "Yes," he said, stretching his stiff neck and yawning. "After you."

Viktoria opened the door and shooed away the curious onlookers, her head swiveling left and right, her shoulders squared and her hand on the holster where she kept her pistol. She beckoned to them, and Vasily followed her out of the carriage and into the dark interior of the inn.

It was simple yet well cared for, and served food in a spacious room on the ground level. Over chicken soup and dumplings, Ayla and Viktoria told him about their training to become royal guards, and he begged them for their war stories, explaining that he'd never had the pleasure of serving.

Ayla held out her arm and pushed up a sleeve. The skin was mottled with burns that had turned it shiny and pink. "I got caught in an explosion trying to remove charges on a bridge at Gorki. They detonated when some asshole corporal moved the wrong wire. The entire right side of my body is like this."

"Ah." Vasily flinched. He remembered Gorki. He'd been the one to order the charges placed on every bridge into the city. When they'd detonated early, they'd accidentally killed thirty-two civilians, along with crippling Alexey's advance for a crucial three-day period. It still hadn't mattered, in the end.

"I only have three toes on my left foot." Viktoria shrugged. "But it wasn't anything heroic or dramatic that did it. Just boot rot and too much marching in the cold." She held up her hands in surrender. "Ayla, I think you win this particular game."

Ayla grinned, and Vasily couldn't help but cringe at Viktoria's bright answering smile, and at the way they were making a game of how the war had damaged their bodies. But war had made broken things of them all, and who was he to begrudge using humor to cope with the pain? The Lord knew he did it often enough himself.

Vasily shoved the bad memories down as they reared up in his mind and turned himself back to the task of gathering information, no matter how meaningless. "Why do you still fight for the Tzar?"

Ayla's face stiffened. "Where else would I go? What else would I do? The palace has been my only home. And it's not as if I alone am keeping him alive and in charge." She bit her thumbnail, and Vasily regretted making her uncomfortable. But it was valuable indeed, to know that even Alexey's personal guard didn't feel much loyalty to him.

"I stayed because the poor can't afford to be picky." Viktoria dropped some coins on the table and stood. "We should keep going," she said gruffly.

Vasily nodded, and they made their way back to the waiting carriage and returned to winding their way through Novo-Svitsevo.

✳

They stopped at another inn for the night, and Vasily insisted on sleeping in his own room, despite Ayla and Viktoria's complaints about his safety. He didn't know what it was like when he talked to Dimitri in his dreams, but he wasn't about to risk speaking in his sleep and having the guards find out he was collaborating with the enemy.

"I'll be fine," he assured them. "I know how to handle myself." He gave them both a winning grin. "I grew up butchering livestock. I think I could take on anyone who came to attack me for long enough that you'd hear the commotion."

"If you insist," Viktoria said with a heavy sigh. "We'll be across the hall. We'll come to wake you in the morning."

Vasily bid them good night, then bathed as fast as he could in the washroom at the end of the hall. He locked the door, put the single rickety chair under the door handle, slid into bed, the rough sheets scratching at his neck, and closed his eyes.

✳

He opened them again in Dimitri's bedroom in the palace at Rav-Mikhailburg. Even though it was a dream, the thick stench of blood invaded his nostrils.

Vasily very deliberately turned his back on the bed and closed his heart to the sound of dream-Dimitri sobbing.

His Dimitri was looking out the window, his arms crossed, his face weary. Vasily sidled up behind him, wrapping his arms around Dimitri and pulling him close, resting his chin on Dimitri's head. He wished there was time to talk about what Dimitri had said the last time they'd met, but he had no way to know when he'd wake up and there was important information to convey.

So instead, he simply said, "I'm on my way. Me and two guards will be there four days from now. I'll tell them to wait until nightfall and sneak into the townhouse using the trellis. We'll come in through your window. If you leave it unlatched, it will make things easier."

Dimitri tipped his head back, resting it in the hollow of Vasily's throat. He sighed. "I can't believe we're going back."

"For a good cause." Vasily held him tighter. A loud thud sounded from behind them. Dimitri's entire body flinched. "Do you know how to weaken him?"

"Yes." Dimitri chuckled, but there was no humor in it. "Believe it or not, I've now communed with an archangel who inscribed the name of God directly on the bone of my forearm, which Anna and Lada had to copy down while Mischka was preventing me from dying of blood loss. I think I'm still passed out from the pain. It must be the middle of the night."

Saliva pooled in Vasily's mouth as his stomach revolted at the image that flashed through his mind, of a flayed arm and unending agony. It was too vivid to be his imagination. It must have been a memory of Dimitri's. "What are we supposed to do with that?"

"Put it in his mouth before I stab him or shoot him or cut off his head, I suppose." Dimitri reached up and wrapped his hands around

Vasily's forearms. "I just need you to get us into the palace. I'll take care of the rest."

"How are you going to do that?" Vasily buried his nose in Dimitri's hair, feeling the other man's heart beat behind his ribs.

Dimitri swallowed. "Alexey will want to believe that I am a broken man, so I will show him a broken man. Alexey will want to believe that I am repentant, so I will show him penance. And he will want nothing more than me back with him, so before nightfall on the day we return, I need you to hide a knife in his bedroom, under the pillows."

"Ah." Vasily's jaw clenched. "I see." He hated the thought of Dimitri crawling back into Alexey's bed. "Will it work?"

"All my sins are written on my bones, Vasya." Dimitri massaged his arm. "But now the name of God is too. If He wills it, then yes, it will work."

TWENTY-EIGHT

DIMITRI

Dimitri blinked back into awareness slowly, wishing that he was still in the dream with Vasily, Vasily's arms wrapped around him. His entire body mourned the loss.

It was dark in the townhouse as he let his eyes open just a little. He was lying on the couch and his head, judging by the delicate thigh he rested on, was on Ladushka's lap, and there were soft hands on his feet that he could swear were Annika's, given the gentle snoring coming from behind him. He was covered in a blanket, distinctly sticky, and missing all of his clothes.

He couldn't feel his left arm. When he opened his eyes fully, he saw that it was stretched out in front of him, draped in a towel, resting on an enormous stack of pillows. Mischa sat in front of him, completely alert, staring at his arm as though they could heal it with their sight alone. A single candle burned next to them, illuminating their face.

"Oh good." Mischa straightened up when they saw his eyes open. "You're awake. I'm impressed you came back to consciousness so soon. You lost an awful lot of blood and I pumped you full of an impressive amount of morphine."

Dimitri tried to sit up, but Ladushka stirred, groaning, and her hand pushed him down. He tried to turn over onto his back, but she kept him pinned in place.

"Stay right where you are," Mischa ordered. "You'll pull out the stitches."

Dimitri's head was pounding and his thoughts were fuzzy around the edges. "What happened after I passed out?" His tongue was thick in his mouth, and it was hard to form the words. He brushed his hair out of his eyes with his right hand and shivered. Annika pulled the blanket up closer around his shoulders, rubbing his back soothingly. Ladushka tucked him closer to her side. The movement sent a jolt through his arm despite the fog of the painkillers, and Dimitri gritted his teeth. "What did you see and hear during the ritual?"

"Well." Mischa licked their lips. "We were all standing in a circle, and then you went stock-still, and *then* you were covered in flames."

"It was terrifying." Annika's hand tightened on his shoulder for a moment before she resumed making comforting circles over his skin.

"We all heard what the angel said and what you said in return, and then the flames receded. And then you were standing there, white as a ghost, with your inner left forearm entirely—and might I say, expertly—flayed open to the bone." Mischa rocked forward, their arms around their knees. "And then you almost killed yourself by puking into your own open wound."

"I remember that part," Dimitri grumbled. "Did you write down the Name?"

"Of course we fucking did," Mischa snapped. "But don't try to look at the paper directly. It renders you temporarily blind if you do. Anna's hand started to blister as she wrote it down."

Dimitri glanced over his shoulder at Annika, who waved a bandaged hand at him grimly. "It was worth it." She swallowed. "And it's a good thing I've seen far worse on the battlefield. It turns out Lada has the weakest stomach of the lot of us."

"It was quite disgusting." Ladushka's voice carried over his head. "But it was also quite fascinating to witness the ritual." She cleared her throat. "From an academic perspective."

Mischa reached out with a hand and pulled the cloth off Dimitri's arm. "You were lucky you didn't bleed out. The artery in your wrist was severed. You lost a lot of blood, Dima. I had to do some impromptu surgery. Can you move your hand?"

Dimitri looked down at his arm, where a perfectly straight line of impeccable stitches marred the flesh, from wrist to the crease of his elbow. The skin was bruised a deep, mottled purple.

Dimitri managed it, wiggling the fingers slightly, but the pain it caused made tears spring to his eyes and he let his hand go limp. Mischa let out a long breath. "Thank the Lord our God."

"The Lord our God had nothing to do with it," Ladushka said from above him. "That was entirely down to your knowledge of muscular anatomy, Mischka."

"So we have what we need." Dimitri took in a deep breath and relaxed into Ladushka's and Annika's bodies. He held Mischa's gaze.

"We do." Mischa's voice was firm.

He carefully disentangled himself from his friends, grimacing as the movement stretched his stitches, his arm hanging like a dead weight at his side while throbbing with pain every time his heart beat. "Mischka, you're going to help me bathe and then I'm going to pass the fuck out again, but in bed this time." He stood up, clutching the blanket around him with his good hand, and Mischa wrapped an arm around his shoulders to steady him.

"Anna, figure out how we can stage a fight with Vasya when he arrives so it's believable. We'll need to know exactly what to do so that no one gets hurt but it still looks like a struggle. We won't tell him, though, so that his surprise can be genuine." Annika nodded. "I just met with Vasya, and he's going to get me what I need to kill Alexey when the time comes." Annika's mouth quirked up at that.

"Lada, I need you to figure out how we put our court back together once Alexey is dead. There are going to be a lot of traitors to be dealt with once I kill him." Ladushka grinned.

"It's time I take back the throne." Dimitri let out a shuddering breath and leaned into Mischa's solid support. "Assuming Vasya can get us back into the palace, it's time we all go home."

TWENTY-NINE

ALEXEY

Alexey had ordered a ball arranged, in Mikhail's absence, to introduce the newly named Ivan Abramovich to the royal court.

The lords and ladies of the noble houses were in attendance, and as they all filed into the hall and sat as the music faded, Alexey surveyed his court. The faction, led by the now-absent Morozov, who supported him. Those who had reluctantly stayed, who he knew secretly hoped for Dimitri's return.

Today, in one stroke of genius, he would unite them both and seize control.

He stood. "My lords and ladies, nobles of Novo-Svitsevo, thank you for your attendance tonight. I have called for this night of drinking and dancing and feasting for a very important reason." He paused and looked around the room, noting which nobles shrank under his gaze and which nobles stubbornly, rebelliously, held his stare.

Despite the portent from God that Mikhail had spoken of, Alexey sensed deep in his gut that Dimitri would never be found. He *couldn't* be found. So this was his solution.

"I am from a noble house, but not a royal one." He gestured to himself. "I am your Tzar by right, but my heritage is not one of leadership.

For generations, one house has led our country. Understandably, many of you feel bound to them and are reluctant to see Novo-Svitsevo led by someone new." He smiled, but aimed a glare at those he knew were his most vociferous detractors, only playing at loyalty. "So tonight, I am pleased to present to you Ivan, son of the former Tzar Abram Fyodorev, brother to the former Tzar Dimitri Alexeyev."

He raised a hand, and Ivan stepped out of the shadows, entering through a side door and making his way to the dais. With his hair newly shorn on the sides, he was the spitting image of his brother. Alexey's heart clenched, just once, as he watched Ivan walk to him, wearing embroidered breeches and a fitted jacket like he had dressed for court all his life, his expression bewildered but his back straight, his eyes locked on Alexey as he walked past the rows of nobility.

"Lord Ivan Abramovich was legitimized by his father before his untimely death." Murmurs rose up from the crowd. Alexey pressed on. "Ivan has accepted my offer of marriage. We will be wed in a month's time." The whispers grew louder, pervasive through the hall. Jaws dropped, hands fluttered to mouths. Yet no one raised an audible complaint.

"You will celebrate my good fortune with me." Alexey raised his hands, and on command the court began to clap. He snapped and the musicians behind the dais struck up a waltz.

Alexey wove Ivan's hand around his arm, to prevent the boy from standing nervously on the dais, and began to circulate around the ballroom, navigating around dancing couples to listen for any hint of mockery that courtiers were bold enough to whisper aloud. He greeted nobles from across the empire, but they all merely smiled and wished him a long and happy marriage.

"I was thinking, for the wedding, we could get flowers from—" Ivan began, but Alexey cut him off.

"Not now, Ivan." His hand clenched around the stem of the glass of champagne a servant had handed him. "I'm working."

"But—" Ivan's fingers tightened around Alexey's bicep. "But if the wedding is in only a month, do we not have to plan it quickly? We'll need to hire someone to decorate the palace, or am I wrong?"

"Later," Alexey said curtly, hating that Ivan was thinking about this now.

"I don't mean to displease you," Ivan stammered. "I'm sorry, *Moy Tzar.*"

Alexey fought the urge to scream and instead pulled Ivan into an alcove, pressing the boy's back into the wall, leaning over him in a way that would look, to those in the ballroom, like they were sharing an intimate moment. It allowed Alexey to pin Ivan's chest for emphasis and hiss into his ear. "You will call me Alexey in public, because if you continue to call me *Moy Tzar*, you will sound like a common prostitute awed by my power instead of the man I am going to marry, the one who commands the wealth and power of an entire region."

Ivan's eyes were filling with tears, but Alexey had no time for histrionics. He set down his champagne glass on the base of the statue in the alcove with them and used his thumbs to wipe Ivan's eyes, then pressed down on the inner corners to try and stop the boy from crying. "I don't have time for this. You will learn your role, and learn it well, without me having to walk you through each and every little action. Find servants to plan the wedding with you. I have more important things to do."

Ivan sniffed but nodded, the tears receding from his eyes replaced with tiny shudders that were working their way through his body. "Yes, *Moy Tz*—" He stopped, and swallowed. "Yes, Alexey." He sniffled as Alexey's name passed his lips.

"Good." Alexey waited until the redness receded from Ivan's eyes, pulling him into an embrace to calm him down, then led them out of the alcove once he was sure Ivan was settled. He looked around to determine if anyone important had noticed Ivan's behavior, but the court was merely eating, drinking and dancing. "Now smile."

He extended his hand to Ivan and led him down onto the dance floor, set in the middle of the ballroom, under the massive crystal chandelier. Their heels clicked on the inlaid marble floor, and the smoke from the candelabras around the room formed a haze that clung to the frescoed ceiling. Alexey took Ivan's hand and began to dance, joined by a swirl of nobles in pastel gowns and somber suits.

"Smile wider," Alexey ordered as they danced, registering a faint yet creeping displeasure at the way Ivan did exactly as he commanded.

Dimitri had hated dancing in public, claiming that it was better done in private when the dance could end with the two of them peeling the clothes from each other, piece by piece. Dimitri was a master at smiling while talking through his teeth, making cutting comments about the nobility they shared the dance floor with, causing Alexey to laugh. He had been the consummate host at Chernitzy's provincial court, had known everyone's name and how to flatter them, the way to throw a party that would be the talk of the region's nobility for the rest of the season. But Alexey knew that Dimitri despised it all and was never happier than when it was the two of them, left alone in the ruins of a ball.

"Are they happy?" Ivan's brow creased with concern as Alexey spun him by two nobles who glared ferociously. Before Alexey could command him to smile again, Ivan remembered and plastered the correct expression back on his face.

"It is not my concern whether they are happy or not." Alexey pulled Ivan in closer to whisper in his ear. "Because if they are not, now they have defied both my authority and the authority of the former Tzars. And that means I will have no choice but to purge them from court."

Ivan stiffened, but then smiled even wider. "You are a talented politician, Alexey." He licked his lips. "You will preside over the greatest court the country has ever seen."

Alexey smiled indulgently but did not reply, merely focused on the way that Ivan's hand was warm in his. He was already calculating who had been placated by tonight's nod to the country's ancient nobility and its importance, and who would have to be killed for their disrespect.

Because Alexey knew that before he made his final move, before he opened the realm of demons and let them walk the earth, he needed no distractions. He would deal with the factions in the court, he would deal with whatever came from the search for Dimitri, and then there would be nothing left to hold him back.

THIRTY

VASILY

Vasily's anxiety grew with each passing day, and by the time they reached the border of Lietuva, he was quite sure his throat had permanently closed up.

Viktoria arranged with the carriage driver to rendezvous at one of the Novo-Svitsevan border towns while Ayla transferred their baggage to the prison wagon that had been following them since Domachëvo. The inside was a great deal less comfortable than the carriage, with just two benches made of rough wood and no windows. But Vasily could have walked over glass and not noticed, because his entire body was vibrating with danger, and with the anticipation of being with Dimitri again, at least able to see the other man.

"What's on your mind?" Viktoria cocked her head at Vasily, sliding into the seat next to Ayla. "You look troubled."

"Oh," Vasily said, perhaps a tad too earnestly. "I just want to find the traitor. I would hate to let the Tzar down."

Both women nodded. "By the grace of God," Ayla said quietly, "we will not disappoint the Tzar."

Vasily didn't miss the way she flinched as she said it. And how, just like Vasily, she too hadn't said which Tzar.

★

After another day of uncomfortable travel, they rolled to a stop and there was a rap on the roof.

"We must be in Wilnetzk," Ayla breathed. She looked through a knothole in the wagon's side. "It looks like they've found somewhere to leave the wagon."

They got out of the wagon and Vasily's shoe landed directly in a pile of horse manure. It seemed, from the sights and the smells, as though the wagon driver had found some kind of stable yard to wait in. They'd agreed that leaving it on a fine avenue in the middle of the afternoon would be too conspicuous.

Viktoria consulted a map she'd brought with her, guiding them through Wilnetzk and to Prospekyii Avenue, Vasily pretending that he didn't know where they were going and deliberately arguing for a few wrong turns. Eventually, they found themselves loitering on the street he'd called home for a year, tucked behind a tree on the street across from the townhouse. Viktoria pulled out a packet of cigarettes and passed them out. Vasily fiddled with his to have something to do with his hands, and looked over his shoulder at the house.

"It's the right address," Ayla said.

Vasily knew that yes, they were in the right place, but instead he made himself bite his lip. "The Tzar said to watch the door, or the windows, and confirm that we can see Dimitri Alexeyev or a member of his court before we break in. He doesn't want an embarrassment if somehow someone else has taken up residence there."

"We'll wait," Ayla said, taking a drag on her cigarette, flinching nervously as a group of people pushing baby carriages passed by. "One of them will walk by a window—"

"There," Viktoria hissed. "There they are. I recognize his court. He's got to be there too."

And God must have been on their side, or maybe He wasn't. Because the window to the parlor had been slipped open despite the chill, and his friends—his family—were fully visible through the pulled-back curtains. Only Dimitri was missing, which was a godsend, because if Vasily had seen him he wouldn't have been able to stay away. But Dimitri was likely lying in bed, on Mischa's orders, trying to recover from whatever the angel had done to his arm. Or chain-smoking cigarettes, staring into the fire in his room.

The court must have been keeping themselves visible from the street at all times, otherwise they wouldn't have known when he'd need them to appear. Even though his instincts shouted that this wasn't safe, he was glad that he wouldn't have to wait around for proof that this was, indeed, the correct house.

Viktoria and Ayla bent their heads together, whispering, and as they did, Vasily felt a tug right through his heart. Mischa was reading one of their journals, Ladushka was at the table writing something, and Annika was knitting yet another sock. She turned her head briefly, and he caught her gaze. She blew him a kiss before turning back to her work, pretending she hadn't seen him, and he couldn't help but smile.

*

Night fell, and Vasily felt as though he were about to burst out of his skin from all the waiting. Eventually, Ayla gave up cleaning her pistol and nudged Viktoria, who had dozed off against the side of the wagon. "It's dark enough for us to move without being seen. Are you ready?"

Vasily nodded. He had never been more ready. He sent up a quick prayer to God that this all went well, that no one got hurt. Ayla rapped on the roof of the wagon, and it started to roll forward, taking them

THE SINS ON THEIR BONES

out of the stable yard and down the roads that led to the townhouse, the wheels of the wagon clattering against the cobbles loudly enough that Vasily was afraid they would wake the entire city.

When they rolled to a stop, he looked at Viktoria, then Ayla. "Do you remember what to do?"

They both nodded, tucking pistols and knives into place. They pushed open the back of the wagon and dropped down onto the empty street, sneaking into the alley between the townhomes. The night was quiet, broken only by the cawing of a crow, the moon barely shining into the alleyway. Vasily felt along the side of the townhouse, pretending not to know where he was going, squinting in the dark, until his hand hit ivy and wood.

He cringed as he stepped on the vines of the roses that Ladushka used the trellis to grow—she'd be devastated at their loss—but he used the lattice to scale to the third floor of the townhouse.

He heard the gentle creaking of the trellis as Ayla and Viktoria followed behind him, the small snapping sounds of the dead vines they were crushing. When they reached the top of the roof, they filed onto the ledge. Vasily looked down, and his stomach lurched at the height as he shuffled along the ledge, the shingles of the roof scraping his back. It had been a long time since he'd done this, to see how easy a route it would be for an intruder to take.

Carefully, and quickly, he used his foot to disable the tripwire that he'd strung across the ledge, which would cause an explosion large enough to hurt anyone caught in it without blowing a hole in Dimitri's wall at the same time. He prayed the guards thought his momentary pause was from the height and that they couldn't see what he was doing in the dark.

He turned back to Ayla and Viktoria, crouched behind him on the roof. His heart was pounding. "Remember," he whispered, "we need them all *alive* for the Tzar. No matter what happens, do *not* kill them."

He tried to thread as much steel into his voice as he could. If either Ayla or Viktoria killed one of his friends, it would be the end of them. Vasily would murder them himself, creatively and with great relish.

They nodded at him, and he paused right before the window. He listened to their soft breathing against the quiet of the night, his palm damp on the handle of the pistol that he'd tucked into his belt.

Vasily took a breath, said a quick prayer to God, and unlatched the window.

Then he eased it open and paused, pretending to observe the room beyond. It was dark, and it looked like Dimitri was alone, tucked into his bed.

Vasily crooked a finger, beckoning for the other two to follow, then dropped through the window and into Dimitri's bedroom. Twin thumps sounded from behind him as Viktoria and Ayla followed, then a thud as Ayla shut the window behind her.

Dimitri's breathing was deep yet suspiciously even. He didn't move as Vasily crept up to him and pulled a pistol out, pointing its muzzle into the soft space under his jaw.

"Wake up," Vasily said in his coldest voice.

Dimitri's eyes slid open and he looked at Vasily. For a second, there was only him and Dimitri, and Vasily's unending relief that Dimitri hadn't died in his absence, that in the last few weeks it looked like he'd gained a few pounds, the circles fading away from under his eyes. Despite the thick bandage wrapped around his arm, he looked healthier than he'd been at any point since the war.

"Get up," Vasily forced himself to say. Even though what he wanted to say was *Come here* and *Thank the Lord you're safe.*

Dimitri sat up slowly, raising his hands. His left arm was swathed in thick bandages and his fingers were so bruised they looked black in the dark. "Who are you? What the fuck do you want?" His nightshirt was slipping off his shoulder, his skin flushing with what Vasily prayed wasn't fever.

Vasily heard pistols cocking behind him. "For you to get up," he said. "You're under arrest."

Ayla stepped around him and put her pistol to Dimitri's forehead. "Dress. Quietly. If you shout for help, I'll shoot you dead."

Dimitri raised an eyebrow but didn't budge. "How about one hundred thousand tolar to climb back out that window?"

"No," Ayla said, although her voice cracked. "Get up."

Vasily chanced a look back at her and saw tears in her eyes, but she swallowed and hardened her expression. Of course she had no way of knowing that Vasily felt as she did, and that the only one who was genuinely excited about having "found" Dimitri was Viktoria.

Dimitri didn't do anything, just stared at her insolently, and so Viktoria stepped forward and slapped him across the face, hard. "Get *up*." She grabbed him by his uninjured arm and yanked.

He stumbled to his feet and Vasily caught him, forcing himself not to ask if Dimitri was all right. Instead, he braced Dimitri against his body, letting him find his footing while pretending to check him for weapons.

"Ayla," he ordered. "Find him clothes." She'd pick warm ones with care.

After Dimitri had dressed, glaring daggers at them, and Viktoria had bound his hands with cord, Vasily pointed at the door. "We're going to open the door. We're going to walk you downstairs. If you make any noise at all, you'll be knocked unconscious. How many people are in this house with you?"

"Two," Dimitri said after a brief silence, chewing on his lip.

Vasily bit back a grin and a flare of pride at how convincing Dimitri's acting was. He wondered who had been deputized to jump out at them. Probably Annika. He hoped he wouldn't have to break her nose to sell subduing her.

Ayla opened the door and they walked onto the landing. Vasily held his breath, his body tensing as the guards forced Dimitri to follow them.

Annika did, in fact, appear out of nowhere on the landing, knives in hand, and slashed at Viktoria, who leapt backwards just in time and started grappling with her. Somehow, Annika disarmed Viktoria and tossed the gun down the hallway, and then sprang up and punched Vasily in the jaw so hard he saw stars.

"The *fuck*," Vasily hissed under his breath. Annika just winked at him from under the curtain of her hair.

"Don't move." Ayla's voice wavered. "Or I'll shoot him." Vasily turned to see her holding her pistol to the crook of Dimitri's jaw, the barrel of the gun shaking in her hand. Dimitri had gone pale and was swaying on his feet—likely from the pain of his injured arm being bound, Vasily thought, but it did help to sell the panic, even if the thought of Dimitri in pain made Vasily want to scream.

"Listen to her, Anna," Dimitri commanded, his voice thin.

Annika had given up after that, holding up her hands and letting Viktoria disarm her. Vasily took Dimitri by the shoulders, shooing Ayla off of him, beckoning to her to lead the way. He guided Dimitri forward, massaging tiny circles into the tight knots in his shoulders, while Ayla hauled Annika down the first flight of stairs to the landing, then continued down, stopping by the door to Ladushka's room to bind Annika's hands and force her to her knees, pistol pointed at her head.

Viktoria burst into Ladushka's room. Vasily watched as Ladushka stabbed her with a letter opener before Viktoria subdued her, tying her hands, and he fought back the urge to bark at Viktoria not to hurt her as the guard hit Ladushka in the head with the butt of her pistol. Viktoria limped out with a snarling, bound Ladushka, the guard holding a hand to her arm, which was dripping blood.

Then there was a loud crash from downstairs. "Get them to the door," Vasily snapped. "He lied, there's someone else here." It was Mischa, then, who was supposed to be the distraction. He reluctantly released Dimitri into the care of Ayla, who used one hand to point a gun at Annika's head and the other to support Dimitri's elbow as he wobbled his way down the last set of stairs. At least there was a second person watching out for Dimitri—he'd need the help. Vasily caught Dimitri shooting his half sister a tender look when Viktoria turned her back.

Once all of them were in the foyer, Vasily rolled up his sleeves and made his way into the kitchen, where Mischa was sitting, legs propped up on the kitchen table, the remnants of a mug shattered against the floor.

Took you long enough, they mouthed, rolling their eyes.

Vasily grabbed a plate off the sideboard and hurled it against the wall. *Sorry*, he mouthed back. *Trying to make sure Dima didn't die in his own stupid plan.*

Mischa pressed the heels of their palms to their eyes, and then pointed at the left one.

Vasily shrugged, made a fist, and punched them in the eye so hard it made his fingers sting.

Mischa started screaming a very realistic set of expletives, then toppled their chair, standing up. They raked their nails down the side of Vasily's face, leaving burning trails, all while continuing to scream about Vasily's eternal damnation and how they'd never be taken alive.

"You could have been an actor too," Vasily muttered in their ear as he tied their offered wrists using a slipknot. "Don't sell it too hard, it will look fake."

He dragged Mischa out into the foyer by the collar of their shirt. "I'm going to go check the rooms one more time and make sure no one is hiding."

He searched the parlor first, palming away their emergency stash of gir and tolar kept under the cushion of the armchair. Two lethally sharp folding knives went into his pocket next, along with the kiddush cup that they'd brought all the way from the palace. He did his best to ignore the massive bloodstain on the carpet, still smelling faintly of iron, and told himself that even if it looked like no one could lose that much blood and live, Dimitri was very much still alive.

He made his way up to his own room, grabbing the thin folio full of forged identity documents for all of them, tucking it into his breast pocket. He twisted together the two exposed wires on his windowsill, completing the circuit that would trigger explosions if anyone opened a window while they were gone.

He checked the fire in Ladushka's room, which was blazing with the remnants of every important document they'd used to strategize against Alexey, along with what looked like Dimitri's bank ledgers. Annika's room was military-neat, everything tucked away except her favorite knife, lying on the bed. He grinned—she'd known he'd go on a collecting mission before leaving the house, then—and slipped it into his pocket.

Dimitri's room would have nothing of value, but Vasily entered it anyway. He reset the tripwire, relatched the window's lock and ran a hand across the covers on the bed, remembering every happy time he and Dimitri had shared there, knowing that whether their plan worked or not, they would never be back.

Whatever happened, there was nothing left for him and Dimitri here.

Vasily swallowed his pain and made his way back down the stairs, then prayed to God that Dimitri was still His favored son, and that He would bless their path back home.

THIRTY-ONE

Dimitri

He had thought he would be able to do it, to make it through. He
had felt so much stronger these last few weeks. But as the prison
wagon rattled across uneven roads, back towards Rav-Mikhailburg
and Alexey, Dimitri was wholly unsure that he would be able to avoid
his fear long enough to do what needed to be done.

He hid the shaking of his hands by tucking them in between his
legs, barely able to feel his left arm, and leaned against Annika's shoulder, closing his eyes. He wanted to dream, wanted to meet Vasily and
seek his comfort, but he never managed to truly fall asleep. His arm
throbbed each time the cart shuddered over a bump in the road,
sending him into convulsing shivers again.

At intervals, the wagon would stop and his half sister and the other
guard would take them out, one at a time, to relieve themselves and
eat. They tossed blankets into the back of the wagon and left them
there at night to sleep, leaning against each other and the rough-hewn
sides of the wagon. At least Ayla managed to loosen the ties on each
of their wrists when the other guard wasn't looking.

The last time Dimitri had been this cold, he was in a war tent full
of holes, huddling with Annika and Vasily under a single moth-eaten

blanket, trying to stay warm as they planned their last-stand campaign, which turned into the disastrous battle at Vysoka.

So he drifted, and shivered, and thumbed over the hard ridges of the playing card tucked between the layers of the bandage on his arm, dreading the moment they would arrive at the palace that used to be his home.

✶

"He has a fever," Ladushka mumbled one afternoon, her hand cool on the inside of his wrist. "He is burning up."

Dimitri couldn't believe that, because he felt as though he were standing outside in the snow with no clothes on. He was shivering, no matter how close the others crowded around him, sharing their warmth.

"Fuck," Mischa hissed. "I thought the salve I used under those bindings would stop infection, but it's not like they've given us supplies to change his bandages. Or time to stop and bathe."

They shifted in their chains and reached into a pants pocket, pulling out a packet of pills. They tossed them to Annika. "Good thing Ayla was the one to 'search' my pockets. She's still loyal to Dima, at least in part, I'm assuming. It would have been harder to get at the ones I've sewn into the hem of my shirt."

Annika opened the top of the packet, then shook his shoulder. He blinked at her blearily, his eyes heavy. His arm was on fire, the only part of him that was not freezing cold. He wondered if it was because he had carefully wrapped the paper containing the name of God between the layers of bandages before Vasily's arrival, along with the playing card and Vasily's note. *Not Yet.* But he didn't want to think of that, not now, not when Vasily was so close to him yet further away than ever.

"Here," Annika said, pressing a pill into the palm of his hand. "You need to take this. Please."

He raised his hand to his mouth slowly and swallowed the bitter pill. "It would be the greatest of ironies if I died of infection before we ever made it back to the palace."

"You'll be fine." Mischa reached forward from the other side of the wagon and rubbed circles on his aching thigh, and Annika shifted so Dimitri could lean further into her warmth.

"They will not let you die, Dima." Ladushka uncurled herself from against Mischa's side as they reached out for Dimitri. "You are far too politically valuable."

"Thanks." Dimitri rolled his eyes.

"Maybe Dima should convince the angry guard to let us stop at an inn anyway." Mischa snorted. "How's Dima supposed to seduce Alexey if he shows up to court filthy?"

Annika shook her head. "Sure, just ask her nicely for an inn and a hot bath." She huffed a laugh.

Dimitri shivered again and pulled the wool blanket tighter around his shoulders. "I hope Vasya's all right." The wagon gave another jolt, and he winced. "I haven't been able to truly fall asleep and check on him." He nodded his head at the front of the wagon, where presumably Vasily was riding.

Mischa tilted their head at him, and then pulled another packet of pills out of their pocket. "Bite it in half." They tossed the packet to Annika, who dispensed a pill.

Ladushka leaned forward. "What does that one do?"

Dimitri put it between his teeth and crunched down, wincing at the metallic taste. Annika grabbed the other half from between his lips before Dimitri could swallow it.

"Painkiller," Mischa said, but their voice was already going soft around the edges. "It will dull the pain, enough to sleep. Hopefully enough to dream."

Dimitri let the soothing heaviness spread through him. His eyes closed of their own accord, and then he was asleep.

✳

"That went well, I thought." In this dream, Vasily was sitting cross-legged against the trunk of an enormous tree. They were in some kind of forest, the scent of loam and rotting leaves drifting through the air. The tree trunk had a hollow in it, with a ratty old blanket, a small stack of books, a candle burned almost to a stub. It was so small that only a child could have fit inside.

Dimitri looked closer and could have sworn he saw an unruly mop of curls with leaves caught in it illuminated by the candlelight. But then Vasily shifted, as if conscious of his dream-self behind him, like he was trying to protect the boy from Dimitri's prying eyes.

"It did," Dimitri agreed. He crawled forward over the leaves and twigs on the ground, until he was on his hands and knees in front of Vasily. "Are you all right?"

Vasily reached out and cupped his face in both hands, bringing him in for a kiss. "I am. Are you?"

Dimitri didn't answer, just tipped his forehead forward. He took in a shuddering breath, realizing that every time he'd seen Vasily in dreams these last long weeks had given him the sense of safety he'd craved since Alexey's death. Since the start of the war. Since his exile to Wilnetzk. Since letting Vasily leave.

It was a feeling that only one other person had truly been able to give him, and something in Dimitri's heart burned with the thought that Vasily's comfort was better, and purer, and more real and selfless and solid than Alexey's had ever been.

He couldn't lose this. He couldn't bear it. This would be the loss that tore him to shreds.

"Dima." Vasily put his hands around Dimitri's waist and pulled Dimitri into his lap. Dimitri winced at the realization that his feelings must have found their way out into the dream, that Vasily *knew*.

"Dima, darling, it's okay. You have to be brave. I'll be right there. I won't leave you, not now. Not like this."

Dimitri couldn't respond. He fought through the tears that were blinding him and leaned forward to kiss Vasily as if it were the very last time.

✳

They did not stop. Instead, in a few days' time, they reached Rav-Mikhailburg.

As the prison wagon clattered over the cobblestones of Dimitri's city, the seat of his power, he looked around at what remained of his court. The foundation upon which he would rebuild his power. They were all dirty from the road, their clothes hanging limp, their faces smudged with dirt. Ladushka had purple bruises under her eyes, and Annika's gaze was wary as she sat up, fully alert again. Mischa had a blank expression on their face that Dimitri knew from the war meant they were terrified.

It hit him that perhaps he should have come alone. If he failed, they'd be shot as traitors and buried in unmarked graves.

But Dimitri knew that had he suggested that, Ladushka would have thrown him a withering glare that told him quite clearly, even without words, that she thought he was an idiot. Mischa would have made a sarcastic remark about how he couldn't possibly fend for himself. Annika would have wrapped him in a fierce hug and told him that he would never be alone as long as she was alive.

And Vasily would have followed him anywhere, wouldn't have even let him contemplate going on his own.

None of them had protested the plan. He had not needed to ask if they would come with him, back to Novo-Svitsevo. Because he knew that even if he was standing at the edge of the world, these four would be behind him, holding him up. They were his friends, his family, his strength, his salvation.

And he could not let them die, which meant that he had to do everything in his power to succeed.

"If I die first," he said, catching their eyes as the wagon ground to a halt, trying to convey all of the love and the trust and the gratitude he felt for each of them in a single glance, wishing he could see Vasily and convey the same to him, "I'll tell you the secrets of heaven."

Not a toast this time. A promise.

∗

The palace was as he remembered it, although he had never entered it in chains.

Vasily stood by as a group of guards pulled them all out of the wagon, blinking in the sunlight, shivering in the wind. Then they were shackled and marched into the palace, surrounded by a phalanx of guards.

Dimitri's hands were trembling, his breaths short, but his mind was clear and his heart was hard.

They walked through the entrance hall, where Dimitri had taken Alexey's hand more times than he could count, the both of them dressed in ceremonial uniforms, before walking out for a parade through the city.

He glanced into the open doors of the formal receiving room, which had not changed since the time that they had arrived back after the coronation and Dimitri had broken down, when Alexey had ordered everyone out of the room and had the doors shut, letting him cry. Alexey had held him and let him grieve everything he had lost and everything he had gained.

He choked on the happy memories, on the tears that pricked at his eyes as he walked through the home he had shared with Alexey.

He stopped dead in front of the ballroom, the mirrors glinting and the floors polished, and remembered every time he'd walked through those doors to see the flush of Alexey's cheeks and the brilliance of his smile before taking his arm to begin each formal ball.

Every memory was sour now, poisoned with the knowledge of what had come after.

Dimitri closed his eyes and walked forward on instinct, stumbling in his chains, letting the guards lead him to what he knew was the throne room.

They stopped before the throne room doors, and a guard slapped the back of his head, hissing at him to open his eyes.

He looked down the length of the room where he had presided over this country. The room where he had been crowned Tzar of Novo-Svitsevo. It was full of the lords and ladies of the court and their retinues, clustered around the edges of the long room, leaving the blood-red carpet stretching down the center clear. Candles still burned in the golden candelabras, and the frescoes on the wall still depicted the history of his family.

He was positioned at the end of the long carpet, and his court was arrayed behind him. He struggled to keep his shoulders back, his stare fierce and unyielding, despite the terror swelling in his chest. Vasily took a place of honor by Alexey's side, staring at him. His gaze was a lifeline, and Dimitri never wanted to let it go.

But eventually he had to, because Alexey was there, and for the good of his country and his friends, he needed to play the part of dutiful, repentant husband one last time.

Alexey sat on the throne. He was dressed all in black, his hands gripping the bejeweled arms of the throne in a way that belied his casual posture. His eyes were haunted, his face gaunt, his jaw stiff. Wrongness radiated off him, stronger than ever before, so much so that the ancient, survival-keen side of Dimitri's brain begged him to turn and run.

Alexey stared at him cooly, his eyes full of black nothingness. Dimitri struggled not to cringe away from his husband's gaze as it traveled down the length of his body, lingering on his face, the bandage on his arm, his filthy clothes. But there was something else there in his searching look, something even more terrifying. Something like concern. Dimitri's hands shook violently, and his knees felt weak.

"Kneel."

Alexey's voice was laced with steel, but there was a crack there, at the end of the word.

Dimitri was forced down by a guard, his knees hitting the floor with a sickening thud. He fell forward on his arms to brace himself, retching when his left hand made contact with the carpet. He looked up at Alexey high on the dais through the curtain of his hair, trying to keep his expression flat through the pain.

He gasped for breath. He thought he could do this. He thought he was strong enough. He thought there was no more love left there.

But that wasn't the truth of it—there was still a small part of his heart that was devoted to Alexey. Maybe it would always be that way, for as long as he lived. Maybe loving other people, moving on, even, would never erase the stain of having loved the wrong man. Maybe it was his curse, to always have that shard of Alexey lodged in his heart.

Dimitri thought he'd feel nothing but relief as he killed his husband, but now he knew that wouldn't be true. He choked on a sob. Alexey leaned forward on the throne, his hands braced on his knees.

Dimitri knew how he looked. He knew what this was. It was a repetition of so many nights when they had played this game, just the two of them, the throne room locked and the guards dismissed. Except now, this was not a game for the two of them that ended in frenzied passion. Now, Alexey would humiliate him in public.

He hunched his shoulders, curling into himself, small and broken and vulnerable.

"Come." The order echoed through the throne room like the crack of a whip.

Something about being ordered around like a dog made Dimitri pause and grit his teeth.

"*Obey me*," Alexey snarled.

Dimitri was playing a part. He was doing it to save his country. But that didn't stop him from flinching, from knowing instinctively what came after Alexey used that tone of voice, the animal that he was obeying without a second thought.

He forced his mind to focus, even as his body started to move. He told himself that Alexey had never realized the problem with games. They required two players, and anything could happen if they were both determined to win.

He started to crawl to Alexey, slowly, painfully, his chains rattling with every motion. The hall was interminably long, the carpet rough under his hands, the weight on his injured arm almost unbearable. Tears pricked at the corners of his eyes, and he let them come.

He heard Annika's choked sob, the titters of the assembled courtiers. He knew Ladushka and Mischa would be upright, impassive, like stone. He knew Vasily would look like he was amused, but that he would be dying inside.

It didn't matter. None of it mattered. Because he would crawl over broken glass to Alexey if that was what it took to get close to him again. If that was what it took to kill him.

He reached the steps of the dais and made his way up on hands and knees, until he was prostrate at Alexey's feet.

He kissed his husband's boots, the leather slick against his lips. Dimitri was shaking, not sure if it was from the fever or the fear or sheer desperation.

His entire life narrowed down to this, to this one moment, this one chance to make it right.

Alexey pulled him up by the collar and slapped him across the face with the back of a hand, the onyx ring he wore cutting a gash in Dimitri's cheek. Dimitri hissed, but kept his gaze averted.

It was miraculous how much he still felt for this man, despite it all. It was astounding how his body responded to Alexey's punishment. Dimitri hated himself for it, for loving this man who had torn the country apart.

But he could love Alexey the same way Alexey had loved him. Unflinchingly, honestly, willing to look him in the eyes and assess his flaws. Willing to betray him, because the love they both felt for their country was more powerful than anything else.

Alexey was breathing hard. He let go of Dimitri's collar, and Dimitri slumped forward, gasping with pain, kneeling before his husband.

"Beg," Alexey ordered, his voice a low snarl but his tone pleading. "Beg for your life and the lives of your court, or I will shoot you myself."

Dimitri cleared his throat and summoned his courage. "Forgive me." He licked his cracked lips and looked up into Alexey's eyes. "*Moy Tzar.*"

He could see every muscle in Alexey's body tense, and it went straight to his heart, the way Alexey looked at him with barely disguised hope in his eyes.

"Go on." Alexey's voice was hard, at odds with the way he reached down and cupped Dimitri's chin in his hand, thumbing away the blood that dripped from his cheek.

Dimitri shivered. "I was wrong." He paused, waiting for the tightness in his chest to recede, the part of him that wanted to lean into Alexey's grip. "I fought you, because I didn't recognize your authority. I did not bow to the realization that it was you, not I, who had been chosen by God to rule." He closed his eyes. "I cede my throne to you and beg for your forgiveness. I beg for you to let us join your court and serve the Lord our God by serving you."

There was a long, horrific pause. Dimitri did not breathe. He did not move. All he did was pray to God that Alexey would not break his neck here and now.

In the utter stillness of the throne room, Alexey breathed out the softest sigh.

Everything in Dimitri's body tensed, his heart pounding, his breath caught in his throat as he teetered on the edge of life and death, his fate resting in the hands of a man never known for his mercy.

And then Alexey dropped his chin, leaning forward on the throne, until their foreheads were touching. "You know, Dima," Alexey whispered, "that was all I ever wanted from you. That was all." He kissed Dimitri's forehead with icy lips.

Dimitri did not flinch.

Alexey straightened up, then rose from the throne, pulling Dimitri up by his arm. Dimitri stumbled, hating that he had to lean against Alexey to steady himself. "You see," Alexey said, addressing the court, "I am merciful to those who recognize when they have faltered. I am willing to welcome back to the fold any who have turned from God's light, if only they repent."

Dimitri caught Vasily's eye. He held his gaze and gave Dimitri a minuscule nod.

Alexey snapped his fingers, and guards unchained his friends. Mischa caught Ladushka as she stumbled when the guards yanked off her cuffs. Annika stood tall and defiant, hate in her eyes as she glared at Alexey.

"My court submits as well." Dimitri let his voice carry to the end of the hall, and his heart clenched as he watched them all bow. They were stiff, like they had forgotten how to show deference to some-one who demanded it.

He vowed to himself that when he was back on the throne, they would never bow to anyone again.

*

Alexey handed him over to the palace guard, and Dimitri was escorted out of the throne room. Guards surrounded Mischa, Ladushka and Annika, and they trailed behind. An unfamiliar steward led them to the wing of the palace reserved for guests, and Dimitri was locked into a nondescript room that would usually host a member of the lower nobility. From the footsteps and the sounds of doors being bolted in the hall, they were all housed together—all the easier to watch over. Because Dimitri knew what this was. Even though Alexey had forgiven them publicly, he would keep them under guard until he'd determined what to do with them.

Or that was what Alexey thought would happen. Dimitri rubbed the bandages on his left arm, feeling the hard ridge of paper hidden there.

He hoped the guards would let him go to his husband tonight, one last time.

There was no knock on the door before it was opened. Servants appeared and bustled into the bathing chamber, the guards stepping in out of the hallway, surveying the scene with alert eyes and hands on the grips of their pistols.

Dimitri submitted to being bathed, shaved and dressed. But he refused the attentions of the physician who came to tend to his arm and breathed a sigh of relief when she put up no fight before leaving. A servant brought in a tray of food and set it on the table. Dimitri ate unthinkingly, not tasting any of the fish he was putting in his mouth. He requested cigarettes and paced around the room, smoking them down to stubs one after the other.

His heart was pounding all the while.

When night fell, Dimitri shed his clothes and donned the black silk nightshirt that one of the servants had left on the bed. The tiles of the washroom were cold on his bare feet as he splashed water on his face and rearranged his hair, then leaned his forearms on the sink basin. His bandage was filthy, and the tips of the fingers on his left hand were beginning to turn a disturbing shade of puce, but he didn't dare to unwrap it. He looked at himself in the burnished mirror, schooling his expression into something contrite, remorseful, devastated by the long separation between him and Alexey. He had to look the part.

The very last thing he did, with shaking fingers, was remove Vasily's note from where it was tucked between his skin and the bandage.

Not Yet, the outside read. Except he might be about to die, so if not now, when?

He broke the seal and unfolded the note. And his throat closed up as he looked down at the king of hearts, folded up with the letter, black ink rendering it into a perfect likeness of his own face.

There was a date on the sketch. It was two years old.

Stunned, he removed the joker from where it had been tucked beneath the bandage, laying the card with Vasily's face next to his on the basin.

He brought his eyes back to the note. *Dima,* he read as his throat closed up.

> *Last night, as I lay awake next to you as you slept, I thought to myself: Could I ever let myself admit how deeply I care for you? Even now, even here, when we might never see each other again?*
>
> *Dima . . . you snuck into the cracks of my heart. You fractured me along all of my fault lines, rebreaking my bones to set them straight. You healed me, because I let myself trust you, even though I told myself that wasn't what I was doing. Even though I swore that wasn't what I was doing.*
>
> *You shifted my entire image of myself. For all this time, I thought I deserved what happened to me as a child. I thought I was the one at fault. But now that instinct just kills me, because I see it in you too. I know you believe, deep down, that you forced this choice on Alexey, that if you had just made the*

right decision, or reacted the right way, or said the right thing, everything would have been okay. And I know no deeper truth than what an utter lie that is.

Every time I saw that flash of fear on your face as you looked at me, that terror after you thought you had done something wrong—and the way you would try to placate me before I even had the chance to say, No, darling, get off your knees, you don't owe me this—*every time I saw that, I wanted to stop you. I* needed *to stop you, so that with the next person, with every person after me, you would look them in the eye and not apologize, instead of paying for imagined slights with your body and your beauty and the entirety of your heart.*

Because it broke me, over and over, looking at you on your knees. Because my heart hurt for you, knowing what had been done to you, but also because it forced me to ask, what if I was wrong, just like you misperceive your own past? What if I didn't bring my old hurts on myself? What if what happened to me wasn't my fault?

That shift in understanding, it just . . . it sent me drifting, because this part of myself, this fundamental unlovableness that I've anchored my identity to, the ways in which I thought I caused other people to break me by being too much and not enough, that wasn't true, was it, Dima? Watching you blame yourself taught me that. I am as entirely faultless as you. I could not believe in your innocence and simultaneously condemn myself.

And that? That healed me more than you will ever know.

Truthfully, I gave you my heart the first time I saw you, and you've been holding it all this time, patching it back together, making sure it's safe. You just didn't know that was what you were doing, and you didn't know how good you were at doing it.

I tried to walk out the door without writing this down. I tried to convince myself it was the right thing to do. But that part of me that's a traitor, that wants to think that you can give yourself to someone to heal you instead of break you, that part of me that fundamentally hopes? That thinks, this is what life is, looking someone in the eye and handing them your heart and saying, I trust you to patch the broken pieces of this and then hand it back to me, whole, mended?

That is the side of me that knows this is the part of being alive that is messy, and beautiful, and painful and raw and perfect. It's the part I cannot bear to give up. It's the part of me in this admission that I'm leaving now with you.

I need you to take this final truth from me—that you are good and kind and deserving of so much care and warmth and comfort—so when I don't come back, you can use it to be safe with everyone who comes after me. I want to die knowing you will survive, that you will believe me, that you will believe these words, and that when you pick who you give your heart to next, it's to someone who will mend it the way I never could because you and I were never meant to be together. Even though I tried to do for you what you had done so selflessly for me.

I hope that, in some small way, I succeeded, because I love you, Dima. I love you. I love you. I've loved you since the day I met you and I'll love you until the day that I die, and for all the days after.

With all my heart,

Vasya

He read it again. And again, though Vasily's neat script blurred in his vision. The third time through, tears fell onto the paper, smearing the ink.

Dimitri slid to the floor, wrapped his arms around his aching, desperate heart, and did his best to stifle his sobs, unwilling to believe that instead of rushing to him—to Vasily, this man who achingly, uncontrollably *loved* him—he'd have to steel himself and head back to the bedroom where a part of him had died, and face Alexey, his husband, the one who had never truly deserved his love, one last time.

THIRTY-TWO

ALEXEY

Alexey had not meant to spare him.

It was the weakness in his heart, the one part of him that could never shake the urge to protect Dimitri. It had betrayed him when he failed to kill Dimitri in the months before the war. It had betrayed him at Vysoka. It had betrayed him again, in the throne room, when he should have ordered them all shot in the head and dumped in the river, but instead he had let them back into the palace.

Alexey told himself that it was benevolence, that it was grace and mercy, all the things that made a ruler great. He told himself that ruling beside Dimitri once more would be even better than having Ivan by his side, that it would truly unite the court. That he would be seen as a model of forgiveness and compassion. A true father for the nation. After all, did the Lord his God not make the holiest day of the year one for forgiveness of sin?

But deep in his chest, Alexey knew there was only one thing he could blame his decision on, and that was the fact that he had always loved Dimitri Alexeyev with all his heart.

"Mikhail." He turned to the other man once the guards had removed Dimitri and his court from the room. "Come with me."

Alexey led him into the council chamber off the side of the throne room and clicked the door shut behind them. "Thank you," he said quietly, "for bringing him back. You have done a great service to the nation. I award you the lordship of Fedorovki, which comes with an estate and its own well-stocked treasury. You will want for nothing, both as a lord in your own right and my general. I will have the papers drawn up in the morning."

Mikhail stayed by the door, his hands clasped before him. "Thank you, *Moy Tzar.*"

Alexey stared into the fire and felt none of the triumph he had anticipated. Just a deep, yawning sadness, bigger and emptier than the void that lived inside him. Dimitri had not returned on his own. And now he was here, back with him, but Alexey was not sure if Dimitri was lying through his teeth, or if his capture had made him realize that the only way this would end was with his capitulation or his death.

If he felt remorse, it hadn't been enough to bring him back to Alexey's side of his own will. He'd had to be brought before him in chains.

"What are you going to do with him?" Mikhail's question was tentative.

Alexey bit his lip. "Whatever God commands."

*

He needed to ask God for guidance, of that Alexey was sure. He ordered his new steward to bar all interruptions and went to immerse himself in the sacred pool.

Submerged in the water, he repented for his weakness.

I ask for forgiveness, the Lord my God.

Alexey floated in the water, weightless, waiting for His voice to absolve him of this sin. *I repent. Forgive me for the weakness of my heart.*

But for the first time since his rebirth, God did not answer his prayers. There was nothing, even when he surfaced and prayed aloud, even when he smashed his fist into the side of the pool and screamed in wordless frustration.

It was not possible that God had forsaken him. This silence was simply God's reminder that he was the Tzar of Novo-Svitsevo, and the decisions that the Tzar made were all blessed by Him. Alexey was not a child who needed to ask permission for every little thing, forgiveness for every small mistake.

Alexey rose out of the pool and wrapped himself in a white cotton robe. He made his way back to his bedchamber, the carpet smooth on his bare feet.

He sat down at his desk, the warmth of the fire barely reaching him, and placed his head in his hands, his fingers knotted in his hair. He would have to find a way to ensure that Dimitri had truly repented, that he had not just decided to beg for his life once he was caught.

Until then, Dimitri would have to remain a prisoner, as would his court.

He rolled his neck, trying to banish the tightness that had settled there, the weight of his indecision about Dimitri. Alexey growled in frustration and wondered if he should call for Ivan, but the thought of the boy soured his mood. He and Dimitri had never broken their marriage contract, and now that Dimitri had been proven to be alive, the court would whisper if Alexey did not divorce him before marrying Ivan, if that was still to be his plan.

And yet, the thought of officially ending his marriage to Dimitri *hurt*.

Alexey had not realized how much he'd missed his husband until he'd seen him again, and it gnawed at his soul. Dimitri was a challenge, a stallion that would never quite be broken, even if he accepted the bridle most of the time. Ivan was tame, a man who would be forever content to rule by his side, the right choice for Novo-Svitsevo, a clean break from the past.

And yet, the thought of marrying Ivan made his skin crawl.

When a knock sounded at his door, he stilled, his jaw working as he attempted to contain his frustration at being disturbed. He crossed to the door in five long strides, pulling it open to reveal Dimitri, looking as lost and alone as the night he'd learned his entire family was dead. Alexey took in the glassiness of Dimitri's eyes, the dark bruises underneath, the way his cheekbones were gaunt and the way he cradled his arm to his chest. He was shaking, his knees quivering as he stood in the hall flanked by guards.

"Lyosha," Dimitri whispered, and started to sob.

In that moment, Alexey's heart stopped entirely, and his world narrowed to the man in front of him, the only one in the world he had ever been weak for.

He could never let Dimitri be seen like this, humiliated like this in front of others. He snarled at the guards to leave, and they saluted and marched down the hallway.

Alexey bundled Dimitri into his arms and shut the door, letting him cry against his chest. Alexey could feel each one of Dimitri's ribs through the thin silk of his nightshirt. He picked Dimitri up and carried him to the bed, sitting down against the headboard, the smaller man cradled in his lap.

He leaned his face into Dimitri's hair as he continued to sob. "Shh," he whispered, hugging Dimitri tight, the way he'd done so many nights before when his husband needed comfort.

Dimitri turned to face him, his eyes wet with tears, shadows in the hollows of his cheeks. Even after all this time, after all they had been through, after everything, he was still undeniably, heartbreakingly beautiful. Alexey put a hand to his face, running his thumb over Dimitri's lips, using it to wipe away the falling tears.

Dimitri shuddered and let out a sigh, then buried his face in the hollow of Alexey's shoulder, going limp.

Alexey closed his eyes, the weight of Dimitri on his lap solid and real. It brought him back to every moment they had shared on his family's estate, curled up together in bed, reveling in each other's presence. It healed something within him that he had not realized was broken, the part of him that would always long for Dimitri, the part that wanted to hold him close.

"Dima," he whispered. His heart pounded, and for a moment, he hesitated. But then he steeled himself. "Why are you here?"

"To say I'm sorry," Dimitri said against his chest. His voice was gentle and laced with sadness. "To wonder aloud if you might take me back."

"Dima." Alexey swallowed against the grief rising in his chest. "I never let you go."

"Do you remember what you said to me, that first night?" Dimitri curled a fist into Alexey's nightshirt.

A lump formed in Alexey's throat, one which he could not will away. "I do."

"Tell me," Dimitri rasped. "Tell me what you promised me."

Alexey closed his eyes, remembering the passion of that night, the way it had felt to cradle Dimitri in his arms after their first time. Dimitri's first time. "I promised you," Alexey whispered, "that I would bring you joy all of your days. That I would protect you with everything that I am. That I would defend you from anything that wished to harm you. That I would always love you. Because you are mine and I am yours."

Dimitri let out another choked sob. "And did you?" Dimitri's voice was rough, thick with tears. "Did you protect me? Did you defend me and love me?"

"I tried." Alexey tightened his grip on Dimitri. "Dima, I tried. Everything I did, I did to honor you. It was you who refused to see it."

"Fuck you," Dimitri said, but there was no heat in it, just resignation. Dimitri finally raised his head to look at Alexey, and tears were glimmering along his lashes. "We're just two broken men, aren't we? Who tried and tried, and yet in the trying, made everything worse."

Alexey recoiled and squared his shoulders. "I am not broken."

Dimitri laughed wetly. "If you refuse to admit it, then, who are we but two people who loved each other to the point of destruction? You and I burned everything to the ground in our wake. I loved you, Alexey, but I *lost* you all the same. I lost you to that fucking Holy Science of yours, and you never came back to me."

Alexey fought back the urge to scream at Dimitri, to reprimand him for how wrong he was. Instead, he just slackened his grip and shoved him away, rolling the other man off him and sinking back into the headboard.

He had thought, for a moment, that Dimitri was truly repentant. "Why are you in my bedroom, Dima? To complain to me that you lost me, long after I had lost you to the throne and to Novo-Svitsevo? To mock me for my desire to protect you? You said you came to apologize. Now you snap at me."

"I'm sorry." Dimitri sat up on the bed, his shoulders hunched, and looked into the fire. He sighed and passed a hand over his eyes. "I didn't mean to start a fight. I came to see if there was still—if there *is* still—love here. If there is some part of this, of us, that we can still save."

Alexey could not bear the traitorous hope that flared in his chest, alongside the grief that Dimitri's mere presence stirred up. "And if there is, what then?"

Dimitri eyed him. "You tell me, Alexey. What then?"

Alexey swallowed, making a decision in between one heartbeat and the next, to let go of his caution and his reservation and to trust in his heart. "If you publicly accept the Holy Science, if you swear by your heart and soul that you'll submit to me fully, if you make restitution for the wrongs you have wrought, I will allow you to live out the rest of your days quietly in the palace"—he paused—"as my husband."

Dimitri could no longer be trusted with the power that a transformation by the Holy Science would gift him, not after the war and his betrayal. But Alexey could offer him this, a mending of their relationship, an offer for Dimitri to stand by his side where he had always belonged.

A tear slipped down Dimitri's cheek. "You would not renounce me?"

"I never did, Dima." Alexey shook his head. "I never did."

Dimitri crawled forward on the bed and took Alexey's hands in his and kissed him. Heat flared low in Alexey's belly, and he felt himself stiffening as Dimitri climbed onto his lap, straddling him. He ran his hands down Dimitri's back, and Dimitri groaned against his lips. Alexey took in each of the imperfections in Dimitri's skin, the freckles dusting the tops of his shoulders, the smell of him, the way his body felt pressed against his.

This was what the scriptures meant when they spoke of the bond between beloveds, the holiness of joining their bodies. Dimitri would always be a part of him, and Alexey had forgotten during these last long years what it meant to be whole.

"Dima," he whispered, pulling back and staring into his husband's eyes. "I love you. I have always loved you."

Dimitri swallowed, his eyes filling once again with tears.

Alexey did not wait for an answer, could not bear if the sentiment was no longer returned. So he simply reached down Dimitri's thighs and grasped the edge of the nightshirt, pulling it up and over Dimitri's head. It caught on the bandage covering Dimitri's left forearm, and Alexey reached down to gently untangle the fabric.

His entire body tensed as his fingers touched the bandage and fire shot through him, the purest agony that he could imagine, as if he were being torn apart.

My son. Stop. The voice of God was back now, thundering through his head, splitting it open with the force of the command. It jarred Alexey down to his bones. He had never heard the voice of God outside of that special meditative state that he had to work to cultivate. He had never had this easy and instantaneous connection to the Lord his God.

Alexey recoiled, shooting up to a crouch so fast that Dimitri fell off him, landing on his back against the sheets.

There is wickedness here, God hissed to Alexey. *I can feel it.* The void inside Alexey was throbbing, the edges stretching, the darkness recoiling and shifting like it was attempting to flee from Dimitri's very presence.

Dimitri was breathing hard, splayed on his back, his eyes wary and his hands fisted in the sheets. "What is it, Lyosha?" His eyes darted to the bandage around his arm.

Alexey slid off the bed and stood, reaching behind the bed frame for one of the daggers he always kept tucked against the wall. His hands were shaking as he took the hilt in his hand. "Dima." Alexey's voice was cold, even to his own ears. "Unwind your bandage."

Dimitri froze and drew in a single sharp breath. "It's just an injury."

"The court physician can rebind it." Alexey flipped the knife in his hand, the blade hidden behind his back.

Dimitri's eyes grew wide, and he scrabbled backwards. "It hurts. I can't."

"You must." Alexey threaded the dagger through the belt of his robe, then leaned onto the bed, his arms bracketing Dimitri's feet, and reached out a hand to grab Dimitri's left wrist. When his skin touched the bandage, fire shot through him again, and Alexey clenched his jaw.

He wishes to hurt you. Alexey could feel God's fury echoing through his own chest.

Dimitri's breaths were coming in audible gasps as Alexey yanked him forward, forcing Dimitri onto his knees, his hand locked in the vise of Alexey's fist.

"I will ask you one last time." Alexey stared into Dimitri's eyes. "Unwind. Your. Bandage."

Dimitri looked up at him, his face contorted with fury. "No," he growled, and swiped a hand under the pillows, somehow producing a dagger with which he lunged at Alexey, as if to stab him.

Alexey grabbed the knife he'd threaded through his belt and had it at Dimitri's throat before he even had the chance to blink, Alexey's body reacting to the threat without his command.

"Do. Not. Move," Alexey growled. Releasing Dimitri's wrist, he reached down and picked at the knot of the bandage, ripping it open, letting the thick cotton unravel.

A scrap of parchment fell onto the sheets. Dimitri looked down at it, scrabbling for it, his chest heaving. But Alexey was faster, snatching it up, Dimitri looking at him with murder in his eyes. Alexey unfurled the parchment with the tip of a finger and fought the bile that rose up in his throat. It was a word, written on the parchment, but he could not look at it or pain lanced through his body.

You know what you must do.

No. Alexey recoiled instinctively.

I am the Lord your God, and I command you to kill him. Love demands sacrifice, Alexey Balakin. Sacrifice for your God.

"May your sins write themselves on your bones," Dimitri spat, "so that when you finally die, you'll never escape them and the Lord our God will punish you for every last thing that you've done."

He lunged again, and Alexey grabbed his wrist, so hard that he felt the bone crunch as Dimitri's fingers spasmed, the knife Dimitri held falling onto the floor.

"Dima." Alexey leaned down to whisper in his beloved's ear. "I am blessed by the righteous hand of the Lord our God, and I will *never* die."

Dimitri jerked underneath him, trying to buck Alexey off. The motion shocked Alexey enough that he loosened his grip on Dimitri's wrist. Dimitri broke free for a moment, reaching out and wrapping his hands around Alexey's throat. Alexey swatted his hands away, crushing Dimitri's windpipe between his fingers, watching as Dimitri's face purpled. "Stop fighting me," Alexey snarled. He grasped harder as Dimitri started to flail, Dimitri's knee kicking him in the ribs so hard that Alexey gasped and dropped the dagger onto the sheets.

He shoved Dimitri down against the bed with a hand on his collarbone and winced at the way the bone cracked. He let go of Dimitri's throat as Dimitri screamed, curling over the shard of bone that poked out of his skin. "Why will you not *obey me*?" Alexey blinked away the tears in his eyes as Dimitri lashed out with a fist, catching him across the jaw.

Alexey grabbed him by the arm and shoved him back against the headboard so hard that the wood cracked. Dimitri lolled forward like a broken doll, blood pouring from a gash in his head, but then he looked up and kicked out weakly, gasping.

"You never gave me a fucking *choice*, Alexey." Dimitri was sobbing. "You could have just *loved* me, you could have been content with me, with *us*, but you had to go and fucking ruin it by making me sin, by turning yourself into *this*—" He lashed out again, raking his nails over Alexey's face.

"Stop *fighting*," Alexey screamed, pinning Dimitri's arm to the headboard, ignoring the way he could feel the bone of Dimitri's arm snap under his hand. Dimitri gagged, tears running down his face, but he kept struggling, kept *fighting* . . .

Alexey closed his eyes and submitted to the will of God. He reached for the dagger on the bed and plunged it into the space between Dimitri's ribs. There was a heartbeat of resistance as metal met flesh, but then Dimitri's skin gave way and muscle and tissue parted, the blade sinking into his heart as easily as a knife sliding through butter.

Dimitri groaned, his hands fluttering down to the hilt of the dagger that was now buried in his chest. "Alexey," he whispered, a bubble of blood gathering at the corner of his mouth. "You—"

Dimitri stared down at his hands, at the blood that was dripping down his body, and fell forward. His breaths started to come in shallow gasps, a rattle echoing from his throat.

Alexey was numb as he pulled the blade out from Dimitri's chest.

"I didn't—" he whispered. "You were fighting—why are you always fighting me, Dima? Why can you not just *obey*?"

He caught Dimitri's shoulders, laying him down on the bed, watching him struggle for breath, watching as the color faded from his skin and the warmth leached from his body. He cradled Dimitri's head in his hands, his tears falling onto Dimitri's face.

Dimitri lifted one hand as his eyes glazed over, smearing his blood on Alexey's cheek as he whispered, "Vasya." And then his hand fell limply to the sheets, and Dimitri stopped breathing. Alexey's heart stopped too, and he was suffused with confusion and a cold, crystal-clear panic, more complete and overwhelming than what he had felt when his own life had left his body.

Alexey finally knew how Dimitri must have felt that night as he watched the man he loved die, knowing deep in his bones that there was nothing he could do to stop it—because he was responsible. He understood, finally, Dimitri's rage and Dimitri's grief.

Except Alexey had died so he could rise from the dead, and for Dimitri, death was the end of everything.

Alexey dropped the knife onto the bed and put a bloody fist to his mouth to stifle his scream.

THIRTY-THREE

VASILY

Vasily knew the exact moment that Dimitri Alexeyev died.

He'd been lying fully dressed in bed, in the room he'd been given in the palace, buried in blankets and praying to God that Dimitri found the knife he'd placed under Alexey's pillow, which he'd slipped in that afternoon during a change of guards. Praying that the whole plan worked, that Dimitri was able to get the name of God into Alexey's mouth and stab him. He'd listened to every creak in the palace, wishing he and Dimitri had talked about what would come after Alexey's death, cursing his oversight.

Dimitri would come to him, he was sure. They'd go find the rest of the court, then spend the night determining which guards were loyal to them and which they'd have to execute. And come morning, they'd have Dimitri back on the throne, and then the nobles would swear allegiance to him because, after all, everyone who lived in the palace was terrified of Alexey. Vasily could practically smell it. They'd probably cry with joy to have him gone.

He'd continued on like this until a sudden burst of pain had split his skull in half. He'd rolled over the side of the bed, gagging from the agony, which passed as soon as it had come on.

And then his head had felt strangely empty, the place where Dimitri had been now hollowed out like the muffled void right after a bomb blast, and he'd put two and two together, sure of what had happened like he'd never been sure of anything in his life, and he'd thrown up all over the rug.

In all of this, in all the time since they'd fled Rav-Mikhailburg, he'd never really let himself imagine what would happen if Dimitri died. He'd thought about all of them dying together—in a shoot-out, in a bombing, murdered by assassins or poisoned or hit with artillery shells—but never once did he really think that Dimitri would die and he'd keep on living.

He spat onto the carpet, trying to stifle his sobs, his chest heaving. He'd never been shot before, but this was what it must be like, his heart turned into a gaping hole that felt like it would consume him from the inside out.

It was so wrong for him to be living in a world where Dimitri was *gone.*

For a brief, horrific moment, Vasily wondered if Dimitri had died having read the note he'd left between his fingers that last morning in Wilnetzk, too cowardly to wake him up and confess to his face, or if it had gone unread. Would it be better if he'd died knowing he was loved? Or would that have been the cruelest thing, having Vasily's feelings shoved onto him with no time to refute them, no ability to let Vasily down and say, *I could never love you the way you love me*?

The question, and the uselessness of the answer, splintered him.

It didn't matter, though. Dimitri was gone. Vasily's ribs were being wrenched apart by invisible hands, or maybe that was the pain from sobbing so hard he couldn't breathe, but silently, the way he'd been taught to cry as a child. Back when pain was hidden inside and kept as a quiet, private thing.

He'd thought that agony was unbearable. This was worse. This was losing the other half of himself.

But he'd done it before and he could do it now, mastering his pain and shoving it down to focus on the present. On getting through the next moment, and the next. Vasily drew in a breath, then another, and straightened up, wiping at his eyes, practicality and training taking over.

If Alexey had killed Dimitri, then they were all in trouble. And Dimitri would never forgive him if he let their friends die.

He slid on his boots and grabbed his coat, the pockets still stuffed with what he'd taken out of the townhome. It would be enough to get them out of the city, possibly into Urushka to start new lives, anonymous, just four people who'd left Novo-Svitsevo because of the war. He slipped out the door, sliding down the hallway, relieved when he didn't see any guards. The hallway was blurry, but not from the dark. He didn't realize until he could barely see that his eyes were swimming with tears again.

Vasily had no idea where Dimitri and the rest of the court had been kept, but it was probably somewhere easy to guard, isolated, close to where Alexey stayed so he could personally keep an eye on the prisoners. He turned down another hallway, then another, passing guards in the hallway who didn't give him a second glance. He wondered if the tunnel in the basement he'd used the last time, the one that came out under the Great Shul, was still there, or if Alexey had found out about it after their last flight from the palace. His mind flipped through all of the other ways he could get four people out of the capital under the cover of darkness, and how many people he'd need to kill to do it.

At least for now, no one else knew what had happened. That would buy them time to escape. He turned down another corner and found himself at the door to Alexey's study. The place where Alexey had spent so much time studying resurrection—

Vasily stopped, his heart pounding. *Resurrection.*

Something tugged at his mind, and he closed his eyes, shuffling through his memories, trusting the bite in his gut that told him he was missing something important.

And then, like a punch to the stomach, he remembered. A cramped, musty room with a talking head that could portend the future and speak prophecies.

You'll be back. Again and again, you'll always come back. He'll bring you back.

He'll bring you back.

Vasily's traitorous heart lurched. Waiting could cost them all their lives. But Vasily knew that Annika, Ladushka, Mischa—they'd all tell him to risk it. They'd all tell him to try, because long ago they'd pledged themselves to Dimitri, and that meant dying for him too.

Maybe he'd gone insane from grief, and he was reading far too much into the ravings of a heretical object in a library owned by a madman, but if there was even a tiny chance that he could bring Dimitri back, he'd do it.

He would do anything for Dimitri, he realized then, except willingly keep on going if Dimitri was dead.

Vasily toyed with the ludicrous diamond earring that had been left in his rooms that evening, presumably compliments of the Tzar, and popped the back off, flicking it onto the ground by the door. He dropped down to his hands and knees and, on the pretext of searching for the missing piece, peered through the minuscule hole he'd had drilled through the bottom of the door years ago. It was too small for anyone to notice unless they bent down and searched, but large enough that if he closed one eye, Vasily could see if there were any feet present in the study.

It was clear. He retrieved the earring back, picked the lock, and slipped himself inside. He took a match from the bowl by the door and lit a taper, setting it on the desk.

He made quick work of picking the lock on the concealed desk drawer as well, the one where he knew Alexey kept his most secret documents, including the contract between him and Tzar Abram, exchanging Dimitri for three and a half million tolar, paid out in full, like Dimitri was some kind of horse that Alexey had bought for breeding. After rifling through it and finding nothing related to Alexey's rebirth or how to bring Dimitri back, he made his way around the desk and went for the books.

He'd been in this room countless times before the war, keeping an eye on Alexey's research. The books on resurrection were together, seven volumes on one shelf at eye level. He pulled them all down and headed back to the desk.

He flipped through the pages as fast as he dared, discarding most of the options as impossible, taking far too much time or needing the body of the deceased. He shuddered as he came across the recipe that Alexey had clearly used to resurrect himself, a frayed piece of ribbon tucked into the page.

And then he opened a thick, dusty volume that was bound in blood-red leather and had no title on the spine. He scanned the title page. *Resurrections of the Soul.*

Suddenly, the candle flame flickered and extinguished. Vasily jerked his head up, looking for the source of the breeze, but then the candle sprang back to life. He flipped the pages, scanning them until he arrived at an entry entitled *Ibbur: The Righteous Possession.*

The candle flame went out again.

"Fuck it all," Vasily whispered to the dark. "I get the point."

He had grown up hearing stories of portents from God, tales of burning bushes and angels speaking to the righteous, rivers parting and floods that washed the world clean. This didn't seem like the same kind of miracle, but Vasily wasn't an idiot and he could take a hint.

He relit the candle and scanned the entry, reading about how, for the benefits of completing a good deed that required a physical form, the dead could possess the living. They had to be invited in to share the living person's soul, and then the connection would be severed once the deed was done, unless a sacrifice was made to the angel of death, who in some cases would allow the possessing soul to return to its original body.

Vasily slumped into the velvet cushions of the high-backed chair, squinting as he flipped to the next page. The entry ended there. There were no instructions as to how it was to be done.

Useless. Utterly, fuck-all useless. These fucking mystics would be the death of him.

Vasily mentally gave himself until daybreak to see what would happen if he tried to invite Dimitri into his soul. It was their last and only chance—Dimitri needed to be the one to kill Alexey, they all knew that, and so Vasily would have to pray that if he *did* manage to summon Dimitri's soul, they'd be able to kill Alexey on a technicality. He tucked the books back on their shelves, arranged everything exactly as it had been, replaced the candle and slipped back through the door, locking it behind him. He made his way back to his room, guilt flaring in him at the fact that his friends were still sitting somewhere in the palace hoping that everything had gone right, when Vasily knew it had gone so very wrong.

He locked himself back into his room, took off his coat and boots, and knelt down before the bed because he could no longer stand on his own two feet, resting his forehead on the silk of the blanket, fisting his hands into the fabric.

Come on, Dima, he pleaded. *You are the Tzar of Novo-Svitsevo, and your country needs you.* I *need you. Please come back.*

Nothing happened. So he tried again. And again. And again and again and again, all through the night, because Dimitri was half of his heart and his soul, and because of that, he'd never give up.

THIRTY-FOUR

ALEXEY

Alexey did not know how long he spent hunched over the body of his husband.

When his throat was raw from screaming, he looked at Dimitri and started to sob, his sides heaving, his breath catching in his throat. All the tears he had bottled up since that night so long ago, that night when he had lost Dimitri, that night his husband had fled from him instead of embracing his vision for Novo-Svitsevo, came coursing out of him, mingling with the blood that was seeping out of Dimitri's rapidly cooling chest. Alexey lay down on top of him, his head in the hollow of Dimitri's throat, grabbing at him as if he would wake up and turn his head, pressing a kiss to Alexey's cheek.

But Dimitri didn't, because Alexey had killed him.

He was struggling to breathe through the sobs, and he got up on his knees to grip the headboard for something solid to anchor him. But the sight of his hands coated in Dimitri's blood made him retch, and he leaned over the side of the bed until blackness darkened the edges of his vision. All the while, he turned his husband's last word over in his mind.

Dimitri had promised to love no one but Alexey. And yet, he had died with another man's name on his lips. Alexey was too mad with grief to tell if he was devastated or furious that Dimitri had called out for someone else as his life had faded away.

Do not mourn him, my son. God's voice echoed in his head, threading its way through the pounding headache that Alexey's sobbing had engendered. *Do not waste your anger and your grief on him. You must dispose of him.*

Alexey's heart lurched at God's command, but he stood on shaking legs and complied. He hoisted Dimitri's body up in his arms, cradling Dimitri's limp form to his chest. Then he laid Dimitri's body back out carefully on the bed and wrapped him in the silken, bloodstained sheets, a funeral shroud for the man whose heart he thought he had recaptured. The pain of realizing he was wrong flayed him.

He would deal with the body further come morning. Right now, he couldn't bear to look at Dimitri for any longer.

Anger bubbled up in his chest as his awareness was drawn to the parchment lying beside the bed. He picked it up from where it had fallen during their struggle, and ignored the way his fingers burned. He tossed it into the fire. The void within him rejoiced as the parchment charred.

You did well, my son. God's voice was reassuring, warm, full of grace. But it was not what Alexey wanted to hear. Not after what he had just done.

Leave me, he ordered God.

It was Dimitri's fault, all of it. Had he just given in, had he just recognized that Alexey was meant to be his lord and master, that Alexey was the one meant to rule, Dimitri would still be here, and alive. They would be curled together under the sheets, sharing in the bliss of their coupling, reunited at last.

Alexey would have forgiven him. Dimitri never gave Alexey that same chance.

Alexey turned away from Dimitri's body and threw on a dressing gown. He pulled open the door to his chambers with such force that it cracked off the hinges. He let it crash to the ground as he stormed across the hall, his fists clenched so hard that blood dripped out of the cuts his nails made in his palms.

He shook as he pulled open Ivan's door, then slammed it shut again. Ivan rolled over in bed, sitting up, clutching the sheets to his nude form. His eyes were red-rimmed, as if he had been sobbing. He probably had, knowing him, over the fact that Dimitri had returned, thinking he'd been replaced. Except he would never be replaced, now, because Dimitri was dead.

Dimitri was *dead*.

For a moment, Alexey stood beside the door, panting, not sure if he was going to vomit or scream or cry, or punch something so hard he would break his own fist.

Ivan swung his legs over the side of the bed. "Alexey?"

In the dark, with his hair shorn on the sides, Ivan was like Dimitri's ghost, come back to haunt him.

Alexey bit his lip and forced down his tears as Ivan strode to him, reaching for the bloody smear on his cheek, gaping at the blood coating Alexey's hands and chest and stomach, splashing down onto his legs. Ivan muttered words of shock and concern that Alexey did not take in, allowing Ivan to unwrap his dressing gown, letting Ivan see that the blood was not his own.

"Dimitri . . . oh," Ivan said simply, when he finally made the realization. "Oh, Alexey."

Tenderness was something that Alexey could not stand, not right now. He reached out and grabbed Ivan by the arm. He slammed Ivan against the wall so hard that the candles rattled in their holders. Ivan gasped and grabbed for Alexey's wrist, but then looked up at him with desire in his eyes.

Alexey should go. He should be asking Ivan or his guards to help him ready the body for burial. He should be rending his clothes and mourning his husband. But he could not afford to grieve Dimitri. If he did not conquer this agony now, he would never be able to rule Novo-Svitsevo come morning. "Can I take you?" he breathed into Ivan's ear, desperate to forget that this was now as close to Dimitri as he would ever be again.

"Yes," Ivan breathed, though his voice wavered. "You are my Tzar, my intended. Everything I am is yours."

It was all he had ever wanted from Dimitri, all he had ever wanted to hear. Alexey picked Ivan up, grabbing him behind his thighs, carrying him back to the bed before slamming him down into the sheets.

Ivan panted and let his knees fall open as Alexey crawled onto the bed. He reached forward and grabbed Ivan's hair, yanking him forward onto his hands and knees. Ivan looked up at him, his pupils dilated, his cheeks flushed.

"Open your mouth," Alexey ordered.

Ivan did, and Alexey shoved his length into it, hitting the back of Ivan's throat. Ivan gagged, but Alexey was merciless, thrusting back in without giving Ivan a moment to breathe. Ivan gagged again, and Alexey shoved a thumb in between Ivan's back teeth so he could not bite down out of instinct.

Ivan's hands wrapped around Alexey's hips, his fingers tightening with every thrust. Tears spilled from Ivan's eyes as Alexey continued to take him, methodically, uncaringly. Ivan eventually took himself in hand, his eyes closing with pleasure, but Alexey pulled away from him and slapped him across the face.

"Not until I say," Alexey growled, and seized Ivan by the shoulders, flipping him around, grabbing for the oil on the bedside. He didn't give Ivan a moment to prepare before he was thrusting into him. But Ivan did not thrash or fight. He merely took everything that Alexey gave him without complaint. He uttered no curses, no filthy words like Dimitri would have, only gasps and moans of pleasure, merely frantic pleas for more, threading his hands into the sheets.

Alexey wiped away tears with one hand after he came, his other hand firm on Ivan's back, where bruises were already blooming. When he was sure his face was clear, he staggered backwards, letting Ivan sit up, panting with exertion and pleasure.

Ivan's face fell as he took Alexey in, standing there, his arms limp at his sides, Dimitri's blood still smeared across his face like a brand.

"Alexey?" Ivan's brows were furrowed with concern. "My love?"

Alexey was hollow, raw, empty. He looked at his husband's ghost, sitting on the bed. Ivan was twenty-three, barely older than Dimitri the first time Alexey had seen him.

It was Dimitri's smile that had made Alexey fall in love.

He remembered every word that he had said to Dimitri that first time, every sensation as he showed Dimitri what it meant to couple with another, every look on Dimitri's face, every sound that fell from his lips. It had been gentle, and tender, and the most perfect few hours of Alexey's life.

And now it was gone. He was gone.

Alexey ran a hand through his hair, and then turned and punched the wall with a scream. His fist went through the plaster and then the wood and into the brick beyond. His hand dripped sluggish blood as he pulled back and punched the wall again, rattling the paintings that hung there. And again, and again, because he was just a vessel for rage and agony that would haunt him forever because he would never die.

Then there were arms around him and he turned with a snarl, grabbing Ivan by the throat and slamming him into the broken wall, choking him. Ivan still did not struggle, just held Alexey's gaze as his face reddened. His lips parted.

Alexey drew in a quivering breath and let go. Ivan gasped and massaged his throat, his eyes downcast. He bit his lip and sighed. "You still love him. You love my brother. You wouldn't have divorced him. You would have cast me aside."

Alexey could not say yes, but Ivan was smart enough to take his silence as assent. Ivan stepped forward and wrapped his arms around Alexey's shoulders, drawing him close. Alexey tried to pull away, but Ivan simply held him tighter and sighed into his chest.

"None of us get what we want in this life." Ivan's voice was laced with such unbearable sadness that it made Alexey choke on a sob. "Not bastards, not Tzars. Not even the chosen one of God."

*

The next morning, Alexey disentangled himself from Ivan's arms, leaving him in bed. He could not have Ivan and Dimitri's corpse in the same room. He couldn't bear having to witness the comparison. It would tear him apart.

Then Alexey rose and returned to his bedchamber. Someone had already repaired the door, and he pushed it open with shaking hands.

Alexey ignored the body lying on his bed.

He bathed himself, eschewing servants, and put on his most severe black jacket, buckled down the front with silver clasps. He needed something to hold him together for what came next. He swung a thick velvet cape around his shoulders. He had never known he could be this heartbreakingly cold, as though he were standing alone in the middle of the fiercest winter storm. His teeth chattered against each other as he turned and snapped his fingers for the steward who waited outside his room.

"Assemble the court," he said, his face as impassive as his voice was dead. "All of them. In the throne room. They have ten minutes to arrive."

The man nodded and bowed, then turned to leave.

"And make sure the captives are brought in too," Alexey added. "In chains."

He shut the door and leaned his head against the wood paneling of the wall.

You are the Tzar of Novo-Svitsevo, he reminded himself. *This is what you must do. This is what his betrayal deserves.*

He shook his head and walked over to the bed, picking up Dimitri's shrouded body.

The walk to the throne room was the longest of his life. He shuddered with every step, the weight of Dimitri in his arms almost unbearable. This was harder than anything in the war, harder than clawing his way back to the world of the living, harder than letting go of the peace of death.

He had no memory of entering the throne room, but then he was there, his court parting around him like ripples in a pond. He passed Dimitri's court, chains around their ankles and wrists, standing in front of a phalanx of guards.

Alexey put out of his mind every night that he had spent around the fire with these people, playing cards, laughing, drinking, plotting how to run the country. He ignored the memory of Ladushka's love of learning and Annika's infectious smile and Mischa's wry, sarcastic jokes. He put out of his mind that before they had been his enemies, they had once been his friends.

He was the Tzar, and they had turned out to be nothing more than traitors.

His every footstep echoed around the chamber. His arms were shaking as they held Dimitri's stiff body to his chest. When he reached the throne, he turned to face the assembled court and dropped the body on the floor.

The thud of it hitting the marble almost made him heave, but he held himself impassive, firm.

He would do this for Novo-Svitsevo. He would do this to ensure he was never challenged again. He would do this to cement their loyalty, to earn their fear.

"This is what happens to traitors." He gazed at his court, his mouth a hard line, his fists clenched. He kicked Dimitri's body and it turned over, the shroud falling away, revealing his bruised, broken form, covered in dried blood. Dimitri's eyes were closed and his face was white, bloodless. His wounded arm stretched towards the assembled court, his finger pointing at them like a condemnation.

There was silence deeper than anything Alexey had ever experienced. Then a thud echoed through the stillness.

Ladushka Zakharova fell to her knees, her hands covering her mouth. Annika Lebedeva began sobbing openly, her body shaking. Mischa Danilleyev stood next to her, blank, impassive, all the color drained from their face.

"A quick death is too good for you," he said, turning to face them, Dimitri's court, his voice thick with grief. "You will stay alive until you repent for what you have done, for the crimes you have aided. Only then may you die."

Guards stepped forward, seizing them by the shoulders, dragging them backwards. Mischa complied, not putting up a fight, Ladushka grabbing Mischa's hands and snapping at the guards who were trying to pull them apart. Annika whipped her chains around the neck of the guard who tried to pull her from the room, strangling him until another guard slammed the butt of his rifle into her head, making her stagger back.

Lord Lebedev—one of his most trusted generals—and his wife stood impassively by as their daughter was dragged from the throne room, screaming Dimitri's name.

Alexey took a long breath to steady himself, then turned back to his noble courtiers, the people whose loyalty he had to ensure. "You see," he said, his voice low, "that there are enemies among us. Last night, Dimitri Alexeyev attempted to kill me. He was not successful. I put a blade through his heart myself." He looked around the room, at the shock written on faces, at the hands covering mouths, at the tears running down cheeks. There was a guard who had collapsed to the floor on the side of the room, her blue eyes full of tears. She was hauled up by a guard with coppery hair, a flinty expression on her freckled face. Next to them, the finance minister emptied the contents of his stomach all over the carpet.

Alexey's eyes landed on Mikhail Haleyvin. He, alone, met Alexey's gaze, his expression unflinching and solid. Alexey looked at him, *into* him, and he felt a tug on his heart like the moment when he first saw Dimitri, bold and beautiful across a courtyard at his Chernitzy estate.

He reached out a hand to Mikhail. Mikhail hesitated, casting his eyes around the court, but then he stepped forward and crossed the expanse of carpet to take Alexey's hand and stand by his side.

"I am creating a new army." He was stronger with Mikhail beside him, holding him up. "With Mikhail Haleyvin as my general. The Holy Science and the Lord my God have opened my eyes to the power of worlds beyond our own. I will use my power to join our worlds together and use the denizens of the middle world to hold back any who would attack us. I will protect Novo-Svitsevo against every enemy, keep you safe against any threat."

He looked down at Dimitri one last time, swallowing past the lump in his throat.

"You can join me." He paused, letting the words settle over the crowd. "Or you can join him." He pointed down at Dimitri's body. "The choice is yours. I am your Tzar, but I force no one to follow me."

He dropped Mikhail's hand and stepped around him, heading for the back exit. There was a rustle behind him, and he turned to see guards hoisting up Dimitri's body as Mikhail looked on, his face a blank mask.

"No," he said, holding up a hand. "Leave his body here. Until it rots." He looked up at the court, his nostrils flaring, his lip curling with grief and disdain. "Let it be a reminder. I will build my empire atop the bones of my enemies, even if those enemies are men I once loved."

THIRTY FIVE

DIMITRI

The throne of God raged around Dimitri like fire, like a blaze that was going to melt his skin and scour his bones clean.

He was aware he was dead. He remembered flashes of a knife in someone's hand, unbearable pain radiating from his chest, tears in his eyes and agony in his heart. He remembered a face hovering over his, its expression glazed with grief.

Dimitri knew he had failed the task he had been doing, even if he couldn't quite remember what it was. It had been peeled away with so many of the other layers of him, lost to the fire.

But it had been important. Had he not been what he assumed was a disembodied soul, his stomach would have clenched with the guilt.

Instead, he was here. Wherever here was, precisely. Whatever he was now.

Dimitri had had a lot of ideas about heaven when he walked among the living. He remembered envisioning a world of endless, quiet forests. His favorite foods, perfectly brewed tea. Huge libraries all to himself, a world he could explore with his friends when they joined him. His sisters and his brothers and his grandparents coming to greet him.

He thought heaven would be something nice. A constant stretch of contentment, a long and eternal rest for the souls of the righteous.

He didn't think it would hurt this much.

Dimitri didn't know how long he had been here, bare and prostrate before his Creator. His awareness drifted as he lay splayed and humbled before the throne of God. There were knives scraping across him, stripping back the layers of his soul, each shred examined, weighed, like he was an experiment Mischa was performing on an animal's corpse. Each action dissected, every thought interrogated, every moment of doubt and faithlessness and sin and shame.

Look. The voice was familiar to him. He had heard it before, in some other place, in some other lifetime. It echoed around his skull. Dimitri tried to ignore it despite the pain gnawing at him. *Look, and if you look, the Lord your God will judge you. His angels will end their examination.*

If he looked, the pain would end. It was worse than anything else he'd felt before, far worse. If he wasn't already dead, he knew he would have died of it.

He wanted to give in, but there was a reason he couldn't, even if he couldn't for the life of him remember what it was.

Look. The raw power of the command was hard for him to ignore. *Gaze upon the burning face of the Lord your God. Submit. Surrender.*

Something about that command pricked at his memory. An annoyance, something that made no sense.

I would rather not. Dimitri rallied against the pain. *If it's all the same to you.*

The flames grew higher around him. *You disobey the Lord your God. You refuse the glory of His burning face. You choose not to revel in His presence. Give in, and the pain will end.*

Dimitri stilled. He had been told not to bow to the pain, in a different time. In another life.

He shut himself off, pushing away the hands that grabbed for him, curling into himself. *No.*

You refuse? The voice was full of ancient rage.

There's someone I abandoned. He could feel it, a tiny, thin thread. It extended from the core of him to someplace else. He followed it, spiraling his consciousness down that thread, sensing at the end of it someplace cool and calm and free of pain.

There's someone I . . . He felt it, reaching for him, pain and tenderness and—

There's someone I . . .

Someone was calling his name. A man's voice, over and over. A name he had not heard in a thousand lifetimes.

Please, Dima, come back to me.

Dimitri laughed at the voice, or maybe he cried. Because he finally remembered why he could not enjoy the secrets of heaven.

You are going to suffer, more than any living man has suffered. The pain will almost break you.

Dimitri understood, now, what the prophecy he'd heard so long ago had meant.

But you cannot allow it to. You cannot give in.

He'd promised the other half of his heart that if he died first, he'd share the secrets he learned from heaven. And now he knew that that love was victorious over death, because here he was, dead but with a heart on fire, burning with love for the man who had saved him.

Love strong enough to bridge life and death. Love strong enough to bring him back.

He let go of the grace of heaven and answered Vasily's call.

THIRTY-SIX

VASILY

Is that my body? Dimitri's voice suddenly filled Vasily's head, and a rush of confusion that didn't belong to him washed over his body, like drawing his first deep breath after nearly drowning, pain mixed with satisfaction.

Thank fucking God. Vasily felt his knees crumple as relief flooded through him, his hand flying to his chest. *Thank the Lord our fucking God. You're back.*

What happened? Dimitri sounded disoriented. It was like he was sharing a mind with Vasily, the other man's immediate thoughts and feelings laid bare to him, so unlike when they had shared dreams. Vasily had never felt this deeply connected to another person, not even in the times when he and Dimitri had been so tightly joined with one another that Vasily hadn't been able to tell where his body stopped and Dimitri's started.

He had thought that was the closest to true bliss he'd ever come. Now, tangled up with everything that Dimitri was, Vasily knew with perfect clarity that he'd been wrong.

Hah. Vasily chuckled inside his mind, even as his face remained impassive. *I borrowed a trick from Alexey's book, literally.*

A shudder went through whatever Dimitri was now.

Your soul is sharing mine, Vasily supplied. *I hope you're enjoying being inside* me *for once, since you're here until we can get you back into your body.*

He could have at least put clothes on me before he dropped me on the ground like a dead dog. Dimitri winced. *Death hasn't been kind to me, has it? What do we do?*

Vasily swallowed hard. *Don't worry, the worst thing that happens is that you're stuck in my mind forever.*

I read your note, Dimitri said as a flash of anxiety passed through his soul. Vasily couldn't tell if it was his, or theirs.

Ah, you did then? He shifted on his feet.

I did, and I—

Vasily's attention snapped away as a steward started to approach him. The rest of the throne room had emptied, the other members of the court having filtered out when he wasn't paying attention.

Go, Dimitri urged. *Pay attention to what he wants.*

Vasily shook his head as the steward addressed him. "The Tzar has provided you with a new suite of rooms in the palace, my lord. Do you wish to have your possessions moved immediately?"

Fucking Alexey, Vasily thought at Dimitri. *As if that's what's important right now.*

Alexey. The thought seemed to send a pang through Dimitri's soul, and it was so distracting that Vasily didn't even hear the response that he snapped at the steward.

Alexey didn't want to kill me, Dimitri thought at him. *He begged me to submit, to stop fighting. Maybe he was right, maybe it was the natural order of things that he should rule and I should be the one by his side. Maybe I am, as my father always said, the weak and foppish third son, the extra spare, the one who brought glory to my family only through seducing a well-placed lord.*

No, Vasily snapped. *You're worth so much more than that, Dima. So much fucking more.* And then he dropped all the walls in his mind, letting Dimitri see everything. Feel everything.

The first time his heart had fluttered, seeing Dimitri at the royal wedding and thinking he was the most beautiful man alive, and—

How it had felt when Dimitri had rescued him, body and soul, by offering him a place in his court, so that he'd never have to face his childhood abuser again. So he could finally pay his own way, finally have freedom and safety that wasn't in the hollow of an ancient tree, and—

How he'd searched for Dimitri's flaws over the years and found none, just goodness that was being buried day by day by what Alexey was doing to him, and how, seeing those tells, seeing those bruises, and knowing he himself carried the same, it had rocked his heart, and—

Finding a family in Dimitri's court, falling for Dimitri with every touch, every glance. Watching Dimitri govern and wanting to sit there beside him. Watching Dimitri dance with Alexey at every formal ball and wishing that it were him instead, the jealousy gnawing through his rib cage even as he maintained his smile and did his job and went to bed alone, and—

Those horrific months where he'd watched Dimitri drift around the palace like a ghost. When he'd held Dimitri as he'd cried over his husband, and Vasily had wished he could bring Alexey back to life himself just so he could murder him for what he'd done to Dimitri. The terror of watching him physically shrink with every passing day when he refused yet again to eat, watching his presence diminish as he folded into himself, how agitated Vasily had been when Dimitri had begged Mischa for a solution only for them to say that, sometimes, you couldn't mend someone who didn't want to heal. How gut-wrenching it had been to see Alexey come back and Dimitri get better, only to fade away again, and—

The all-encompassing panic, a desire to protect Dimitri that went far beyond duty when Vasily had found the plans for Alexey's coup, rushing them all out of the palace in the dead of night, his only thought *I have to keep him safe*, and—

The pure, unadulterated joy that had flashed through him when Dimitri had asked him to bed in a small tent in a muddy field, both of them shaking from cold and desire, and everything that came after, and—

Finally, most of all, because it was at the core of everything, at the heart of each one of his memories, the agony of realizing that all of this was because he loved Dimitri Alexeyev, the Tzar of Novo-Svitsevo, a man who would never be his, because Vasily Sokolov was the most minor of lords, so unworthy of a political marriage that people would laugh at the thought. The persistence of that love anyway, through every hardship, through every time he knew that Dimitri was looking at him and seeing Alexey, through every moment where he would joke and laugh and kiss Dimitri's hair and massage his feet and hold him close, because if he couldn't have him, then he could have this, this stream of perfect memories that felt like the only thing worth living for. His love for Dimitri was life returning to a soul that had been laid barren by loss and abuse and war, and even though he knew it was hopeless, Vasily couldn't help but nurture it.

Do you understand now? he asked Dimitri as the steward retreated. *You said you read my letter. Can you feel what I've been hiding from you all this time?*

Dimitri was quiet for a long moment before he finally spoke, and Vasily caught himself holding his breath while he waited for something, for any answer at all. *That first time, in that flimsy tent in the dead of night, what I was really saying with my body and my soul was, I want you, I want you, I want you to be mine because I trust you and I don't want to be alone anymore.*

Vasily stilled, the only movement the beating of his heart.

It was me saying, I trust you to hold me together while you take me apart at the edges and pick at my scabs and my seams and my scars. And it was me saying, I trust you to uncover me, to excavate me. Because I know what it is to hurt, and the part of me that still hopes and loves and dreams looks at you and knows that you don't have it in you, that you could never have it in you. That was what I was saying to you when I lay down next to you in that godforsaken tent. It wasn't about the sex, it never was. It was about the trust.

Vasily felt Dimitri reach out and wrap himself around all of Vasily's heart that he could hold. *It was about the love, Vasya. And you didn't see it. You wouldn't let yourself see it, just like I couldn't see it in myself. I only recognized it in you, that we are the same.*

Dima, Vasily thought, tears pricking at the corners of his eyes. *Dima, I—*

Let me finish, Dimitri begged. *I thought the night I killed my husband, the man I knew as my whole world, was the worst moment of my life. But I was wrong. I was so terribly, terribly wrong. Because there was nothing worse than reading your confession right when the distance between us was biggest. Right when I was going to walk back to the man who shattered me in the first place, without even being able to tell you first, Yes, you are right, and, It's you, Vasya, it's always been you. Even when I didn't know it, it's always been you. We were inevitable, you and I.*

Vasily had moved while Dimitri was talking, his movements instinctive, his body taking control. They were in a hallway now, and Vasily shouldered through a door into an empty parlor, sliding down the wall as he started to sob.

It will always *be you, Vasya,* Dimitri continued, as if he needed to get it all out, to come clean. *There will be no other men. There will be no other lovers, there will be no other great romance. There will merely be this, between us, this recognition of the perfect hurt and pain that honed us into blades, so we could cut each other free. I wanted so badly to tell you that if you died, I would follow, because it's no longer the secrets of heaven I would wish to whisper to you. It's that I love you too.*

I am yours, Vasya. For however long I have left. For whatever this is.

Then Vasily felt Dimitri suffuse all the love he felt, every last scrap of it, through his mind, painting the picture of the two of them for Vasily to cling to, and in that moment Dimitri was his anchor the way that Vasily had always been for him.

Eventually, Vasily's crying slowed, and he drew in a deep breath, blinking his eyes until they cleared. *Are you all right?* Dimitri asked.

Happy tears, darling. Vasily wiped his eyes on the sleeves of his suit. *Happy tears, love. Too bad you don't have a body, or I'd kiss you senseless right now.*

Vasily felt his entire being effervesce like the bubbles in champagne, Dimitri's happiness flowing into him and merging with his own.

I wish we could too, Dimitri replied. *But for now, we have to set Novo-Svitsevo free.*

∗

Vasily flipped the small piece of parchment over in his hands, staring at the note that the steward had just delivered on a silver platter. Apparently, Alexey had decided his transformation would take place the next morning, in the council chamber, so everyone in the court of Rav-Mikhailburg could watch the dawn of a new age, or some bullshit like that.

He really wastes no time, does he? Dimitri lurked in the back of his skull, a ball of agitation. Vasily had been pacing around his room, the two of them arguing back and forth about what to do now that their first attempt to kill Alexey had failed.

It's fine, because we have no time to waste. Vasily rubbed a hand over his tired eyes. *If we leave Anna and Lada and Mischka in a prison cell for longer than a day, they're going to be fucking irate.*

Better than them being dead. At least they're safe down there, Dimitri quipped back. *So we have until tomorrow morning to figure out what to do.*

The problem is that we no longer have the Name, Vasily said for the fifth time. *And we need that in order to weaken him before we kill him. Too bad Anna didn't make a copy when she wrote it down.*

Dimitri's consciousness quivered. *Now that I think about it, there is a copy.*

Oh God, Vasily replied, horror dawning on him when he realized what Dimitri meant. *Oh my God. I don't know if I can.*

You have to, Dimitri replied. *Because it's the last chance we've got, Vasya.*

And you're okay with it? With ... that part? Vasily cringed, an uncontrollable shudder sweeping through him.

I would give every bone in my body to Novo-Svitsevo, Dimitri said. *I've already given this country my life. What's a little bit more?*

✳

Vasily begged off lunch and then dinner. He figured he'd need an empty stomach for what came next. Instead, he sat at the table in his room, sharpening Annika's knife as much as he could without warping the blade.

I wish Mischka could be the one to do this, he groused to Dimitri.

Except they're not here. Dimitri rustled around in the back of Vasily's skull, restless. *Just think of it like butchering an animal.*

Except it's not an animal, Vasily snapped back, before taking a breath and putting his head down on the table. *Sorry. Last chances clearly make me tense.*

It's going to work, Dimitri soothed. *He'll never suspect you. He'll never suspect this.*

Now would be a good time to start praying, Vasily retorted. He went back to sharpening the knife and listening to the ticks of the clock, praying that night would fall quickly so he could get this over with, and either die or save Novo-Svitsevo. Because there were no longer any other options. It was only death or salvation.

*

Vasily left his room in the dead of night, weaving through the hallways of the palace, deserted now with the lateness of the hour. There were guards at the throne room entrance, so he turned down the corridor and pressed on the hidden panel that led to a concealed entrance right behind the throne, to allow the ruler to slip away in the event of an emergency.

The sick tang of blood wafted through the air. Vasily raised a handkerchief to his nose, the smell overpowering him, making him retch.

He stepped out into the throne room, his heart pounding a deafening beat in his ears. The vaulted ceiling was too tall, the cavernous space causing his footsteps to echo. Without the court here, it was barren, the marble floor and gilt-covered walls cold and imposing. His eyes flitted to every corner of the room, scanning it for guards. He took another step and his heel clicked on the tile, and he seized up, his heart pounding even harder. He paused and strained his ears, listening for any sign of movement. He hadn't been this nervous in a very long time. Not since he'd been young, listening for footsteps outside his bedroom door, listening for the creak of the knob.

I'll kill him, Dimitri growled inside his head.

Now isn't the time for anger, however righteous, Vasily snapped back. *I need to concentrate.*

Dimitri tucked himself away as Vasily skirted the throne on the dais and gazed down at Dimitri's lifeless body, still mostly covered by the sheet, lying on the floor in a puddle of moonlight from the windows set into the ceiling.

Vasily shivered. The skin around Dimitri's eyes had begun to hollow, and Vasily blinked spots out of his vision at the sight of Dimitri's bruises, his bones jutting from his skin.

Maybe you shouldn't watch this. Vasily wondered if there was a way he could metaphorically cover Dimitri's eyes.

At least I won't be able to feel *it.* Dimitri shifted around in his mind again, a sensation that Vasily was quickly deducing was a sign of his anxiety rising. *The first time it hurt like you would not believe, and I was conscious.*

Vasily swallowed hard, closing his eyes. Then he steeled himself, pulled Annika's knife out of his pocket, and knelt down beside the body, next to Dimitri's left arm, still pointing towards a court that was no longer there.

He cut the stitches holding the wound together one by one, undoing what must have been Mischa's careful work.

When he reached out to pull the thread from Dimitri's skin, the flesh was cool against his fingers. He shifted the arm to an easier position, wincing when it resisted him, still stiff with rigor mortis.

He took a steadying breath and went to work, picking the stitches out of Dimitri's ruined flesh, letting the sides of the wound gape open as he did. A few sluggish drops of blood leaked out of the wound, joining the bloodstains that had pooled on the carpet, and he quickly wiped them away from Dimitri's frigid skin. Alexey could not know what they had done if he came to look at Dimitri's body tonight or tomorrow morning. But judging from the purpling of Dimitri's skin where it met the carpet, most of his congealed blood was pooled on the side of his body pressed against the floor. Vasily breathed a sigh of relief.

At least I won't ruin the carpet any further. Dimitri's voice was strained, his presence tense. *It's going to be impossible to get those stains out of the weave.*

Vasily ignored him and kept uncovering the wound, peeling away the newly healed flesh until he came to the bone.

It hurt to look at, his vision going dark around the edges.

Go on, Dimitri urged, *you've got to. You're the strongest man I know.*

Vasily used the tip of the knife to dig into the bone. The ulna, his brain supplied ridiculously, something from a long-ago discussion of anatomy with Mischa. He used his left hand to steady the hilt of the dagger, then brought his right fist down on the hilt.

The bone snapped with a crack like a gunshot.

Vasily paused, his breathing ragged, listening for any disturbance from outside, anything that would sound like the guards coming in to see what the noise was. But there was nothing, just the beating of his own heart. Even Dimitri was quiet now.

He snapped the other side of the bone, and then dug his fingers into Dimitri's flesh, closing around the slickness of the bone, retching while pulling it free.

Good, Dimitri said.

We're not going to be able to get the Name in his mouth. Vasily fought back his nausea. *I can't imagine how we'd do that. He's going to be far too suspicious of anyone coming at him with a parchment that they want him to eat.*

The rebbe of Rav-Mikhailburg once said to me that Ludayzim was a religion built on technicalities and arguments, and that if you asked two rebbes a question, you'd get three answers. We need to not think literally. Couldn't it be symbolic? Dimitri shifted around in Vasily's head, restless.

Stabbing someone in the mouth isn't likely to kill them. Vasily hated that he knew that, but anatomy lessons with Mischa were running through his head. *Do you think the throat would count? A dagger to the throat would be fatal. And if the Name is on the weapon, maybe that would count too, enough to weaken Alexey and make his death hold?*

Dimitri gave the mental equivalent of a shrug. *Maybe.* He paused. *I'm scared that getting this wrong will end all of us, but we're going to have to pray that you're right. I . . . I can't think of another way to do this.* Dimitri's voice didn't quite shake, exactly, but Vasily heard the pang of something hoarse in his words. *This will be an exercise in faith. Desperate times, and all. Now finish up, in case someone comes. You'll just have to sharpen the end before morning.*

Vasily took a hold of himself, wrapping the bone in a spare shirt he'd tucked into his waistband, securing it down his back, wiping his hands off. It burned where it touched him. Then he pulled the needle and thread he'd begged off a seamstress from his pocket and did his best to close the wound again, recounting the number of stitches, using the old punctures in the skin.

I hate to leave you here, he said, straightening up, the room spinning slightly around him.

Not for long, Dimitri replied. *Tomorrow, we'll return me to my body. Then you won't have to carry me with you anymore.*

Dima, Vasily said, slipping back through the secret panel and into the hallway, *I'll carry you with me for the rest of my life.*

Dimitri stilled, a flare of surprise flashing through him.

I know, Dimitri finally said, his voice full of all the unspoken things between them, the matters that would have to wait until after their work was done, because duty to the empire was more important than the love between two men, and it always would be. *I know, Vasya. I know.*

∗

Vasily spent the night sharpening Dimitri's bone into a dagger, wearing gloves he had found in the wardrobe so that touching it didn't blister his skin. After a while, the motions became methodical enough

to soothe him, to make him forget what he was working on and what
he had to do. He thinned it out, until it was sharp and slim enough to
sever an artery, and by the time the sun rose his hands were aching
but his mind was clear and his body calm.

This is it, then, Dimitri said, stirring for the first time in hours.

Yes, Vasily agreed. *This is it.*

He dressed himself before the servants could come in, tucking the
bone up his sleeve. When they came for him, he squared his shoulders and followed them to the council chamber, where the first thing
he noticed—in a ridiculous part of his brain that was still noting and
filing away information—was that the tables in the council chamber
had been arranged in the shape of a star.

He has such a flair for the overdramatic, he thought at Dimitri. It
was easier to joke than to think about how, if he fucked this up, he
was going to die, Dimitri was going to die, and then the entire country was going to go up in flames.

He always did. Dimitri's voice was thin and strained.

Vasily tried to swallow as he was escorted by a steward to the head
table. The nobility of Alexey's court were seated, people who looked
like they would rather be anywhere than here, judging by their drawn
faces and the fact that no one was eating the lavish breakfast spread
in front of them.

*He thinks they're going to watch him experiment on a person while
eating herring?* Dimitri shuffled around in a way that quite clearly
indicated disgust.

Vasily was about to respond when the door opened again and a
demon walked into the dining room.

One of the ladies promptly fainted forward, her long black hair
spilling into a dish of eggs. Another one vomited into a teacup, and
several others went rigid with terror.

Vasily could understand why. The last time he had seen Morozov, he had been grotesque, but he was still distinctly human—albeit with entirely black eyes, clawed hands, and the feet of a bird.

Wow, he got fucking worse.

Darling, Dimitri drawled, halfway between terror and amusement. *You're much too beautiful to be turned into that.*

Because Morozov was now clearly giving in to whatever demon was possessing him. He was bare chested, his skin laced with black veins and dark purple bruising, his shoulders horrifically displaced around the wings that had sprouted from his back. He still had a human's face, but he was hairless, his jaw broadened to house pointed teeth. His talons clicked on the wood of the floorboards as he prowled forward, rounding the tables, the lords and ladies shrinking back as he passed their seats to hunch in the corner of the room.

He emitted an overpowering odor of sulfur and garlic that made Vasily gag.

Fuck a goat, Vasily thought. *He's gotten . . . much, much worse since the last time I saw him.*

Serves him right, Dimitri replied. *He was always such a sycophant.*

Vasily was about to retort that Alexey definitely wouldn't find Morozov fuckable now, but then Alexey walked into the room, his head held high, his cape flowing over his shoulders and rippling across the floor as he swept through the doors. His face was drawn, though, his eyes red-rimmed with purpled bruises underneath, as if he hadn't slept a wink.

At least he has the good grace to look distraught, Vasily thought. *I hope he cried so hard he puked, and had no one to help him clean himself up.*

It was chilling, seeing the man who had killed Dimitri walking around, doing business, carrying on as though he had not just murdered his own husband. Moving forward, when decency dictated he should be grieving.

Alexey looked at Vasily and smiled. Vasily forced himself to smile back. Ivan trailed behind Alexey, his eyes downcast.

He's even made Ivan wear my clothes. Dimitri's disgust made the corner of Vasily's mouth turn down, his smile dropping just as Alexey's gaze left his face. *He couldn't even buy the poor boy his own?*

The nobility rose as one. Vasily forced himself to his feet. He was shivering and he couldn't stop it, his body gone cold. The enormity of what they were about to do, and the fragility of the theory on which they were basing the next step they took, reverberated through him. If they were to fail now, that meant they were both about to die—but Vasily, strangely, was all right with that. They were together, at least, and for him that was enough.

No, what weighed on him was that if they failed, everyone in the world was going to die too. Slowly, not today, but perhaps far more horrifically than even he could contemplate.

The only thing that was keeping him upright was Dimitri there with him, his conviction and his strength and his courage wound around Vasily's spine, threaded through his heart.

Alexey reached him and gestured for the lords and ladies to sit, but when Vasily went to settle back into his chair, Alexey caught his elbow. Vasily jerked back before he could correct himself, but Alexey didn't even notice.

"You no longer need to show deference like a lord, Mikhail Haleyvin. You are above them all. From now on, you are a general. You rule beside me." He stroked Vasily's upper arm with a thumb, and Vasily grew nauseous at the smirk on Alexey's face.

But he nodded all the same, keeping his face impassive as Alexey dropped his hand and turned to face his court. "Today you will witness the power of the Holy Science. You will witness the power that our Creator has endowed me with. You will bear witness to the beginning of a new army, one that will keep Novo-Svitsevo, and all of you, safe from any enemy."

Alexey kept talking, gesturing animatedly with his hands.

You'll have to be the one to do it, Vasily said to Dimitri. He was desperate, now, to see this through. *That's what the demon said, yes? So do it. Use my hands.*

He thumbed the bone shard out of his sleeve. Alexey was still speaking, his arms held wide as he surveyed the ashen-faced lords and ladies seated around the tables. He was paying no attention to Vasily, his eyes shining with a maniacal light. Morozov was hunched behind Alexey, opening and closing his clawed hands, his night-black eyes tracking Alexey's every movement.

I will. Dimitri was as tense as he was.

His heart beat frantically, and Dimitri's along with it. Vasily's focus narrowed to a single moment, a single point, the exposed hollow of Alexey's throat—the only target left that mattered, the only place to sink a blade and end the war for good. Every soldier, every death, every war crime and heartache and night spent in fear in a tent on the edge of a battlefield, it all came down to this.

And so together they raised the bone shard up high, the name of God blinding Vasily's eyes, and thrust it deep into the hollow of Alexey Balakin's throat.

There was a heartbeat of silence, of perfect stillness, Vasily's hand clenched tight around the bone, the wetness of Alexey's blood staining his fingers, the two of them suspended in time as he turned his head to look at Vasily, his lips parted, his eyes wide, choking on the last of his words.

And then Vasily was forced to his knees as the destruction began.

THIRTY-SEVEN

DIMITRI

Darkness was pouring out of Alexey.

Dimitri felt every sensation hitting Vasily's body—first the feeling of immense pressure, like standing in front of an oncoming storm, the air crackling with electricity, then the shock wave of energy exploding outwards from Alexey as he fell forward against the head table, sliding down to his knees, his hands scrabbling at the tablecloth.

Alexey opened his mouth as if he was trying to scream, but the sound that emerged instead was inhuman. Dimitri felt Vasily cover his ears, but it did little to muffle the horrific grating noise, like jagged pieces of metal were being ground together. The demon that had been Morozov jumped forward, its arms outstretched towards its master, but it was thrown back against the wall by the waves of energy crackling out of Alexey.

Shadows crept out of his open mouth, leaked out of his eyes and ears and nose, trickling down his chest and limbs like blood. Alexey was choking, his hands grasping weakly at the bone protruding from his throat.

Dimitri could barely force himself to look. It was too much like that night, too much like Alexey grabbing for the hilt of the knife he'd thrust into his own chest. Dimitri shuttered his emotions even as Vasily refused to avert his eyes.

Alexey slumped to the floor, his hands falling away, his mouth opening and closing weakly as he tried to speak but couldn't. The waves of pressure kept coming off him, rattling everything in the room.

Vasily drew in a ragged breath and finally turned his head away, looking at the rest of the nobility. They were rooted to their chairs, some of them bleeding from their noses, some passed out. The rest of them looked terrified. The lord closest to Vasily was gripping the table so hard that the bones of their knuckles showed through their skin.

Dimitri's own half-brother was as white as a sheet and looked like he was struggling to stand and reach for Alexey. Alexey flung out a hand and Ivan took it, but a wave of darkness knocked Ivan violently back into the table, his head cracking the edge.

Then, as suddenly as it began, whatever was happening ceased.

Alexey lay still and unmoving on the floor, his eyes open and blank, reverted in death to the warm brown of Dimitri's memories. Dimitri looked at the corpse of his husband for the second time in his life, except now he felt nothing but numbness.

For a moment, no one moved.

Then a shrill cry sounded, like a wounded bird. Morozov swooped down and gathered Alexey up in his arms, his wings beating and sending food and debris flying everywhere.

Do we stop him? Vasily asked Dimitri, both of them still fighting through the shock that Alexey was dead.

I don't think so, Dimitri said back, sounding equally stunned. *What's he going to do with a dead body that has the name of God embedded in it?*

Some disturbing experiment, Vasily thought back. *I don't want to know. But fine. Time to leave.*

As Morozov rose unsteadily into the air, holding Alexey aloft, it broke the spell over the council chamber. The lords and ladies started screaming as they scrabbled over each other, fighting for the exit as guards attempted to pour in through the same door. In the chaos, Vasily expertly shouldered through the crowd and into the hallway, while Morozov punched through a hall window, sending a shower of glass down on the screaming knot of nobility as he took off over Rav-Mikhailburg, Alexey's body limp in his arms, his head dangling grotesquely, the bone dagger still sticking out of his throat.

Wait. Vasily paused. Lords, ladies and guards were surging around them, so no one noticed when he darted back into the council chamber, scooping Ivan up.

What are you doing? Dimitri hissed. *We've got to get the rest of the court.*

He's hurt. Dimitri felt Vasily swallow hard. *We can't just leave him here. Maybe Mischka can help him.*

Ivan's eyes were shut, blood trickling down his head, and he was dead weight in Vasily's arms as they reemerged into the corridor. Injured and unconscious, Ivan looked even more boyish and vulnerable than usual. Dimitri didn't think that Mischa was going to be able to do anything for Ivan, not now, but he could feel Vasily's grief. There wasn't truly harm in letting Vasily try to help, even if Dimitri was fairly sure it would be futile in the end.

Turn here, Dimitri instructed.

He guided Vasily down a hallway, then another, until they came to Alexey's study.

You can open the door, right? Dimitri's mind, sharpened by the chaos, was thinking through what they needed to do.

Vasily nodded, and propped Ivan up against the wall to pick the lock. He swung the door open and grunted as he picked Ivan back up, pulling him into the room and sitting him in the closest chair.

The room was as Dimitri remembered it, except for a small, catlike creature with wings curled in a birdcage in the corner. The thing was chittering nervously, its huge eyes turned on Dimitri. One of its ears was crinkled, like it had been injured in a fight.

What's Alexey doing keeping a demon as a pet? It was an asinine thing to think, but Dimitri couldn't help it.

He could feel Vasily's brow furrow. *There's nothing there, Dima. And we have more important things to think about than Alexey's atrocious decorating.*

Vasily turned his attention to Ivan. His head lolled forward, blood flecking the corner of his mouth. Vasily went to try to prop him back up against the back of the chair, but Ivan merely slumped forward again, boneless. Vasily sighed. *He definitely needs help. We should go get Mischka. And the rest of the court.* Vasily's panic was making his fingers twitch.

No, Dimitri insisted. *They're safe for another few minutes. My body first.*

✳

This one was harder.

As soon as Vasily stepped out of Alexey's study, he came face to face with one of the lords who had been seated next to him in the council chamber and who had just watched him stab the Tzar of Novo-Svitsevo in the throat with a length of bone.

The man didn't take it well. He started to scream for guards before Vasily clapped a hand over his mouth, then pulled out Annika's knife and slit his throat. Two guards, a man and a woman, turned down the hallway and, seeing Vasily standing over a mostly decapitated body, started sprinting for him.

Vasily sighed. *I'm getting a little worn out. Ivan was heavier than he looked.*

I'd help you out if I were corporeal, Dimitri quipped as the male guard tried to slam his shoulder into Vasily, only to find himself thrown forward as Vasily used the man's momentum against him. In sidestepping the guard, Vasily swiped his pistol, then dispatched him with one neat shot to the back of the neck.

Vasily turned to find himself face to face with Ayla, who was standing there, mouth agape, her ice-blue eyes flicking back and forth between him and the two dead bodies lying on the ground.

"Mikhail?" she said, her voice wavering. "What are you doing?"

Oh. Dimitri brightened. *Thank God. Help.* He'd always had good relationships with all of his half siblings, but he loved Ayla in particular. He'd realized from the start that Ayla was bright, and unlike with Ivan and the others, he'd deliberately cultivated a closer friendship with her, as close as he was allowed without crossing the invisible social boundaries that separated his father's illegitimate children from his legitimate ones. They'd corresponded for years after he'd moved away to Alexey's estate, and he'd insisted she attend university when he ascended the throne.

This is going to be fucking weird, Vasily thought, tucking the pistol into his belt and pinching the bridge of his nose, taking a deep breath. *But I'm pretty sure she supports you. It seemed like it while we were on the road.*

"Ayla," Vasily began. "Good to see you."

Her hand drifted to the pistol she wore at her side. "Did you just . . . murder two people?"

We don't have time for this, Vasily said, urgency making his eye twitch.

Dimitri was numb with the shock of dying, coming back to life as a possessing spirit, and then murdering his husband. But he realized the acute danger of the situation—unless they could get him back into his body, he and Vasily had just left Novo-Svitsevo completely rulerless, utterly adrift. He could feel the same realization hitting Vasily, the other man's concern a half step behind.

They had to fix this, and fast. *Tell her the truth*, Dimitri insisted. *All of it.*

Vasily didn't hesitate. "Three, including Alexey Balakin. My name is Vasily Sokolov. I'm Dimitri Alexeyev's—your brother's—spymaster. He's currently possessing my spirit. I need to get to the throne room and retrieve his body."

"That's a load of horseshit," Ayla barked, unholstering her pistol.

Tell her that I taught her how to ride a horse. Its name was Lizetta.

Vasily held his hands up. "He taught you how to ride a horse named Lizetta."

"What the fuck?" Ayla paused, her pistol half-cocked.

Tell her that she confessed to me that she skipped classes to go kiss Anastasia by the pond, and that I didn't blame her even though I was paying for those classes because I agreed Anastasia was quite beautiful. She sent me a drawing.

"He also thought Anastasia was beautiful and didn't blame you for skipping classes to kiss her by the pond," Vasily rushed out, taking a step backwards. Dimitri could hear Vasily thinking about how he'd tackle her if she raised the pistol.

"Oh." Ayla's eyes went round. "What? How do you know that? I only ever told . . ."

"Dimitri," Vasily finished for her, letting his hands drift down as she holstered her pistol again, confusion sliding across her features. "I know. I told you, we're somewhat inconveniently sharing a consciousness at the moment."

Not that I'm not enjoying the closeness, my darling, Vasily purred hastily in Dimitri's direction.

"Oh," Ayla said again, still frozen in place, her face very pale now.

There were footsteps and voices getting closer, clattering down the marble of the main hall. "Help me," Vasily ordered her, gesturing to the bodies. He grabbed the nobleman's ankles and dragged him back into Alexey's study, Ayla following with the guard, leaving a smear of blood on the ground.

Cover that, Dimitri nudged. Vasily grabbed one of the rugs from in front of Alexey's hearth and threw it over the bloodstain before reentering the study, clicking the door shut and beginning to strip.

"What are you doing?" Ayla's head was swiveling between Vasily, undressing, and Ivan, his eyes half-open and unfocused now, looking as pale as parchment and gurgling slightly as he breathed.

"Changing." Vasily divested himself of his bloodstained clothes, slipped on the guard's trousers and jacket, and then used the man's undershirt to wipe blood off the back of his cap. "It's a good thing we're roughly the same size."

"What—" Ayla's eyes were gradually glazing.

She's going into shock, Dimitri warned.

"Ayla, dear." Vasily finished buttoning up his jacket and clasped her on the shoulders. "Do you love Novo-Svitsevo?"

"Y-yes," she stuttered out.

Dimitri felt Vasily smile, a warm and reassuring one. "Then you're going to come with me, help me fetch your brother's body, then some prisoners, then we're all going to put Dima back into his body and back on the throne, and everything will be well."

"I'm dreaming," she replied.

"Sure," Vasily said. "You're dreaming. Now let's move."

✶

It was much easier carrying his body with Ayla helping them, but Dimitri still felt every strain on Vasily's muscles as if it were him doing all the work.

You owe me a massage for this, Vasily complained, gritting his teeth.

If you get me back into my own body, I will gift you a thousand massages. Your own bathhouse. Anything. Dimitri tried to hide his agitation, but he was growing more and more uneasy the longer they took. Being so close to his body, wrapped in the shroud Alexey had carried him into the throne room in, felt wrong. Like his soul recognized that it was a hands-breadth out of place, that it had been wrenched out of the only home it had ever known and now was being forced to look back in through the window. It was a taunt, a deep and unyielding homesickness, that even his enmeshment in Vasily's solid warmth, his steadily beating heart, had no power to soothe. His soul wanted to break back into his body, to shove itself forward until it rejoined with his corpse. But Dimitri knew in the sliver of himself that was still rational that if he gave in to the desire, he'd be flinging himself outwards into nothingness. That if he let go of his connection to Vasily, he wasn't going to return to his body. He was going to vanish into the same void he'd seen in Alexey's eyes, into sheer eternal blankness, because he had rejected the offer of the Lord his God and there was no longer a place for him in heaven.

He breathed, and curled his awareness tighter around Vasily's spine like it was his anchor. Because it was, and he wasn't going to let Vasily go. Not when Vasily's soul was reaching for him in the midst of the chaos they were wading through, telling him, *You've got to stay*, and, *I'll help you hold on.* Dimitri would stay, for him. Dimitri would try, for him.

And as they skirted through the hallways, the extent of the confusion overtaking the palace was laid bare—several people appeared to have been injured in the rush, and they were laid out in the main hall, moaning as the physicians tended to them while palace guards milled about, directionless. There were nobles stripping the tables of valuables and stuffing them into pockets, and a huge knot of them appeared to be trying to leave, but Alexey's personal guard had taken it upon themselves to bar the doors to the palace and were engaged in a screaming match with the lords they were apparently determined to keep captive.

Satisfaction washed through Vasily as they went unnoticed, walking calmly through the chaos.

People see what they want to see, he told Dimitri. *Right now, I'm just a guard, carrying a very oddly shaped package. I should try this particular disguise more often.*

I just want my body back, Dimitri groused. The gut-wrenching feeling of loss was now accompanied by physical pain, like he was being pricked with pins over and over, the sensation of a limb falling asleep the only thing he could feel.

We'll get you there, Vasily replied, his reassurance soothing not one bit of the pain, but helping Dimitri focus on holding on.

They made it undisturbed to Alexey's study once more and deposited his body next to the corpse of the noble and the guard, at Ivan's feet.

"We need to help him." Ayla turned to Ivan as soon as she was relieved of Dimitri's body, pressing a hand to his cheek.

"Yes," Vasily said brusquely. "Except he very clearly needs a doctor, not us. Luckily, we have one on hand. They're stuck in the dungeons."

More hallways, several flights of steps down. Dimitri's consciousness now felt like it was fading, floating, struggling to keep its hold on Vasily's mind, the anchor of Vasily no longer enough to weigh him down.

Hold on, Vasily said, his heart speeding up. *Don't leave. Not yet.*

Not yet, Dimitri echoed as he slipped, and drifted.

✳

Hey. Vasily nudged him with a poke of his mind. *Dima. Say something, please.*

Dimitri blinked back into awareness, looking through Vasily's eyes right into Mischa's, back in Alexey's study.

"Is he still there?" they said, tilting Vasily's chin back and forth.

Yes, Dimitri answered, bleary. *I feel . . . stretched out.* It was the only way he could describe it, like trying not to fall asleep when one was exhausted. There wasn't anything else. No pain, no longing. Just the need to rest.

"He's being pulled back," Vasily said, although it sounded far away. "I invited him to possess me for a purpose. Now that purpose is done, and his soul is being called back."

Stay, Vasily begged, turning his attention to Dimitri. *Stay with me.*

I will, Dimitri replied, so weary that he could hardly stand it.

"We have to figure out how to put him back in his body." Vasily turned to the bookshelf. Dimitri felt his consciousness flickering like a candle with barely any wick left. "Mischka, take care of Ivan. The rest of us, read like your life depends on it—because it does."

"I will start with the books on the right, Anna the left," Ladushka ordered. "Vasya, you take Alexey's journals. Work quickly, since it seems as though we have very little time."

Dimitri tried to focus on what was happening, at the words Vasily was frantically skimming in Alexey's journals. But it was too difficult to stay anchored without Vasily's voice to pull him back from wherever it was he was going.

But he had to hold on, he told himself. He had to hold on for Vasily. Because with every beat of Vasily's heart, he felt him beg, *not yet*.

✳

Vasily's flash of triumph was what stirred Dimitri back to awareness. He looked through Vasily's eyes, and saw him holding one of Alexey's journals aloft.

"So," Vasily said, addressing the court. "Which one of us—who isn't currently housing an extra soul—is most interested in dying for Dima?"

"Me," Annika, Ladushka and Mischa all said at once.

Dimitri felt like breaking down, seeing the way his friends would always give everything that they were for him.

"Not that we need to know, but why?" Mischa scratched the side of their neck.

"Because that's how Alexey's journal claims one can induce a soul to repossess its original body. It says you summon the angel of death, *Malakh ha-mavet*, and if you're found worthy, you must sacrifice a life for a life, to be resurrected. Alexey told me over a meal about how he bargained with this angel during his own resurrection, so it caught my eye when I saw it here." Vasily swallowed. "I would obviously prefer it to be me, but unfortunately, I think if I die before Dima is back in his body, he's going to be gone for good."

"I would die for Dima in a heartbeat," Ladushka said, her expression deadly serious as she dropped the book she was holding unceremoniously. She loosened the collar of her dress, exposing her throat. "And because my death would save Dima's life, whichever one of you kills me would not be violating the sacred commandment against murder. Saving his life would absolve you of the sin."

"Who says it gets to be you?" Annika snapped. She pulled a blade from her boot and pressed it into Vasily's hand. "It should be me. I'm ready."

"I really would prefer if I was the one to die," Mischa said, plucking the knife out of Vasily's hand before Vasily could protest. "I don't even need any help with it. I know exactly what to do. Just give me two minutes to bleed out, and forgive me for the mess I'll make of the carpet. I'm not a noble, it's not like me dying is going to disrupt the social fabric of Novo-Svitsevo. No one will even remember who I was once you're all dead."

"But we couldn't function as a court without you. We *need* you," Annika said, practically vaulting over the desk to grab the knife back. "I'm the one who's next to useless. I'm the general that lost us the war. It really should be me. And with luck, Dima won't be fighting any more wars anyway, so what does he need with a general?"

"You are the most brilliant general of our age. And besides, by the logic of who failed the worst, it must be me." Ladushka had given up trying to get the knife that Mischa and Annika were now grappling over, and had simply removed a jeweled letter opener from Alexey's desk, holding it aloft like she was half a second from slitting her own throat. "Because I was the chancellor who failed to predict Alexey's betrayal, and—"

"Fuck that," Mischa snapped as Annika finally wrested the blade from their hand. "War and strategy are difficult, medicine isn't even *hard*, there are thousands of doctors in this country and only one of each of you—"

"Um," Ayla said tentatively, breaking in as Mischa, Ladushka and Annika all started to bicker viciously over who would get to die for him. "I know it's important to figure out the Dimitri thing, but I think Ivan really needs help. Like right now. He's getting worse."

She was kneeling in front of her brother, who had started to shake, his eyes open but rolled back in his head.

"What's happened now?" Mischa snapped their head around, then crossed over to Ivan and peered into his eyes, prodding around his skull. "It looks like the back of his head has caved in. How long ago was he injured?"

"About an hour ago, when Alexey was dying." Vasily's fist was clenching and unclenching, and Dimitri felt Vasily's growing horror as he came to the same realization that Dimitri had. "Alexey threw him against the table, hard enough to crack it. The poor kid . . ."

Mischa turned a pitying look on Vasily, and Dimitri wished he could wrap him in a hug. Dimitri did the best he could, winding himself even tighter around Vasily's heart and soul.

It's not your fault, he whispered to Vasily, because there was guilt there too. And a memory of spies hanging from a bridge, informants who had never come back, innocents who had been crushed under a bridge that was supposed to blow only when there was no one around. *It's not your fault, Vasya.*

I should have forced him to run, Vasily thought bitterly. *Like I said, he was just a kid. He was just a kid in love with Alexey, who didn't realize he loved a monster who was treating him ill.*

Vasily trailed off, watching as Mischa rocked back on their heels, but Dimitri knew what he would have said next, if he'd continued on. Because Vasily didn't need to tell him for Dimitri to feel the sentiment, bone deep. *Like Alexey had abused you.*

"He's not going to make it," Mischa finally said into the quiet that had fallen over them all. "He's experiencing what we call brain death. His brain is no longer functioning, and his body hasn't yet caught up. He's dying, but slowly. Although functionally, he's already gone, and there's nothing more we can do for him."

Ladushka let out a small, sad sigh, and Annika started whispering the prayer for healing, even though it wouldn't do any good.

Vasily stepped forward and put a hand on Ayla's shoulder. She had tears shining in her eyes. "He had such a sweet heart. He was always the one bringing us together for holiday meals, all of the Tzar's bastard children. He made us into our own little family, or tried to, at least. I got too busy with school to keep attending, and now I wish I had . . ." She trailed off, choking on a sob.

"I think," Vasily said shakily, "that at least he got what he truly wanted before he died. When Alexey legitimized him. Even though it was forged, even though it was false, at least he died knowing he belonged."

Alexey couldn't legitimize him, Dimitri said, feeling Vasily's grief at yet another senseless death. *Not really, even with forged documents. But I can. As the true Tzar of Novo-Svitsevo, I can grant him the title and name of Lord Ivan Abramovich, who shares in my estate as my legitimate brother.*

THE SINS ON THEIR BONES

You would do that for him? Vasily wiped away a tear. Mischa stood up to put an arm around Vasily's waist, and Vasily leaned his head on top of theirs.

He's my brother. Dimitri felt the weight of it pressing him down, watching Ivan's breathing become labored. Yet another member of his family dying, with him unable to do anything about it. *It's the least I can do for him, letting him die a proper Abramovich.*

What do you need? Vasily's gratitude was a small balm to the hurt.

Nothing. Dimitri gave the mental equivalent of a shrug, although his soul was growing so tired and strained that even the thought of movement was difficult. *I will it, and so it is done.*

"Dima says he's legitimized Ivan," Vasily choked out, his voice cracking. "He's Lord Ivan Abramovich, by order of the Tzar of Novo-Svitsevo."

"Lord Ivan Abramovich," Mischa said gently, "is probably going to die very slowly and painfully over the next hour or so."

Ayla laid her head on Ivan's knee, holding his hands. "We should . . . we should do something about that. You said you needed someone." She bit her lip. "You said you needed someone to die. He's dying. It would be a kindness to not let him suffer."

"No," everyone said reflexively, identical expressions of horror dawning on their faces, but Dimitri's selfish, selfish heart said *yes.*

Do it, Dimitri ordered Vasily. *Do it. I command you. I'll take his death on my conscience. And as Ayla said, it will be a kindness. Are we going to murder someone else, and then watch Ivan pass on too? We are commanded to save lives where we can by the Lord our God.*

"He commands us," Vasily whispered. Dimitri felt him recoiling from the idea, but sharing in Dimitri's relief that there might be a way to do this that didn't involve watching one of their friends die too. "He commands us to."

No one spoke for a long, long minute. Then Ladushka looked at Annika and nodded. Annika chewed on her lip, then nodded too.

"I'll show you how to make it quick. And painless. But there's another problem." Mischa bit down on their thumb. "Dima's body is . . . a little worse for wear."

Vasily turned to look at the wrapped corpse on the floor. Dimitri felt Vasily's head spin before his eyelids fluttered shut.

"So fix it," Annika urged. "That's what you do." She sat down in a chair and pulled Ladushka into the one beside her. Vasily went to stand beside them, and Ayla stayed with Ivan, holding his hands.

Mischa sighed, then knelt on the floor next to the body. They rifled through a bag they'd procured somehow, pulling out medical supplies. "This will be difficult, so all of you may want to avert your eyes."

Annika snorted. "After the war, I doubt it's anything we haven't seen before."

Mischa's hands stilled on the bundle. "It has nothing to do with the ways in which bodies can break, and everything to do with loving the person who has been broken."

I won't look away. Vasily's voice was reassuring. *Unless you want me to.*

No, Dimitri replied, as fiercely as he could manage with what little energy he had left. *Let me see what he has done to me. I want it to sear itself into my memory. Let me remember.*

Vasily's eyes flicked up to Ladushka's, then Annika's. They were both leaning forward in their chairs, their faces drawn but their eyes flinty with resolution. Ayla's face was tight with more than grief. Anger, too.

"I am here to bear witness," Ladushka said slowly, "to the crimes of the late Lord Alexey Balakin, governor of Chernitzy, usurper of the throne of Dimitri Alexe—Dimitri Abramovich."

Dimitri released some of his tension shakily. He never thought he'd be overcome with emotion at someone invoking the law, to condemn his husband in place of a jury and a trial. And he hated how hearing his birth name made him feel free.

"I bear witness." A single tear snaked its way down Annika's face.

Mischa gave a curt nod as they began unwrapping the sheet covering Dimitri. "Me too."

Vasily hummed in wordless assent. Dimitri could feel the lump in his throat, too solid to let him speak.

"And I witness the quorum," Ayla whispered. "As a daughter of the late Tzar Abram Fyodorev."

Mischa laid Dimitri's body bare.

"Two broken toes," they whispered, their hands starting their examination at Dimitri's feet, working their way up his body. "Severe bruising of the left thigh. Dislocated right hip." They paused, and wiped roughly at their face with the back of their sleeve.

Their fingers crept up Dimitri's ribs, prodding the skin. "Ten broken ribs on the right side. One has—" They stopped and drew in a breath. "One has likely pierced the lung."

Vasily sat down and wrapped his arms around Annika's legs as she made a choked noise. Ladushka simply sat, rigid and impassive, her eyes following Mischa's fingers. Ayla's face went gray.

"Open fracture of the collarbone. Heavy bruising around the throat consistent with strangulation. Hairline fracture on the back of the skull. Right forearm fractured, right wrist crushed." Mischa paused. "Left arm has been . . . resutured postmortem?"

"That was me," Vasily admitted. "We have quite a story to tell you once Dima is back."

Mischa cocked their head at him. "At least your stitches are neat." They turned back to Dimitri's body. "All injuries caused immediately prior to death. Cause of death, penetrating wound of the heart that likely severed the aorta." They sat back on their heels and covered their face for the briefest moment, then stood.

"I find the late Alexey Balakin guilty of murder," Ladushka whispered. "Do you concur?"

The rest of them muttered their assent.

Dimitri exhaled, and looked through Vasily's eyes at each one of the wounds in turn, studying the carnage that Alexey had wrought on his body. Hearing Mischa say it, hearing the recitation of the hell that Alexey had put him through in his last minutes of life, seeing the bruises and the breaks and the evidence of pain, was one of the hardest things Dimitri had ever done, like going to war, like letting Vasily leave.

But it also, finally, after all these years, hardened his heart. If this was Alexey's love, he no longer wanted it.

"I have a lot of work to do." Mischa pulled wads of gauze out of the bag. "A *lot* of work. And Dima, I want you to know, if this resurrection doesn't miraculously heal your body somehow, you're going to be in a world of agony for a long, long time."

I know. Dimitri was not afraid of the pain. He had lived with pain haunting his mind and his heart long enough that it was no longer a stranger.

"Well," Mischa breathed, flipping a scalpel in their hand, "I hope I remember how to do surgery on a heart. At least it's not beating."

*

It took Mischa another hour to finish cleaning and binding Dimitri's wounds, setting his bones, and injecting his body with what they claimed were enough antibiotics to sanitize a latrine. Dimitri felt Vasily's gaze continually flickering to Ivan, making sure that he was still breathing. Ayla nodded minutely each time.

Mischa stood up and wiped their hands on their shirt. "That's all I can do. His left arm will be useless without actual surgery, and maybe even then. Now we pray for him to be resurrected, then we pray that he doesn't die right away from a raging infection."

Ladushka looked to Vasily. "Vasya, Dima. Can you do this?"

Vasily didn't respond. *Yes,* Dimitri answered for them both, even though Ladushka couldn't hear. *We must.*

"It will be right here." Mischa stepped forward and pressed a blood-coated finger to Vasily's sternum. "Push the blade in here, and he won't feel a thing. It will all be over in a moment."

Mischa beckoned to Ayla, who gathered her brother up in her arms and laid him flat on the carpet, next to Dimitri's body. She smoothed his hair back, kissed him on the forehead, and stood, tears falling freely down her face now.

Vasily was crying too.

For a moment, Dimitri looked at his brother's unconscious form, feeling yet another piece of his heart breaking off, never to heal. Seeing his own broken, dead body next to the living form of his brother, still breathing, still rosy with life, was jarring. Knowing that Ivan was dying anyway was cold comfort, because the only reason Ivan was dying at all was because of Alexey. Because Dimitri had brought Alexey here, to the palace, and then brought him back to life, and then left him . . .

No, Vasily broke in, fierce and unyielding. *It's not your fault, Dima. It's not your fault, and I'll be here to tell you for the rest of your days that it's Not. Your. Fault. Alexey did this. Alexey was the one to kill Ivan. We're merely granting him mercy, in the end.*

Dimitri didn't know if he believed Vasily, but he wasn't going to make this harder for him by arguing. He felt Vasily's hand close around the knife that Mischa had pressed into his palm.

I'm doing this, Dimitri bargained with God. *Don't blame Vasya for this crime.*

He prayed that God would listen. He should be the only one held responsible for Ivan's murder.

He reached out for Vasily. *We're going to do this. We have to do this. But does this make me as bad as Alexey? Using someone for my own ends?*

No, Vasily responded after a beat. *You could never be. This is—this is fucking horrible. This is sad and awful and wrong. But think of what will happen if you don't return to yourself, Dima. The country will descend into chaos. People will go to war again over who has the right to rule. Maybe someone we know would win, maybe someone else. Maybe someone even worse than Alexey.* He paused and breathed in deep, and Dimitri felt that breath hitch in his chest and felt the lump in Vasily's throat as he swallowed, the hot wash of tears filling his eyes as if they were Dimitri's own. *All I know is that if we can kill one man to save the lives of thousands, we must. And maybe we'll pay for it in the afterlife despite our reasoning, but that's simply what we need to do to keep Novo-Svitsevo safe.*

Dimitri steeled himself, because he trusted Vasily and Vasily was right. *Let's get ourselves an angel, then.*

He took control of Vasily's lips and ordered his court to stand back. They did, and he let his consciousness drift, creating a space in Vasily's mind like the one that he found when he meditated and prayed to the Lord.

Malakh ha-mavet, Dimitri prayed, trepidation threading its way through him, manifesting in a trembling in Vasily's fingers. *We call on you.*

The temperature in the room dropped as the light dimmed. The candles flickered in their holders, illuminating his court, backed up against the wall, huddled together, holding each other.

Offer to me. The voice was as cold as the grave, as fiery as heaven. *Blood and flesh.*

Dimitri knelt in Vasily's body, and put his hand on his brother's chest, feeling him draw in what would be his last breaths. He unbuttoned Ivan's shirt, revealing the pale skin beneath, marred by a string of bruises in various states of healing scattered across his ribs and circling his throat like a grotesque necklace. Dimitri's entire being shuddered in revulsion and sympathy.

Is that what I looked like? Dimitri couldn't help but think at Vasily. *Is this how you felt, looking at me?*

Yes, Vasily replied simply. *Each and every time. It never got easier.*

He finished laying his brother's chest bare, watching the last beats of his heart pushing gently against the hollow of skin between his ribs. Dimitri wished he didn't have to do this, but he did.

I offer him to you.

He took the knife in Vasily's hand and did as Mischa had shown. The knife slipped into the skin of Ivan's chest, lodging there just as it had when Dimitri had killed Alexey all those years ago. Blood spurted out of the wound, soaking Vasily's arm, warm and sticky. Dimitri drew in three tortured breaths before his brother's heart stopped beating under his hand.

I'm sorry, he said to Ivan, even though his brother couldn't hear. *I'm so sorry.*

Now the flesh. The angel's voice was greedy, hungry, a ravenous darkness that Dimitri knew would consume the world whole, if it had enough fuel. Dimitri reached out with Vasily's hand and grasped one of the candleholders, then tipped the flame down onto Ivan's unmoving chest. It caught slowly on his shirt and then spread, rippling across his body, reaching his neck and then his face, filling the room with the smell of charring flesh.

Vasily retched, and Dimitri felt his own consciousness convulse.

I accept your sacrifice. The angel's voice filled Dimitri's entire being. *What do you wish?*

Dimitri shivered. *To restore my soul to my body.*

For the righteous who sacrifice to me, I shall perform miracles.

The angel's presence touched him, the cold hand of Death itself. Dimitri's consciousness was yanked forward, stretched into an unbearable thinness, pulled through the world until he finally let Vasily go with three last, whispered words.

✸

Dimitri Abramovich, Tzar of Novo-Svitsevo, took a gasping breath, awakening to agony that lit every one of his nerves on fire.

He let out a choked sob of gratitude, opened his eyes, and gave thanks to the Lord his God for restoring him to life.

THIRTY-EIGHT

VASILY

"Come here," Vasily said, lounging against the pillows.

He was exhausted, the kind of tiredness that came from a long day's work. In the weeks that Dimitri had been back on the throne, Vasily had imprisoned more Alexey supporters than the dungeons could hold. Between him and Mischa, the dungeons filled, then emptied, in a constant wave. And that was before the work of rebuilding his spy network, reaching out to his contacts in the contingent of western nobility that had come at Dimitri's call, reestablishing correspondence across the continent, and overseeing the search for Morozov, who hadn't been spotted since the night Alexey died. Watching, as always, for threats.

But his work didn't end when the sun set. He shifted the covers of the bed off of himself, letting the fire-warmed air caress his skin.

"One more minute." Dimitri's head was bent over a piece of paper, the scratching of his pen slow and painful. He'd insisted on learning how to write with his right hand. Mischa had done their best to repair the missing bone with a length of metal, but it hadn't healed. Instead, Dimitri's left hand could only hang useless by his side, scars rippling down the flesh to match the ones that now coated his body.

Vasily let him write. Dimitri never needed to know that Vasily rewrote the almost illegible letters in a forged version of Dimitri's script before they were dispatched across the empire.

Eventually, Dimitri snuffed the candle and stood up out of his chair, making his way over to the bed. There was a lightness about him in the flickering candlelight, despite the sling that held his arm, despite the way he limped now and sometimes had trouble breathing.

His body may have been damaged, but like Novo-Svitsevo, Vasily thought, Dimitri was finally free.

Dimitri shrugged off his nightshirt and sling, one-handed, and splayed out beside Vasily, turning burning eyes his way. Vasily stroked a hand over the healing scar on Dimitri's arm, but Dimitri didn't even blink. He couldn't feel anything there, now.

Vasily licked his lips, feeling his chest tighten as he decided that yes, tonight was the night. "I want something from you."

Dimitri's eyes widened as he looked at the bottle of oil in Vasily's hand, the way that his left leg was hitched up. Vasily's heart started pounding as he handed the bottle of oil to Dimitri.

"Are you sure?" Dimitri propped himself up on his right arm, his wrist still in a splint, and looked at Vasily. "Are you sure you want this from me?"

Vasily reached out and ran a finger down Dimitri's face, memorizing it. "Yes." He swallowed past the thickness in his throat. "I want to be yours, the way you are mine."

Dimitri just nodded slowly.

Vasily fought every one of his body's efforts to tense up, to block Dimitri's careful exploration, telling himself that he was safe, and he was here, in the present. Dimitri pressed kisses to the edges of his jaw, to the creases of his eyelids, whispering encouragement and praise and finally a constant stream of words that all amounted to just how much and how deeply he was loved.

Dimitri edged into him, and it was like fire and pain and pleasure, and also like he was finally being scoured clean. Vasily let himself cry as Dimitri cradled him, unmoving except for the tiniest stuttering of his hips, until finally Vasily caught his breath and nudged him to move and Dimitri did, and it was resplendent.

He knotted his fingers through Dimitri's deadened hand, even though he knew Dimitri couldn't feel it, and stroked his palm with a thumb.

Because even if Dimitri couldn't sense it, even if Dimitri didn't know it, Vasily would always, always be there. He loved Dimitri, and would be his until he had nothing left to give.

✶

Dimitri fell fast asleep in his arms, Dimitri's right hand curled into the blanket, his head on Vasily's chest, a leg splayed over his stomach. His breathing was slow and steady over Vasily's skin, which was stretched so tight with happiness and contentment that he thought he might burst. He turned to snuff out the last candle, the one illuminating the king of hearts, folded and creased but whole, that he kept on top of the joker on his nightstand, stained with Dimitri's blood.

Vasily looked at him, in the dark, measuring out each one of Dimitri's breaths, matching it with his own. He could spend a thousand lifetimes like this, looking at Dimitri.

But the Tzar of Novo-Svitsevo had never been his to keep.

For now, though, he was holding the man he loved. He gathered Dimitri Abramovich close and kissed the top of his head, breathing in deep, Dimitri safe in his arms.

It was enough. For now, it was enough.

THIRTY-NINE

DIMITRI

Dimitri's body might have been pain incarnate, but his mind, after all these years, was finally at ease.

He blinked awake at the weak winter sunlight making its way through the curtains and gave thanks to God that he was alive. And then he turned his head up to Vasily's and woke him with a kiss.

It didn't hurt, anymore, to share a bed.

They made their way through their morning routine, Vasily doing up Dimitri's shirt buttons as Ladushka came in to brief him for the day. He was already tired, but in the way that came from honest effort, day after day. It was going to take months of work to put the court at Rav-Mikhailburg back together. Half of the lords and ladies had fled when he'd stumbled into the throne room, battered and broken, and had Vasily help him onto the throne. It hadn't been his best showing, though the shock had been enough to have a sizable contingent of the nobility bowing at his feet once more.

But the reprieve was short-lived. Already the western provinces were sending delegates and engaging in the delicate dance of bowing to their true Tzar while negotiating for far lower taxes than he needed them to pay. Already there had been two assassination attempts by Alexey sympathizers. Already he was being thrown into court politics while keeping an eye on the restive Urushkin border and the political machinations of the Free States.

He wouldn't have been able to do it without the steady knowledge that he had Vasily to return to, night after night. That Annika, Ladushka and Mischa would always be there too, holding him up when he faltered, his buffers against the ravages of memory when they came for him, whether in nightmares or flashbacks or triggered by snide words slipped into palace conversation.

He didn't miss the way his friends sometimes stopped, their eyes glazed over or their shoulders gone rigid. He was not the only one struggling, nor the only one who was too weak to admit what plagued them. They were all haunted by the war, by Alexey's crimes, by having huddled over Dimitri's dead body. He didn't miss that Vasily had found an excuse to spend every night with him since Dimitri retook the throne, even if Dimitri's recurring, vicious nightmares often led to Vasily being punched instinctively. Vasily never complained when Dimitri woke up in tears, thrashing around in bed, in terror at the feeling of Alexey's hands around his throat. Vasily just held him close and let him cry, and then soothed him back to sleep.

Vasily whispered that no matter what, he would always love him.

Dimitri didn't miss that on the mornings when he rose with red-rimmed eyes, Ladushka would subtly clear his schedule of any fraught meetings, or that Annika would distract his mind with funny observations when she saw that he was anxious. He did not miss that Mischa watched him like a hawk, making up excuses to pull him away from court to "check in on his health" while surreptitiously giving Dimitri a space to talk through his complicated feelings about Alexey, free of judgment.

And so, for his court, he tried to express his love and support in turn.

For Mischa, he founded a hospital in their name in the center of Rav-Mikhailburg, where anyone, regardless of their ability to pay, could seek treatment, and where Mischa's name would carry on long after they were gone. They had smirked when Dimitri presented them with the deed to the building and a formal endowment, saying that Dimitri had finally found something decent to spend all his money on, but their face had lit up with gratitude.

For Ladushka, he signed a decree into law that no one could be forced into a marriage without their consent, and that only one party to a marriage had to petition for divorce for it to be granted. She had looked at the paper in that calculating way of hers, and had merely bitten her lip and nodded, whispering about how it would do good for many people and that she would file it with the judiciary right away. But then she had looked up at him, and her blue eyes were just a little bit brighter.

For Annika, he gleefully, finally, exiled the father who had forced her into a career as a general so she could follow in his footsteps, making her deny all that she was. Then he'd relieved her of her position and held her while she'd cried with gratitude after he told her that her new job was to design a program to help children orphaned by the war.

And for Vasily, he sent mercenaries to hunt down the man who had hurt him as a child. When Vasily had opened the gilded box that Dimitri presented him, Vasily had raised an eyebrow and joked, *Dima, you remembered what I wanted from him. How lovely of you. It's much smaller than I remember. Age wasn't kind to him.* But Dimitri saw the tears shining in his eyes, and that night, Vasily hadn't insisted on locking their bedroom door.

For Vasily, but also for himself, he carefully hid away each of the offers of marriage that had come in from the royalty of far flung countries, locking them into the newly added hidden drawer in his desk that he hoped Vasily never discovered, telling himself that they both deserved a bit more time.

He deserved a bit more time with a man who loved him, and he deserved a bit more time to love someone in return, with the entirety of his scarred, ruined heart.

They had survived. They were broken, but they had been healed through their own determination not to give in. And they were more beautiful for the cracks that threaded through their souls, the big ones they spoke of and the small ones he sensed in the quiet moments they shared.

They had all been through hell. They were all haunted by the past. But he had Vasily, and the rest of the court, and they all had Novo-Svitsevo. And for now, it was enough.

FORTY

ZEMONYII

It had borne its master's body aloft, traversing the long miles to its master's ancestral home.

It had been told, when it was a man, what to do should people hurt its master. It had committed the instructions to memory, and its master had been wrapped around its mind too, whispering the steps, directing its preparations.

It had done what it was told to do. And now it waited.

And waited, as the snow stopped falling and the grass grew green, its master shifting inside his new confines and growing restless with the waiting.

And on the appointed day, it had checked its master's shell. It reached for the power within itself, releasing the soul that had been gifted back into its master's body. It feared it would be too little, that its master had slipped away.

But then its master opened his eyes, and it knew it had been enough.

AUTHOR'S NOTE

The Sins on Their Bones is a work of fiction. Novo-Svitsevo isn't real and the Ludayzist religion doesn't exist—like so many fantasy authors, I wanted to transport my readers to a place they'd never been before. But the world of this book is hardly a work of pure imagination. In fact, it is very deliberately inspired by legends, myths, folktales and forms of religious practice that are firmly rooted in Eastern European (Ashkenazi) Jewish culture—my culture.

If you are familiar with Ashkenazi Jewish history and culture, you probably already gathered this. Maybe you recognized the prayers, the rituals, the culture, or even the echoes of the real-world locations that inspired me. The fantastical elements in this story, from Annika's protections against demons to Alexey's method of resurrection, are drawn from existing sources. And the religious practices depicted are accurate to my personal lived experience of Judaism, from Friday night Shabbat services to Saturday night *havdalah* prayers.

But you shouldn't need to be familiar with any of that to enjoy this book. I intended *The Sins on Their Bones* to be understandable by anyone and immediately relatable to everyone, regardless of their background. After all, at its core, this book is about universal themes— love, loss, pain, belonging, fear and healing. If you aren't yet acquainted with Ashkenazi Jewish culture and religion, and you enjoyed the book anyway, then I have accomplished one of my goals.

While *The Sins on Their Bones* is a work of fiction—I am not a scholar of religion, and I have at times taken liberties with my source material—many scholars have written excellent commentary on the myth, magic and folklore of Judaism through the ages. In writing this book, I relied on too many texts to recount here, but some of the most useful to me are cited below. If you are interested in exploring the themes and subjects in this book further, I urge you to engage in the very Jewish act of learning and questioning and read them for yourself.

I also want to use this author's note to share a few thoughts about two of the themes that drive *The Sins on Their Bones*—love and belonging.

On all sides of my family, I am descended from Eastern European Ashkenazi Jews. My great-grandparents on both sides were from Eastern Europe—my mother's family comes from Vilnius, Lithuania (which was then Wilna, Russia—the inspiration for Wilnetzk), while my father's family comes from what is now Warsaw, Poland. They all made their way to America in the late 1800s and early 1900s because of the difficulty of life as a Jew in that place at that time, fleeing death, destruction, insecurity, erasure and outright ethnic cleansing. My father recalls my great-grandfather telling of his escape from war by crossing out of Poland hidden under hay in a horse-drawn cart. My mother's family escaped forced conscription and pogroms.

Through all of it, they remained unabashedly Jewish, some of them religiously and others culturally. My family has carried my great-grandfather's kiddush cup, like Dimitri's, through war, and it is used by us to this day to celebrate Shabbat. My mother's family ran a Jewish deli in Brooklyn called Hy Tulip; my childhood was full of the kinds of food that Mischa would love to cook and the old-world sentiment that gives Annika comfort.

Like so many immigrants to America, their children, grandchildren and great-grandchildren are fully assimilated into the fabric of society. That story is my story—but it's not so different from the stories of so many people, Jewish or not. But as a teenager, I often wished that I wasn't so different from everyone else—something as close to a universal wish as I think teenagers can experience. I tried to divorce myself from my Jewishness, the religion and the culture that I had grown up with.

This, too, is not a unique story. At least a part of the history of Judaism in the modern era is assimilation into dominant cultures—as a source of belonging, but also as protection. Reformers in the eighteenth and nineteenth centuries sought to reinterpret Judaism in a nonmystical way during the so-called Jewish Enlightenment. The tension in this book between the old ways of Zalman, Dimitri's version of Ludayzim, and Alexey's Holy Science is meant to invoke, albeit imperfectly, the different strands of Judaism that I chose to put in conversation with one another—folk religion, Enlightenment Judaism, and the mysticism of Kabbalah. For me, the most intriguing part of writing this book was discovering the rich cultural and religious heritage that had been shed during the Enlightenment, by people like my great-grandparents. The research I did for this book introduced me to the magic and myth that likely would have been part of my ancestors' lives in Eastern Europe, from herbalism to superstition to outright magical spells.

As an adult, I have come to be deeply connected to both the religion and the traditions of my ancestors. At a time when antisemitism is reaching heights not seen in decades and Jews face very real physical threats to their lives and livelihoods, it is more important to me than ever to be proud of who I am and where I come from. Part of my goal in rooting *The Sins on Their Bones* in the folklore of my own people was to demonstrate that a world not rooted in Christian mythology is no less interesting, or universally accessible, than a world that is. If you've been entertained by *The Sins on Their Bones*, then I've achieved this, my central goal as an author. If I have made readers root for characters that are born out of my traditions and my perspective, perhaps it will encourage tolerance—and eventually acceptance—of those who are different and reside in the real world, instead of on pages in books.

And finally, speaking of acceptance, readers may have noticed that I have also crafted a world where queerness is normative. As a queer person with a complex identity, in a world where the LGBT+ community is increasingly under threat, I wanted to craft a narrative where sexual orientation wasn't a source of trauma or an obstacle for characters—unlike the way it is for so many people today. My readers for whom this is meaningful, I hope you felt at home—and that one day, this world we live in will echo the diversity and inclusion of the one I've crafted here.

SELECTED FURTHER READING

Ausubel, Nathan, ed. *A Treasury of Jewish Folklore: Stories, Traditions, Legends, Humor, Wisdom, and Folk Songs of the Jewish People*. New York: Crown Publishers, 1963.

Bialik, Hayim Nagman, and Yehoshua Hana Ravnitzky, eds. *The Book of Legends, Sefer Ha-Aggadah: Legends from the Talmud and the Midrash*. New York: Schocken Books, 1992.

Cohen, Deatra, and Adam Siegel. *Ashkenazi Herbalism: Rediscovering the Herbal Traditions of Eastern European Jews*. Berkeley: North Atlantic Books, 2001.

Dennis, Geoffrey W. *The Encyclopedia of Jewish Myth, Magic, and Mysticism*. 2nd ed. Minnesota: Llewellyn Publications, 2020.

Greenberg, Steven. *Wrestling with God and Men: Homosexuality in the Jewish Tradition*. Madison: University of Wisconsin Press, 2004.

Schwartz, Howard. *Lilith's Cave: Jewish Tales of the Supernatural*. Oxford: Oxford University Press, 1988.

Schwartz, Howard. *Tree of Souls: The Mythology of Judaism*. Oxford: Oxford University Press, 2004.

Trachtenberg, Joshua. *Jewish Magic and Superstition: A Study in Folk Religion*. New York: Behrman's Jewish Book House, 1939.

Unterman, Alan, ed. *The Kabbalistic Tradition*. New York: Penguin Classics, 2008.

ACKNOWLEDGEMENTS

Unlike Dimitri, I've never lost a throne—but *The Sins on Their Bones* came out of losing my sense of security and self. I wrote this book in June 2021, a time when my body had betrayed me and the world had turned upside down. In the midst of COVID-19, I had been diagnosed with a mysterious condition that would later turn out to be tuberculosis, but that had left me very ill and with few answers. Worse, it had shattered my view of what my future would be, reshaping what I thought I could accomplish and what I was capable of enduring.

I was furious—at myself, at the world. I was so deeply sad I couldn't even process the emotion and just shoved it down. I was worried that somehow I had brought this upon myself, but also that I didn't deserve to be wallowing in the pain because it could be so much worse. So I poured my feelings out into a story about a ruler who had lost everything, who blamed it on himself, and whose inability to look at the situation and his lack of agency unflinchingly, honestly, led him to bury his grief so deep it festered.

It can be hard to admit that bad things happen to people who did nothing wrong—or whose only fault was loving too much, trusting too deeply, being too willing to believe that other people are good and kind and just. It can be hard to look unflinchingly at your past and reframe everything about yourself that you thought to be true. I have been where Dimitri sat in more ways than one. His story is my story. His struggles are my struggles. The horrors he faced are ones I've shared, but the beauty and catharsis of writing this book was that I realized his strengths are my strengths too. I am blessed with friends as strong as Dimitri's, a love as deep as the one Dimitri finds, a family as comforting as Dimitri's, and the resilience that Dimitri eventually discovers in himself.

The first thank you, therefore, goes to my characters—for allowing me to live through them, to process my past through their experiences, and to use their journeys as mirrors for my own.

Just as Dimitri's court was his backbone, I could never have done this alone. So many, many thanks are in order.

To my team:

To Amanda Ferreira: there would literally be no book without you. You are the most extraordinary editor, and I knew from that first email where you saw straight to the heart of the story that you were the one to help me tell it. Thank you for your dedication and immense hard work, your patience in answering all my questions, that fanfic suggestion that one time, and for figuring out who *really* had to break into the palace. I hope I made you proud, and that we get at least a few Real Human Tears. You have made my dreams come true, and there's no real way for me to express the enormity of my gratitude to you. I hope you know how much it means to me that you loved Dimitri, and took a chance.

To the entire Penguin Random House Canada team: Sue Kuruvilla (for her early support of the book and her championing of my vision), Evan Klein (for helping the book to find its home on shelves), Anaïs Loewen-Young (for coordinating an extraordinary marketing effort), Danya Elsayed (for the wonderful ad copy and marketing assistance), Deirdre Molina (for bringing together so many parts of PRHC to work on the book), Catherine Abes (for helping create the gorgeous, gorgeous ARCs), Diyasha Sen (who taught me about the origins of adhesive price stickers on books), Geffen Semach (for being the best supporter of "cockslit of a dirtbag" an author could have asked for), Tilman Lewis (for lovingly removing my hundreds of extra commas), John Sweet (for preventing my typos from sneaking through), Talia

Abramson (for the truly, utterly stunning cover of my dreams, and all the interior page design), my publicists (for getting my book in front of as many eyeballs as possible), and Matthew Broberg-Moffitt (for helping me tell this story with the utmost care). My book couldn't have found a better home, or stronger champions. Thank you for taking a chance on this queer Jew, and this queer Jewish story, even as antisemitism and intolerance rose around us. It means the world to me to get the opportunity to tell my story. I hope my story means something to the world.

To Hannah VanVels Ausbury: my original champion, the one who saw something in my writing that made her say yes. None of this would have happened without you, my agent extraordinaire. I'm so lucky to call you both a business partner and a friend. I hope to be playing brilliant or bananas with you until the end of time. Thank you for teaching me how to write and enabling all these wild, weird, wonderful stories.

To Mark Merriman: thank you for being my advocate, and the most patient lawyer I could have asked for. Having you in my corner means so much to me.

To the artists who have lent their talent to *The Sins on Their Bones*, most especially Ashe Arends, whose immense talent resulted in the perfect interior art—thank you for bringing my characters to life.

To my friends:

Kamilah Cole: my newest friend, but a dear one nonetheless. Thank you for your warmth, humor and compassion, for welcoming me into your circle and loving my characters—and letting me love yours right back.

Therese Horn: this book wouldn't—couldn't—be here without your friendship. You inspired me to write, and I'm so thankful to be able to grow with you through the years, as authors and as people. And thank you for lending the perfect name to Alexey's *zemonyii*.

Karissa Plachecki: thank you for being there for me through thick and thin, TB and tumors, all the ups and downs of life. I didn't think when I tweeted at you that I'd be gaining a deeply treasured friend. Thank you for rooting for me, always—and for letting me root for you in turn.

Aden Polydoros: thank you for talking to a writer on sub terrified that we were somehow both writing identical books about dour gay Tzars. I'm indebted to you for teaching me how to rip people's hearts out and smash them to bits.

Elana Stern: when you stole my spot in that lecture hall, I lost my seat but gained a sister. I can't believe it's been a decade. Thank you for your unwavering support of me and being there for me through thick and thin.

Amanda Woody: thank you for being my bestie, my petty bitch-in-arms, and my perennial cheerleader. Thank you for believing in Ivan even when he was a playboy boytoy with literally two lines and no name. All my room descriptions are dedicated to you. Thank you for letting me fill up your Google Docs with notes from here until we're ancient.

My writing community: shoutout to the Ash and Sheyd Discord for hosting the best group of Jewish writers ever who answered so many of my obscure folklore questions; the supportive querying group I landed in on Twitter named after a trademarked character I shall not mention here (thank you Gabi, Eliza, Amanda, Emily, Jennifer and Joan, for being there for me since the very beginning); the 2024 fantasy debut Discord (special thanks to Sarah and Koren, for filling this with the snippets that keep me going); and the 2024-ever debut Slack, as well as everyone else on the Internet who has shown me so much love and support through this whole journey. And thank you as well to every author who took the time to read and blurb *The Sins on Their Bones*—your words and support mean the world.

To my family:

I couldn't have done this without you. Mom, thank you for always being there for me without question or hesitation, the model of unflinching support, love and acceptance that I based Dimitri's court on. Dad, thank you for teaching me everything that you know and guiding my path through life (and binding all those "books" at the office way back when). Without parents who nurtured my dreams, I would be nowhere. Allison, thank you for answering all my grammar questions and being the brightest, best sister I could ask for. Mitchell, thank you for making me laugh and being the most wonderful little brother I could hope to have (and not making fun of me too much for all this). I love you all more than I can say.

I am privileged to have an extended family too large and spectacular for me to call out by name and thank here. So to all my grandparents, aunts, uncles and cousins: thank you for your wisdom, humor, love and support. To my in-laws, brother-in-law, and recently acquired extended family, thank you for welcoming me with open arms and blessing me with yet more people to kibbitz with.

To Grandma, thank you for always being there for me, for loving me and teaching me your recipes and talking to me until we can only conclude with "and that's the story." To Aunt Stacey and Uncle Howie, thank you for being the runners to my chaser. Grandpa, z"l, I'm sorry you're not here to read this. I hope you can see the trees where you are—and I also hope you don't mind that I made you a talking head that could tell the future. I hope it would have made you laugh. I hope my writing has made you proud. I miss you every day.

To Sacha: we were inevitable, you and I. I could do none of this without you. Thank you for teaching me what a love story is so I could go on to write one. And thank you for supporting me in this writing endeavor of mine, even though I'm pretty sure it was nowhere in the ketubah. Nothing I could say with mere words would ever be enough, so I just hope that you'll take it on faith that yes, I love you more.

To Tory and Bertie: thank you for providing me with all the extra cat hair I could ever need, all the cuddles I could want, and endless hours of Cat TV. I appreciate all of the words you tried to insert into this manuscript by stepping on the keyboard, and I apologize that none of them made it into the final text.

To Laura, author, age eight: thank you for daydreaming your way through childhood so that twenty years later I could finally put pen to paper. Thank you for not giving up on that dream you had, to publish a book. You did it!

And to you, reader: thank you for taking this journey with me. If this book meant something to you, know that you are not alone. Know that the stories you tell yourself aren't always true. Know that it can get better, no matter what *it* is, and sometimes all it takes is time to mourn and mend. And so, darling, let the grief out.

LAURA R. SAMOTIN and her spouse live with two enormously large felines. When she's not pursuing her academic research on military tactics, power politics, and leadership, she relishes her role as a full-time cat servant.